# Profiled

## Renee Andrews

Interior by
The Killion Group
www.thekilliongroupinc.com

# Dedication

This book is dedicated to my agent, Tamela Hancock Murray. Thanks for the insight and the faith you've had in this novel. You rock!

# Acknowledgments

I wish to thank my agent, Tamela Hancock-Murray, to whom this book is dedicated. Thank you for loving this story! I also want to thank the Jacksonville State University Forensics Department for allowing me to invade their courses and ask countless questions that occasionally made the students wonder where I'd buried the body. I'd also like to thank the Alabama State Troopers who didn't mind providing detailed information to this writer's most obscure questions. And I want to thank beta readers Amanda Tankersly and Sadie King for your meticulous observations and recommendations for this novel. Last, but certainly not least, I want to thank my family for cheering me on through every book and understanding when I didn't get around to cooking...again.

# Other Books Available

Inspirational Books Available by Renee Andrews:
Her Valentine Family
Healing Autumn's Heart
Picture Perfect Family
Love Reunited
Heart of a Rancher
Bride Wanted
Mornings with Jesus 2013

# PROLOGUE

May 17, 1985

"I miss Mommy and Daddy," AJ repeated for the twentieth time since they left her home.

Aunt Bev turned the volume down on Foreigner's number one hit, wiped tears from her eyes and stopped singing about wanting to know what love is. She sniffed, peered in the rearview mirror and attempted to smile at the eight-year-old in the backseat.

"I do miss them. I'm not gonna stop." AJ crossed her arms.

"I know, honey." She blinked through her tears. "Tell you what. Why don't you try to relax for a while? Get some sleep. By the time you wake up, we should be at Granddaddy Truman's house. Aunt Carol said she'd make your favorite cookies, chocolate oatmeal." Bev sniffed again and wiped beneath her nose with the back of her hand. "And I'll let you tell Granddaddy Truman and Aunt Carol all about the names we picked for the baby."

There was no use changing the subject back to Mommy and Daddy. Aunt Bev wasn't listening. "All right. I'll sleep *if* I can unbuckle."

AJ's aunt sighed from the front seat. "We've barely left home. It isn't safe."

"Then I won't sleep."

Another heavy sigh, and Aunt Bev rolled the window down. "Go ahead. I'm too spent to fuss with you."

"I love you, though."

"Love you too, sweetie."

AJ unbuckled. Even with three big suitcases in the trunk of the Buick, Aunt Bev had tossed extra clothes on the floorboard. AJ shimmied beneath them and enjoyed the warmth of feeling covered, protected and safe. Daddy's scent, like Old Spice and soap, enveloped AJ with the fabric. Mama's scent, a combination of lavender and Downy, wasn't as strong, but it was there too. AJ had asked to bring some of their things along so she could remember.

The engine vibrated through the car, made a soft rumble against AJ's ear on the floor and provided a soothing belly tickle that should've lulled any kid to sleep. It wouldn't have taken long to surrender to the pull of exhaustion if her aunt hadn't slowed the car.

From within the cloth cocoon, AJ blinked. The engine purred to a stop. Were they there already? No, they couldn't be, but they'd passed all the town's stoplights. They were on the little two-lane road that led the way to Granddaddy Truman's.

Why had they stopped?

"Do you need help?" Aunt Bev called out.

"No offense, ma'am, but I believe I need a man's help. Your husband with you?" The male voice wasn't as deep as Daddy's had been, but it wasn't a little boy's voice either.

"I'm not ma—," Aunt Bev started then paused mid-word. She gasped, then whispered a near silent, "Oh, no."

Footsteps on gravel penetrated the car.

AJ's skin bristled.

"Do you need any—," Aunt Bev started again, her voice quivering.

The hinges on the door squeaked as someone yanked it open.

AJ heard her aunt's muffled attempt to scream. Shifting beneath the covers, she peered between the layers of Mama's summer sweaters and Daddy's dress shirts to see her aunt's blonde head pressed against the seat. A big hand covered her mouth, and her eyes sought out AJ, then widened. Her head moved in that "no" motion AJ recognized. Before today, Aunt Bev had made that motion when AJ had done something wrong.

This time, it meant something else.

*No, AJ, don't yell. Don't scream. Don't speak. Don't let him see you.*

AJ swallowed. Tears burned, as the man released her aunt's mouth and hit her face with his fist. Aunt Bev screamed. He growled. Pounding and yelling and screaming and crying.

*Aunt Bev.*

More cries. More pleas. More screams. More growls.

And then...nothing.

AJ's throat stopped working. It tightened and clenched and burned while she listened, struggling to hear anything at all. Maybe her ears had stopped working too. Maybe this was a bad, terrible dream, and in a minute, she'd wake up and her throat would work and her ears would work and Aunt Bev wouldn't look at her with those big scared eyes, silently telling AJ to be quiet, telling her not to scream.

AJ *couldn't* scream. She could barely breathe. And she struggled to hear...

There it was, the first sound wedging through the fog in her head. Aunt Bev's breathing. Breathing? No. Gurgling.

Another sound, a louder sound, found its way in through the haze. A car roaring to life, then tires spinning on gravel as it sped away.

*He's gone,* her mind whispered. But maybe—just maybe— he could still see the car. She couldn't let him see her. If he did, she might not be able to get help for Aunt Bev, and she had to get help. Aunt Bev made another sound, like trying to vomit, and AJ forgot about waiting. She pushed the clothes away, jerked up from the floorboard then peered over the seat.

Blood. Everywhere.

She grabbed at the door handle and fumbled her way out of the car, her legs slamming against the gravel road as she fell forward. Her knees stung as she ran, the raw flesh full of dirt and blood, but AJ didn't care. She had to run, and she had to run fast. Aunt Bev needed help.

AJ's lungs swelled, sucking air as she tore her way down the endless road. Her heart pounded so hard it hurt her head. Any moment, her ears would burst open, eardrums ripping apart and making her scream, but she couldn't stop. And her heart would calm down. It had to, before time ran out.

The center of her chest tightened, while her breakfast swirled in her belly and burned as it crept up her throat.

*No.*

She swallowed past the bitterness and ordered the toast and eggs Aunt Bev had served this morning to stay put. No time to get sick. No time for anything but finding help.

*Aunt Bev.*

She shouldn't have waited so long before leaving the car, shouldn't have listened for the evil man to leave. It'd taken too long. He'd taken too long. Too much time had passed between her aunt's last gasps and the sound of his car roaring to life then driving away.

But Aunt Bev had given her the look. The same look that Mama used to give AJ to stay quiet. So AJ stayed quiet. And because she had, Aunt Bev...

*No.*

She blinked back the tears, swallowed past the disgusting taste of vomit in her throat. Mama was dead, but Aunt Bev wasn't *yet*. AJ would not believe she was dead. She could find help. She'd find someone and bring the person back to the car. They'd stop Aunt Bev's bleeding, and then they'd help the baby too.

AJ turned to run uphill, over the rough road and back toward the city. Why weren't any houses around? Where were they? Didn't someone—anyone—live here?

Mama had always talked about the "pretty countryside" between Macon and Granddaddy Truman's. But there was nothing pretty about it. Nothing at all. It was ugly. It was horrible. It made AJ sick.

She tripped on a loose rock and fell forward, her mouth slamming into hard red clay. Gritty dirt and metallic blood combined and pooled in her throat. "God, please. Help me."

Her eyes squinted to view the road ahead, the nothingness ahead. Pushing forward with every ounce of strength her body possessed, with legs burning and lips bleeding, she moved her feet in a frantic pace that matched her thundering heart.

Help. Aunt Bev needed help. And the baby needed help. They needed AJ, and she wouldn't—couldn't—let them down.

Panting and crying and hurting, AJ climbed the next hill

while her side cramped. "Please, God, please." She whimpered, pressed forward, peered in the distance and saw a man.

Who was he? The one who would help? Or the one who had hurt Aunt Bev?

Praying she made the right decision, AJ took a deep breath and yelled.

Time swirled in the aftermath of her scream. The man did help. His wife called the police, and they came. An ambulance came. The lights and screams and sirens blended together while they all tried to save Aunt Bev.

A big policeman held a strong arm around AJ as two men put Aunt Bev in an ambulance. Then he put AJ in his police car and they followed the ambulance moving faster than AJ thought possible down the rough back roads. The policeman hadn't said much to her while they'd been by Aunt Bev's car, but he'd been there, standing beside AJ and holding that strong arm around her as her world, once again, fell apart.

While trees and fields and roads soared past, she forced words from her throat, scalding sore from her frantic screams. "Is she—" AJ tried to ask him, but she couldn't say the last word.

"They're taking your mama to Atlanta. They've got some doctors there waiting to take care of her and the baby."

"My aunt." AJ swallowed. "She's my aunt. Mama died last week, in a car wreck." As if she couldn't hold back the rest, she added, "Daddy died too." She sucked a deep gulp of air, then set the emotions free, her chest heaving at the weight of her tears.

The policeman's face tightened then big fat tears trickled down his weathered cheeks. "I'm so sorry."

AJ sniffed, nodded, and kept crying. She cried and cried, until they pulled into the emergency room area of the huge Atlanta hospital and Aunt Carol helped her out of the policeman's car. Aunt Carol thanked the policeman for bringing AJ, then hugged her close. She smelled like Mama. She smelled like Aunt Bev.

AJ cried harder.

"Come on, honey." Aunt Carol's voice shook.

They moved into the emergency room, noisy and wild, with

doctors and nurses moving back and forth and yelling things AJ didn't understand. "Is she going to die? Is she?"

"I don't know." Aunt Carol squeezed AJ while she let her own tears fall.

AJ twisted in Aunt Carol's embrace. "Where's—where's Granddaddy?" She squinted through her tears to look toward the emergency room entrance. Why hadn't Granddaddy come too?

"He wasn't home when they called, but he's coming." Aunt Carol's body trembled all over. "Dear God, I don't know how much more we can take."

And as if he'd also heard her words, Granddaddy Truman hurried through the sliding emergency room door, his eyes blinking, adjusting from the blinding sun outside to the dimness of the room. "Where are they? Somebody tell me where they are. Bev! AJ!"

AJ lurched from Aunt Carol and ran toward him. His face, normally all sturdy and business-like, was a mass of worried lines filled with watery tears, just like it'd been a few days ago at her parents' funeral. He lowered to the ground and opened his arms, then let her run inside. "Oh, darling. Oh, my little darling."

Then his body tensed, and AJ turned to see why.

A doctor in green hospital scrubs exited the back of the emergency room and walked toward them with his surgery cap in his hands. "Senator Truman."

AJ's Granddaddy gave her a final squeeze, then stood and eased her toward Aunt Carol, who took over holding her while they listened to the doctor speak.

"I'm sorry, Senator. We did everything we could to save your daughter and the baby, but she'd lost too much blood. We weren't—"

The doctor never finished. AJ's Granddaddy made an awful sound, between a gasp and a scream, and grabbed his chest. Then he fell face-forward on the hospital floor.

# CHAPTER ONE

March 28, 2013

Lexie McCain took her place in front of the yellow crime scene tape, held her microphone to ward off the evening chill associated with Georgia this time of year and watched for her cameraman's cue.

Henry performed one last adjustment to the backlighting, then held his earpiece for instructions from the station. He nodded while listening, drew his eyes to Lexie and mouthed, "We're live in three, two, one," then he gave her the single nod and finger point that said late-breaking news would now broadcast throughout all of Macon and middle Georgia, courtesy of WGXA's dominant transmitters.

Adrenaline pumped through Lexie's frame as she began to speak. No matter how many news stories she'd done throughout her years in Atlanta and now in Macon, she still couldn't control the sickening urge that occurred with each and every reported homicide. The niggling, burning curiosity that questioned whether she'd announced another of *his* kills, and the intense yearning to be the one who proclaimed that the Sunrise Killer had been caught. But while she'd wondered several times if she'd get the chance to cover the story, tonight's anxiety was different. This time, she didn't feel curious about the killer's identity; she knew.

She gripped the microphone even tighter and looked into the camera. Was he watching her now? "This is Lexie McCain with late-breaking news. Macon Police have recovered a victim of homicide at this home in the western part of the city." She shifted her weight so Henry could film the tiny white clapboard house. "The victim, Camille Evelyn Talton, known as Cami, was found by her landlord this evening and had reportedly been murdered several weeks ago. Ms. Talton was employed by Dowdy Paper Mill and was in her sixth month of pregnancy. Police are investigating possible motives and suspects; however, if you have any information regarding the case, please call the Macon County Police Department at the number listed on the screen." She paused, swallowed, fought the urge to go ahead and let the public know that they were, once again, dealing with the Sunrise Killer then concluded with, "This is Lexie McCain reporting in Macon for WGXA."

Henry put his camera back in the news van, then disconnected cables and lighting, while Lexie turned and looked at the tiny house where the murdered woman had lived. Had she known the man? Had she called for help? And then, the obvious questions, given the police had already informed the public of her prenatal status. Was she blonde? And was she single? Because if Cami Talton was blonde, single and pregnant, then she met every criteria of the Sunrise Killer's victims, and she would authenticate Lexie's belief that, once again, he'd returned to Macon.

"You ready to head back?" Henry packed the last of his equipment in the cluttered van.

Lexie nodded then turned away from the house where a woman and her unborn child lost their lives.

"You think they'll get him?" Henry asked as they crossed through the darkened city.

"I don't know." *But, I promise, this time, I will.*

After her segment aired again the following morning, Lexie stepped outside the station to get a breath of fresh air and nearly walked right into John Tucker. As in Detective John Tucker, the one man in town who made her nervous and the man she'd be dealing with 24/7 *if* she got the story.

"Lexie McCain." His deep voice caused a ripple of goose bumps along her skin.

"Detective Tucker." She nodded. "It's good to see you."

His smile said he knew she wasn't so certain of the statement. "Good to see you too."

She worked to control her racing heart and made herself smile until he disappeared inside the building. Then she shook her head to clear it from the fog the mesmerizing male had on her senses. No man had ever had this effect on her, not even Phillip, but the tall detective with the baby blue eyes, waves of black hair and daunting smile did *something*. He would be the head detective on the case, no doubt. And if she got the ongoing story, she'd work with him around the clock.

Fine. She could handle the notable detective. But could she handle everything she'd learned about him over the past eight months? Could she handle knowing he'd been a potential suspect in the 1999 murders?

But he hadn't been found guilty, and the District Attorney, Warren Young, insisted the profiler's claim unfounded. There'd been no evidence beyond the detective's match to the FBI profile generated for the killer. Nevertheless, John Tucker had worked to prove his innocence ever since, begrudging the marring of his stellar reputation as Macon's best guy in homicide.

Last fall, Lexie had covered Tucker's heroics when he'd gone head-to-head with a child killer and emerged the victor. She'd admired his honesty, been impressed with his determination and believed in his innocence regarding the Sunrise Killer's crimes.

So why did he still make her nervous?

She waited a moment to gather her bearings then went inside to start working on her formal request for lead reporter of the story, a bigger story than everyone realized. A premeditated plan that began twenty-eight years ago with a killer that had haunted Lexie's nights just as long. She couldn't let it fade into the background. Therefore, she remained at her desk the majority of the day banging out her frustration on her computer keys as she generated the extensive report that would prove to her boss that they were indeed dealing with the Sunrise Killer.

And she fought to keep her mind off the handsome homicide detective and the way those blue eyes seemed to see straight to her soul.

Clipped articles, photographs and notes wallpapered her

cubicle. Not her own award-winning stories from twelve years as a television news correspondent in Atlanta, or even from the noteworthy segments that had aired during her current stint at WGXA, Macon's smaller station. Oh no, nearly three decades of details regarding Macon's Sunrise Killer covered every stitch of gray particleboard. A constant reminder of the reason she moved back eight months ago. No way would she allow another broadcast journalist to get the story of a lifetime, the story of *her* lifetime, seniority or not.

She read the last words on her computer screen, decided she'd covered the reasons she should receive the coveted story and hit the print key. Then she waited for twenty-four pages of information to spit out while preparing to hit her boss with her biggest request yet, one that Paul Kingsley better grant. Unless he wanted to battle Lexie on a daily basis.

True, she was the newest correspondent on WGXA's talented team, but she was also the most renowned. Lexie made a name for herself in Atlanta. The people of Georgia knew her, respected her and appreciated her tenacity for the truth. However, she hadn't used her name to get more money from the station, hadn't asked for any favors in order to take the job at the smaller station and hadn't bucked any other reporter from the bigger stories. Until now.

Although Kingsley didn't know it, and she'd never confide the truth, she'd worked so hard in Atlanta to get to this station, *this* story. It'd been her sole motivation for returning to Macon, in spite of her comfortable life in the bigger city. And she'd waited for *this* story since...well, longer than any of her coworkers realized.

She snatched the first three pages off the ever-chugging printer and scanned her text. Perfect. Succinct. Would Paul give her the assignment? Would he agree they were dealing with the Sunrise Killer? Because Lexie knew it as well as she knew *she* had to cover the story.

Kingsley couldn't argue with her abilities. He'd described her on more than one occasion as the "best investigative reporter in Georgia," which meant Lexie McCain had the best chance of helping the police stop the monster who'd plagued her for years. A monster that deserved to be caged.

She grabbed another handful of pages, shuffled them into place, then stacked them on her desk while the printer spat, coughed and jammed. Clenching her teeth, she popped the lid, yanked out the paper obstruction, and hit the reset button. Then she noted the last printed page and kicked off the remainder of her report once more. She needed to get this thing printed and on Paul's desk.

For the past twenty-four hours, since Cami Talton's body had been found, Lexie had pleaded her case for this story, the full story, not the one she'd already covered on the evening and morning news. However, Paul had yet to admit Macon's notorious serial killer had returned.

"It's been seven years, McCain," he'd said. "How can you be sure this murder is related to the others? We don't want to scare the public without cause. The mayor has already called over here more times than I can count to ensure we don't panic, and that we don't cause his community to panic."

"It's him." In two more days, Lexie would know for sure. Easter Sunday. His very first kill occurred on Easter Sunday, and in each series that followed, he'd had an Easter kill. He would again; Lexie knew it. Why didn't Paul? They needed to warn the city. They needed to warn all women who were blonde, single and pregnant. And they needed to do it fast.

Her printer jammed again and she banged the side of the hunk of junk. How she missed the state-of-the-art equipment she'd left at the Atlanta station. But the killer reigned in Macon; therefore, she was where she wanted to be, ancient printer or not.

"You okay, Lex?" Melody Harper poked her head around the side of Lexie's cubicle. A plump woman in her late fifties, she had purple-gray hair and granny glasses daring to tip off the end of her nose. Melody hadn't bothered getting out of her chair, but instead wheeled it across the threadbare carpet to check on her friend.

"Yeah." Lexie managed a grin while fighting a grimace. She pressed reset, and the thing started up without requiring her to resend pages.

"You think it's him, don't you?" Melody leaned into Lexie's space, keeping her chair outside the narrow opening.

She looked around, cupped one hand around her mouth and whispered, "The Sunrise Killer." She indicated the multiple forms of media lining her friend's walls.

"Don't you?"

"I hope not." Melody frowned. "My daughter-in-law, Delia, is expecting. And she's blonde."

Lexie's chest clenched. "Maybe it isn't him this time." Did that sound reassuring?

Melody's round face drained of color. "Yeah, maybe it isn't him."

"And Delia's married."

The older woman's tense shoulders relaxed. Then she scooted her chair back to the next cubicle and banged her keyboard to prepare the lead-in to tonight's news, or to send an email of warning to her daughter-in-law. If the latter were the case, Lexie wouldn't stop the woman. Lexie also wanted to warn the world. Before Easter, if possible.

Her printer stopped, and the paper light flashed.

"God, please help me." She flipped the latch on the tray, pulled a ream from her supply shelf and ran a finger along the end to remove the outer cover. The thick paper sliced her flesh, and a thin smudge of red marred the end of the white sheets. Lexie popped the stinging finger in her mouth, jabbed paper in the tray and slammed it closed. The printer moaned but then continued, while Lexie focused on the very first newspaper article identifying the madman.

April 7, 1985. Easter Sunday.

A murder rarely happened in Macon at that time. Molly Taylor's bright smile, big round eyes and long blonde hair seemed to bring her to life from the center of the front page. But nothing could bring her back. He'd taken her, and since then, he'd taken twenty-seven more. Yet it had all started with Molly Taylor, and no one knew why. What role did she play in this maniac's plan?

Lexie had learned through covering Atlanta's I-20 rapist that the first kill spoke volumes about a serial killer, but no one had ever determined how Molly Taylor factored into the killer's initiative. Why her? And what did the church where they found her body have to do with it?

That year, as they did every Easter, a group from several Macon churches met at the Coleman Hill Park downtown for the sunrise service. However, on that particular year, they saw more than a pristine yellow-gold Georgia sunrise. A young blonde woman, her belly swollen with the child she'd lost, lay dead in the center of the park.

At eighteen, Molly Taylor had been pregnant, blonde and single, three factors later determined as the killer's signature criteria. He'd beaten her and strangled her, killing both the woman and her unborn child, then left her face up in the center of the park with her hands resting on her belly, the same pose in which the remaining victims were found that year. Macon lost six women at his hand in '85 and never had the first lead toward identifying the killer. When 1986 came and went, the city thought it'd seen the last of the monster. But seven years after his first kill, he returned. And at the end of 1992, seven more women, all blonde, pregnant and single, were dead.

Then in 1999, he was back. And once again, at the end of the year, the police had no leads and no killer behind bars. But seven more women dead.

Ditto for 2006.

Now, seven years later, another blonde, single and pregnant woman had been murdered in Macon. Yesterday, Cami Talton's body had been found in her home. Although his killings occurred outdoors during that very first year, he'd since veered from the pattern. The last twenty-two women had been murdered in their homes, where they should have been safe, and left presented atop their own beds with each blonde head resting on a pillow, hands resting on the stomach of a lost child and the covers beneath smooth and unwrinkled. "Not even a hair out of place," one cop had claimed, when interviewed about a victim in the 1999 spree.

Why hadn't the police acknowledged he'd returned? Why hadn't her boss? Because they didn't want to scare the town? In Lexie's opinion, the town needed to be scared. Very, very scared.

She snatched the last of the printout, added it to the rest of her notes and stormed the short distance to Paul Kingsley's office. A glass window formed the top half of his outer wall allowing him to view employees with a quick glance. Not that he did. Too busy to play overseer, Paul Kingsley instead played the king of multi-tasking. Right now, in fact, he had his phone trapped in the crook between cheek and shoulder, one hand scribbling on a yellow steno pad and the other using the Bible method, seek-and-find, on the keyboard, while his glance darted to the television screens on one wall, where WGXA's current broadcast played, along with several additional stations, and where CNN announced the latest headline news. Lexie knew his inbox held her report, but she was certain he hadn't opened it yet, so she held the hard copy. He *would* read it, one way or another.

She knocked on the door, watched his head bob—yet another task added to the mix—then entered. He sat tall in the chair, his starched white shirt smooth except for one thick crease near the right shoulder. A red power tie had been knotted at his neck when he began the day; now it hung an inch below the top button of his shirt. His skin had a golfer's tan and crinkle lines at his eyes and mouth to go with it. Mid-forties, Lexie would guess, though without the salt-and-pepper hair—heavy on the salt—he could pass for late-thirties.

He ceased keyboarding and waved her to a chair, but kept his right hand writing on the page. "Right, Tucker. I've got it. Yeah. So what time is the first meeting?" He looked up at Lexie then frowned as he scribbled numbers at the bottom of the page and circled them. "I'll send her over."

Lexie straightened in her chair. Tucker. So he *had* been talking to Tucker about the story.

Paul finished the call and hung up the phone. "Okay."

"Okay, what?" She watched his pencil continue to circle the numbers at the bottom of the yellow page. A time. 6:00.

"Okay, what did you need?" His chair creaked as he leaned forward, steepled his fingers beneath his chin and examined her with steel gray eyes. "Coming to beg for the story?"

"If you're airing it, then I deserve it. I don't beg."

He smirked and shook his head, causing a wavy silver lock to shift against his right temple.

Lexie waited for his response. A word, a nod, any sign of affirmation. She received none. But their relationship was peculiar at most, odd at best. Boss-employee for Lexie, but he wanted more, had made it no secret he wanted more. However, Lexie didn't feel nervous around Paul Kingsley. As a matter of fact, she didn't feel anything. A good-looking man, Paul had divorced three years ago and was ready to move on, but he was her boss, plain and simple. She didn't need complications in her life when she was so close to getting the story she'd always wanted, the killer she'd always wanted. Going out with Paul Kingsley qualified as a complication.

She'd left her ex-husband and his wife of ten years in Atlanta, but the three of them had an amicable relationship. In fact, she and Phil had always gotten along in areas involving Phillip, Jr. Their marriage lasted eleven years on paper, even if they hadn't had a real marriage beyond the first three years. In spite of the son they created and her desire for Phillip, Jr. to have a "real home," she couldn't do it. Couldn't give Phil her heart, her soul. The memories hurt too much. The nightmares cut too deep.

Even knowing about Lexie's past, Phil never understood her distance, and when he met Ginger, he fell for her. Lexie attempted to save the marriage, but she couldn't correct a problem that she didn't understand. And why *hadn't* she been able to love, to trust?

*Because of what happened back then.*

Now, with Phillip, Jr. in college and with Lexie financially secure and having passed her thirty-sixth birthday, her life was settled and her lifetime goal close to complete *if* Paul gave her this assignment.

"I know you don't beg." Leaning back and clasping his hands behind his head, he took his attention from CNN and focused on Lexie. "I don't either. But I have with you, haven't I?"

Lexie took a deep breath, gathered her composure and prepared a rebuttal.

"No, save it." He shook his head. "You don't have to humor me. Besides, this ended up not being my call."

Her eyes widened, pulse skittered. "What ended up not being your call?"

"The request for you to cover the story." His gray-eyed stare penetrated her like piercing daggers from across the desk.

"Who requested me?"

"Tucker."

"Detective Tucker?" She knew the answer. This case called for Macon's top guy in homicide and tainted reputation or not, that meant John Tucker. And Tucker got what he wanted regarding his cases. This time, he wanted Lexie to air the story. Her stomach quivered. John Tucker requested her, the most recent hire at the station, rather than one of the hometown favorites. Why? Because of her previous history covering the Atlanta series? Maybe, but Lexie couldn't fight the gnawing reporter's instinct that told her it was more.

"Tucker, that's the one. Seems he was so impressed with the way the two of you worked together that he wants you involved with the task force."

"Task force?" She swallowed. Lexie had been prepared to argue her right to the story, but what did Tucker mean, involved with the task force? And why couldn't she control the excited surge of adrenaline that raced through her at the possibilities?

"The cops seem to be under the same impression as you, McCain. And if it is true, if the Sunrise Killer has returned, then we all know what's going to happen on Sunday. The police department has formed a task force to try to stop him from succeeding, to try to catch him once and for all."

"They had a task force last time." She'd read all about the group and about the profiler they'd brought in from the FBI. She wondered who they'd send this time. Though she suspected—hoped—that she knew.

"Yeah, but they're trying it again. In 2006, they didn't get the force organized until after the fifth murder. Not a lot of time left by then. This time, they're grabbing hold from the get-go. According to Tucker, they don't intend to let the guy make it through another killing spree. And if at all possible, they don't want him to accomplish the next kill."

"On Easter."

"Right. So that gives them two days to warn all women who fit the killer's criteria."

"They want me to warn them?"

"Can you think of anyone better, given your past experience with that serial rapist in Atlanta?"

"No. No, I can't." And although Paul didn't realize it, Lexie had more "past experience" with this killer than anyone.

"Good. The task force is meeting at the Macon P.D. at 6:00. I expect they'll meet again tomorrow and Sunday, so this will be a full weekend assignment."

"That's fine."

"Tucker said he'd like to talk to you before the others, since you'll be the newest member on the team. He wants you up to speed." Paul tapped his pen against the paper as he spoke.

"Did he say when?"

"Whenever you can get there." He circled the numbers on his pad again, taking those gray eyes from hers. "I can extend your deadline until 4:00 a.m. for tomorrow's morning news segment. That should give you the time you need to provide the most up-to-date story. We'll intersperse breaking news pieces throughout the day then air an update at the evening 6:00 and 10:00. Does that work for you?"

"That's fine. And Paul?"

"Yeah?"

"I'll do a good job."

"Never questioned it." He tore the top sheet of paper off and handed it to her. "Here's the information you'll need for the meeting." He paused for a moment when she touched the page, looked at her and swallowed hard enough for her to see his throat pulse against his collar. His mouth flattened, then he released his hold on the paper and exhaled.

"Thanks." Lexie stood and turned to leave, but stopped when he cleared his throat. "Is there something else?"

"For what it's worth, McCain, I never doubted you were the best reporter to cover the story. And I never doubted your theory about the killer's return."

"Then why didn't you give it to me the first time I asked?"

His jaw stiffened. "Because I agree with you. I think it's him. And I don't want you having anything to do with that monster. He killed twenty-eight women, and he won't appreciate the one who airs his dirty laundry on TV. The guy's not right, Lexie."

The back of her neck tingled. She'd never heard her first name from Paul Kingsley's lips. A waterfall of goose bumps trickled down her arms. Grateful for the long sleeves of her pantsuit, she forced a smile. "I don't fit the criteria."

"You're blonde and you're single."

She held up two fingers. "Two out of three. And I don't plan on becoming pregnant anytime in the near future."

At his audible groan, she added, "Don't worry. I'm a big girl, and I promise I can take care of myself."

"I'm going to hold you to that. But if you sense anything, anything at all that doesn't feel right, I want you to let me know."

"Deal."

Vickie Jones stepped into the afternoon sun and shielded her face from the blinding glare. Her eyes were ultra sensitive today and burned the same way they did after they'd been dilated by an optometrist, because she'd been crying for the past hour.

But she hadn't visited the eye doctor today. And the doctor she had visited couldn't prescribe a pair of contacts to fix her problem. Matter of fact, there wasn't a doctor in Macon who could prescribe anything at all to fix the problem of having her ex-husband's baby growing inside of her. Vickie didn't want to do anything to harm her child, even if that child was his.

She'd gotten a raw deal from the divorce, but she could handle that. Her new life in Macon, away from Florida and her ex, was going okay. And the new job at the Waffle House helped pay the bills for her tiny apartment, but she didn't know what she'd do when the baby came. Her weekly check and tips couldn't support her and pay for a good daycare, and she wouldn't put her baby in just any ol' place.

Digging through her canvas tote, a big cream bag stamped with the Waffle House logo, she located her sunglasses, slipped them on and walked the short distance from Dr. Weatherly's office to the city bus stop. Typically, at least one other person sat on the wrought iron bench and waited for the next pass of the green trolley-like shuttle. Today, however, bare black metal awaited her arrival, and Vickie plopped her body, and her troubles, on the cool seat.

Things would be much better if her mother were still alive. No doubt Omadee Cutter would've been thrilled about a grandbaby to love. She'd have been happy watching the baby while Vickie went to work each day, and Mama would've given the child more love than it could handle. Too bad the cancer took her last year. Vickie could sure use her Mama now.

She sniffed, slid her fingertips beneath the big round lens of her cheap sunglasses and wiped her tears away. "Suck it up, Vickie. Crying isn't good for the baby."

A cloud passed over the sun, and the instant shift in temperature made her shiver. A soft rain misted through the thick Georgia air and added the final punctuation to her miserable day. She released another full dose of pity tears.

"Super." Pulling her sweater together, she arched her shoulders in an attempt to keep the front of her body dry. Her pants were already a tad tight, due to the eight pounds she gained after her wedding day. She'd need maternity clothes soon. How would she afford them?

"Here."

Vickie raised her head toward the deep male voice. She hadn't even heard him approach. Then again, she'd been lost in her misery. In spite of the rain, the afternoon glare and her sunglasses cast his face in shadow, but she viewed the item in the hand he'd extended. A black umbrella.

"Just press the silver button. It'll open on its own. I believe you need it more than I."

She smiled. So there were some people in the world who'd help her after all. Things could get better, couldn't they? "Thanks."

"I saw you leaving the doctor's place over there." He pointed toward Dr. Weatherly's office.

Vickie nodded, popped the umbrella open then lifted it above her head. "Do you want under here too?" The proximity required the two of them to fit under the dome-shaped shelter, but he'd given her his only protection from the increasing rain.

"No thanks. I like the rain." He sat on the other end of the bench and tilted his head heavenward as if emphasizing the truth of his statement. Then he looked at her and smiled, his face wet and his eyes friendly. "Not many people at the park today." He nodded toward the city park nearby. "I guess the weather kept them away."

"I guess so." She wished the trolley would hurry.

"Dr. Weatherly is a baby doctor, isn't she?"

"Yes, she is."

"You got a little one on the way?"

Vickie nodded, sniffed and managed a half-smile. In truth, she'd always wanted a child, even if she wasn't happy about the entire picture.

"Your first?"

"Yeah."

"Well, I'm sure you'll do fine." He leaned over and patted her thigh.

Vickie fought the urge to jerk away from the physical contact. He'd given her the umbrella, after all.

"No reason to be nervous, you know. No reason to cry. A baby's a gift from God." He moved back to his side.

"I know," she said, relieved to regain her personal space.

"Have you told your husband yet? Bet he's excited." The stranger let rain mist his face.

Vickie inhaled, then blew it out. "I don't have a husband." Might as well get used to saying it.

"Oh." The man seemed to care, the single word apologetic and his smile disintegrating. And she needed someone to care. Sylvia, the oldest waitress at the Waffle House, had taken Vickie under her wing, but other than her, Vickie didn't have a friend in town. It felt good to know a stranger would offer kindness. She prayed she'd meet more people like him in Macon.

"It's okay. I'll be all right." She touched her belly, where a ten-week-along baby slept. Everything would be okay. Somehow. The man was right. God had given her this baby. "We'll be all right."

# CHAPTER TWO

One down, six to go, then this mission would be complete. They were all so stupid, the cops, the FBI, thinking they could stop the inevitable. Thinking they could prevent what had to be done, what *he* had to do. It wasn't as though it was his choice, after all. He followed the plan that had been set in motion long ago; he didn't start this, after all. Hannah did.

Now the followers would start to understand. They'd know, and while they'd proclaim that it didn't make sense, that it wasn't a part of their existence, of the rules that they'd all believed and lived by, inwardly they would see the truth. Rules were made to be followed, and his plan ensured that they were, the best way, the only way. Too many of them had forgotten the wisdom of Brother Moses, the wisdom he'd shared before he too had doubted the plan.

Like Moses, the current believers had also turned their heads and ignored the ones who didn't follow the rules. But he knew there were those among them who cheered his resolution to see justice served, to maintain that the power wasn't distributed to the sinners that hid their darkness beneath a veil of purity. They weren't pure. Hannah wasn't pure. She should have been pure; she should have been his. But she followed the darkened path, and she paid the price. Just like Cami Talton. And just like the other six, the ones who would be delivered to him at the appropriate times. Seven that would pay the price for the sins of so many. A shame he couldn't rid the world of all, but he was only one man. Still, he'd been selected to make a statement, to remind them of the destruction that would come to those who wrongfully take the power.

He noted the people surrounding him in the Internet café. No one paid any attention to another coffee lover out to check his email and have a cup of strong java to start his day. He powered up the computer then logged on to the familiar site, noted the number of followers participating in an active session in the chat rooms. Did they suspect he'd returned? Did they know? And if they did, would they be grateful this time? Or would they slander him again for doing what's right? How many years would pass before they embraced the dedication he had to the goal?

His generic screen name, TRUTHLUVR, blinked to life at the end of a long list of similar pseudonyms filling the active chat area. He'd never entered a single message under the identifier he'd selected so long ago, yet he used it to lurk within the depths of the believers and to see how close they were to the truth. In the chat room, an aggressive discussion ensued regarding the return of the "Anti," their preferred reference to him during the predestined years. Anti. As though he was the opposite from all of them, rather than the same. Or rather, *better* than the same. *He* fulfilled the plan, reminded the sleepy town of Macon of a greater power and rules to be followed, rules that they embraced so long ago, back when they embraced Brother Moses and his teachings. Before he too went astray.

He watched as another visitor to the site logged on and the new screen name displayed beneath his own. PROTECT&SRV had entered the chat room. Smiling, he relished the thought that he'd brought the high and mighty individual out of hiding once more. As if every believer online didn't realize that the one man on the Macon PD who had served dual duty as detective and suspect on the case had now entered their midst. "Welcome back, Tucker."

Detective John Tucker thumbed through almost three decades of reports regarding Macon's Sunrise Killer. Twenty-seven murdered women, or twenty-eight, if Cami Talton marked the beginning of another killing spree, which she did. John knew the killer had returned. And he had to end it this time for good. And for Abby.

He flipped through page after page of documented evidence, autopsy reports, crime scene photos and pictures of each victim. All blonde. All pregnant. All single.

The same signature. The same MO. And the same sick feeling in the pit of John's stomach.

Each woman smiled back at him from the page, but one pierced his heart more than any other. He moved through the six women of 1985, the seven from '92, then slowed his progression as he started through 1999's victims.

"Why, Abby, why?"

Abigail Lynette Tucker beamed from the page and looked as beautiful as she had the day of the photo, their wedding day. The questions that had plagued him throughout the past fourteen years whispered through his mind once more.

*Was it a boy or a girl? Why hadn't she told him she was pregnant?*

The police hadn't requested a DNA test to verify paternity for the child, had assumed John was the father, since he and his wife had been separated for a couple of weeks when the murder occurred. But Abby started cheating well before they separated. She'd admitted it, even if she hadn't acknowledged whom she'd fallen for when he'd spent his days and nights trying to capture the Sunrise Killer.

While he put everything he had into sparing additional victims, his marriage disintegrated. Then Abby fell in love with someone else, got pregnant and became the perfect target to be murdered by the very killer John had been chasing. And then, as if his life couldn't get any worse, the FBI profiler penned him as the perfect fit for their wanted man.

Fourteen years had passed since the nightmare of 1999, and John still had to overcome the whispers, the memories, the suspicions. Even though the Feds never had enough to bring him in, that hadn't stopped folks around town from talking. And it sure hadn't kept them from dragging his name through mud as thick and unforgiving as Georgia's red clay.

He forced his clenched teeth apart and took a deep, cleansing breath. He'd made it through 1999, then 2006 and another set of murders and rumors, unscathed. But he'd also ended both years without apprehending the killer. This year would be different. One way or another, he'd put an end to this thing. One way. Or another.

His phone rang, and he snatched it from his desk. "Tucker."

"Detective Tucker?"

"Yeah."

"Leon Hawkins."

John closed his eyes. Knowing that this call would come didn't make the reality any easier. "Agent Hawkins, what can I do for you?"

As profile coordinator for the FBI's Atlanta field office, Leon Hawkins would deliver the news that John would, once again, have to work with someone who'd see him as the perfect depiction of a serial killer. Although he had expected Leon's call, John had hoped the Feds would give him full reign this time.

No such luck.

This morning John had received the District Attorney's direct order to send his list of potential task force members to Atlanta to be authenticated and accepted by the powers that be. The Feds had evaluated his prospects and were ready to get the show on the road which meant, he assumed, sending their own person, or people, to join his team. John didn't know how he'd control himself if Stanley Carlton stepped one foot in Macon.

Stan, a young, determined, egotistical jerk, had placed a glaring spotlight on Tucker during the 1999 murders. The FBI and Macon PD hadn't generated an official task force that year, but Carlton drove in from Atlanta in his big black car and delivered his spiel identifying John Tucker as a manipulative, conniving killer. Then he left town, while John faced endless speculation.

But Carlton couldn't put Tucker with his wife at the time of her murder. He had an airtight alibi, meeting with the father of victim number three. John had watched the wind deplete from Stanley's sails when the girl's father corroborated his story.

Tucker vowed never to forgive the guy for his part in that nightmarish year. Because of Carlton, he hadn't been able to mourn Abby the way he should. He'd been too involved with proclaiming his right to be at her funeral instead of a four-by-eight cell. John attended the memorial, but the whispers and stares followed him, taunted him, haunted him. Yeah, he and Abby had problems, but he still loved her. And he'd wanted that baby she carried.

In 2006, Stanley Carlton returned, and although his profile of the killer hadn't changed, he didn't put a name to the description. He even had the nerve to attempt an apology, which John accepted, even though he still wanted to wrap his hands around Carlton's skinny neck and squeeze.

"I wanted to verify the task force has been established." Leon cleared his throat. "I know you sent a list to the other guys here, but I'd like a copy as well."

John punched a couple of keys on his computer and brought up the list. He would have sent it to Leon anyway. Hawkins wasn't the enemy in this thing, far from it. Matter of fact, Leon Hawkins had been John's main supporter in 1999, when Carlton had been ready to issue him a death sentence. "Sending it now."

"Fine. Hang on, and I'll check it out."

John listened to Hawkins move around his office, then heard the phone rattle a bit.

"Let's see here. Captain Ed Pierce. He's your chief for homicide and sex crimes, right?"

"Right."

"Deputy Chief Lou Marker, Lieutenant Ryan Sims and Sergeant Zed Naylor."

"That's it from the department." John eyed the four names on his screen.

"Same guys as before, minus Sergeant Brooks?"

"Right." John didn't want to talk about Brooks any more than necessary.

"He was there in '99 and 2006. Why not now?"

"Transferred to Birmingham." Of course Leon didn't know the details. Most people didn't. John liked it better that way.

During the Sunrise Killer's 2006 series, Ed Brooks and John Tucker worked side-by-side trying to identify the killer and clear John's name. Their partnership forged a friendship for a time, until the end of the year, when Ed found the guilt too heavy a burden to bear and confessed his affair with Abby. They'd struck an agreement, John and Ed. Brooks would leave

Macon posthaste without telling anyone what he'd done, and Tucker would refrain from killing him.

"Fine. I'd rather keep the original group intact as well, and I feel you've got your bases covered, if you added the media personnel the guys up top requested."

"Lexie McCain has been assigned to the story and the task force."

"Lexie McCain." Hawkins whistled. "She's the best we could ask for. Good job, Tucker. I'd forgotten she moved down there. Gotta say, I always enjoyed her coverage of Atlanta's news. The woman gets so involved with her stories that the public relates to her." He paused. "She's got heart, but she doesn't hold her punches either. Excellent. I can't imagine anyone who could do a better job."

"Me either." John remembered the intelligent blonde and her interview with him last fall. She told John's story in a manner both truthful and appealing. Since her piece ran, he'd noticed a definite shift in the public's portrayal of his brief turn as a potential suspect. Thanks to Ms. McCain, he'd been redefined as a near-victim rather than a near-killer.

"Sounds like you've got things moving well. I'm assuming you're working over the weekend, correct?"

"This is the killer's weekend. Today is Good Friday."

Leon grunted. "Right. We used to get the day off."

"Yeah." And John used to be as religious as the next guy regarding Christian holidays, and way more knowledgeable of scripture than his friends in high school, thanks to his father. He waited, knowing what came next in the conversation, but Hawkins remained silent. Tired of playing wait-and-see, he asked the million dollar question. "When's he getting here? The profiler."

"Not a *he*, this time, John. *She*."

Tucker blinked, pressed the phone closer to his ear to make sure he heard correctly. "She?"

"Stan Carlton is working a case in Miami, so you're getting one of our newer profilers."

"They're sending me a rookie? For this killer?" True, John didn't want to deal with Stanley Carlton again, but he wanted—needed—someone who knew what they were doing.

His task force still believed the FBI profiler had hit the nail on the head, even if the head Stan kept focusing on was his. Tucker hadn't murdered anyone, but with all the reasoning Carlton provided, even John agreed he fit the bill. And if someone else in Macon also hit the mark, a profiler would help them find him before he killed again.

"She may be younger than Carlton, but she's no rookie. None of our profilers are rookies; you know that. At the bare minimum, they've had two years of agent training, additional time as a profiler coordinator in a field office, then served in the Behavior Science division at Quantico. In fact, this woman has surpassed every other profiler in the unit, based on her success rate for recovery."

Recovery. Such a deceptive term. It sounded as though she'd found all the victims alive. However, recovery meant the body had been found, didn't mean it'd been breathing at the time. John almost asked for the details of her success rate, but he didn't need to rock the boat. Yet.

"Fine. What does she need and when will she get here?"

"She's on her way now."

"Our first meeting is scheduled for 6:00. Think she'll make it?" John glanced at the clock on his computer.

"I'll give Angel a call on her cell. She'll be there."

"Angel?"

"Angel Jackson, the profiler assigned to the Sunrise Killer. She's topnotch, Tucker. I believe she'll help you find your man. You won't have any problems working with Angel." Leon didn't have to add, *"like you had with Carlton."* It was implied, and John understood.

"As long as we find him and stop him before he kills again, I'd accept help from anyone, problems or not."

"Carlton was just doing his job. He was still green and jumped the gun in pinpointing a suspect. Besides, our unit only provides the profile. It's up to the cops what they do with it. But Stan did what he thought was best, even if he was a bit overzealous."

"That's one way to describe it."

"Angel will get the job done right. I'll call her and make sure she knows about the meeting. She'll let you know everything she needs from you at that time."

"Thanks, Leon."

"No problem. And keep me posted on things down there."

"As if you won't know what's happening before I do." John hadn't found one of the killer's victims yet when the FBI hadn't stomped on his heels in the pursuit, if they weren't ahead of him forging the trail.

"Still, keep me informed."

"Will do." Tucker disconnected as a knock sounded at his door. "It's open."

Lexie McCain entered, and his day brightened. In fact, his day had been a bit brighter ever since he ran into her outside the television station this morning. He noticed her cheeks flush, the same way they did earlier, and he wondered if it were due to nerves, or to him? "You got my message?"

"I was in Paul Kingsley's office when the two of you were talking. Guess it was no secret I wanted the story. I appreciate you asking for me." All business-like and efficient, yet friendly and approachable, what his task force needed for their media link to the public.

He motioned to a chair and waited while she sat down. She wore a crisp navy pantsuit and navy heels, which gave every impression of her professionalism, but the hint of satin camisole peeking above the top of her suit provided a blatant reminder that Lexie McCain was every ounce a female. As if the loose blonde curls framing big green eyes and pale pink lips didn't announce the fact to the world.

John cleared his throat. Now wasn't the time for observing females. "I didn't do you any favors, Ms. McCain. I requested you because you're the best."

She smiled, a big bright Julia Roberts smile that claimed her face. "You're right. I am the best."

He laughed at that, grateful for her ability to provide him that luxury today. The calendar might declare the day Good Friday, but before she stepped through his door, there hadn't been much good about it. However, even though Lexie McCain was a welcome relief from the bulky men who would soon fill up the conference room as part of the task force, he hadn't requested her for visual appeal.

She placed her thin leather briefcase on the floor beside her chair then withdrew an overstuffed file from its center. "I brought my notes. After Cami Talton's body was found, I gathered everything I could find on the past murders." She opened the file, but paused and looked at him. "You haven't learned anything else about her killer, have you?"

"Nothing. Everyone who knew the woman has an alibi, and all indications point to the Sunrise Killer."

She nodded, and her mouth dipped at both ends. "But we'll find him. And stop him."

"That's right, we will." He indicated her file of information. "However, I do need to add some details for you before the remainder of the group meets. As you know, the task force has worked together on the two previous murder series."

"In 1999 and 2006."

He nodded. "Although they weren't identified as a task force in '99, the same officers were all involved and know the killer's history. During those times, we didn't have a reporter onboard, although I can see why the FBI and the District Attorney believe you'll help us get the word out."

"I agree." She straightened the papers in her file. "And I've gathered every scrap of information I could find from the past killings. What details am I missing that the rest of the group has?" Her throat pulsed as she swallowed and she straightened in her chair. Although she tried not to seem anxious, Lexie McCain wanted to know everything about the case. Good. If they were going to catch this madman, she'd prove a key factor in the equation.

"I'll give you the current info sheets along with everyone else at our meeting. However, I needed to ask you something before the remainder of the group arrives."

"I'm listening."

"The fourth victim from 1999," he said and watched her thumb through her notes.

"Abigail," she paused, "Tucker."

"My wife."

She nodded, her awareness evident in those big green eyes.

"You've seen the profiler's statement released in 1999."

"I did." She peered at Abby's photo on the front page of the

Telegraph. "And that's the part that didn't fit you. He thought
the first victim would have been someone the killer knew. You
never met Molly Taylor, the first victim."

"When Abby and I separated, and then she became one of
the killer's victims, Carlton, the profiler, set his sights on me.
In his mind, regardless of my non-relationship with the initial
victim, the remainder of the profile had been covered, and her
death sealed my fate as their best fit."

"I'm sorry." The concern in her voice, in her eyes, made his
throat tighten. She'd made the statement before, during that
interview last year. He'd never learned how to respond to the
appropriate statement concerning his loss, so he remained
silent. But most stopped with "I'm sorry." Lexie McCain
didn't. "I'm sorry about your wife...and your baby."

John's pulse quickened, gut tightened. He swallowed
through the physical response and shrugged. And he praised
God for the fact that Ms. McCain didn't know the baby wasn't
his. His main purpose for meeting with her this afternoon was
to see if she believed in his innocence. He couldn't work with
her if she didn't. Her broadcast last year insinuated she
believed him, but he had to know that hadn't been to add
emotional appeal to her "local hero" story. Judging from the
sincerity in her eyes and her body language as she shifted
forward in her seat, she believed Tucker.

He could handle Stanley Carlton pointing the finger at him.
He could even handle an occasional whisper when he ran into
certain people around town. But he couldn't handle Lexie
McCain, a woman he admired and respected, and whose
opinion mattered to him more than he dared admit, believing
he was capable of killing those women. Of killing Abby.

Her head tilted and she glanced back down at the article
detailing Abby's murder. Then she turned the page and ran her
finger down the transcript from the televised news reports
covering the case. Each member of the task force had the same
information, and each had noted the discrepancy in tone
between the newspaper's coverage and the televised version,
the one from WGXA, Lexie's station. She flipped back and
forth, comparing the two.

John knew her question before she asked. "Paul Kingsley."

"What about Paul?"

"You want to know why the article attempts to crucify me, but the news correspondent didn't go for blood when a homicide detective was suspected of murdering his wife."

She flipped the pages again. "Based on the newspaper's account, you were the prime suspect when this broadcast aired, yet the context of the televised version implies the police suspected the wrong man."

"Paul Kingsley is a friend, a good friend. The two of us hung out together as teens, and he and his ex-wife, Kathleen, were friends of mine and Abby's. He knew I hadn't hurt Abby, that I'd never hurt her. There was no way he'd let WGXA insinuate that I did. He ran the truth, the basic facts, and left it at that. In a town this size, even if something isn't spelled out, everyone knows. Plus, the newspaper reported the truth too, the FBI version."

"You're right. I heard about your suspected involvement when I moved here. But, being a reporter, I've learned that you can't believe everything you hear, and—"

"—and only half of what you see."

She smiled, and again he enjoyed the gesture. Smiles were rare in a homicide detective's world. "And when I interviewed you, I knew. Even though I'd already read about the evidence clearing you as a suspect, I knew when I talked to you that you weren't a killer. And you loved your wife. I can see that now when you look at her photograph."

He *had* loved Abby, enough to forgive her. "Journalistic instincts?"

"I suppose so. Or perhaps it's the ability to realize when someone isn't a killer. You aren't a killer." She gave him another reassuring smile.

"You have a side job as a profiler now? Because if so, I'd much rather recommend you to the FBI than the last guy they sent."

A small laugh bubbled forward. "Not a profiler. But I can read most people. It's part of the job."

"And it's the part I'm counting on to help us nail this guy." His chair squeaked as he leaned forward. "So, do you have any questions for me, before the task force meets?"

"Just one."

"Shoot."

"Who do you think it is?"

She'd asked the one question that'd haunted him for over a decade. Who killed Abby? Who killed all the others? He shook his head and gave her the truth.

"I don't know."


Angel Jackson crossed the Bibb County line, while Special Agent Stanley Carlton's voice filled her SUV. She'd memorized the previous profiler's assessment, but she had waited her entire career for a chance at the Sunrise Killer and wanted every bit of ammunition available. That included all of Carlton's observations, even if, on some counts, they disagreed.

She wasn't about to assume he'd reached all the correct conclusions. Everyone knew he missed the mark when he pegged the detective with the foolproof alibi. But Stan had been too young, too ready, too eager. Angel wouldn't make the same mistake. She had no doubt Carlton's error cost him his case. *Her* case now.

True, Carlton had been conducting an investigation in Miami when Cami Talton's body had been found, but the guys at the top knew they were dealing with the Sunrise Killer. And they'd left Carlton in southern Florida.

That told Angel plenty. They didn't trust Stanley to get the job done. He tried twice, and both times he failed. Angel's track record, on the other hand, neared ninety percent. And she wouldn't let her numbers fall now, not with this killer, the one she wanted more than any other.

"Therefore," Stan's voice continued on the CD, "the rationale for Detective John Tucker as the key murder suspect is due to his direct correlation to the profile detailed earlier and outlined within the case files. Unfortunately, his alibi has been authenticated, so that Detective Tucker could not have committed the crime, at least not in regards to the murder of Abigail Tucker."

"Unfortunately? Stan, what did the guy do to you to make you so certain he killed his wife? You sound like you hoped he did it." Merely a month ago, Angel had fallen prey to the charm of Stan Carlton and had briefly thought she'd fallen for her handsome fellow profiler. Then she'd thought better of the notion and broken ties, telling him they shouldn't mix business with pleasure. He'd been fine with the break, and then he'd left for Miami. And Angel got the assignment he'd wanted, right here, in Macon. She ejected the CD as she crossed the Macon city limits sign at three minutes past six, while her windshield wipers beat a staccato rhythm against the glass. She never arrived late for anything, but she also never sped in the rain. Too many post-accident photos engrained in her memory kept her from battling the elements for a few extra seconds.

Thick, gray clouds cloaked the city, making it much darker than she'd expect at this time of day in March. Dark and ominous and foreboding, they were in direct association with the case she'd come to conquer, but she would conquer it. And conquer him.

"Welcome to Macon," she whispered, "Ninety-one thousand residents and no telling how many are blonde, single and pregnant. Perfect victims for a hungry killer with a unique appetite."

She found the police station, parked her black SUV in a visitor's spot and eyed the building, while one part of Stanley's theory kept ringing through her thoughts, the main part they agreed on. The killer would want to be close. Close to the information. Close to the case. Close to, if not part of, the task force.

"If even half of Stan's theory is correct, there's a good chance I'm about to meet the man who killed my mother." She dropped Carlton's CDs in her briefcase and gathered her thoughts, while waiting for the rain to slack off.

Within seconds, the drizzle converted to mist, and FBI Profiler Angel Jackson climbed out of her vehicle and headed inside. Time to meet the good guys. And maybe, the monster.

Heaven help her if she couldn't tell the difference.

# CHAPTER THREE

Angel's boots slapped a shallow puddle as she darted toward the building. At least she hadn't worn open-toed sandals. Although she'd been on her own for the past ten of her twenty-eight years, she still followed her aunt's rules of fashion etiquette. No exposed toes, white pants, or pink lipstick prior to Easter or after Labor Day.

Two more days until open toes. Which also meant two more days until the Sunrise Killer attempted another strike.

A large dark-skinned woman, her hair pulled back so tightly her eyes slanted and an exaggerated hairpiece bobbing atop her round face, waited in the entry of the police station and opened the door for Angel. The wind rushed in as well, making the other woman squint even more, while her long green and gold floral skirt whipped around her ankles.

"You're the FBI?" The woman eyed Angel's SUV as though only government personnel would dare bring a black Tahoe into Macon.

Angel peered through the parking lot and saw no fewer than two additional vehicles identical in color, make and model to her own. "I see you've got several FBI folks here today."

The woman laughed. "A sense of humor. Good. Folks around here will like that when they're pulling extra hours over the holiday weekend."

Angel had never celebrated the Easter holiday—or anything else involving religion—and she didn't plan to begin this year.

The woman yanked the door shut, away from the rain and wind that had, once again, picked up speed. Then she extended a hand. "Etta Green." Multiple silver bangles jingled and jangled as she pumped Angel's arm.

"Nice to meet you, Etta. Angel Jackson, and you pegged me right. I am FBI. Did the jeans give me away?"

Etta laughed again. "I was just sticking around to glare at the gorgeous creep from last time. Didn't want him thinking I'd forgotten what he did to Tucker."

Angel smiled; she couldn't help it. Southern loyalty ran thick as sorghum, and this woman had a soft spot for the previously accused detective...and an ax to grind with Stanley Carlton. "Stan won't be making this trip, but in all fairness, he was just doing his job."

The woman jerked her hand away, propped it on her rounded hip and cocked a suspicious brow. "That mean you think John did it too?" She frowned. "The man's been through enough, Ms. Angel, and we don't take lightly to folks roughing up good men around here, let me tell you. That there is a good man, and I won't hear no different. It's taken me a decade to keep folks from whispering and talking and bad-mouthing him everywhere from the grocery store to church on Sunday, but it's about near stopped. We sure don't need you coming back and stirring up his misery." She stopped long enough to inhale. "What we need is someone to catch the real killer."

"Which is what I mean to do."

The woman looked skeptical, but then smiled again. "Good." She reached out and touched the butter soft yellow leather of Angel's jacket. "Ain't seen one of these before. Looks like something my oldest daughter would love for her birthday coming up next month."

"I ordered it online. I can give you all the details later, but right now I need to get to a meeting."

"Yeah, the task force. Third hall down, turn right, pass the break room on your left, where a few over-muscled field cops are joking and the overweight desk jockeys are taking their umpteenth Snickers break. Conference room is two doors later on the right."

Angel eyed the woman in a whole new light, as a bubbling fountain of knowledge and hearsay, not always a bad thing for a profiler's investigation. "I didn't catch your position here."

"That's because I didn't give it." Etta broadened her grin

and flashed a gold tooth on one side. "Dispatch, the day shift, Monday through Friday."

Angel glanced at her watch. "Kind of late for you to still be here, isn't it?"

Etta shrugged. "My girls are in high school now and can start supper on their own. I like it better that way. They're turning out to be decent cooks. Besides, I had to make sure the other guy didn't come back in here waving his finger and causing another heap of trouble for Tucker."

Loyal indeed.

"Tell you what," Etta motioned for her to follow, "since I'm still here anyways, I might as well get you settled. Come on, I'll show ya where you're headed. Chances are you're gonna be there most o' the weekend."

"I'm sure I can find it." Angel didn't see the need for an escort, or an introduction. She'd form her own assessment of the killer, without the input from the group meeting down the hall. They may help her with the victims, but she didn't want help regarding the killer. Their interpretation of him might throw her off the right track, and she wouldn't allow anything to hinder this investigation. She didn't have time for it. One woman had been murdered, and the killer wouldn't stop until six more had joined her.

Unless Angel stopped him first.

"Nonsense." The woman grabbed Angel's bicep. "Whoa, Nellie. These fellows got nothing on you, have they, child? All that muscle hiding in that jacket. Who'd have thought?" Etta bobbed her head in appreciation, which made the spray of ringlets on her hairpiece jiggle. "Not bad at all."

"Thanks." Although small in comparison with most folks at Quantico, Angel had worked to prove herself in each and every physical challenge throughout her special agent's training period. And she never missed a daily workout. Who knew when the bad guys might need a dose of real southern hospitality?

Etta led the way down the hall, while Angel listened and noted each officer's name as Etta provided curt introductions to those they met along the way. When they passed the break room, Etta jerked a thumb in the direction of the hefty snack junkies and buffed up field officers. "Told you."

Angel grinned and continued following her informative guide. After a couple more brief introductions, Etta stopped walking and pointed toward the second door. "Okay. A quick run down." She grabbed Angel's arm again, her manner of saying she expected her to listen, and listen good. "Captain Pierce is all business and major ticked we're having to deal with this killer again. I think he was the only man in town who the other FBI guy almost convinced that Tucker was guilty, but Pierce changed his tune when John's alibi checked out. I ain't thought as much of him since, even if he is a captain." Etta stopped talking as a geeky-looking guy too skinny and too old to be sporting a flattop neared.

"How're things going, Miz Green?" The stench of stale tobacco and strong coffee wafted toward them with his progression. He stuck out a bony hand. "You're new here, aren't ya?"

Angel accepted the clammy palm and shook it, then made a mental note to wash her hands as soon as possible. "Angel Jackson."

"Elijah Lewis."

"She's here to help with the task force." Etta's face tensed as though she were trying not to inhale.

Angel didn't blame her.

"Really? Well then, I guess I'll be seeing you on the sites, huh?" His excitement pulsed through each word.

"Or maybe you won't." Etta's eyes narrowed. "I know we need you around here, Elijah. But more work for you, when it regards this task force, isn't a good thing."

He snickered, and the hissing sound made Angel's skin crawl. "Right. Guess I hadn't thought of it that way." Then he stretched his grin into his cheeks and displayed a speck of black tobacco stuck to one of his front teeth. "Well, maybe I'll see you around here then." He stalked away.

Etta inhaled, then blew it out. "Sorry about that. Elijah's our crime scene photographer."

Angel watched the slight fellow slither down the hall. "He works here fulltime?" Macon wasn't known for an abundance of crime scenes.

"No. He's freelance. He works for a photo studio in town and for the Telegraph, but he also does the crime scenes for yet another on-the-side kind of thing. He does a better job than the field cops, so we keep him around." She shrugged. "Plus, he works for cheap. Problem is, I think he enjoys it. And something about that just ain't right."

"I agree." Angel remembered a detail she'd thought about during her drive over, a detail Stanley had missed. Not all of the people who worked on the case were meeting in the room behind her. She needed to learn how long Elijah Lewis had been involved in his moonlighting stint.

"Okay, let me finish up on the folks you've got helping ya. Deputy Chief Lou Marker is a good ol' boy who's in the department for all the right reasons. The guy believes he can save the world and still thinks all Boy Scouts walk around looking for little old ladies like me to help across the street."

Angel wasn't sure whether Etta's insight about the task force would help her after all; however, the woman hadn't made an effort to stop speaking, and Angel had already determined she wanted to befriend the lady. Etta seemed to know everything about everybody, and before this thing ended, Angel suspected that kind of inside information, not provided in the FBI's resources, could prove invaluable.

"Then there's Lieutenant Sims. Ryan is an odd sort, but he's still okay in my book. Doesn't smile a lot and doesn't talk a lot, so there ain't much to tell. He does a good job, though, and is neater than any man I've ever met in my life."

"Neater?"

"You know, his desk, his locker, all that. Neat and orderly. Wish he'd give my girls a few lessons." When she grinned, her gold tooth caught the light and sparkled.

Angel considered Etta's observation. John Gacy had been a neat freak too. So neat, in fact, he'd placed the bodies in his crawl space then created a detailed map identifying each victim's location beneath his home.

"And then there's Sergeant Zed. Zed Naylor has been here through all the Sunrise Killer's sprees, so he knows more than most. He's a good ol' boy too, with emphasis on the ol'." Etta laughed at her own joke.

"Got it."

"And I'm assuming you know pretty much everything there is to know about Detective Tucker. In my opinion, you don't get no better. Never once has he forgotten my birthday, or to send me a card on Christmas." She shook her ringlet-embellished head. "You don't get that from most guys in here. Not that anything's wrong with any of them; they just ain't got time to humor an old fat girl like me. John's different."

Angel controlled her facial response and the impulse to ask how John Tucker differed, besides remembering birthdays and holidays. "Is that it?"

"Oh, Ms. McCain is in there too. She's a big time TV news reporter from Atlanta moved to Macon, I guess it's been almost a year now. She's the best reporter we've ever had, that's for sure, though no one can figure out why she left her cushy job in Atlanta to move to Macon." Etta tilted her head as if expecting Angel to guess the woman's reasons.

"Maybe she got tired of life in the big city." But Angel knew exactly why Lexie McCain had returned to Macon.

"Maybe, but in any case, I sure enough like hearing her report about stuff. She's the kind of person that can make your heart hurt with her stories, you know. Takes someone who cares to make you feel that kind of thing for people you've never met before. She'll have you hating the bad guy, or loving the good one, or ready to write a check to help some family having a hard time. Whatever she tells, it moves you, you know what I mean?"

Angel's eyes burned, throat tightened. She blinked past the impulse to set the tethered emotion free. "I know what you mean." And she now knew everyone who awaited her on the other side of the conference room door.

Although she hadn't needed Etta's sneak peek at the task force team, the knowledge proved to be valuable. She might not have controlled her surprise when she opened the door and saw Lexie on the other side. Angel knew she'd see her in Macon; however, she hadn't expected the news reporter to snag a spot on the task force. Good for Lexie. She, like Angel, wanted, a chance at the Sunrise Killer.

With her poker face intact, Angel thanked Etta.

"I'll check back in tomorrow, just to make sure everything's going okay and y'all don't need me for anything. It's my day off, but I know how big a weekend this is for the department. Maybe I'll do a bit of baking and bring some stuff over if y'all get hungry. I ain't a bragger, but some folks say they'd kill for my banana nut bread."

Angel didn't so much as flinch at the woman's expression. She'd worked on cases where people had killed for less. "Thanks."

With her bangles bumping down her forearm, Etta saluted, turned around and retreated, a vibrant color combination of green and gold swishing down the hall. Then Angel stepped forward and placed her hand on the knob.

To knock? Or not?

Knocking expressed subservience to those inside, or rather, to the one leading the discussions, which would be Detective John Tucker. Although determined to be an influential player in resolving this case, Angel was just as determined to gain the trust of the six individuals within this room. It'd be easy to barge in, spout her surplus of information gained from victimology and pronounce the FBI in charge.

And it'd be easy, after Stan Carlton's mess, to "put a rise in all their tail feathers," as her aunt used to say. But Angel didn't need any tail feathers ruffled. In fact, she needed the cooperation of everyone in Macon and the task force. Especially if one of them could be the killer.

She listened to Etta's footsteps fade, removed her hand from the knob and knocked. Within two seconds, the door opened.

Angel recognized John Tucker from the photographs in her file. Before seeing the detective in person, she'd have claimed he took a good picture, but the photo had nothing on the real deal.

He seemed taller than she'd expected. True, his background information put his height at six-two; however, she'd been around tall men at the field office. Several who were well over six feet. So six-two shouldn't intimidate her. Right now, however, it did.

Was it because of everything she'd read about the man? All the cases John Tucker had closed unassisted? Or because Stan

Carlton assessed John Tucker as the best fit for the Sunrise Killer's profile?

She didn't think so.

Maybe the contrasting elements composing the man threw her world off-kilter. A guy who'd seemed as sensitive as steel when depicted by Stan Carlton, but who had never forgotten a birthday or Christmas card for his daily dispatcher. And the guy whose sky blue eyes didn't seem to belong within a forest of black lashes, whose forehead seemed a tad too high, nose a bit too straight to match the full lips and cleft chin.

Plus, there were those love spots, as Aunt Carol called them. The two smatterings of gray at both temples that hadn't been present in the previous photos. They added an even stronger appeal to the man wearing the detective's badge. Aunt Carol claimed men gained those appealing sprinkles of silvery hair when they'd been well loved and given love well. It took time to obtain that notable mark of achievement, she'd said.

Funny thing though, Angel had never looked at love spots as anything but gray hair. On this man, amid the jet-black waves, they propelled his appeal clear off the chart.

"Special Agent Angel Jackson. I've been assigned as profiler on your task force." She noticed his jaw relax a fraction when she clarified the task force as his, which was what she'd intended. The man had been roughhoused by Carlton and didn't have a sweet taste in his mouth for the profiling unit. She needed to gain his trust, even if she hadn't ruled him out as a suspect.

"We've been expecting you, Agent Jackson." He opened the door wider. The other task force members, sitting in mismatched office chairs and gathered around a long conference table that'd seen better days, peered toward the stranger invading their space. "I'm Detective Tucker, but I'm sure you knew that, didn't you?"

She nodded.

He stepped aside and waved her toward a vacant chair at the center of the table. "You haven't missed much. We were briefing the killer's history, as well as our general assessment of who we're dealing with."

Angel opened her mouth, but he didn't give her time to

speak. "Don't worry. We may not be FBI, but we all know the drill. We're not to give you any of our assessments or opinions about the killer. That's your job, right?"

She wasn't known for staying silent, but Detective John Tucker didn't leave her much of an option. So she nodded. Again. Soon though, she'd have her say, and she'd be patient *if* he didn't take too long.

"We decided to get our own opinions in before you arrived. Now, though, I'm assuming you'd like to meet the team."

She took the last file from the center of the table and sat down, then pulled her own notes and her iPad from her briefcase and placed them beside the others. Aware of all eyes scrutinizing her every move, she shuffled the papers into place, turned on the iPad then raised her head to peer at the team. Scanning the table, she scratched off two of the six as suspects.

Her killer wasn't a woman, so the female at the table wasn't a threat, not that she would have considered Lexie McCain a threat anyway. Angel fought the urge to smile at the news journalist. She found it gratifying to see a woman who'd made such a name for herself, and Lexie had accomplished more in her lifetime, and more in regards to this case, than any of the men surrounding her realized.

But Angel knew.

Lexie McCain's arched brows lifted. None of the men noticed, but Angel did. Lexie knew Angel wouldn't unearth her secret. She tossed the reporter a nice-to-meet-you smile and nodded, as though they'd never seen each other before, and Lexie's shoulders relaxed.

In fact, the notable news journalist looked calm, cool and collected amid the brutish group of men. Yes, Angel had wanted this assignment, wanted to catch the Sunrise Killer more than any other UNSUB in her past. But she'd be the first to admit she hadn't merely wanted to catch the killer.

She wanted to help Lexie catch him.

Therefore, she scratched the TV lady off the list of potential suspects. And the old man at the end of the table, who she suspected was Zed Naylor, based on Etta's description, wasn't a possibility either. Though his eyes were alert and eager, his body was fading fast. She had no doubt he'd offer insight to the case, since Etta said he'd been around since the first series of murders, twenty-eight years ago. But he'd been around much longer than that. Aunt Carol would classify the weathered fellow with one of her favorite quips...

*"The wheel's still turning, but the hamster's dead."*

Angel bit against her inner cheeks to keep from chuckling. However, the urge to laugh out loud died a quick death when she caught a glance from Lexie. A look of admiration, and perhaps something more, toward John Tucker. Now if that wouldn't make things difficult.

No problem. Angel could deal with complications, and with keeping those she cared about from facing them. Right now, in any case, she had to deal with her potential suspects on the task force and with narrowing that list by Sunday, if possible.

Two down, four to go. And perhaps the introductions would help her even further in her process of elimination. Of the task force, at least. She had no doubt there were more people than those in this room who were close to the case. And whether her killer stared at her now, or whether she'd yet to meet him, he'd want to be close to the investigation.

"Yes, I'd like to meet everyone."

"Fine. Then we'll get started with the intros." John Tucker dropped in his seat at the end of the table in complete control...for now.

The woman who'd commanded their attention the moment she entered the room impressed Lexie and reminded her of a younger version of herself. Although Lexie listened to the men's brief bios, she wasn't as interested in their answers as in the profiler's questions. Even Lexie realized Angel Jackson considered them potential suspects, yet most of the men seemed oblivious to the fact. John Tucker, however, gave the profiler a look that would melt steel.

Angel didn't seem to care.

Lexie's chest swelled with admiration.

In her yellow leather jacket, tight blue jeans and Timberland boots, the young woman with the long blonde ponytail didn't fit the "guys in black suits" image Lexie had always associated with the FBI. But regardless of her attire, her sex, or her beauty, Angel Jackson composed one tough female, intent on finding a killer.

Lexie had every intention of helping her accomplish that goal. Since she had also met some of these men for the first time today, Lexie jotted notes during their introductions.

After each task force member finished his spiel, Angel asked him the same series of questions. In a normal meeting, no one would've thought much of her queries; they'd have seemed commonplace in a getting-better-acquainted discussion. In this room, and in the midst of this investigation, they took on a new meaning.

"How long have you lived in Macon?"

"Are you married? Divorced? Single?"

And if they'd been married, Angel jumped right into, "When did you marry? Any children?"

Lexie wrote each detail, and the manner each man responded, when he realized he was under Angel's meticulous scrutiny.

Captain Ed Pierce scowled about providing the information, but quoted his wedding date, 6-13-86 as though captured by terrorists and providing name, rank and serial number, then he added they had no children and hadn't wanted any anyway. "You can't be a cop without seeing the evil out there, and I wasn't about to bring another kid into it."

"And how long have you lived in Macon?"

"Moved here in '92. Before that, I was on the force in Valdosta."

The corners of Angel Jackson's mouth dipped for a brief second, but then she nodded and moved on.

Lou Marker stated he'd been born and raised in Macon, quoted his wedding date, pulled a photo from his wallet to show Angel his new grandbaby and noted his twenty-fifth anniversary would occur next month.

Acknowledging his turn, Ryan Sims shifted in his seat. "I've lived here forever, got married in 1985, divorced in '92. No kids."

Angel opened her mouth as if she were going to ask more, but then nodded at Sims and moved to Zed. Zed coughed and sputtered through a ten minute tribute to his "dear sweet

Ruthie" and elaborated on how their thirty-two years together weren't enough.

Although Lieutenant Sims looked as though he wanted to put a hand over the older man's mouth to shut him up, he didn't. No one did. And Lexie was glad no one stopped him from expressing affection toward his wife. At the end of his monologue, he withdrew a white handkerchief from his back pocket, wiped his eyes and blew his nose.

Next in line, Lexie gathered her courage then followed their lead. "I moved to Macon eight months ago from Atlanta. I'm an investigative news correspondent at WGXA and hope to inform the city as to what they should watch for regarding the Sunrise Killer." She paused, then added, "And I plan to air the story informing the world that he's been caught."

Angel nodded, and Lexie expected her to move on to the last person in the room, John Tucker, but the profiler didn't let her off the hook.

"And are you married? Divorced? Single? Have any children?"

Lexie blinked. Angel knew the answers to all of the above. However, the men at the table weren't aware of that, and she'd had to ask, to maintain consistency. Lexie should've anticipated the questions.

"Divorced. And I have a son attending college at the University of Georgia."

"Shoot, you ain't old enough to have a kid that age." Zed Naylor tilted his head and tried to pinpoint her age.

"I married young." Though answering Zed, she looked at Angel. "And I had my son at nineteen."

Angel gave her a tender smile then drew everyone's attention to the man on Lexie's left. "And you, Detective Tucker?"

Lexie's face had burned when she provided the information about her failed marriage and her son. Something about baring that information in front of John Tucker made her more aware of her past, more aware of the things that had happened and the things she couldn't change.

He leaned forward in his seat and looked at Angel when he spoke. "I was born in Macon. Married in '91. Abby was

murdered in 1999, as I'm sure you know. Any more
questions?"

"No." Angel inhaled, and Lexie leaned forward, curious to
hear what she'd tell about herself. But Special Agent Jackson
acted as though revealing her own information wasn't part of
the deal. None of the men asked. Instead, Captain Pierce asked
the question all of them wanted answered. "So, did we give
you what you're looking for, Agent Jackson?"

"What I'm looking for?"

"The profile. How many of us fit?" He glanced in John
Tucker's direction.

Angel didn't bat a lash. "Three are close, but none hit the
mark."

Lexie swallowed. She had determined *that* from their brief
responses? Or did she look at people and know whether they
were capable of murder? Lexie scanned the men around the
table; they didn't look at all surprised by the quick assessment.
Three potential killers, but none hit the mark?

Which three?

"You're saying your profile differs from the previous guy's
profile?" Captain Pierce didn't attempt to mask his glance in
Tucker's direction this time.

"I'm not saying that at all. Special Agent Carlton identified
several aspects that I still believe are associated with our killer;
however, I do have some additions to his evaluation, which
you'll see on the profile I've generated." She withdrew a
packet of papers from her file, removed the black binder clip
from the top then passed them around the table.

Lexie accepted her page and scanned the FBI profile, while
Angel Jackson read aloud.

"We're looking for a white male, since the first victim in
1985 was Caucasian. The first victim is almost always the
same race as the perpetrator. The killer starts out within his
comfort zone. Sometimes he will move beyond that barrier, but
in this case, he didn't."

Captain Pierce nodded.

Angel read, "He's in his forties to mid-fifties, which means
he'd have been a teenager or in his early twenties during the
first series. He would have lived in Macon during the time

periods of all preceding series. Our guy knows his way around and appears to have entered several victims' homes without sign of forced entry which, as Stan Carlton noted, could indicate he wore a police uniform or another uniform identifying a trusted profession. Or he could have a face they all recognized and respected."

Unimpressed, Captain Pierce crossed his arms. "We knew that much."

"But what I've added to Agent Carlton's evaluation follows." Angel continued, not swayed by his skepticism. "Our perpetrator was married, or began a serious relationship, between 1985 and 1992. My reasoning for this addition is his MO changed between those two series of murders. In 1985, all of his victims were attacked outside, beaten and left to suffer the elements until their bodies were located. When he returned seven years later, he approached victims from within their home and stopped beating them. Instead, he strangled them then placed them almost reverently on their beds to be found."

"Which means?" Lieutenant Sims prompted.

"Remorse. Our killer began seeing his victims as more than mere bodies after 1985. This means the UNSUB had a change of heart, so to speak, with regards to his interpretation of humans and life in general. However, it wasn't strong enough to stop his urge to kill. In past experience, our unit has found that a change of MO such as this means one of two things."

When she paused, Pierce scowled. "We're listening."

"Either we're dealing with a copycat killer, or the original murderer experienced a life change during that time, which I believe is the case in this series. Although the modification in the number of women murdered during each series still doesn't make sense in the scenario outlined here. Why he only killed six that first year, then maintained his number at seven for the following three series is still anyone's guess, but I feel certain there's a reason for the change. We just have to find it."

"So how do you know it wasn't someone different, a copycat killer, like you said, starting in 1992?" Lou Marker asked.

"I don't. However, with the signature remaining the same, it would appear we've got the same UNSUB. All victims were blonde, single and pregnant. They were all strangled until they, and their unborn children, died." She looked at Lexie, then back to the remainder of the group.

"From the criteria I've already listed, three of the people within this room fit our target suspects: Deputy Chief Marker, Lieutenant Sims and Detective Tucker. Captain Pierce wasn't living in Macon at the time the first murders were committed, and Zed Naylor is, I'm assuming, above our age range."

Zed ran a wrinkled hand through his thin crop of stark white hair. "I'll say I am."

"But, if you'll notice the item in red at the bottom of the page, none of you meet the last criterion. Our killer knew Molly Taylor, the first victim. In some way, shape, or form, a serial killer almost always selects that very first victim due to past experience with that person. From my files, and from Special Agent Carlton's reports, none of you ever met the girl. But our killer did. And because of her death occurring on Easter, I believe the way he knew her had something to do with religion. Or non-religion."

Lexie listened to the men at the table mumble their suspicions regarding Molly Taylor, how every lead about her killer had turned up nothing and how the potential suspects for the girl's murder had been exhausted throughout the past twenty-eight years.

She started to keep her thoughts to herself, but one thing had been niggling the back of her mind all day, and the reporter in her couldn't resist bringing it to light. True, she wasn't a cop or an FBI profiler, but her dedication to reporting the news did cause her to ask pertinent questions. And since she hadn't been involved with the case before, she had no idea whether the question had ever been answered.

"Special Agent Jackson?"

"Yes?" Angel's green eyes studied Lexie's face as if trying to determine the question before she asked. After the profiler's quick analysis of the men at the table, Lexie wasn't so sure she couldn't. Even so, she'd ask. There was no such thing as a stupid question.

"Has the FBI considered the killings could be more religious-geared than they first realized? I'm sure you have," she added, not wanting to insult the government, "But as I looked over the days of the week for kills in each series, I couldn't help but notice that when the dates were definite—that is, when the body was quickly found and the coroner didn't have to estimate the date of death—several of them also coincided with the same day of the week."

Angel Jackson's chair scraped against the floor as she scooted forward. "Go on."

Lexie sifted through her notes until she found the page she needed. "In 1992, the first victim was found on Tuesday, the tenth of March. Then the second one that year was found on Easter. In 1999, the first body was found on Tuesday, February twenty-third. The second one, again, on Easter. In 2006, the first body was also found on a Tuesday, March seventh. Then another Easter for the second kill. This year, however, Cami Talton's body wasn't found immediately, but the coroner stated she died four to five weeks ago, which could have put the date of death on Tuesday, February nineteenth."

"You're saying that since 1992, the first murder has always happened on a Tuesday?" Captain Pierce asked.

"No, what I'm saying is—" Lexie started, but stopped when Angel, flipping through her pages, nodded her head. Her eyes widened as she got it.

"What she's saying is the first murder always occurred on the same weekday. And that, in fact, every murder in the series occurred on the same day of the week."

"Yes." Lexie nodded. "The first murder in the series seems to have always occurred on Tuesday, except for the very first murder in 1985, on Easter. And the third murder is always on a Friday, the fourth on a Wednesday, and so on. But even though that's what I noticed, I don't think that's the pattern."

"You said you believe it has to do with religion." Lou's interest tuned in on Lexie's observation.

"It does. His first kill is always forty days prior to Easter, isn't it?" Angel directed the question to Lexie.

"It looks that way. And even though the remaining dates each year don't appear to hit any religious holidays," Lexie continued, while everyone at the table searched through the murder dates with renewed interest, "they all occur on the same day of the week, with response to the previous murder."

"Because they're all forty days apart." Angel wrote several notes in her file. "Forty days and forty nights. I should've looked for more Biblical references. Good job, McCain. This gives us something to work with. The guy's got a knowledge of religion, albeit a sick interpretation, and it goes deeper than including an Easter kill in each series. He's following a pattern, and we need to figure out why that pattern was established, what it means."

"Then why didn't he follow it the first year?" Lou asked. "It makes no sense. There was no murder that year forty days before Easter. Everything started with Molly Taylor on Easter Sunday."

"Maybe not." Papers stopped rattling and whispers ceased as everyone turned their attention to John Tucker.

Angel looked up. "What are you saying, Detective?"

But Lexie knew, and she agreed. She turned in her chair to hear him convey the same thing she'd been thinking since she'd first noted the pattern in the past three series.

"I'm thinking they missed a murder that first year. Yeah, I know his MO changed, and I think you're right about him humanizing his victims after that point, due to a marriage, or a kid, or something along that line, but I don't think he changed the number of women killed between '85 and '92. Someone was murdered on that Tuesday, forty days before Easter in 1985, and that's the *real* first victim. That's why you haven't been able to match any suspects to Molly Taylor."

"She wasn't the first victim." Angel nodded as though the theory had potential.

John agreed. "After hearing what Ms. McCain brought to light tonight, I think there was another woman murdered in 1985. It makes more sense than any of our previous theories, I'm surprised we didn't question it earlier."

"Kind of hard to say a murder was committed when you haven't got a body," Ed Pierce droned from his seat.

Lexie watched John Tucker's jaw twitch, listened to his deep inhalation, then the steady whoosh of air as he released the breath. She'd bet money he had counted to ten. Or a fast twenty.

"No, we didn't find another body, but after the following series, we should've gone back and taken a better look at that year."

"We did. I've got the reports right here." Ryan Sims lifted his copy of the information the police had gathered throughout the past twenty-eight years, information on the murders, autopsies, victimology and crime scene photos.

"We checked out the information on the murders and the victims," John corrected. "We should have looked more at the year in question to determine if there could've been an additional murder, as Ms. McCain suggested. Missing persons' reports, number of recoveries, number unrecovered. That information would provide a good starting point in identifying if there was a different initial victim."

"You think Molly Taylor wasn't the first?" Zed Naylor looked skeptical. "He left all the bodies out to be found back then. Why wouldn't we have found the first one?"

"Maybe because he knew that kill would point to him," Angel said. "Because it *was* personal."

"You know, that could be right." Captain Pierce changed his tune and sounded interested in pursuing this new avenue. "We *haven't* connected any possible suspects to Molly Taylor. Her family checked out, friends checked out and the girl had never done anything out of the ordinary or produced any enemies, from what the department learned back then."

"And I think if we find that first victim, then we'll find the link between that person and the people who fit your profile. All of it, including the last item on your list, Agent Jackson." John Tucker underlined the item on his page. "The killer did have some type of relationship with the first victim. We just haven't identified the first victim yet."

Angel looked at Lexie and gave her a slight smile, then nodded in appreciation. "Maybe I should always request a media professional for my cases."

"Thanks," Lexie said, thrilled to be an active member of the group, and even more pleased they were getting closer to finding, and stopping, the killer.

"Missing persons?" Zed Naylor asked, rising from his chair.

"Yeah," Captain Pierce answered. "Pull January through

April of 1985 and let's see what we've got."

"It'll take a while." Lou Marker stood beside Zed. "That stuff's still in hard copy and handwritten. Don't think the techies have scanned that far back. Nothing will be in the system, and it's combined with the rest of the state's records."

"Fine." The captain's tone emphasized his determination. "See how many people we can put on it, and let's try to have something together by morning."

Lexie looked at the big round clock on the wall. White circle, black numbers, and both hands pointing straight up. Midnight. Twenty-four hours before the murderer planned to kill again. Her pulse raced. They were on the right track; she could feel it. If they identified that first victim, she believed they'd find the killer. And perhaps, put an end to her personal nightmare.

# CHAPTER FOUR

In spite of Zed and Lou finding the surplus of boxes with missing persons' data from 1985, the reports weren't as detailed as their modern counterparts. To locate those identified as missing from Bibb County, they had to go through the state files one by one and search the victims' addresses. By 3:00 a.m., tempers flared, patience was fleeting, and the group realized they needed sleep if they weren't planning to kill each other before they finished.

Captain Pierce announced they would call it a day, leaving Zed and Lou to continue perusing the files until 6:00 a.m., when Tucker and Sims were scheduled to relieve the pair. The captain wanted somebody on it until all potential victims surfaced and the team could determine which of them, if any, was the Sunrise Killer's initial murder. He'd have additional police personnel to help sort the information by morning, and the task force would reconvene at 8:00 a.m. Not a lot of time for sleep, but time was a limited commodity.

Weary from the stress of putting the pieces together and from the painstaking chore of searching for Macon addresses within those endless files, Lexie gathered her things.

"Ms. McCain." John Tucker stepped close.

She tried not to react to the prickle on her skin, an immediate response to hearing him say her name, and a response she neither understood nor could control. Fear, or something else? "Yes?"

She had to tilt her head to look at his eyes, blue eyes that gazed straight through her, and seemed to see more than she wanted to show. How much did John Tucker know about her, anyway? Nothing. No one knew her part in what had happened so long ago. That portion of the records had been extinguished from public access years ago. Angel had even verified the fact when she joined the Bureau.

"You're an asset to this team." His mouth crooked up on one side. "I admit I wasn't sure anyone from the media would help. But then again, you're not the average run-of-the-mill reporter, are you?"

Relieved, she smiled. "Guess not. And thanks for the vote of confidence. I hope to help catch him." He couldn't realize how much.

"We'll get him this time. We have to." He leaned closer, those blue eyes making her stomach quiver. "I—" He didn't get the chance to finish before Captain Pierce interrupted.

"Tucker, I need you to take a look at this." He held up a file.

"Right." He gave Lexie an apologetic look. "Duty calls."

"Of course." She added her surplus of new notes to her briefcase and started leaving. Then, aware she had an hour to get her story to the paper, she searched out Agent Jackson and found her walking toward the lobby.

"Angel." Her voice bounced off the tile walls.

The profiler turned around, peered beyond Lexie and shook her head.

Realizing her mistake, Lexie whipped around to verify no one had heard her casual reference to the FBI agent. She mouthed, "Whoops," but Angel motioned her to come on.

Lexie neared and matched Angel's steps toward the exit.

"No problem." The profiler looked around once more, lowered her voice. "You doing okay?"

Lexie shrugged. "You would know better than I. I may know how to cover the stories, but I'm a rookie in this type of thing. Who would have thought they'd ask me to join the task force? So, how am I doing?"

"Fine. I can't tell you how pleased I was when Etta told me you were inside. Figured we'd better keep our distance while I'm in Macon, all things considered, but working together on the task force will make communicating much easier. I'd requested an investigative reporter, but wasn't sure who they'd get. Of course, I assumed they would realize you were the best person for the job."

"Your boss doesn't know about me? I assumed the FBI knew everything."

"Quantico knows, of course. The Atlanta field office, however, doesn't. Until this guy is caught, it'll stay that way. Safer for both of us, according to the guys at the top."

Lexie nodded. "Tucker didn't tell me the name of the profiler, but I knew if there was any way for you to get this case, you'd try." She smiled. "By the way, I was impressed with how cool you seemed when you came in and saw me sitting there with the cop crew. I should've realized Etta stuck around and filled you in."

"Checked me out was more like it, although she'd staged her one-woman ambush for Carlton. That lady's mighty protective of the town's number one homicide detective."

Lexie didn't comment. It seemed odd to say she also felt protective of him, given he was a walking mountain, but for some strange reason, she did. This killer had ruined his life. Granted, not in the same manner as he'd ruined the lives of his victims, but John Tucker had also been violated. He'd lost his wife, his baby and his credibility due to the Sunrise Killer. And he seemed as committed as Angel and Lexie in making the man pay.

The two women kept walking, passing through the lobby then exiting the building. Thankfully, the rain had taken a break.

Angel indicated the vacant parking area. "We're all clear now. Did you need to ask me something?"

"Yeah." Lexie looked behind her to make sure no cops headed their way. She didn't want to seem too chummy with the FBI agent assigned to the case. They didn't need anyone suspecting the truth, but she had to ask this question. "Paul Kingsley, my boss, extended my deadline until 4:00 this morning to let me get the most up-to-date story for the early news segment."

"Sounds good. What do you need from me?"

"I'd like to broadcast the updated profile, as well as the fact that we now know the first kill of each series occurs forty days prior to Easter and subsequent murders are also spaced forty days apart. Bring up the whole Biblical aspect that may be associated with each series. During the 2006 series, they aired Stan Carlton's evaluation; however, with your additions, the changes between 1985 and 1992, I think the public deserves to be informed of what they're looking for. It'll help us pinpoint him, narrow down our list. And maybe convince a witness to come forward, if they know of someone who fits the description. Knowing the guy probably married or had a serious relationship between those years might spark someone to put two and two together. And the whole religion theory might also spark a memory."

Angel stopped walking, seemed to consider the ramifications of the information hitting the airwaves, where the killer could hear every word of their progress.

"Would it be a good thing? Or would it set him off to do something else, something not in his plan?"

"That's what I'm trying to decide," Angel admitted. "In all honesty, if our UNSUB believes he's conducting some sort of religious objective and that he's supposed to perform his duties on specific dates, I don't think anything you do will change that plan. It'll just make him more aware that we're onto him. And that might make him nervous, might even make him slip up."

"So you think I should? Granted, I'll be the first to admit I'm hungry for the story, but I don't want the guilt of knowing someone died because of my news segment."

"That won't happen. Maybe with some killers, but not this one. He's too detailed, too precise. I don't believe there's anything that'll make him veer from his plan. He hasn't had a fear of getting caught before. Maybe if he thinks we're watching for him to act, that we may anticipate his next strike, he won't find it so easy to hit his target."

"All right. I'll include the specific dates that we suspect he'll strike; that should remind the public how serious this is and how deranged he is. I'll write the copy now."

"You're going to your office? Now? Alone?" Angel shook her head. "I don't think so. I'll go with you."

"I don't have to go in. I'll email the text from home. One of those amazing modern conveniences we all love. But thanks for the offer."

"When will you tape the broadcast?"

"I'll call Henry, my cameraman. We'll bring a van here and tape the footage in front of the police station."

"In the middle of the night?"

Lexie grinned. "The news doesn't sleep." She held up a hand when Angel started to argue. "I've been doing this a long time."

"What about this Henry guy? Can he protect you? And do you trust him?"

"Yes, I trust him, and since when have I needed a man for protection, anyway?"

Angel glared. "Lexie..."

"I'll be fine, and I'm counting on producing a story that throws the killer's careful plan off-balance, or at least exposes it to potential victims."

"I never doubted your abilities," Angel clarified. "I just don't want you getting hurt."

"Still determined to even the score?"

"Hey, I've never denied it."

"Problem is, like I said, I can take care of myself."

Angel held up her palms in defeat. "I'm not going to argue with you anymore. And I have to tell you, the Biblical reference, the whole forty days and forty nights thing, that was crucial. You did good catching that." She shrugged. "Religion isn't my strong suit."

"It could be."

Before she could say more, Angel added, "Listen, I think it's fine that you turned to church and all to help you cope with what happened. But for me, I'd say God let me down before I even got started."

"He didn't let you down. The world let you down." Lexie cleared her throat. "I'm planning on going to an Easter service Sunday. Why don't you come? It will be like old times."

"The only way it'd be like old times is if Aunt Carol was dragging me against my will." Angel laughed. "But the fact that you think you'll get to go to church Sunday—and that we won't be spending the day dealing with the aftermath of another Easter kill—proves that you're still the glass-half-full girl. Mine is still half-empty." She pressed the keyless remote to unlock her SUV. "Where are you parked?"

"Right there." Lexie gave up on coaxing Angel to try God again, for now. She pointed to a silver Lexus.

"Wow, guess it pays to be a big time newswoman. Last time I saw you, you still had the dirt brown minivan."

"My minivan was silver, thank you very much. It was just dirty from running Phillip, Jr. to baseball, football, basketball..."

"Quite the athlete, isn't he?"

"Yeah." Lexie gushed with pride. He'd moved on campus last summer and had become a confident, self-assured young man who would make it in the world. God had blessed her with an amazing son.

"So when did you get the new toy?"

"I bought it as a celebration of Phillip Jr.'s scholarship to Georgia. I saved more in tuition expenses than what the car cost."

"And did he get anything out of this deal?"

"His daddy bought him a Jeep for high school graduation, so I figure we both made out like bandits."

"I guess you did." Angel turned to look at the police station. The rest of the group remained inside. "Listen, I saw the way you looked at him, John Tucker."

Lexie's mouth opened to protest, but then she saw Angel's eyes, and knew it'd be wasted breath. "Okay."

"You realize he's still a suspect."

"He didn't do it, Angel. Besides, he had an airtight alibi for when his wife was murdered. You know that. You've seen the reports."

"And I also believe it doesn't appear to be a copycat killer. But I've been wrong in the past."

"Funny, I never remember you admitting that before."

"Yeah, well, it doesn't happen often."

"You being wrong, or admitting it?"

Angel grinned. "Both. Just be careful, okay?"

"Don't worry. I will."

"And try to watch what you let happen with Tucker, or anyone, at least until we catch this guy."

"Understood. But if memory serves, I'm older than you. Older equals wiser, right?"

"Not necessarily." Angel climbed in her SUV.

"And speaking of wiser," Lexie countered, "A wise FBI profiler would get some sleep tonight so she'd be ready for the rest of the weekend."

Angel's blonde ponytail swished across her left shoulder as she jerked her head toward Lexie. "And when are you going to sleep? Before you write the copy? During the broadcast? Or after you've taped, when I know you'll edit the segment until the minute it airs?"

"Guilty." Lexie couldn't deny the truth. "And you'll search Internet sites for info on whacked out religious buffs all night, right?"

"Admit it. If you didn't have to produce your story, you'd do the same thing, but I requested six books on Biblical numerology to be left at the front desk at my hotel."

"Why am I not surprised?"

"After I read them, then I'll sleep."

"Sure you will." Lexie did another scan of the parking lot to verify they were still alone then lowered her voice to a soft whisper. "Have you seen him lately?"

Angel's smile converted to a thin, solemn line. "Last Monday."

"I went Saturday. He looks good, doesn't he?"

"Yeah, he does. When are you going back?" Angel held up a finger as an officer exited the building and crossed the lot. "See you tomorrow, Ms. McCain, Agent Jackson." Lou Marker waved at them, then entered a car parked two spaces away from Angel's Tahoe.

Lexie watched Angel start her SUV, then drive away. Disappointed they didn't have more time to talk, she moved toward her car.

"Hey." The deep voice startled her, sent an icy finger down her spine.

She turned to find Lieutenant Sims standing behind her. Why hadn't she heard him? Had he been in the parking lot all along? Had he heard their conversation? And did he realize the two women knew each other? Or why?

The lamppost cast a shadow across his face, but she could still see his sandy hair, more ruffled than it'd been in the building. He cocked his head to the side, and a beam from the light behind him made her squint to make out his face in the darkness.

"Wanna go get a cup of coffee?" With hands stuffed in his jacket pockets, he appeared nervous, like a teen asking for a date, instead of a forty-something inviting her for coffee.

Lexie scanned the parking area, but she couldn't see well with the lieutenant towering between her and the light. Her eyes smarted from the bright beams pulsing over his shoulder with each shift of his weight from one foot to the other.

*Was* he nervous? Should she be?

She caught a glimpse of the multitude of surveillance cameras pointed at the parking area. They were in a parking lot outside the police station. She shouldn't be so queasy here. "I need to get home and write my piece for the morning broadcast. It's due by four." She wished someone else would come outside. Not that she thought Ryan was the killer or anything, but based on Angel's profile, he fit.

"It's a cup of coffee, Lexie." He took a step toward her. "Or do you not go out with cops? Is that it? You got something against cops, McCain?" He chuckled, but it sounded like a wet hiss.

The old feelings returned. Panic. Fear. She could hear the screams. Her screams.

*No. Not again. Not now.*

Where were the others? Where was...

"Tucker." Ryan turned his head toward a large shadow, making its way toward them in the parking lot. "I thought you were going to stay and help Pierce."

"I did." John Tucker stepped beside the lieutenant. "Everything going okay out here?" he asked, while Ryan stepped away from the light and Lexie's eyes adjusted.

"Just fine." Sims braced his stance as though daring the detective to assume otherwise.

"I was telling Lieutenant Sims that I have to go work on my story." Lexie's heart slowed to a near-normal beat. "I want to air the updated profile information on the early news broadcast."

"Guess I'll see you tomorrow then, Sims." Tucker stood his ground.

Although Lexie still couldn't see his face, she heard a thick grunt from Ryan. Then he mumbled something incoherent, turned and walked away.

Detective John Tucker stood there, unmoving, until the lieutenant entered his car and left the lot.

Funny how she didn't feel the same kind of panic next to the formidable detective. On the contrary, she felt protected, safe. "Thank you. I'm sure he didn't mean any harm."

"No, but he made you uneasy."

She nodded. "Not his fault. It's mine, I'm sure. Guess even at thirty-six, I'm still afraid of the dark." She tried to laugh, but it came out watery and weak.

"Where do you live?"

And with those four words, her heartbeat kicked right back into full gear. She couldn't control her gasp. Not him, too. She'd felt so certain. He'd seemed safe, hadn't he? Or had she just wanted him to be?

He shook his head then reached out and touched her cheek.

Lexie jerked away as if he'd slapped her. She couldn't help it. Those old reflexes, the ones that cost her a marriage, were too strong.

He turned to the side, exposing his face to the light and the pain etched on his features. "You told me I wasn't a killer."

"I know." *Dear God, help me. Help me control my fear.*

"Still believe that? Do you still believe I'm a good guy, Ms. McCain?"

She wouldn't—couldn't—let her anxiety win this time. "Lexie." She needed to let him get more personal, let him see she trusted him. She did, didn't she? She just had to trust herself enough to let go of the fear. "Call me Lexie, please."

*I can do all things through Christ who strengthens me. Give me strength now, Lord. Control my fear.*

"All right." He studied her, his gaze searching her eyes to see the truth. "Lexie. You still think I'm okay?"

She nodded past the tension in her chest, the tight squeeze around her heart, and her pulse began to slow. She'd been drawn to him last fall, and she suspected the emotion that churned deep within her wasn't one-sided. But she'd stayed away from the man since they'd met. Why, she wasn't sure. Didn't she deserve a chance at knowing what could happen? At seeing if maybe she could move past the memories? But could she ever move beyond them if the killer wasn't caught?

"Then let me follow you home."

"Follow me?" She hated the way her voice snagged between the words. She'd been dubbed one of the strongest television personalities in the South, had been praised for her tenacity and her ability to obtain the facts. She'd even been the primary media source for the I-20 rapist case. So why did John Tucker's request feel like a vise around her neck?

"We both agree I'm not the killer, but we also agree there's one out there. And there's no way I'm going to let you drive home alone without making sure you get there okay."

She swallowed. "All right." Then her gaze darted to where Angel had driven away. "Oh. Oh no."

"Don't worry. The FBI has someone watching her hotel. They take care of their own."

She blinked. "How did you know what I was thinking?"

"You're a female. Females watch out for other females." He lifted one shoulder. "Females watch out for others, period."

Lexie believed him. He didn't know Angel's role in her past. He didn't even know her past, and she planned to keep it that way, for now. The fewer that knew, the better. Because if the killer found out what she knew, Lexie would be dead. Then again, it wasn't what she knew that could get her killed; it was what she couldn't remember.

Vickie Jones dangled one leg out of the covers, her mouth open and one hand threaded through her hair on the pillow while she slept. In spite of the cloudy night, the moonlight filtered through the drizzling mist to emphasize her blonde locks, her angelic face. An angel who'd sinned, like Hannah. And a foolish angel too, sleeping with her window open and a mere screen providing the scant appearance of safety. She probably liked listening to the rain while she slept. Hannah had always liked the rain, too.

The weather forecasted rain again tomorrow, which would make his mission easier. She'd leave the window open again, and he'd step through, accepting her invitation.

He could take care of her tonight, but it wasn't time. Not yet. He had to follow the plan, maintain order, accomplish the necessary completeness to fulfill his destiny. That's what Brother Moses would have wanted when he taught them the truth. He wouldn't have approved of his followers going astray, turning weak in the face of adversity. Brother Moses would have known that the Supreme One would be pleased, would even praise his dedication to the Fellowship.

Vickie Jones had a child, a creation from God, growing inside of her, but she didn't deserve its power, in spite of the proclamation of purity that crowned her pretty face. Like Hannah, Vickie embodied a multitude of contradictions, appearing all good and pure while hiding a demon in her soul.

The demon had to be captured before it gained the power of the child. That power made him strong. He'd be stronger if the child were his own, but that hadn't been the plan. He'd tried. And failed. Not because he'd sinned, but because he was meant to save these children, to capture and control the power that'd been bestowed in error.

Not the Supreme One's error, of course, but the other.

He placed a gloved hand against the mesh screen covering Vickie's window. Tomorrow night, at the right time, he'd return. Tonight he'd prepare. And that meant visiting Hannah.

The rain thickened as he traversed the vacant streets of Macon, his windshield wipers beating, thud, thud, thudding against the glass. The rhythm matched his pulse, strong and steady and deliberate. Tomorrow night, he'd feel her pulse, a more frantic rhythm, drumming beneath his fingers as he pressed them into her throat, shutting off her chance to breathe, squeezing the life away.

After he finished, he'd feel peace, inner strength at his accomplishment, the power over evil. That would satisfy him, for a while, until the next appointed time. Six more to be complete. Six more to quench the thirst, fulfill the fire. Then he'd wait again. Wait for the precise amount of time necessary to prepare, to expend the power granted then conquer again.

The cycle tired him, a burden no soul should bear, but bear it he must.

Because of Hannah.

If only she'd seen the truth and realized the power they could create together, what they were meant to accomplish. Together.

But no, she'd fallen prey to the other, had heeded *his* calling. She let a heathen claim what wasn't his to take, what should never have been given to anyone but those who'd proven themselves worthy.

The child should have been his. Then again, in the end, it became his, living within him now, its power keeping him strong, as did the power from the other children after. The ones who fulfilled the balance, generated completeness.

His gloved fingers gripped the steering wheel so tightly his wrists stung, and he continued, away from the city, toward Hannah...and her lover.

They'd never been found, their bodies not worthy of a formal farewell from family and friends who didn't understand why they had to leave, why they were required to forfeit their child. And didn't that confirm the truth? No one had mourned them. No one had cared.

Because they didn't deserve to live.

The others, those that had followed to fulfill the requirements, had received their due, the grief from loved ones and friends. He didn't mind that; he understood. Those females were offered because of Hannah's sin. They'd come forward to offer their children and give him what he should have had all along, power from the child. Power that he and Hannah could have had together, if only she'd seen the truth. If only she'd understood.

She belonged with him. She belonged to him. He'd known it from the moment they met, but she fought her destiny. She fought fate. And her lover convinced her they could flee, that she wouldn't have to pay the price for what they'd done. But she did pay. And so did he.

Overgrown brush and weeds hid the dirt road from view. He turned the wheel and flinched as wet branches slapped against the glass, caused the wipers to stall and sputter. Pine needles stuck to the sides of the window and obstructed his view even more. But he had to continue. He'd never killed without going to Hannah and her lover, telling them what they'd done and what they'd caused him to have to do. They needed to know, needed to feel the guilt they deserved. He'd have never had to continue, would have never had to kill in the first place, if it weren't for their deceit.

He flicked his lights on bright, stopped the car and climbed out, his shoes sinking in leaf-covered mud. Within seconds, he stood above them, above the very spot where he'd buried them deep, their bodies entwined in the same manner as they'd been when they committed the sin. Hannah's enlarged stomach displayed the evidence of what she'd done. Of how she'd hurt him.

Big, thick drops of rain fell through the trees, drenched his hair, his face, his clothes. The pungent scent of damp earth and pine overpowered his senses, made his head spin at the memory of what had happened so long ago.

His knees buckled and he fell forward, letting his body crumple to kneel against the cold, hard ground. "Can't you see what you've done, Hannah? Don't you understand?" His hands clenched fists full of dirt, the earth that hovered above her body, naked beneath him and beside her heathen lover. Then he turned toward the spot where Brother Moses had once preached fire and brimstone, good and evil, and he knew Moses could see him now. And even though Brother Moses hadn't been able to see it through, he'd known what had to be done. It took someone strong enough to make those sinners pay, starting with the two disgusting lovers buried beneath him.

"See what you've done!" He lifted his hands and flung the filth toward Heaven.

# CHAPTER FIVE

*Help. Aunt Bev needed help. And the baby needed help. They needed AJ, and she wouldn't—couldn't—let them down.*

*Panting and crying and hurting, AJ climbed the next hill. Her side cramped. Just a few more steps to the top. "Please, God, please," she whimpered as she pressed forward, peered in the distance and saw him.*

*Who was he? The one who would help? Or the one who had hurt Aunt Bev?*

*Praying she made the right decision, AJ took a deep breath and yelled.*

Covered in sweat, her pulse pumping so hard her skin burned, she jerked awake in the bed. She wasn't eight, wasn't on that never-ending, rock-covered road. And she wasn't trying to save her aunt. She couldn't. No matter how many times she returned in her dreams, the ending never changed.

Aunt Bev was gone.

She stood from the bed and stripped the sheets. They were warm and damp, smelled of sweat and fear. She hated the smell. She'd always hate that smell.

At 7:45, Lexie entered the conference room and found Angel surrounded by stacks of books, several of which were opened, with bright yellow post-its on some pages, dog-eared tabs marking others. "Where's the rest of the team?"

"Marker and Naylor left at 6:00 to catch a bit of sleep, but they should be back soon. Tucker and Sims are down the hall in one of the other rooms going through the missing persons' data." She marked her page in the book. "I saw your broadcast this morning. Good job."

"Thanks. I thought you said you were going to get some sleep."

"I said I'd sleep when I finished reading. I didn't finish." Even with red rimming her green eyes and makeup missing in action, Angel Jackson still gave the presence of having everything in order. Matter of fact, she looked alert and ready to tackle anything, even a killer. Her yellow leather jacket draped over the back of her chair, and she wore the same tight jeans and brown boots she'd had on last night.

"No time to change clothes?"

"Nope, but I did manage deodorant."

"We appreciate that, Agent Jackson." John Tucker entered the room, and Lexie's skin tingled in response.

Angel smirked at the detective. "Sure you do."

Lexie forced her gaze from Tucker back to Angel. "I thought you requested six books." She lifted Bible Mathematics and thumbed through to read the pages Angel had dog-eared.

"I did. And then I requested more." She reached for one of three large Styrofoam cups sitting beyond the books, took a big sip, then squinted through the swallow. "What do they put in this stuff?"

"We don't ask," Tucker looked at Lexie. "You do okay last night? Get some sleep?"

She nodded. "About an hour. Thanks again for following me home."

Angel's head jerked, her vision lifting from the pages of Numbers in Scripture, but she made no comment.

"You're welcome." He drawled, Southern accent giving him even more appeal. Lexie was used to Southern accents, of course, but still, his had a deep, rich confident cadence.

"Well, if you two are done visiting, I think I've found a few points of interest here." Angel's tone held a hint of irritation and her look said she'd caught Lexie staring at the man.

Lexie felt her cheeks blush, and she concentrated on Angel's words rather than Tucker's accent. "A few points of interest?"

"The lieutenant and I found a couple too." John took his

chair as Ed Pierce and Ryan Sims, both carrying steaming cups of coffee, entered the conference room.

"You go ahead." Angel closed one book and peered at the men.

"Want me to tell her?" Ryan took his seat.

"If you want." Tucker answered Ryan, but Lexie noticed his attention didn't waver from...her. She opened her briefcase and removed her files without looking at the man. And silently told herself to get a grip on the attraction, or energy, or whatever existed between her and Detective John Tucker.

"Good news first, or bad?" Sims asked.

Angel took another sip of her coffee, her mouth grimacing as she swallowed. "Good."

"We've located three subjects reported missing in Bibb County during January, March and April of 1985."

"What about February?"

"That's the bad news. The February files are missing."

She placed one hand on her forehead, spread her fingers and rubbed her temples. "And since the date for the first kill would've been," she moved her hand away and consulted her notes, "February 26th that year, that's the month where we'd find who we're looking for, right?"

"That's the date I got too." Lexie located the same date in her notes. "Forty days before Easter."

"Any idea what happened to February's information?"

"Seeing as it's the only month missing for the year, I'd say someone didn't want us finding it," Sims answered, while Captain Pierce shot a not-so-discreet glance at Tucker.

John Tucker placed his palms on the table. "For the record, I haven't accessed the missing persons' files from that year prior to this morning, in Lieutenant Sims' presence, I might add. And also for the record, a variety of people have had access to those files throughout the past twenty-eight years, and all of their names are logged in records."

"You see, that's another bizarre thing." Pierce cut his gaze to Tucker. "We're missing a records book too."

"What year?" John pushed the two words through gritted teeth.

"1985."

"Who has access to those records?" Angel's query brought the conversation back in the direction they needed and away from the unspoken insinuation that Tucker had something to do with the missing files. "Anyone other than police personnel?"

Lexie watched Angel's eyes and prayed she wouldn't draw additional attention to Tucker. She'd thought a lot of the man before, but after his offer to follow her home last night, plus the fact that he'd done nothing more than verify she made it inside, Lexie didn't want his name brought back up in this case.

Ryan Sims shrugged. "With older records, anybody could've taken them."

"What do you mean?"

"Folks come in all the time to take a look at those files. If they didn't, the things would never be of any use to anybody."

"Well, they'd sure be of use to us now." Angel looked appalled. "*Who* comes in to look at them?"

"Kids from the college doing reports, family members wanting to check out the old case information, see if they missed any clues about what could've happened to their kids, cops looking through old cases." He shrugged again. "Lots of people."

"That's true," Lou Marker confirmed as he and Zed entered the room. Both of them were still in the same clothes they'd worn last night and although they looked like they'd had some sleep, they hadn't had much. "Lots of folks have access to those files."

"I called the state this morning," Tucker said. "They have the February info, but they said it'll take them a while to find the files."

"Did they say how long *a while* would be?" Angel's frustration with this additional kink in their plan was evident.

"Estimated it could be up to a week."

"We don't have a week. We don't even have a day." Lexie looked to Angel for guidance. "Can you pull some strings with the FBI to speed things up?"

No one in the room seemed to think her question over the top, judging from the way they looked toward the profiler to hear her answer.

"I'll make a few calls. I'm assuming the state still has the files on hard copy as well? They haven't scanned them into their database?"

"That's what they said," Tucker answered.

"Super. Well, I'll light a fire under them but if they're going through everything by hand, I won't be surprised if their estimate is on the money. And we can't afford to wait a week." She slammed the cover closed on Bible Numerology. "What did you find in the other three months?"

"Two boys and one girl," Tucker said.

"A description of the girl?" Pierce asked.

"Brunette. And she was only eight."

"Not our victim." Angel sighed. "I'm going to make those calls." She withdrew her cell phone from her purse and left the room.

Lexie's stomach churned. So many women were in danger, and the task force was at a dead end. "What are we going to do now?"

"Media." Pierce surveyed the remainder of the task force for their response. "I don't like dealing with them any more than you guys." He gave an apologetic one shouldered shrug to Lexie. "No offense."

"None taken."

"But in this case, the more coverage the better. I saw your broadcast on this morning's news, McCain. It was good, but I need you to do more."

"Okay, what do you want?"

"Tucker, what are your thoughts on this? Any ideas on how far we take it?"

Tucker didn't miss a beat. "All the way."

Pierce nodded. "Agreed. Okay, we're going to come up with a statement for the press, and we'll let McCain deliver it as soon as possible. It will need to be covered in all forms of media, the Telegraph, all local radio stations and on television, with Ms. McCain our primary link to the public. Make sure it gets in all of today's newscasts." The captain looked at the group. "All of Macon needs to be aware of the situation."

Lexie also agreed with the captain's direction. "What do we want to tell them?"

"Everything, the profile as well as his signature. We need

every woman fitting his criteria to be protected. No one who fits his target base should be alone. They shouldn't so much as step foot in their front yard without someone with them."

"What if he goes for the chosen victim *and* her friend?" Sims asked.

"It isn't his MO. He takes one victim at a time, every forty days, starting forty days prior to Easter."

Angel returned to the room with strands of blonde hair falling from a band barely containing her ponytail. She looked tired...and determined. "You're going to tell the public everything?"

"Yeah," Pierce answered. "I realize most folks who've lived in Macon for years are already aware of what this guy will do, but for the ones who've just moved here, or for the teens who may not remember, we have to put it all out there."

"Exactly. We need to bring him out into the open. That's the best method to combat his plan of action. Plus, I have additional information to add to our profile." She plopped down in her chair, grabbed one of the books in front of her and started quoting, "Seven, the number for completeness. Seven is formed by taking the perfect world number, four, and adding it to the perfect divine number, three. Human physiology is based on a law of sevens. Gestation for humans is two hundred eighty days, divisible by seven."

"Forty weeks." Lexie followed Angel's reasoning. "But he's committing the murders every seven years and spacing them forty days apart. That doesn't match those numbers."

"I know." Angel flipped pages in another book. "Forty is the number for trials and tribulations. I believe he spaces his kills forty days apart because he feels tested during that time. That's when he is supposed to refrain from killing, to hold off on what he wants, like giving up the thing you want most during Lent. It's been proven that serial killers are addicted to the act. That's why we have so many repeat offenders. He wants to kill again, but he holds off for forty days, denying himself of what he wants most during his temptation period."

"Why the seven years between?" Lou asked. "And why seven women murdered each time?"

Angel shook her head. "I don't know. Maybe seven

symbolizes his wait is complete? For the seven years between, the best scenario I've found is the seven years of plenty, then seven years of famine in the days of Joseph, though that would almost insinuate he should kill for seven years, then go seven without killing." She studied a page in Bible Mathematics. "Our guy is religious, but he seems to make his own rules, variations of the Biblical facts. Or maybe he was taught a deviation of typical Biblical numerology. Either way, with him starting the killings forty days prior to Easter, always committing an Easter kill and spacing all murders by sevens and forties, I'd say we've got ourselves something of a fanatic."

"A fanatic who thinks we haven't figured out his system," Pierce said.

"Right. And if he believes we're onto him, even if we don't understand why he's picked the dates and years he's selected, he may feel as though his plan has been altered. Maybe he'll believe things have changed."

"But if he does think his plan has gone haywire," Lou countered, "would he stop the cycle, or would he swap to more convenient dates and times?"

"He's too much of a perfectionist, too intense a planner, to vary from the structure. However, if the women in town know what to watch for, if they're all aware of what he's looking for and when, then maybe we'll eliminate the opportunity to accomplish his goal on the specified date," Angel continued. "Then, once a date is missed—"

"The cycle will be broken," Tucker completed. "You're the profiler. What do you think he'd do, if we were able to prevent tomorrow's murder?"

"In all honesty, I haven't dealt with a case like this before, based on Biblical numerology, but given the information we have on our killer, I believe he'd see the series as ended. What good would it do to commit the murder if it weren't on the specified date?"

"Fine." Captain Pierce grabbed a pen and a pad of paper from the center of the table. "What do we want in the broadcast?"

"I say we tell them everything," Angel said. "There's no

better way to find a snake than to remove his rock."

For over eight hours, the group wrote and submitted their articles and announcements to every form of media available in Bibb County and the surrounding areas. A draining process, but worth it—if they stopped the killer.

Lexie didn't have to assist Henry in editing footage at the station for tomorrow's broadcast. He was capable of getting the segment done right on his own. But she didn't want it right; she wanted it perfect. Moreover, she wanted to verify it depicted the horrendous person they were after. Like before, they taped the footage at the police station, after the remaining task force members verified the content. The group wanted her to cover each and every scrap of detail they had about the killer, his profile, his signature, his MO. And they wanted to make sure the city knew how instrumental the next twenty-four hours would be in their effort to stop the madman's cycle.

The police department tripled the number of officers on duty, and 911 operators were ready to field any and all incoming calls referring to the killer. Every local radio station and television newscast gave a word-for-word account of the killer's updated profile, with all details noted and a list of things to watch for. They cautioned women fitting the criteria of his signature not to be alone for any reason. In theory, every blonde, single and pregnant woman should've heard the warning and, if Lexie did her job right, understood the gravity of its message.

She prayed they did.

"You said there wasn't anything else you could do today." Paul Kingsley leaned against the opening in her cubicle. "I think it's time you call it a night, McCain. The story is set and it looks good. Besides, the short piece is airing in our breaking news segments, with the full footage scheduled as the top story in all of tomorrow's broadcasts. Not bad for a day's work."

"I don't care about the notoriety." She didn't. "I just hope we save her, whoever she is."

"I can't imagine any woman fitting the description who wouldn't heed your warning. You did a good job, as usual."

"I hope you're right." But her insides twitched with fear that he wasn't.

"Come on, it's late, and I'm betting you didn't get much sleep at all last night. There's nothing you can do now but wait."

"I know." Wait. She hated the word. Wait to see if her article worked. Wait to find out the identity of the first victim from 1985. Wait to see whether the cycle ended, or whether he committed a second murder. Wait to see if the task force did its job.

"Lexie, you're exhausted. Let me walk you out."

She nodded, grabbed her briefcase and her purse then numbly followed him from the building. "You're right. I am tired." What an understatement. Her head felt like a bowling ball atop a golf tee. She needed to go home and sleep. And maybe, when she woke tomorrow morning, all single, pregnant and blonde females would still be breathing.

*Please, Lord.*

They exited the building and walked toward her car. "Want me to follow you home?"

"No, I'm okay."

"Your footage tells women not to be alone."

"Pregnant, single and blonde women. Two out of three, remember?"

He smiled. "Fine. But take care of yourself, and get some sleep. Maybe we'll have nothing to report on this guy tomorrow."

"I hope not," she said, as he closed her car door. She waved goodbye, backed up her car then left WGXA.

A few all-night restaurants showed signs of life, but most of Macon had turned in early and locked up tight, knowing a killer was on the prowl.

Would he find a victim?

Had they warned her in time?

Lexie's eyelids were heavy. She fought exhaustion to see her way down the streets leading home. Finally, she pulled in her driveway and parked her Lexus beside John Tucker's truck. She looked at the bulky man sitting in his vehicle. Her awareness magnified tenfold as she exited her car and watched him do the same. "What are you doing?"

He circled in front of her car, and the dimming headlights spotlighted his muscled frame in motion. "I heard you tell Angel you were going to the office, so I called Paul and asked him to make sure you got to your car. Told him I'd take care of things on this end."

She let him take her briefcase from her hand. His fingertips brushed her palm and sent a shiver of warmth up her chilled arms.

"Come on." Starting up the brick pathway, he led her to the front door. His scent, all musk and brisk and male, somehow made her feel...safe.

"Seems every man in town has decided tonight's the night to tell me what to do." Yet she couldn't deny the pleasure in knowing both Paul Kingsley and John Tucker had partnered to watch over her tonight. It'd been a long time since she'd understood the luxury of having a man around. "You walking every woman in Macon to her door tonight, Detective Tucker?"

"Nope, just the one who impresses me most."

She stopped walking, fumbled to get her house key out of her purse.

"Hey." He placed his finger on her chin, then tilted her face to look at his.

The porch light illuminated his blue eyes, accented by tiny crinkle lines at the corners. His black hair, a bit too long, needed a cut, but it suited him, with those rippling waves and sparkling flecks of gray at both temples.

Her chin quivered above his finger.

"You didn't jerk away."

Her eyes widened. "No, I didn't."

"That's progress." He gave her an easy grin.

"I guess it is." Her nerves simmered down, a little.

"Lexie?"

She swallowed. "What?"

"I won't hurt you." Had he moved toward her, or had he been standing this close all along?

She thought about his words. "I know you won't." He still believed she thought he could be the killer. But why wouldn't he? He had no way of knowing why he made her jittery, why all men did. But she didn't want to be afraid, not anymore. And not with Detective John Tucker. The monster, whoever he may be, had hurt him too. And Lexie wouldn't let the killer rob them of experiencing life, and of experiencing each other. "I'm not afraid of you." She wanted him to understand, but felt unable to tell him more.

"Yeah, you are. But we'll work on that."

She nodded. How could she argue? His words were true, but at least he wasn't giving up on her. Phillip had given up on her. John Tucker was willing to work on it.

So was she.

"Go ahead. He nodded toward the key she held between her thumb and forefinger.

She looked at the shiny silver metal and wondered when she'd located it in her purse. Her attention had been on the handsome detective escorting her to her door and making her feel things she hadn't felt in a very, very long time.

"You're leaving?" She blushed when extra crinkle lines formed at the edges of those vivie blue eyes.

"Yes, Ms. McCain, I believe I should." He smiled brighter. "Trust me, I don't want to go, but it isn't the right time for us yet."

Another blush heated her cheeks. "Oh, I didn't mean—I thought you might want to come in for coffee, or something."

"I'm heading back to the station. Going to be available tonight, just in case. But I appreciate the offer for coffee, and I appreciate you letting me see you to the door."

"No problem. And thanks."

"My pleasure." He withdrew a card from his wallet. "Here. All of my numbers. Call if you need me, or if you just need to talk."

"Okay." She entered her house, listened to his words instruct her to turn the deadbolt, clicked it into place then moved to the window and watched him leave.

Even though she'd been bone tired when she prepared to leave her office, Lexie hadn't planned to sleep, not with the killer preparing to murder again. But after her encounter with John Tucker, she relaxed. They'd done what they could to protect potential victims. Paul and John were right. She couldn't do anything else at this time.

She walked to her bedroom, dressed for bed and climbed beneath the sheets. No nightmares. No terrors. Then she said a prayer that all single, blonde and pregnant women in Macon would be safe.

Vickie slid her time card in the slot at six minutes past four. She rolled her head from shoulder to shoulder, stretching the muscles that had tensed from looking down at the orders on her pad. Why had she been so preoccupied tonight? She hadn't been able to memorize orders, nor could she even remember the snappy Waffle House slang the cooks expected. Waffle on two. Scattered, smothered and covered. Why couldn't she remember what they meant?

Because her mind had been on the baby in her stomach and the ex who'd put it there.

She started to tell Sylvia about the child, a baby she wanted in spite of the difficulty he or she would cause in her life. But one of the high schools had bombarded the Waffle House for a late night breakfast, and Vickie ended up without even a bathroom break...and without any time to tell Sylvia her news. No matter. Sylvia, such a dear person and an up-and-coming best friend, had invited her to church in the morning and then to her home for Easter lunch. Vickie couldn't contain her excitement at the invitation. It'd been years since she enjoyed a real family Easter. Sylvia said they even planned on helping the grandkids dye eggs then hunt them around their farm. Vickie couldn't wait. What better way to celebrate having a child than spending an afternoon playing with kids?

She smiled, slung her tote over her shoulder and headed out. Her cab waited.

"See you tomorrow," she called to Sylvia. Then she paused at the door. "Sure you don't want me to bring anything?"

"No indeed, child." Sylvia continued wiping down a table. "You just bring yo'self. We've got everything covered."

"I'm looking forward to it." Vickie exited the restaurant with her emotional load a bit lighter. She'd begun making friends in the city, had a good job and a beautiful baby on the way. Things weren't so bad after all.

Jeremiah Wilkins waved at her from the front of the cab.

He'd gotten used to her late night pickups, even if she'd only been working this shift for a few weeks.

"Hi Jeremiah." She climbed in the cab.

"Hello, Miss Vickie. You had a good night?" He drove from the parking lot.

"It was fine, but I'm tired. How about you?"

"Not too busy with the news of that killer coming back."

Vickie had scanned the front page of a paper one of her customers left behind, and she'd even heard a few folks talking about the girl's body that'd been found Thursday. She'd been pregnant, according to the talk Vickie heard. And Vickie had also learned all of this killer's victims had been pregnant, blonde and single. Her heart ached for those women. Now she knew what it felt like to carry a baby, to want to protect that child with every part of your being.

She leaned her head against the cool window glad she hadn't told Sylvia, or anyone else at work, about the baby. Who knew who could be listening to their conversations as they chitchatted while serving plates? No need in broadcasting that she now met all three items on the killer's checklist.

"It's Easter, you know. You gotta work?" Jeremiah asked.

"I have the day off. Going to church, then eating dinner with friends." Boy, it felt good to say that.

"Sounds nice." He continued driving without speaking, then pulled up in front of the tiny duplex she rented. The other half was empty; the landlord had a big *For Rent* sign in the front yard emphasizing the fact. Vickie looked forward to having some new neighbors. Maybe she'd get another batch of friends out of the deal. Perhaps even a friend who had a car and wouldn't mind driving her places. She'd help out on the gas, of course. But it would be handy to have someone around to get her where she needed to go, the hospital, for example, when the baby came.

"I'll watch you make it inside," Jeremiah said, as she placed some of the cash from tonight's tips in his hand.

"Thanks." She climbed from the cab and walked down the short path to the house. Then she waved bye to Jeremiah and went inside. It'd be nice to wind down a bit, watch a little television, read for a while or even have a late night snack. But the baby made her so exhausted, or it could have been standing on her feet an extra two hours, since she agreed to work over when all the high school kids came in. Either way, she wanted to climb in bed and forget everything but sleep.

Within four minutes, she'd washed her face, brushed her teeth and slid under the covers. Two minutes later, Vickie let the soft whooshing of the wind whistling through the trees outside her window lull her to sleep. She dreamed of babies, a chubby blonde-haired boy, a cooing blue-eyed girl. They were beautiful. They were happy. They were hers. Which one would come first?

The covers twisted around her as she snuggled into the mattress and wondered how incredible it'd be to snuggle her baby to her chest, to feel it latch on to her breast to nurse. Vickie smiled in her sleep. She had a baby to take care of, hers to hold, hers to love. She couldn't wait.

An odd sound echoed through her dream. It wasn't a baby's sigh, or cry, or giggle. It wasn't the wind whistling through the branches outside. Vickie stirred in the covers and tried to decipher between dream and reality.

A gloved hand covered her mouth, and she knew the difference. The man in her bedroom was real.

*No.*

She fought to get away, but couldn't move. *My baby. No! Please!*

She tried to bite his hand, but his thick leather glove voided her effort. She'd made him mad. The hand around her throat gripped her tighter.

*Can't. Breathe.*

Vickie closed her eyes, saw her Mama, then her baby girl...and went to them.

# CHAPTER SIX

Removing his shoes, he placed them in the deep mud sink in his laundry room then started the washing machine. He stripped off his gloves, dropped them into the swirling soapy water, then pulled off his clothes and did the same. The items moved and shifted beneath the bubbles. In a short time, they would be clean again. Pure. He wished he could clean the world of sinners this easily, but he couldn't. And that's just the way it was.

He left the laundry room, walked through the dark empty house then paused to power up his laptop. While the computer came to life and illuminated his bedroom, he moved to his bathroom and started the shower. Turning the water nozzle to the hottest setting, he waited for the steam to envelop him then stepped beneath the scalding spray. His skin burned at the attack, but he gritted his teeth and bore the pain. The water would cleanse the filth away, much like the water in the washing machine cleaned the dirt from his clothes.

By the end of his shower, with the grime of the kill gone, he experienced the euphoria after-effect, the thrill of knowing he'd accomplished his goal and claimed the power. He dried off, then used the towel to wipe the steamy film from his mirror and stared at his body, red from the burning water and exhilarated from the kill. He wrapped the towel around his waist, left the bathroom and found his laptop ready and waiting. He typed the site address for the Fellowship, and within seconds he'd logged into a chat room, abuzz with visitors, even at 6:00 a.m. Did they realize he'd fulfilled his next requirement? That the day had barely begun, yet he'd already accomplished the goal? Were they praising his efforts now?

He scanned the chat list. Disappointment ebbed through him when he didn't see PROTECT&SERV in the list. He'd so wanted to know what the great John Tucker had to say about his newest kill. But in any case, there were others talking...about Easter. The entire board seemed filled with announcements for sunrise services around Macon, Easter egg hunts and afternoon theater presentations reenacting the resurrection. Frowning, he searched the topics of discussion for something—anything—about his plan, about him. Nothing. The Anti hadn't been mentioned after the posts regarding Cami Talton's body being found. Didn't they realize he'd started the plan? This year he had to fulfill his duty, to teach the city that the rules were to be followed. Didn't they know?

The last topic caught his eye, as did the number of posts beside the subject line. Over 400 throughout the night. He clicked on Local News then found what he'd been looking for all along.

LIVE4HIM: What Lexie McCain said on the news makes sense. It could be a religious fanatic, as she called him, and it could be the one from before. If there's another kill today, it is.

IBELIEVE: The Anti? Let's pray it's not. And if it is, what is he trying to accomplish?

LIVANDLEARN: Obviously, he's from the old school. He still believes, you know, what our parents believed. He doesn't think these women deserve their children. It isn't right, but what can we do about it? How do we stop him? How do we tell him he's wrong?

LIVE4HIM: WE don't. The police are on the right track. They will figure it out.

IBELIEVE: What if they don't? What if they have no idea why he's doing all of this?

LIVE4HIM: They know. They may be denying it, or may not realize the connection, but too many of our guys in blue were in the Fellowship back then. There's no way they haven't put it together, even if they don't want to admit it could be tied to everything.

LIVANDLEARN: Today's the day. Let's pray they stop him

before another innocent person dies.

IBELIEVE: I'm uncomfortable discussing this here. We don't want to give any of our number reason to think the Fellowship condones what he's doing. Let's end this chat now and spend our time praying that the killer isn't affiliated in any way whatsoever with us. If he's from the old school, then let's leave him there and not let him mar what we've worked so hard to obtain.

LIVE4HIM: I agree. I hadn't thought about it like that. If it is the Anti, if he is back, then if we talk about him here, we're giving him what he wants. Plus we're tying him to the New Fellowship, whether we realize it or not. Like IBELIEVE, I think we should spend our time praying.

LIVANDLEARN: Agreed. We'll end this chat session right here and pray that another innocent person doesn't die.

The chat room went silent, with the screen names one by one logging out. His disgust rose like bile up his throat. How dare they disregard his efforts? Refusing to acknowledge that he gave them what they wanted deep inside. A pure world. How he wished he could put faces to the cheesy screen names; he'd teach them a thing or two about the one they'd misnamed Anti. He wasn't the Anti in this; they were. His eyes narrowed as he reread the last post.

"Innocent?" He glared at the screen. What ungrateful trash they all were, what hypocrites. They knew what had to be done yet they acted oblivious to the truth. His hands clenched into fists. If it were up to him, he'd kill them all. They weren't doing anything for the Fellowship by sitting in their homes and typing their ludicrous assumptions on a screen. Were any of them out in the world, doing the will of the Supreme One? Did they think He accepted their tiny church functions and plays for remembrance? He wanted them battling the enemy, and they were twiddling their thumbs, and all smiles about it. And how dare they "pray" that he be stopped? Who were these people anyway? And PROTECT&SERV hadn't participated in any of the ignorant interchange. Where was John Tucker?

Lexie attended the sunrise service at the Community Church. It'd been tiring to get up that early after such a stressful weekend and hardly any sleep, but she'd been so uplifted by the service. Today, on Easter, she could feel God's comfort in her soul. He helped her now, gave her the strength to face her fears, her increasing trust toward John Tucker a testament to her progress. But deep down she knew she would never be rid of her fears until they caught the Sunrise Killer.

*Did we stop him, Lord? And will You guide our path in our effort to catch him?*

She parked her car at the police station at a quarter till two on Sunday afternoon. Fifteen minutes until the task force reconvened, and no sign of another murder...yet. She felt relieved. All indications from his previous kills depicted him as a nighttime stalker, a man who entered homes late in the evening. When last night came and went with no victims reported this morning, Lexie thought they were in the clear.

But were they?

There were still ten hours left in the day, and if he hadn't made his mark last night, he could strike later. That would still be within the restrictions of his bizarre plan. So even though Lexie felt more at ease, she knew their worries weren't over until the day had passed and all women fitting his criteria were accounted for.

Church bells rang in the distance. They'd played all morning in tribute to the religious holiday. Lexie had passed the church of her youth on the way in. Ever since she returned to Macon, she'd attended the Community Church instead of the tiny church where she, her mother and her father had spent many Sundays when she'd been a little girl. She would love to visit the old church and see if it stirred memories of her time before she lost her parents. However, the slight chance someone might put two and two together, and realize the true identity of Macon's newest television correspondent, even after so many years, kept her away. True, the city saw her on the evening—and currently, the morning—news, but there was something to be said about a face out of context.

Lots of people could see her and realize the face looked more familiar than other TV personalities, but not be able to put their finger on the reason why. Going back to her old stomping ground, on the other hand, might help them put it all together.

She wouldn't take that risk.

However, she looked nothing at all like she did back then. People change in thirty years. Plus, she had a new name, different hair color, and she hadn't stepped one foot back in this city since that awful day—until eight months ago, when she became tired of being the victim and ready to be the vindicator.

She closed her eyes and prayed, *Lord, it if be Your will, help us stop him. Help us keep more innocent women and babies from dying at his hand. In Jesus' name, amen.*

A knock on her car window made her jump. She turned to see John Tucker, tall, dark and handsome standing outside.

Lexie unfastened her seat buckle and opened the door. "Have you heard anything?" She grabbed her purse and computer bag, then climbed from the car.

"Nothing yet. You okay? You've been sitting there a while."

"Just thinking and praying."

"Been doing a bit of that myself—thinking, that is—and wondering if we stopped him." He inhaled, then let it out with a shake of his head and a hint of a frown.

Lexie resisted the impulse to ask why he wasn't praying. "What do you think?" They started toward the building.

"I honestly don't know. Agent Jackson called me this morning to ask some questions about the last series and to discuss how our killer always commits the murders around the same time of day."

"Always at night, usually very late."

"Yeah. She's thinking if it didn't happen last night, we may have pulled off stopping his pattern. Not many hours of darkness before midnight tonight, but then again, if he's determined to get a kill in today, that might not be a strong enough deterrent. In fact, I believe if he hasn't already killed someone, he'll be even more determined tonight."

"That's what I think too."

A gold full-sized conversion van pulled in the parking lot and parked in front of them. They stopped walking and watched Etta Green bustle out, her hands full of dishes.

"Hold on, I'll help you." John moved toward her car.

"Oh, no you don't." Etta shooed him away with a twitch of her head, sending big wide curls waving in all directions. Longer than yesterday's hairpiece, today's had tiny flowers stuck here and there, undoubtedly for this morning's Easter service. "I've got everything balanced, and all you'll do is mess with my system. Tell you what, though, you can open the door." Her orange skirt swished as she trekked across the parking lot, while John and Lexie tried to keep up.

John opened the door and let her shuffle through.

"I talked to your profiler a little bit ago. Poor thing has been here most of the night, from what I can tell. I figured she might need a bit of home cooking. The girl's way too thin, needs some meat on her bones."

"You've taken a liking to Agent Jackson, haven't you?" John grinned as Etta continued down the hall.

Etta stopped walking, turned her head back and gawked at John. "Tucker, you're the one who should be spoiling her rotten. The last FBI guy wanted to lock you up and throw away the key; she believes you're half-decent, which you can thank me for, if you want to know. And it ain't that I like her so much," she corrected. "I'm just trying to fatten her up so she can't wear that coat. I think it's the perfect size for my CiCi."

He laughed out loud. "You're something else, lady, you know that?"

"And don't you forget it," she instructed with a sharp nod, before barreling ahead toward the conference room.

"You think we should catch the next door for her?" Lexie peered down the hall.

"Nah, she'll round someone up from the break room to help. Etta has no problem getting folks to jump through her hoops."

"Sounds like she jumped through a few for you."

"No doubt about it. My main salvation in this place during '99 and 2006 came in the form of Etta Green. She never backed down from her claim that I was innocent." He shrugged. "I helped her out when her husband died in '92. Didn't do much, but I checked on Etta and the girls. I think it meant a lot to her to know someone cared. He was only forty-four when cancer got the best of him. That's how old I am now."

"I'm sure she appreciated your help."

He laughed. "Etta didn't need any help. She's about as self-sufficient as they come, but I think it meant a lot to her that I tried. Truth of the matter is, she's happiest when she's got someone to take care of, and she took care of me during those last two murder series." He stopped at the vacant break room and stepped inside. "Guess the guys smelled Etta's banana nut bread and followed her down the hall." He tossed four quarters in a soda machine. "You want a Dr. Pepper?"

"No thanks."

"Anyway," he took a sip of soda from the can, "it looks like Etta has decided Angel Jackson needs her attention now. Leave it to Etta to decide the FBI needs help in the form of good ol' Southern cooking."

"And what do you think about the profiler?" Lexie asked, curious about his take on Angel.

"Considering the last FBI guy pegged me as the prime suspect, I'd say she's a definite improvement." He held up his can in mock tribute to the new profiler then took another drink.

Lexie laughed, partly because she enjoyed Tucker's sense of humor, but more because she enjoyed being so at ease around a man, and around this man.

They left the break area and headed toward the conference room, where three police officers walked out stuffing their faces with big hunks of something that looked like cake and smelled like bananas. One held up half a slice. "You're too late, Tucker."

"Right. As if Etta didn't bring enough for an army." John held the door for Lexie, and they walked inside, where Etta distributed nut bread to the group. The smell of bananas and pecans filled the tiny area and made Lexie's stomach growl. She'd forgotten breakfast and had eaten a plain bagel for lunch. Not much of an Easter dinner, but she hadn't been in the mood for more. She looked at the end of the table, where Angel eyed her slice, triple the size of everyone else's.

"You didn't have to do this." She broke off a piece of the steaming bread and popped it in her mouth. After swallowing and rolling her eyes toward the ceiling, she added, "But we're glad you did. Don't guess you'd share the recipe?"

"You give me the information on where to buy that jacket, and I'll share my granny's secret recipe."

Angel smirked. "Deal."

Lexie sat down and took a bite of her bread, added her own praise to Etta's culinary talents, then watched the lady, beaming, leave the room, while promising to bring more goodies when she came to work tomorrow.

A new, packed file of information rested on the table in front of each task force member. Lexie flipped hers open. Molly Taylor's background sheet topped the pages. Lexie examined the pretty girl, then lifted the page and viewed the next victim's photo.

"Since we're still at the wait stage for today, and since we still don't have the missing persons data from February of '85, I thought we'd concentrate on the next best way to determine more about our killer," Angel tapped her file. "Victimology. We're going to look at all of the victims to see if they have more in common than the three signature criteria we've already noted."

"We've been through this with each series." Lou tossed an oversized chunk of bread to the back of his mouth while he flipped through the pages. "It hasn't changed. The women have nothing in common except they were single, blonde and pregnant. Evidently that's enough for our killer."

"At this point, until we get that missing persons data, victimology is our best resource."

Lexie knew Angel well enough to know she wasn't pleased with Lou's flippant attitude. They were dealing with a killer, and whether or not he murdered again today, they still needed to find him.

"Well, if we're going to look at victims," Ryan said, "we should be able to look at all of them."

"What do you mean?" Captain Pierce fanned the corners of his victim sheets. "We've got them all right here."

"Not this one." He lifted a page. "They never gave us much more than her name. But considering the name, I guess they thought that was enough."

Lexie's throat tightened. She'd turned past that page in her own file and had hoped no one noticed she didn't examine it like the rest. But now, with him holding it up for the group, she found it difficult to control the natural reaction. Angel wasn't immune to the effects either. The profiler's mouth flattened, as if she had no response to Ryan's comment regarding the prominent senator's daughter, but Lexie knew better. Angel's teeth were undoubtedly clamped against her inner lip and helping her maintain composure, the method she had always used to mask her pain.

"I understand they wanted to protect Truman's family, but all we have here is the same information available on public record. We've never found out if the killer selected her because she fit his signature criteria, or if it was more political than that. They never even questioned Truman," Ryan explained.

Angel cleared her throat. "According to the information I received, he wasn't able to answer questions. His heart attack and subsequent mental breakdown left him incapable of helping with the investigation. And all evidence suggests that Beverly Truman had been selected like every other victim, because she fit his criteria, not because she was Nicholas Truman's daughter."

While they continued discussing the most notable victim, Lexie fought to maintain composure. She hated that Angel had to listen to their speculations, their theories, about something so personal, so painful. But Angel Jackson's professionalism kept her part of the killer's history private. Then again, Angel hadn't seen the Sunrise Killer.

Lexie had.

She stood from her chair. "Excuse me. I left my tape recorder in the car." Then she exited the room and put some distance between her and the photo that pierced her heart. But she'd seen the concern in Angel's eyes before she left the table. Angel wanted to follow her, to make sure Lexie could deal with the past until they caught the killer. But she couldn't, and Lexie would be even more upset if she did. They'd come too far to let everything fall apart now. It had all started with the two of them, together. And if they caught him now, it would end the same way, with the two of them, together.

They could do it, Lexie and Angel. They'd help the government put him away for good, but both of them knew the risk they were taking by coming back to his domain. If he learned Lexie's identity, or Angel's, before they identified him, they were as good as dead.

She held her emotions in check as she moved down the hall passing officers and forcing cordial greetings through a throat pinched tight. She exited the building, filled her lungs with thick air and returned to her car. Then she let the tears fall in silence.

In contrast to yesterday's rain, the sun beamed, filling the Lexus with warmth and cloaking her pain with heat. The memory fought to be reclaimed, and Lexie fought just as hard to keep it at bay. She couldn't stop now. She had to find him, had to stop the nightmares.

Closing her eyes, she decided to wait a few more minutes before returning inside. Let them discuss the prominent senator's daughter and the way she died without Lexie having to hear. She didn't need anything to remind her, didn't need to hear about Senator Truman's heart attack, didn't need to remember how his entire world had shattered during the two weeks when he lost his two oldest daughters. And she didn't want to remember how he'd have made his way to the White House.

Lexie didn't want to remember. But she did. In fact, she remembered the sirens, the way they'd blared on that day so long ago. And the screams. If she could only block out the screams...

Opening her eyes, she saw John Tucker climb in his truck then peel out of the parking lot.

*Dear God, what happened?*

She punched the unlock button on her door. Her stomach rolling, she tried to open her door, but she'd hit the wrong button and locked it again. Two black-and-whites sped past, Ryan and Lou in one, Zed and the captain in the other. Lexie pounded the button again and flung her door open, nearly falling to the pavement with her momentum.

Angel sprinted from the building and hurtled through the parking lot toward her SUV. Her hair unbound now, it billowed behind her as she ran.

Lexie knew something big had happened. "What is it?"

"Another murder. No time to explain—follow me."

Her heart raced. "He found someone, didn't he? He got someone else?"

Angel's grim face answered Lexie's question. "Come on!"

"I'm right behind you." And then they left, Lexie following Angel, the two of them headed to the scene of his kill. Another single, blonde, pregnant woman was dead. Lexie could feel it. She tightened her hands on the steering wheel. It had happened, the monster had murdered. Again.

Angel pressed the accelerator and tore through town, her mind repeating the directions Sims had given her before they left. All of the locals knew where they were going, and she hadn't taken the time to program her GPS, just listened to the turns and, like everyone else, made a beeline toward death. Tucker hadn't stopped long enough to translate anything, but she hadn't expected him to. As the homicide detective in charge, he had to get first and foremost to the scene.

She looked in her rearview mirror and saw Lexie, following so closely Angel couldn't see the front of her car. Lexie. How would she handle this scene? Simple, Angel thought. She wouldn't. Even though Lexie McCain had secured a spot on the task force for the investigation, she still counted as media, and no way would the crime scene investigators allow a reporter near the body. Thank goodness. Lexie didn't need to see someone else who'd been attacked by the Sunrise Killer. Although Angel knew what he was capable of, had seen the crime photos verifying the fact, she'd never seen the victim firsthand. Lexie, on the other hand, had. And viewing the scene this soon after the murder would intensify those memories. Lexie didn't need to sharpen that image. Remembering the details meant reliving the pain, and no matter how many times Lexie McCain revisited that scene, one detail remained unchanged...

She didn't remember his face.

Angel started to think she'd picked the wrong street, but then she saw the telltale red and blue lights flashing outside a tiny brick house. She pulled in behind Tucker's green Grand Cherokee and jumped from the Tahoe.

Lexie parked behind Angel and hopped out as well. "When did it happen? Who is she? Who found her?" Lexie ran toward Angel in full investigative reporter mode. But Lexie the reporter wasn't asking the questions; these questions came from Lexie, the woman who wanted the killer stopped, just like Angel.

"I don't know anything yet. The call came in a few minutes after you left the conference room, and I followed Tucker's lead."

"Well, we need to find out." Lexie stepped toward the house.

Angel didn't want to stop Lexie's progress, but she also knew the reporter wouldn't be allowed on the crime scene. Plus, knowing Lexie's past, Angel would be the first to declare Lexie McCain didn't need to see the body. But she didn't want to be the one to tell her she couldn't. Thanks to the two cops who'd responded first, she didn't have to.

"I'm sorry, you'll have to wait here." One of them stepped between Lexie and the house.

"But I'm on the task force."

"You're Ms. McCain, right?" the second cop asked. "The news lady?"

"Yes."

"Right. Detective Tucker told us to have you wait out here. He'll be out to update the media as soon as the scene has been analyzed."

"The media? I'm not just the media. I'm helping the police with this case. I'm *on* the task force." Her words were sharp, clipped and determined.

Angel hadn't been sure whether she'd see eye-to-eye with John Tucker about anything in this case, but right now, she did. He could've foregone typical protocol with Lexie on the task force, but he didn't. Maybe he realized the truth, even if he didn't know why.

Lexie didn't need to go inside.

"I'll keep you posted on what's happening." Angel started toward the front door. She stepped around a *For Rent* sign, but stopped when another field cop, the size and build of a professional wrestler, centered her path.

"I'm sorry. Only authorized personnel inside."

Angel displayed her badge. "FBI." Then she moved past him without a backward glance.

Two additional police officers stood inside the door. She flashed her shield again, then proceeded down the hall to the bedroom, where Elijah Lewis backed out of the doorway and stepped on her foot.

"Whoa." He cradled his camera as he moved away. "Sorry, didn't hear ya coming."

"That's okay." She cut her gaze to the photographer. "You got here fast. When did they call you?" She understood how the cops who'd been first on the scene already had everything roped off and moving. She even understood how the CSI guys had been at the ready position for the 911 call telling them he'd struck again. But the crime scene photographer wouldn't have been one of the first called.

"Heard it on the scanner. Been waiting to hear something since last night, so I was ready." He grinned, excited, and this time two specs of tobacco dotted his top teeth. "Didn't want to miss getting the gig."

Angel fought the urge to grab him and fling him into a wall. "The gig is a murder. A woman who was alive yesterday is dead today. I'd say that qualifies for a stronger term than *gig*."

"I meant the homicide." He grinned. Then he turned and snapped more pictures.

"Looks as clean as the others." Ryan Sims stood beside Tucker and eyed the woman on the bed.

"Tell me everything was documented before the scene was contaminated by overzealous cops." Angel glared at the flurry of uniforms at the scene.

Tucker shifted to look at her. "They're on our side, remember?"

Angel breathed in, cringed at the foul odor of death, then let it out—and reminded herself not to inhale any more than necessary. She had no reason to get mad at the local law enforcement. *They* hadn't murdered the woman. "Did they find anything?" She noted two CSI guys searching the room.

Lou Marker grunted. "Nope, place is as spotless as all his other scenes were. The guy's a pro."

Angel looked again at the blonde woman on the bed. Wearing a blue waitress outfit, she had her Waffle House nametag above her right chest. The yellow rectangle had her first name inscribed in black block letters in the center. "Vickie."

"Vickie Jones." Tucker stepped away from the body.

Angel's gaze moved to the woman's flat stomach. "She wasn't pregnant?"

"EPT kit in the bathroom has a big plus sign that says she was." Ryan Sims nodded toward the open bathroom door.

Tucker shook his head. "The thing is, she wasn't far enough along to tell, and the waitress who found her said she hadn't said word one about being pregnant."

"Who found her? What waitress?"

"Sylvia Rawlins. She's out back talking to Dan Faust, the first responder. According to Ms. Rawlins, Vickie Jones divorced a few months back then moved here from Florida to get away from the ex."

"Why was the Rawlins lady here? Does she live here too?" Angel scanned the Spartan room. A bed, dresser and nightstand composed the entire furnishings. No pictures, no knickknacks. Vickie Jones hadn't even settled in.

"No. She'd invited Ms. Jones to church and Easter lunch and was worried about her when she didn't answer her phone. Since Vickie didn't have any family, the other waitress decided to come check on her and see if she wasn't feeling well." He pointed to the cell phone on the nightstand.

"We'll want to check those phone records." Angel stepped forward and viewed Vickie Jones, the bedding beneath her as wrinkle-free as if it were on display in a mattress store. Other than the marks on her neck and the defecation beneath her pelvis, Vickie Jones could have been sleeping.

No doubt about it, their killer was John Gacy neat.

Angel's glance darted to Ryan Sims, talking to one of the crime scene investigators in Vickie's bathroom. Etta had described the lieutenant as overly neat. Was he neat enough to strangle a woman to death and leave a crime scene this clean?

"What's your take on this, Agent Jackson?" Ed Pierce stepped into the bedroom from the hall.

Angel turned toward the captain and saw Zed Naylor and Lou Marker through the bedroom window. Zed pointed to the ground outside, while Lou annotated his observations.

"She left her window open. And he saw it as an invitation. Plus she fit all of his criteria." Angel looked back toward Vickie Jones. "He may have known she was single. News like that travels quick in a town this size, but how did he know she was pregnant? If she had no family, and if she hadn't yet told her friends, how did our killer find out?"

"There was a doctor's receipt on the nightstand," Tucker said, pointing toward a bagged yellow paper. "Dr. Weatherly, OB-GYN."

"What's the date on the receipt?" Angel asked.

"March twenty-ninth, two days ago, on Friday. And the receipt said initial visit."

Pierce lifted the bagged receipt, scanned the doctor's writing. "She found out two days ago?"

Sims left the CSI guy and returned to the group. "What's your take, Agent Jackson? Same guy?"

She decided not to judge Ryan Sims. True, he was a potential suspect, but several people were, for now. Stan Carlton had made the mistake of speaking too soon with this case; she wouldn't do the same. However, she also planned to keep her eyes and ears open regarding Lieutenant Ryan Sims. And Elijah Lewis. That photographer got here too fast.

"Yeah, it's our guy, but he wasn't nervous, wasn't rushed. He had plenty of time, and he took advantage of it. He had to remove the screen and climb in, but he didn't leave any evidence of entry. And he removed the mesh obstruction, rather than slashing it."

"There were shoe marks outside the window," Marker said, "Size ten, but no tread."

"It was muddy out, but there's no mud inside," Angel noted. "So he either took the shoes off before coming in, which is doubtful, or he took the time to clean up his mess on the floor before leaving. I'm thinking it's the latter. Our guy took his time entering, took his time killing the victim and took his time leaving. He wasn't the least bit scared by our broadcasted warnings. He's still conducting his plan as scheduled, without any regard to the cops—or the FBI—on his tail." She surveyed the room, the ordered and clean room. "We haven't shaken him. Yet. He'll strike again in forty days unless we do something to throw him off, to make him think we're onto him, or catch him before he commits the crime."

"Well, did you learn anything else about him from this scene?" Lou entered the bedroom with his notepad in one hand and a pen in the other.

"Yeah, we can add agile to our profile. That window may be on the first floor, but it isn't close to the ground. Our killer was able to enter without waking the victim, judging by the lack of signs of struggle. I'm betting she didn't even hear him until he had a hand on her throat."

"But how did he know she fit his specs?" Lou asked. "How did he know she was pregnant if she'd just gone to the doctor and hadn't told anyone?"

"I don't know. Let's check for a Facebook page, Twitter, and any other types of social media. If she announced it somewhere online, maybe that's how he found out."

"I'm going to pay a visit to Dr. Weatherly," Tucker said. "Our guy may be privy to doctor records."

"That wouldn't fit the profile," Angel started then stopped when John Tucker snarled, "but it wouldn't hurt to check it out."

"Thanks."

She couldn't stop staring at the woman on the bed. "She looks perfect, doesn't she?" Other than the bruises on her neck, Vickie Jones seemed almost peaceful.

"So what does that tell you?" Captain Pierce asked.

Angel's head throbbed from lack of sleep, eyes stung from reading all those books on Biblical numerology. *Biblical.* Why hadn't she thought of it before? "Oh my."

"What?" Zed asked.

"He did see her as perfect. A perfect sacrifice, provided by God, like the lamb mentioned in some of those books I read this morning. Perfect and unblemished. Except, in her case, maybe it was the child inside of her that was still untainted. He saw the child as pure. Perfect."

"If that's the case," Tucker followed her line of reasoning,

"Wouldn't he have wanted to save the child?"

"You would think." Angel mulled over the possibilities, which were endless, if they were dealing with a fanatic with his religious perspective way off the mark. "But look at the bed, her clothes, her position. She's on an altar, and she's being offered."

"Along with her child?" Ryan asked.

"Seems that way." Angel took a step closer to the bed. This woman should have a full life, and a beautiful child, ahead of her. She'd been robbed of what she deserved, the same way Lexie and Angel had been robbed in the past. And by the same man.

"A perfect body. A perfect bed. A perfect sacrifice." The banana bread churned in her belly. Then, unable to control the physical response to the reality, Special Agent Angel Jackson darted out the back door.

He watched the pretty profiler throw her guts up on the back lawn. She held her long hair away from her face while her lunch hit the grass and big, bulbous tears fell to join it.

Bless. Her. Heart.

He found it hard not to smile at his success, at their failure. Didn't FBI Profiler Jackson know she couldn't stop the inevitable? The last FBI guy had failed. She would too.

The pattern, the process, had started years ago. Twenty-eight years ago, when Hannah had chosen the way of the sinner. Like Eve, she led the way for the women who came later, the women who would pay for her transgression, sacrifice for her fall.

They had no idea they'd followed in the steps of their predecessor, a woman who mirrored their own image and also carried a child. A child who had done nothing wrong, who carried power that should be bestowed on those deemed worthy, not granted to a woman who couldn't even keep a vow. Women who, like Hannah, hadn't followed the divine law. And women who, like Hannah, paid the price.

He watched Lexie McCain, the savvy news reporter, leave her cameraman and maneuver her way down the crowd of media personnel held back by a thin plastic strip of yellow crime scene tape. Concern evident on her face, she reached her point of destination, the profiler, doubled over at the edge of the lawn.

McCain shifted her gaze to the cops at the door then frowned at her inability to cross the flimsy barrier. Determined, she dug in her purse and withdrew a couple of white tissues. Then she extended her arm over the yellow tape and handed them to Angel Jackson.

The profiler looked up, accepted the offering and gave her a weak smile.

Funny, the way women ran to help each other, tried to assist one another in bearing the burdens of life. And death. It didn't matter whether they knew each other or whether they'd just met. Women were strange that way. They had a camaraderie he didn't understand, didn't want to. Because, whatever they had, it wasn't enough. No female had shown up to save Vickie Jones last night. Her tears had fallen, streamed down her exquisite face, without anyone offering a single tissue. And no female had ever shown up to help any of her fellow partners in crime. Partners in sin.

He watched the two women, Lexie McCain and Angel Jackson, exchange a few words, then McCain returned to her place amid the other TV people. Such a pretty woman, with her short blonde curls framing a petite face and turned up nose, big green eyes amid an abundance of thick lashes, she radiated with curiosity. Yeah, Lexie McCain looked like she wanted answers, to tons of questions, and the determined set of her jaw said she expected to get them.

*Curiosity killed the cat.* Again, he refrained from smiling. There wasn't anything funny about this situation, after all. He'd done what he had to do, and he'd do it again, in forty days.

Angel Jackson finished with an ending punctuation of dry heaves adding to her noticeable display. He'd swear she staged the whole thing, to get the cops and the public feeling sorry enough for her to come forth with the proverbial witness who'd been holding out all these years.

*Give up, pretty profiler.* There were no witnesses. Well, there were. But now they're dead. Guess those don't count.

However, as he watched the profiler head back toward the house, he saw her wipe her eyes and sniff, then inhale, a lone crusader ready to tackle the world. She wasn't fishing for sympathy, he realized. She was sorry the girl had to die. Well, he was too. It wasn't as if he enjoyed what he had to do, but he had to do it. Period. Maybe Angel Jackson would figure that out.

He watched her move. In spite of her trademark outfit of t-shirt, leather jacket, jeans and boots, she had a graceful gait and a definite air of femininity. Near perfect. Then again, he thought, turning his attention back to the pretty news reporter, so was Lexie McCain. A shame neither of them had a baby on the way. Every other aspect hit the mark. But he'd find the chosen woman in time for the next kill. The one who had the power growing within her, but who wasn't worthy of the child. He always found the perfect sacrifice. And he always killed her...perfectly.

# CHAPTER SEVEN

John Tucker exited the police station at five minutes past midnight. The day had ended, and the clock ticked once more. Forty days until the Sunrise Killer murdered again. He knew no more about him now than he did during his prior sprees.

No, that wasn't true. Thanks to Angel Jackson's assessment of the "sacrificial lamb," John had a good idea *what* they were dealing with. But he still didn't know *who*. And now that he understood more about what the killer did, the possibilities were endless. It'd been over twenty-five years since the Fellowship had ended, or so John had thought, but one of its members still practiced. Not only that, but the person still believed the outlandish assessments posed by Brother Moses.

Had Macon's notorious cult from way back when resurfaced? And if someone had begun practicing again, then who? And when should he bring up his theory to the remainder of the task force? If he did, then what? They'd want to know why he put two and two together when they hadn't. Why hadn't they? Three of them were affiliated with the congregation. Surely Lou and Ryan had thought the same thing today, when Angel saw everything. Or even Zed. He'd been a deacon, along with Tucker's father.

But ol' Zed hadn't said a single word. Neither had Lou or Ryan.

Because no one wanted to talk about it anymore. No one wanted the reminder of how they'd lived back then, looking for demons, searching for power. Power that, according to the deranged Brother Moses, could only be obtained...from a child.

"God help us." Tucker dropped into the seat of his truck and

shook his head. It'd been fourteen years since he'd prayed, and
he wasn't sure the three words counted as a prayer, but he
knew one thing; if they were dealing with someone still warped
by the Fellowship, then they needed all the help they could get.

It'd been so long, so many years, since the assemblage had
met. They'd dismantled, after learning that their leader
abandoned his congregation, with everyone agreeing they'd
been wrong in their views. Everyone *had* agreed. Hadn't they?

Someone didn't.

His cell phone rang. He knew he'd see Paul Kingsley's
name before checking the caller identification to verify the fact.
"Tucker."

"How's it going?"

"All right. How's she doing?" Thankful for an inside track
on Lexie McCain's work environment, Tucker appreciated
Paul watching out for Lexie. He couldn't deny that he felt
something growing between them, but he also couldn't deny
her skittishness. He needed to take things slow, but he also
needed to watch after her. True, she didn't fit all the killer's
criteria, but there *was* a killer roaming Macon, and he didn't
want Lexie anywhere near the man's line of fire. Of course,
it'd be easier to protect her if he knew who he was looking for.

If the killer was one of the former members of the
Fellowship, it could be anyone. Half the city, not to mention
more than half the task force, had belonged to the
congregation.

"She's hanging in there, been mulling over every word of
her broadcast, but I'm about to kick her out."

"I'll wait at her house to see her in."

"Quite a tag team we've got going. Almost reminds me of
how we used to gang up against Kathleen and Abby at
Canasta."

John smiled, remembering. "Yeah, it does."

During his marriage to Abby, they never passed a Saturday
night without getting together with Paul and Kathleen for hot
pizza, cold drinks and cards. It'd been good, clean fun. They
laughed, cut up and enjoyed each other's company, as though
both marriages would last forever. Neither marriage did, with
Paul's ending in divorce a few years back and John's ending

with Abby's murder. Through it all, the two men grew even closer, sharing a bond they could neither discuss nor describe. And right now, that bond fused once again in a joint effort to keep the valiant news lady safe.

After an awkward pause on the line, Paul broke the silence. "You did the right thing today, you know."

"How's that?"

"Keeping Lexie away from the primary crime scene. You knew she wanted to go inside." Paul arrived on the scene after Lexie then waited outdoors with all of the remaining media circus, which meant he knew firsthand how frustrated she had been with having to stay away from the remainder of the task force.

Did Paul also know John could've let her in if he'd wanted? "Lexie didn't need to see that, even if it was a clean kill. She's too close to the investigation. I can see it in her eyes when she examines the prior cases. I assume it's because she's female and fits two out of three of his criteria."

"Yeah, but you've gotta admit her empathy toward the victim helps her portray this guy the way he needs to be defined, as a ruthless killer. You can't see her segments and not feel as though those victims were someone you knew. When I watched tonight's footage about Vickie Jones, I could've been hearing about my sister, or even my wife—" He cut off the word, but not fast enough.

John's chest tightened. "It's okay."

"No, it's not. I wasn't thinking. It's late, and it's been a long day, but that's no reason for me to forget about Abby."

"You didn't forget about her. You just said what was on your mind. None of us will ever forget her."

"That's true." Paul changed the subject. "Anyway, when you told the other media folks you'd deal exclusively with Lexie, that was a stroke of genius. It kept her busy relaying the information to the various news crews, and I think it helped her cope with the reality that last night's attempt to save that woman failed."

John leaned his head back and let his neck brace against the headrest. "Why was that woman, Vickie Jones, so alone in the world? Who knows how long she'd have been there if that waitress hadn't come over to check on her? Even her Facebook page had remained stagnant since she moved here from Florida, as though she had no friends, no life."

"Cami Talton was a loner too," Paul reminded. "No one even checked on her when she missed five weeks of work at the paper mill. They assumed she'd quit. She might not have been found at all if her landlord hadn't started smelling something."

"Maybe the killer is targeting women without ties now, but that wasn't a factor in the past. Abby had ties."

"Could be he thinks the cops are getting close, so he's trying to pick victims who won't be missed.

"Maybe. I don't know." Tucker's thoughts were muddled from two nights without sleep. "But I still can't figure out how he knew Vickie Jones was pregnant."

"You checked with the doctor to see who knew she was there?"

"I'll see her first thing in the morning. She was out of town today for Easter. All I got was the answering service."

"Figures. Well, it was a smart move to have Lexie over media coverage. It's also a good way to get the information you want out there, instead of some lowlife reporter's interpretation."

John had to smile at that. According to Paul, all reporters who didn't work for WGXA were lowlife. But he'd done the right thing selecting Lexie as their media rep instead of someone more set on portraying the facts than the emotion. Lexie delivered both. Plus, the public loved her.

He couldn't blame them.

"So, you got any ideas on suspects?" Paul asked. "Off the record, of course."

John watched a swarm of gnats circle around a lamppost in the police department's parking area. Flitting and floating close to the light, but never landing. Never getting burned.

How close to the light was the killer? Or was he trying to land, trying to find a way to that proverbial light, the one they heard about so many times at kids, listening to fire and brimstone from the pulpit. He and Ryan and Lou and...Paul.

"Did you look at Jackson's update to the profile?" John

asked. "Lexie included it in her broadcast, I'm sure."

Paul exhaled through the receiver. "Yeah, I did."

"Well then, you tell me. Any ideas?"

Paul waited two telling beats before answering. "You know folks around here don't believe that mess anymore." He confirmed that he'd thought the same thing as Tucker, that the killer's plan could be linked to the Fellowship.

"I know that's what we were told, but she pegged it, didn't she? It was a sacrifice. Vickie Jones, and all the others before. Every one of them pregnant. Children growing inside of them, Paul. Children, the symbol of power."

"I think you better make certain you know what you're doing before you go stirring up that kind of trouble."

"I'm not stirring anything yet. We still haven't got the missing persons information from back then, but when we do, if there's some tie to the Fellowship, we won't be able to deny the truth."

"And what do you think that truth is?" Paul's voice lowered to a hush, even though John knew he was locked tight in his office.

"Same thing you do. Someone in the Fellowship has developed another set of rules, inspired by Brother Moses, another creed that wields power. And that someone has been fulfilling his personal requirements for that power every seven years." Relief spread through him as he said it out loud. "Go ahead. Admit it. You thought it too."

"Yeah, I thought it. But we can't jump to any conclusions. Besides, you realize if it's true, almost every man our age living in Macon is a potential suspect. *Everyone* was part of the Fellowship back then. You and I would be suspects, Tucker. Is that what you want?"

"What I want is to catch the killer and stop him before he kills again."

"I want that too, but I thought we'd put all of that behind us." He cleared his throat. "Did you say anything about this to the profiler? Or to Lexie?"

"Not yet."

"Don't. Not until you're sure. One thing you have to remember about pointing a finger, John. When you point one straight out, you've got three pointing right back at you."

Tucker grimaced. That'd been one of his father's favorite sayings when he led his chapter of the Fellowship. "I remember."

"Twelve-thirty. Time to hit the hay before tomorrow's run. I'm gonna send Lexie home." Paul paused, then added, "Tell me something, John."

"What?"

"You've got your eye on her. I'm assuming the feeling's mutual?"

John sat straighter in his seat. "I think it may be."

When Paul didn't respond, John leaned his head back again, stared at the flitting bugs once more. "You interested in Lexie too, Paul?"

"We always went after the same girls, even back in high school. But I saw the way she acted every time you stepped out of that house today."

Tucker could've pointed out that every reporter perked up when he exited the crime scene today, given he led the homicide investigation and therefore became their primary source of information. But he didn't point out the obvious. Besides, he liked thinking Lexie wanted to see him for more than information about the case.

"She'll be home soon. I'm assuming you're gonna be there before her?"

"Yeah. I'll make sure she gets in okay."

"You do that." Paul's voice sounded more crisp than usual, but Tucker's exhaustion rendered him too tired to care.

They disconnected, and John started his truck. Then he drove away from the swarming bugs, away from the station, and toward the woman who had become his primary source of light.

Lexie pressed the accelerator a little harder than necessary, and the Lexus surged forward at her command. Finally, something in this day that she could control. She reached toward the passenger seat, slid her hand inside her purse and fingered the contents until she found her industrial-sized bottle of Ibuprofen. At the next stoplight, she opened it and popped two pills dry.

Darkness covered the town, again. And the city housed a killer, again.

Again? No. Chances were he always lived here, even during the years between killing sprees. He drove the same streets Lexie drove, went shopping in the same stores where Lexie shopped and communicated with some of the same people Lexie communicated with on a daily basis. Then again, he could *be* one of the people she communicated with on a daily basis.

The pills hit her empty stomach, and she cringed. Or did she cringe because of the reality? The killer had been here for twenty-eight years. Closing her eyes, she tried to make her brain focus. Why couldn't she remember? If she had interacted with him, if she had seen him, wouldn't she remember?

Lexie wasn't sure. But that wasn't the question that bothered her most.

Would *he* remember *her*? Did he ever see her on the evening news and think her face looked a little too familiar? Did he ever wonder why?

A car horn sounded, and she jerked her eyes open. How long had she been sitting at this light? How long had it been green? Thank goodness the horn pulled her out of her daze, the same killer-induced daze that had crept upon her throughout the past twenty-eight years.

Within minutes, she approached the "cozy cottage" she purchased eight months ago. Built in the 1920's, the house wasn't large, but it had tall ceilings, stained windows and two bedrooms, so Phillip, Jr. had his own room for visits. Plus, the neighborhood had been dubbed one of the safest, according to the realtor and the police reports. Lexie had checked the latter before moving in. She always checked police reports. Some habits never die.

But even though there'd been hardly any criminal activities recorded within a mile of her quiet little street, and although she should feel comfortable going for an evening walk without locking her door, she didn't. Especially tonight, after she'd witnessed firsthand the aftermath of the killer's actions. Well, secondhand, since Tucker relayed the information. Lexie hadn't seen Vickie Jones' body atop an unwrinkled bed in her waitress uniform with her hair combed and her makeup flawless.

*That* had been what bothered her most about John's description of how the woman had been found. If Vickie Jones had struggled, her hair would've been mussed. And after a long night of waitressing, she shouldn't have had any makeup left at all, much less after trying to fight off a killer. But she did. "Coffin ready," as Elijah Lewis had told Henry. His phrase choice had bothered Lexie as much as the killing itself. Almost.

Her front porch light illuminated a crescent of asphalt on the street ahead. *Home.* After this horrendous day, and after two nights of hardly any sleep, she would rest. For a while. Tomorrow she'd provide a brief segment on the aftermath of the murder, since the task force wasn't scheduled to reconvene until Tuesday. Captain Pierce had determined the police would work on their own processing the crime scene information from today's murder before they added Vickie Jones to the growing bulk of Sunrise Killer victimology. Plus, another day gave the State a chance to locate and send the missing persons data from February of 1985.

She yawned, tired. Could she sleep? She didn't know, but she had to try. She nor Angel could accomplish their goal if they continued running on empty. She knew her pounding headache wasn't due to today's stress. Her body needed to rejuvenate, and tonight she'd sleep—if it killed her.

She shivered at her train of thought. Sleeping wouldn't kill her. The Sunrise Killer, though, would…*if* he knew Lexie had seen his face. Then again, he'd laugh out loud if he knew the rest of the story—that she'd erased it from her memory.

At just past 1:00, she pulled her car into the driveway beside Tucker's Grand Cherokee. She'd known he'd be here when Paul told her it was, "time to go home," then escorted her to the car. She didn't mind the two of them playing tag team. Paul had always taken a special interest in her because he wanted a relationship, but even when Lexie told him she didn't feel that way about him, he'd understood and backed down from pressuring her for more. Now though, he'd become something of a big brother, someone who watched over her and made sure no one hurt his friend.

Her connection with John Tucker, however, didn't feel sibling-like at all. His presence reminded her of what it felt like to be a woman and to want a man, something she hadn't experienced in quite a while. Maybe because of that emotion, and the fact that she was letting her guard down with the detective, she wanted nothing more than to punch him. Hard.

She climbed out of her car, turned on her heel and headed down the brick pathway leading to her front porch without so much as a wave goodbye at the mountain of a man sitting in his truck.

Her dismissal would've made a stronger impact, however, if she didn't have such a big purse, and if her keys didn't always find the perfect cranny somewhere in the bottom. She dug her hand around, her fingertips hitting lipstick, loose change, a wadded tissue, everything but the essential strip of metal that would get her beyond the big oak door with the stained glass center.

She heard his truck door slam, then footsteps approaching.

So much for a flamboyant statement.

He eased his way on the porch, while Lexie continued to look down, shaking the purse and hearing the jingling keys defying her goal. If she'd have felt her cell phone within the clutter, she could've used it to light her bag. But it was MIA too.

"I see you made it home."

She didn't answer him. How many compartments did this purse have anyway?

"I could have let you come in her house today, could have authorized your presence on the scene."

Lexie stopped searching and looked up to view his strong face, solemn from the events of the day, his eyes sad and forlorn, like a man who'd seen...a woman's dead body.

"Why didn't you?"

He stepped forward but made no effort to touch her, a smart move, since she hadn't dismissed the impulse to hit him.

"You didn't need to see her, Lexie. You've been hurt. I don't know what happened or who did it, but I'd have to be blind not to see the signs. Plus, I'm a cop. We tend to pick up on these things." He offered her a slight shrug and a curve of a smile.

She blinked. Did everyone see what he described? People always commented on how "together" she was, how calm, how cool. It wasn't until she started getting her chance to report on the Sunrise Killer, that she'd felt that old tinge, that nightmarish fear, niggling its way back into her life. But she'd disguised it well. Or so she thought.

"Only me." He read her thoughts without a word from Lexie. "I haven't heard anyone else comment on it." Then he shifted from one foot to the other and one corner of his mouth twitched. "Other than Paul."

She should've assumed that, of course. The two men who were around her most and who both expressed an interest in "something more" would sense the truth. Maybe she shouldn't have let them get close enough to see.

"What is it that the two of you think?" Her strained voice defied her usual confidence, but Lexie didn't have the wherewithal to fake it tonight.

"That you've been hurt by some man in the past. I don't know what he did, but I know you're fearful of another relationship. I can tell that you don't want too much too soon. And that's okay."

She stuck her chin out. "What does that mean?"

"Well, it doesn't mean I'm throwing in the towel. I'm just willing to give you whatever time you need. I felt it, Lexie, last fall. That connection, that spark, between us. I think you felt it too, and I'm willing to bet that's the reason I didn't see you at all between that interview and when I ran into you Friday morning outside your office." He paused, swallowed, and Lexie's eyes were drawn to the thick pulsing of his throat with the action. "Am I right?"

"Maybe." Her stomach fluttered with the admission. Goosebumps trickled down her arms.

"Are you scared of me, Lexie?" He moved even closer, so close, in fact, that if he wanted to, he could kiss her.

She blushed, looked down at her purse and saw her keys, cradled within a wadded tissue. "There they are." Smiling, she pulled them out.

"Do I?" He didn't let her off the hook. "Do I scare you?"

"No, you don't, but—"

"But what?"

"But what I'm feeling toward you, *that* scares me."

"I'm thinking that's not a bad thing." He grinned, a big beautiful smile that set another round of goose bumps traipsing over her flesh.

"And," she continued.

"And what?"

"And being alone, while he's still out there, *that* scares me." Her heart hammered against her ribcage as though it would bust right out of her chest if it weren't confined.

"Let me stay—"

Lexie didn't wait to see whether there was more to his request before she answered. "I don't—I won't be with a man that way outside of marriage." She wouldn't admit it to John Tucker, but—thanks to her past—she'd barely been "that way" with a man within the boundaries of marriage.

"You didn't let me finish."

Her cheeks tingled from the blood rushing beneath her skin. "Okay."

"Let me stay out here, in my car, while you sleep." His blue eyes caught the light, and Lexie saw everything she needed to see. A man who wanted to make her feel safe and didn't mind keeping watch all night in a cramped vehicle to meet that goal.

"You don't need to do that."

"I was only asking to be polite. Whether you say yes or no, I'm staying till daybreak. You're going to get some sleep. And don't worry; this isn't my first stakeout."

Shocked, and moved, by his declaration, she realized he hadn't given her any options. "What am I supposed to say?"

"You might as well say yes."

She couldn't hold back her smile. "All right, then. Yes."

# CHAPTER EIGHT

Lexie's feet tingled against the gritty, warm sand as she walked along the beach. The water looked too inviting to pass up, so she ventured closer, until the chilled liquid slapped against her ankles, licked her calves and knees.

When had she felt this happy? This free? She turned to smile at the man who'd provided her this luxury, the man who'd made her safe enough to close her eyes and dream of sandy beaches prickling her feet, salty air tingling her nose, cool water splashing her legs and beaming sunshine warming her flesh.

John Tucker.

A shrill ring echoed through the turquoise sky and carried on the ocean's breeze.

*Her alarm clock?* Lexie didn't want the fantasy, the beautiful, blissful dream to end.

No, it wasn't her alarm. She hadn't set it last night, when she'd crawled into bed and drifted to sleep with Detective John Tucker parked outside.

*The phone.*

Lexie's eyes popped open. Shaking her head, she rolled over and picked up her cell. "Hello."

"You didn't call yesterday. Everything okay?"

She shimmied up in the bed taken aback that she was still fully clothed. But she'd been so exhausted that she hadn't done more than crawl under the covers. "Hey."

He laughed. "Mom, since when do you sleep past 6:00?"

Her eyes darted to the red numbers on the digital clock beside her bed. 7:22. She should be on her way to work by now. She'd need to call Paul later and let him know she'd be late. Not that he required her to call in, but he'd expect her to, because he'd already come to terms with her work ethic, which was that she worked—ethically. As in more than she needed to, doing more work than necessary, and providing the best possible stories for her viewers. Paul liked that about her and Lexie liked that about herself, too. But right now, she wouldn't worry about calling Paul. Right now, she'd enjoy her son's thoughtfulness.

"I had a busy weekend." She yawned as she crawled from the bed and walked to the front of the house. "I know I always call on Sunday. I hadn't realized, however, that you'd miss it if I forgot." A maternal grin crept into her cheeks. "Have to admit, that's rather appealing." She peeked out the window and saw no sign of John's vehicle. Then she spied a sheet of paper on the floor by the front door with a note written in thick black ink.

*I left at daybreak, as promised. Hope you slept well.*

"I didn't call just because I didn't hear from you yesterday."

She blinked, dropped the note on the desk by the door. "Is something wrong? What do you need?"

"Not me, Mom. You. I got up to get ready for Psych 101 this morning, flipped on the news and saw you on the screen. They carried your broadcast on the Atlanta stations. Figured you might want to talk about it."

*That* got her attention. "They carried it in Atlanta?"

"Yeah. You were standing outside that house where the woman was murdered and talking about how the Sunrise Killer was back and had murdered on Easter again."

"Oh." She didn't know what else to say. She hadn't thought of Phillip seeing her there, at Vickie Jones' home. But she also hadn't realized her segment had been picked up by the Atlanta affiliate.

"I know that kind of thing is part of your job, but I gotta tell you, when you investigated that I-20 rapist, well, I was worried. You got too close to it. I'm learning about that kind of thing in Psych, and it isn't good."

Lexie sighed. She *had* gotten close, so close in fact that she became the public's point of contact with the victims. They looked to her to know how each girl felt, what she'd experienced, how horrendous the crimes were. And she'd provided what they wanted via interviews with the sole survivor, the one woman who'd lived to tell about the man's heinous acts. And the woman who, with Lexie's support, had found the strength to face the monster in court. "Maybe I did get close, but that's what it takes to get the story right. You know that."

"But you had me at home then. I was there for you to talk to and protect you."

*Thank You, God for blessing me with this boy.* "You're worried about me being down here on my own?"

"Well, yeah."

That maternal pride rippled through her once more. "Would it help if I told you Angel's here?"

"Angel is in Macon?"

"She's here, working on the case with me."

"Which means she has her gun handy."

Lexie smirked. His favorite thing about Angel, her sharpshooting. Little did he know, Lexie had her share of talent in that area too. He also didn't know about the .22 his doting mom kept by her bed. "Well, she *is* FBI. I'm sure she has a weapon with her most of the time."

That sounded non-technical, didn't it? Something a normal mother would say? A mother who hadn't hit the firing range with Angel on numerous occasions to make certain she could shoot as well as the FBI Special Agent. Or better.

"All right." His tone eased. "I'm glad she's there. Although it'd be better if she were male."

Lexie's eyes bulged. "Excuse me?"

He laughed. "No offense, Mom. I agree there's not much a man can do that you can't, but when it comes to protection," he let the word hang.

"I'm going to pretend you didn't say that." Another call beeped through on the line. She decided to let it beep. The caller wasn't more important than her son, a son who worried about her and never failed to touch her heart in all the right spots.

He chuckled again, and she noticed the sound had grown

even deeper since he left for college. It seemed like only yesterday he toddled around in the backyard.

*"Mommy, watch this. Mommy, watch that."*

Yeah, parts of Lexie's life would never be the same thanks to what happened so very long ago, but she'd done a good job raising Phillip.

"I'm gonna be late to Dr. Morland's class. One of the amazing things about being a freshman, the low men on the totem pole get all the 7:30 classes. But I wanted to tell you to be careful. There's a killer down there."

"Don't worry," another beep interrupted her words, "I will."

"Bye, Mom."

"Bye." She clicked the *end* button then accepted the other call. "Hello."

"Why didn't you answer?"

"Angel? I thought you weren't going to call me while you're here." Then realization dawned. "What happened? What's wrong? Is it the killer?"

"No," Angel said, her voice a single, somber syllable, the tone someone used to deliver bad news, news that someone had died.

"Oh no."

"He's okay, but he left again yesterday. They have no idea where he went or what he did while he was gone. And he's not speaking. Jacqueline tried to call you. When she didn't get an answer, she called me. I told her I'd let you know."

"I didn't even think about him when I didn't take the call."

"That's okay, she can always get one of us, and she knew I'd get in touch with you. But I wanted to see if you could drive over. I can, but I'm supposed to have a powwow with Pierce today about the case. Plus, Leon Hawkins has a conference call scheduled with me and Quantico to see if they can provide a bit more insight into my new theory."

"That he's offering his victims as sacrifices?" Lexie had a hard time fathoming the possibility when John first relayed the information to her for the news, but after thinking about it, she realized a warped twist on religion would fit the type of person they were dealing with.

"Yeah. I'm not sure if the profilers have ever handled

anything like this before with Biblical numerology, but that doesn't mean they won't be able to help me stay focused on the big picture. We can find him, and I'm betting when we get that missing persons' data from the State, we'll be able to narrow our search even more."

"I hope you're right."

"Anyway, if I head out of town, the rest of the task force is liable to get suspicious. Today's meetings are important to the case, and it'd look odd for the profiler to take a hike now. On the other hand, you're not due back in to meet with us until tomorrow, so I was thinking you could go and check on him, then get back in time for tomorrow's meeting, and we wouldn't have to tell anyone about us yet. Is that possible with your job?"

"I'll leave right now." Lexie climbed off the bed, then pulled her overnight bag out of the closet. "I'll call Paul and let him know I need a personal day. It's not a problem at all."

"And why didn't you answer the phone? I thought—well, why didn't you answer?"

"I was talking to Phillip, Jr. He saw me on the Atlanta news this morning and was worried."

"Is he okay now?"

"Yeah, and I told him you were here, which seemed to help."

"It's hard to live up to being an eighteen year old's hero."

Lexie knew Angel didn't mind trying. "Somehow I think you'll manage. And don't worry, I'll get down there. I'll stay tonight and drive back in the morning before our meeting. That way I'll get to see him after he wakes up, make sure he's still doing okay."

"Sounds good. Tell him I'll be there later in the week. I know, he probably won't remember whether you tell him or not, but tell him, just in case."

"I will." Lexie disconnected then got ready for a trip to Valdosta.

John checked his watch. Again. 10:43. He'd been sitting in Dr. Yvette Weatherly's waiting room, along with six women whose bellies looked ready to explode, for two hours and forty-three long minutes, while reruns of TLC's *A Baby Story* aired non-stop from the TV. One of the doctor's patients had gone into labor during the wee hours of the morning, and the good doctor was still involved in the delivery. According to her receptionist, things were progressing nicely, and she'd be here soon.

He decided a doctor's definition of soon and a homicide detective's description weren't even close. And during the past two hours, he'd viewed two cesarean sections, complete with each mother muttering a drug-induced, "Oh, I feel something," when the doctor yanked the baby from her sliced belly, as well as four vaginal births with no drugs. In one of those, a woman had the Lamaze breathing down pat. By the time she pushed the baby out, which he equated to pushing a watermelon through a keyhole, she'd done that hiii-huuu hissing so much the waiting room had depleted of oxygen. John sure felt lightheaded. But that could've been from the final three births. Vaginal, no drugs, no Lamaze. *Ouch.*

However, he couldn't help but be amazed witnessing the women's pain, in screams and thrashes and clenched fists, words of pure venom spouted at husbands who looked like they wanted to keel over. Then John watched those agonized faces relax, cry and smile at the first sight of their newborn. He would describe it as a Jekyll-Hyde type transformation, beyond incredible. As many times as he'd wondered about Abby's baby, it'd never hurt as much as it did right now.

On the screen, a new father passed out during his wife's delivery, and several moms-to-be in Dr. Weatherly's waiting room giggled. John turned his attention from the television. Too much pain. He didn't need any more.

While one of the expectant mothers exchanged the DVD, another entered the office with her husband in tow. She looked calm, peaceful and had that pregnancy glow, with her belly protruding, and her navel poking out, a fabric-coated bump in the center of her stretchy top.

"You sit down, honey," the man instructed. "I'll get us signed in."

She waddled through the room, one hand on her lower back and the other cradling her ripe belly. "Hi," she said to Tucker as she passed. Then she continued through to the only two chairs remaining side-by-side and eased her way into one of them, while meeting and greeting each of her fellow moms-to-be as she progressed.

Short, blonde curls framed her face, fuller than usual, John knew, due to the impending birth. Her eyes were green, like Lexie's. Hair neat, but touchable, like Lexie's. His gaze fell to her belly. What would Lexie McCain look like, her stomach swollen with a child?

John shook his head. Yeah, he'd spent last night protecting the incredible woman, but he'd been close to women since Abby and hadn't jumped into thoughts of seeing them pregnant. Maybe because Lexie had been pregnant before. She had a son, as she'd told the task force during Agent Jackson's interrogation.

It felt good taking care of her, caring about her, even from a distance. He hadn't wanted to leave. But Pierce's mandatory 6:00 a.m. breakfast meeting forced him away.

He looked at the women in the tiny waiting room. Three were blonde. All were pregnant. Were any of them single too?

The theme music for *A Baby Story* geared back up from the television's speakers as another episode started rolling. By 11:30, John had deemed waiting out a child's birth worse than an all night stakeout, any day. He stood, figuring he might as well head back to the precinct. He sure wasn't getting anything done here.

He'd taken two steps toward his exit when the door beside the reception area opened and a black-haired nurse poked her head out. "Detective Tucker?" She eyed the badge.

"Yes?"

"The doctor is back and will see you now. You did say it would only take a few minutes, right?"

"Right."

"No one out here in labor?" she asked the women in the chairs.

"Not yet," one of them answered, and they all laughed.

The nurse smiled. "Then we'll get you back as soon as we can."

"No problem," one of the moms-to-be responded. "We'll

watch a few more births and get ready for our big day."

"I don't know about you, but I'm ready right now," another said.

While the women continued chatting, John followed the nurse, clad in turquoise and purple scrubs covered in teddy bears, to the back of the building. They found Doctor Yvette Weatherly sitting at her desk looking tired, but cheerful.

"Good morning, Doctor. I appreciate you seeing me on such short notice."

"I want to do whatever I can to help you catch Ms. Jones' killer, Detective. She'd been surprised at her pregnancy, even though she said she'd already taken a home test, but still, she'd seemed pleased. However, it isn't Ms. Jones you're looking into, right? You said you wanted to talk to me about my staff?" She looked concerned. "I have to admit I'm curious why."

"May I?" He indicated a chair.

"Oh, yes, of course. I'm afraid I've had a busy night and sometimes forget common courtesies when I'm running on two hours' sleep."

Knowing how she felt, he sat down and smiled, then noticed her loose jacket, and the belly protruding beneath.

She patted her stomach. "That's right. I'm not only the doctor; I'm a patient. Baby's due in ten weeks."

"Congratulations."

"Thank you. And this little fellow makes me even more anxious for you to stop that maniac. I can't stand the thought of him killing those women, and of those children never getting the chance to experience life."

"I agree." His attention moved to her hair, short, bobbed and brunette.

"I know. Even if I wasn't married, I wouldn't fit the bill." She pointed to her hair. "Kind of makes me want to tell all my blonde, single patients to dye theirs."

"It isn't a bad thought, but we're going to get him. We can't let women continue to be scared to live, to leave their houses alone. It isn't right."

"So how can I help?"

"I need the names of all male staff members, with those who worked on Friday noted."

"I can't give you any names. I'm sorry."

John frowned, but continued, "I have a warrant signed by Judge—"

"It isn't that, Detective. We don't have any men on our staff."

John closed his eyes. He'd suspected as much from viewing all the nurses as he walked through, but he'd still hoped. "Doctor, did she mention anyone when she was here on Friday? A man? A friend? Anything?"

"I'm sorry, but no, she didn't. It was my first time to see Ms. Jones. She was new to the area and hadn't been to the office before."

"Can you think of any way this guy learned she was pregnant within one day of her finding out? Assuming he wasn't a friend, and she didn't voluntarily tell him."

She shook her head and looked sorry she couldn't help. "I'm afraid not."

"Have you heard about our profile for the killer?"

"On the news. I'm sure most of Macon has either seen it on the news or read it in the paper."

"Well, if you do see any men hanging around fitting that description, or hear of your patients being approached by strangers, or anything that seems the least bit odd," he withdrew his card and handed it to her, "please call me."

"I will."

He stood, and the black-haired nurse rushed in from the hall and nearly barreled into him. Her eyes were wide with excitement.

"Mrs. Schuler's water just broke in the waiting room."

Doctor Weatherly smiled. "Never a dull moment. I should've expected it, though. It's a full moon."

"Full moon?"

"More babies are born on full moons." The nurse grinned. "No idea why, but it's been proven."

"That so?"

"That's so," Dr. Weatherly agreed.

They followed the nurse to the front, where all the women who'd been waiting were gathered around the lady who'd brought her husband along for the ride.

"Okay, Mrs. Schuler, I need you to go on down the street to the hospital and get checked in. The staff there will set you up in a birthing room and get everything ready for us. I'll be there shortly." She smiled at the women surrounding the "lucky" lady. "I'm going to let each of you see Nurse Langston today, but we'll reschedule all of your appointments with me for later this week, if that's okay. If not, just let my receptionist know what works best for you."

They all nodded, their eyes as excited as the nurse's had been. John didn't blame them. Excitement pulsed through him as well, and he'd never seen Mrs. Schuler before today.

"Can you drive her down there?" The doctor looked to the husband, who'd turned a bizarre shade of pale green.

"I—don't know."

John stepped toward the shaken man. "I'll take you."

"This is Detective Tucker from the Macon Police Department." Dr. Weatherly had a small smile in place as she spoke. "I'm sure he can drive you to the hospital, and then you can return later to get your car. I'll be there momentarily."

"Thank you, Doctor." Mrs. Schuler seemed much more at ease than her husband, who nodded.

"Come on, let's get her to the car." John snapped his fingers in front of the man's blank face. "I think we should hurry."

"Right." The guy surged to life, then grinned. "This is it, Anna, isn't it?"

"Yes, honey, this is it." She took his hand and led him along with Tucker.

"I'm going to mess up your seat." She indicated her wet pants.

"Doesn't matter." This was the most exciting, most thrilling thing that'd happened to John in a long time. And that included catching killers.

Within three minutes, and with his lights flashing, he'd herded Mrs. Schuler and her dumbfounded hubby into the Family Ties Birthing Center at Coliseum Medical Center. After giving the nurses his card and asking them to call with information regarding the birth, he left her in the capable care of the hospital and the semi-capable care of her husband.

John pulled out of the emergency parking area. He wanted

to stay, to see what had started at that doctor's office come to fruition and to witness the miracle of a child's entrance to the world. But that was something meant for the doctor, the expectant mother and the eager father.

The brutality of Abby's murder, of losing his wife and the child she carried, sucker punched him once more. He had never experienced what took place in that hospital now. Then again, he wouldn't have experienced it with Abby anyway, since the baby she carried in all probability belonged to Ed Brooks.

He pulled into the parking area at the police department, parked the car and thought of Lexie. With all the pent up anger from what happened fourteen years ago beckoning for release, he focused his attention on the one good thing in his life right now. The inquisitive news reporter with big green eyes, soft blonde hair and a smile that had the power to melt his hardened heart.

The task force wasn't scheduled to meet today, so she'd be at the TV station preparing for the evening broadcasts. She'd need a break for lunch. Or dinner. She might even need someone to guard her tonight while she slept. He withdrew his cell phone and dialed WGXA. The newspaper's switchboard operator answered.

"Lexie McCain," he requested.

Three rings, then it went straight to her voice mail. He hung up without leaving a message and dialed Paul.

"Kingsley."

"How's it going?"

"Fine. Any news on the case? You checked things out at the doctor's office yet?"

"Struck out. There aren't any men who work at her clinic, and she hasn't noticed anyone fitting the profile loitering."

"Well, you tried. Something else will come up, though."

"It better. Listen, I'm trying to reach Lexie. She off on a story?"

"Nope. I kind of figured she was with you, helping to find answers."

"She's not with me." An uneasy feeling slammed John's senses. "She didn't come in?"

"Called and left a message that she was taking a personal

day. Like I said, I figured she was trying to find answers for the Sunrise Killer story so she could prepare for the next segment."

"Not unless she's working on it on her own." John tightened his grip on his cell. "You don't think she'd do that, do you? Chase a lead by herself?"

"She's been known to before. That's the best way to one-up the other guys for the lead story, and Lexie likes getting the lead, but she's not stupid. She wouldn't go chasing this guy."

"No, she isn't stupid, but she might think she can handle him, that she's smarter than him." John tried to remember if she'd said anything last night, hinted to anything that would give him a clue what path she'd taken this morning. If anything happened to her...

"I've got her cell number."

"Give it to me."

Paul recited the number, then added, "But it won't do you any good."

"Why's that?" John saved the number to his contacts.

"I've been trying to call her all morning. No answer. She must be in a dead zone."

John winced.

"Bad word choice."

"I'll say." John stared at the number. "You know of any areas where a signal won't pick up in the city limits?"

"No."

"Why were you calling her all morning?"

"I have a lead on another story and I wanted to see if she was interested."

John knew better. "How about the truth?"

Paul groaned. "All right. I'm afraid she might be doing something stupid. She tends to be a little too brave and determined for her own good."

"I'm thinking the same thing." John straightened to relieve the tension causing the muscles in his neck to bunch. What had she done? Where had she gone?

"So what're you gonna do?"

"I'm a detective, right?"

"That's what I've been told."

"Then I suppose I should be able to detect where she

headed."

"Any idea how you're gonna do that, if she doesn't want to be found?"

"I'll find her."

"Good. And John?"

"Yeah?"

"Call me when you do. I want to know she's okay."

"Will do." He disconnected, climbed out of his truck and stormed into the police station. If he did his job right, he'd soon know where Lexie McCain had gone.

He prayed he found her before she did something she'd regret.

It should've taken Lexie two and a half hours to make the trip from Macon to Valdosta. She made it in two.

After parking beneath an aged magnolia, she climbed out of her car, retrieved her overnight bag from the trunk, then headed up the familiar rock pathway leading to Murrell's Assisted Living. She had visited the large pink Victorian house for the past twenty-eight years, but her stomach still twitched each time she stepped on the wooden slats of the front porch. Not nervous from fear. Nervous from hope. Hoping for something that never seemed to occur, something that never would occur, according to the doctors. Nevertheless, as she entered the foyer, she felt it stronger than ever before. *Hope.* And, although she hated to admit it, this time she also felt an ounce of fear.

"Oh, Lexie dear, I'm so glad you came."

Lexie turned toward the silver-haired woman sitting in the small office to her right. The lady, Jacqueline Murrell, had a gentle face and an even kinder heart. She'd been like a grandmother to Lexie, ever since Lexie first met her so many years ago. "Jackie. How is he?"

"Here, child, let me get Donovan to take your things."

Lexie knew better than to argue.

"Honey, Lexie's here. Can you give her a hand?" Jackie moved to the open doorway at the back of her office, looked in and smiled. "Were you napping?

Donovan Murrell, his stark white hair disheveled and his glasses lopsided, emerged from the room. He kissed his wife on the cheek as he passed. "Just resting my eyes, Jacqueline."

Jackie chuckled and followed him out.

He had extra wrinkles on one side of his face from sheet marks, and his eyes blinked behind his brown-rimmed glasses to focus. "Hello, Miss Lexie." He reached for her bag.

"Hello, Donovan, how are you?"

"Haven't heard any complaints." He winked at his wife.

Jackie shook her head, but grinned. "Well at least now I know you're awake."

He winked again, this time at Lexie. "You're planning to stay next door, I assume?"

"Yes. I'll have to leave early in the morning, but I thought it'd be nice to stay overnight and see him again tomorrow."

"He'll like that." Jackie's rosy cheeks plumped with her smile.

"Sure he will." Donovan started toward the exit with Lexie's bag slung over one arm.

"Come on, dear." Jackie hugged her as they crossed the foyer. "I'm sure you're anxious to see him. He's doing fine now. I just thought I should tell you and Angel about him leaving again. She called you, I guess?"

"Yes, she did. Do you have any idea where he went?"

"No." Jackie turned down a long hallway, where four rooms branched off each side. Most of the doors were open, and the elderly residents, all familiar with Lexie's visits, smiled, waved and spoke as she passed.

She greeted each of them by name, wanting them to know someone cared, even if they might not remember her visit tomorrow.

Murrell's Assisted Living was divided between those older individuals who were still sharp-minded but needed a place to stay and those who were lost inside themselves while their outer bodies continued to thrive. Most of the latter group were diagnosed with early Alzheimer's. However, the one Lexie came to see had stopped wanting to remember twenty-eight years ago and even though he probably couldn't tell whether she came or not, even though he may not remember her visits after she left the confines of his room, she would continue to come, continue to visit and continue to hope.

"You know, this isn't the type of place where I can keep my residents from going outdoors." Jackie's tone indicated her guilt that he'd wandered off again. "And he isn't getting hurt or anything when he leaves. But I still feel responsible."

Lexie stopped walking just shy of his door, the only one in the hallway that remained closed. "It isn't your fault. He loves it here. On the few times he's said anything to us, that's been the one thing that he made clear. And I don't want to move him, nor do I think he needs to be in a lockdown facility. He must've wanted some fresh air, which a lot of your residents want, right?" Lexie didn't believe her own words, but she didn't want Donovan and Jackie Murrell blaming themselves. They hadn't caused the mental shutdown.

Jackie nodded, but her eyes glistened. "Yeah, but most of our guests go out to the gardens for a while, or sit by the pond. I don't know where he went, Lexie. He had dinner with everyone Saturday night, but at breakfast Sunday morning, he didn't come out of his room." She shrugged. "He does that sometimes, you know, when he wants to sleep in, so we didn't disturb him. Then, right before lunchtime, he came walking in the front door. He looked tired, and he'd been crying." She clasped her hands together at her chest. "I was worried, but since he's done it before, and since I have no authority to stop him from going where he wants to go..."

"You didn't do anything wrong, Jackie. I have no idea where he went either, but you said he's doing okay now, right?"

Jackie blinked her tears away and nodded. "And he does seem better today. Whatever he does when he's away, I think it helps. But I still get worried about him leaving, since I never can tell when it's going to happen, or how long he'll stay away. As far as I know, nothing upset him to make him leave. He was in the TV room with several of the other residents then everyone thought he went to his room. But the next morning, he wasn't there."

"What were you watching on the television?" Lexie feared the answer.

Jackie shrugged. "The news."

Lexie tamped back her anxiety. Even if he'd seen her on the

TV and even if he knew the killer had returned, that didn't mean he'd gone out looking for the guy, did it? But where had he gone? And *had* he seen Lexie on TV? Had her broadcast been picked up by Valdosta too? And if he had seen her, would he have even recognized her? Then again, last time she visited, he'd said her name.

"You said he seemed better after he got back though, right?" Lexie needed reassurance before she entered his room.

"Oh, yes, and he looks very good today. Hasn't spoken yet, but he ate a big breakfast this morning and smiled at his little brother."

"Little brother?" He didn't have a brother. As a matter of fact, he didn't have anyone anymore, except Lexie and Angel.

"One of the local churches started a program where teenagers come into the centers around town and visit with our guests. His little brother's name is Jacob. I thought I told you about him, Jacob Zimmerman. Must've been Angel I told."

"Must've been. Is Jacob here now?"

"Oh no, he came before school. He'll come back on Thursday morning. Mondays and Thursdays are when he visits, always before school. Sometimes on Saturdays, if he doesn't have anything else going on."

Lexie nodded, glad he had other people visiting when she and Angel couldn't be here. But she wondered if this teen had anything to do with his disappearance. Had he gone out looking for Jacob? Had he found him? "The next time Jacob comes in, will you give him my number and ask him to call me?"

"Sure."

"Anyway, he ate real good this morning while Jacob was here."

"I'm glad." Maybe the teen reminded him of Phillip, Jr. It'd been a while since Phillip had made his way to Valdosta since he'd been so busy with school. Maybe this teenager filled that void. If so, she'd have to thank Jacob Zimmerman.

"I'll go make sure Donovan got your things over to the guesthouse."

Lexie smiled, then turned the knob and entered the room that, for the past twenty-eight years, had been her grandfather's home.

Nicholas Truman's striking emerald eyes were fixed on the large screen television composing the majority of one wall in his room. With his hand on the remote, he nodded, agreeing with the anchorwoman, then flipped the channel and listened to another newscast. He stopped on CNN, then moved on through the local stations. When he hit Macon's news, his trigger finger for the remote stayed at a standstill.

She knew what he wanted to see. Or at least she thought she knew. Why hadn't she or Angel thought about him seeing her broadcasts about the killer? Had he realized seven more years had passed and the monster who tore his life apart had returned?

Lexie looked at the tray resting on the table beside his bed. "Granddaddy, you never ate your pudding after lunch." She indicated the white ceramic bowl filled with his preferred dessert. "It's chocolate, your favorite." Jacqueline Murrell spoiled him, but she spoiled all of her guests. Murrell's Assisted Living had been dubbed the best facility in the south, and for the mighty Trumans, only the best would do.

The mighty Trumans. Lexie couldn't bear to think of her heritage in that light anymore. True, the money still abounded, but the strength of the family disintegrated on that day so long ago.

Lexie swallowed hard and took a seat beside his bed. While her grandfather stared at the television and dozed throughout the afternoon, she sat, hoping against hope that he'd turn his head her way, that he might speak her name again, or that he'd do something indicating he remembered her for good.

Nicholas cleared his throat, straightened in the bed, then pushed the sheet aside.

"You need something?"

He smiled at her, and Lexie's heart squeezed within her chest. Then he stood from the bed and went to the bathroom. In a few minutes, he returned. He looked at her again, but didn't smile. Then he grabbed the remote from atop the bedding and sat in the chair on the opposite side of the room.

At 5:30, Jackie brought both of them dinner. "Thought you'd want to eat in private." She placed the trays on a circular wooden table by the window. "You've got a great view of the magnolia grove. Might as well enjoy it while you eat."

"Thank you." Lexie moved to one of the chairs.

"Enjoy your meal, Nicholas." Jackie gave Lexie a soft smile then left.

When the door closed, he moved to the table and sat across from his granddaughter. They ate in silence, while the news chanted from the television screen.

Then it happened. Nicholas Truman's fork, filled with a healthy hunk of garlic mashed potatoes, dropped from his hand to the plate, and Lexie turned her attention from her grandfather to the television screen, where the pretty brunette news anchor, a woman who had worked with Lexie in Atlanta, updated Georgia on Macon's Sunrise Killer.

"Granddaddy?" Lexie jerked her head from the television back to her grandfather.

Tears streamed down his slack cheeks.

She moved from her chair to kneel in front of him. She knew better than to turn off the television. He'd waited for this all day.

"Granddaddy." She made certain her voice sounded strong and determined, in spite of the emotion making her insides churn. "We're going to get him this time. Angel and I will get him this time. I promise you, we will."

He inhaled a ragged breath, closed his jaw and swallowed. Then those vivid green eyes stared at hers. "Yes. You—will."

# CHAPTER NINE

Angel's behind was numb from sitting. Perched at this conference table for over ten hours, she'd participated in the call with Quantico and met with each member of the task force, except Lexie, at some point throughout the day. They hadn't scheduled an official meeting, but Ed, Lou, Ryan, Zed and John had taken turns reviewing the bulk of information they'd gathered, then each had followed his respective lead on the investigation. Most followed up with victimology, studying autopsy protocols and CSI files from the past murders. Lou Marker had returned to Cami Talton's house and Vickie Jones' duplex to see if they'd overlooked any details at the most recent murder sites. Tucker left Macon altogether, saying he had another lead that would take him out of the city and that he'd report the details as soon as they were available.

Angel didn't know why she trusted him, but she did. He meant something to Lexie, and she'd never known Lexie to misjudge a person's character. Therefore, for now, he'd moved down on the list of potential suspects. Not that she'd removed him from the list, but he wasn't as near the top.

She grabbed her cup of coffee, her fifth cup today, judging from the empty Styrofoam containers littering the table, and she worried that her perceptiveness was slipping. The stuff tasted half good.

Captain Pierce poked his head in. "Still here, huh?"

"That's what I'm paid for."

"You eat today?"

"I'm planning on it, but right now the caffeine is keeping me sustained."

He grunted. "If that caffeine is satisfying you, you've got some serious issues."

She laughed. "I was thinking the same thing."

"Here." He entered and plopped in the chair beside her. "It's tuna salad. My wife makes a mean tuna salad." He placed a brown bag beside her empty coffee cups.

"Don't you want it?"

"She never knows how late I'll be working, so she always sends extra. Today, she made three. I ate two. There're two bags of chips in there too. I'll take one of them, but you can have the other."

Angel opened the brown bag, withdrew a sandwich covered in foil and unwrapped it. The scent of tuna filled the room, and her stomach growled.

"That's what I thought." He pointed to the sandwich. "Go on, start eating, and tell me what you're working on. I haven't got the profiling experience you do, but I've solved my share of cases. Maybe I can provide a bit of insight."

She took a bite of the sandwich, then closed her eyes and enjoyed the delicious conglomeration of tuna, boiled eggs, sweet relish and mayo. Aunt Carol used to fix tuna sandwiches for Saturday lunches. She swallowed then looked at Pierce. "This is delicious."

"I know." He grinned. "I'll tell her you said so, though. Always means more when it comes from a stranger."

Angel laughed and took another bite.

"So tell me what you're following here." He indicated the stacks of books.

She had to consider how much to disclose, but Ed Pierce wasn't on her list of suspects since he didn't live in Macon at the time of the first murder series, and he seemed to want to help her solve the case. When she'd first met him, she'd had the suspicion he had his eye on John Tucker as a suspect; however, as she'd watched him interact with the remaining task force members, she'd come to realize Ed Pierce didn't merely suspect Tucker. He suspected everyone, and that suspicion could help her narrow her list, since he knew more about the task force members, and the additional personnel involved with the case, than Angel. Past experience told her the killer would be close to the investigation. What she hadn't determined, though, was how close.

"After my conversation with the guys at Quantico, I realized I may have focused too much on the signature and not enough on the modus operandi."

"But the signature is the more reliable guide to the behavior of serial offenders." He removed one bag of chips from the lunch sack, opened it and popped one in his mouth. "It's static; MO is dynamic. Chances are, if our killer has come up with a better means of pulling off the crime, he's done it. What he won't change is the signature."

"I know, but that's just it. His signature has stayed the same. He strangles blonde, pregnant and single women. Seven of them, every seven years. However, his MO changed between the first series and the second."

"He stopped leaving their bodies outdoors." Pierce followed her train of thought.

"Right. And his method for abducting them changed as well. He not only left the bodies indoors; he also attacked them within their own homes."

"That's still the case, based on the past three series." He ate another chip. "What about the MO bothers you?"

"The part we haven't covered." She took another bite of her sandwich, then flipped back in her notebook to find where she'd annotated her theory. "Okay. I was thinking about the case I completed before I came here, involving a serial rapist in Oklahoma City. His MO was to scope out upscale restaurants for attractive women arriving alone. He'd wait until his target entered the restaurant, then he'd give her enough time to get seated. Afterwards, he'd drive through the parking lot and note the license plate on her car. Then he called the restaurant, told them he had just finished eating there and was on his way out when he noticed a car with its lights on. He'd recite the tag number, then he'd wait."

Pierce followed the scenario. "They'd tell her she left her lights on, she'd go out to turn them off, and he'd grab her."

"Then he'd abduct her in the parking lot, take her away to a remote location, torture her, rape her, kill her and leave her body in the woods."

He shook his head. "You got him?"

"Yeah, we got him."

"How does his MO remind you of our guy?"

"His MO involved taking all of his victims in the same manner. At a nice restaurant, with the ploy that they'd left their lights on."

"Our guy always comes to their homes," Pierce said, not following her point.

"But the guy I mentioned found the women he wanted at restaurants. He always found them in the same manner."

"We don't know how our guy finds them. That's the whole problem with Vickie Jones. She apparently hadn't told anyone she was pregnant, so how did he know? How could he have found her, when he looks for such specific criteria, and she wasn't showing any signs of pregnancy yet? Do you think he's keeping track of all EPTs purchased in the city? Because if he is, he still wouldn't know which ones were positive."

"No, I don't think it was the EPT that did it. I believe it was her trip to Dr. Weatherly's."

"That's what Tucker thought too, but you talked to him this morning after he visited the doctor. There aren't any male staff members, and she hasn't seen any men fitting the profile hanging around."

"Just because she didn't see him doesn't mean he wasn't there."

"You think he's finding his victims at OB-GYN offices?"

"I think he's finding them at one particular OB-GYN's office."

"Dr. Weatherly?"

Angel nodded while she opened her bag of chips. "I called Cami Talton's mother today, asked her if she'd mind telling me the name of her daughter's doctor." She popped a salty chip in her mouth.

"Let me guess. Weatherly?"

"Yeah. Mrs. Talton said Cami loved her doctor. She said since Yvette Weatherly is the only female OB-GYN in Macon, that's the only doctor Cami wanted. She went on to explain Cami wanted a female doctor because she wasn't happy with males at the time."

"That makes sense. If some guy got you pregnant then abandoned ship, you wouldn't want to go to another guy to discuss what happened. If you could go to a woman, someone who would understand, you would."

"Right. And, according to these statistics," Angel withdrew a report she'd generated earlier, "during the past twelve months, Dr. Yvette Weatherly has handled eighty-five percent of all pregnancies in Macon involving single mothers."

"He's stalking her patients." Pierce's eyes widened with disbelief. "Whether the doctor has seen him there or not, our perp has his eye on her patients."

"I think so." Angel snatched another salty chip and popped it in her mouth.

"All right. Tucker's already got what he needs to access her files. He can get a list of Dr. Weatherly's single patients by tomorrow, I'm sure. Then we'll know who to watch. And I'll put a guy on her office as well to keep an eye out for anyone fitting our profile. We'll catch him." He finished off the last chip. "Good observation, Jackson."

"It'd still be better if we were on the offensive. Pro-active, that's the way to catch this guy. We won't have to worry about trying to pick the right victims if we catch him first."

"I agree, and maybe putting someone on Weatherly's place will help us do it. By the way, the State called today. We should have our missing persons info by tomorrow morning. That'll help, but I still plan to keep an eye on the women most at risk. Matter of fact, I'm going to call Tucker right now, let him know we want that list by our meeting tomorrow."

"Sounds good." Angel watched him leave then looked back at her notes. How he learned they were single, Angel didn't know, but she knew without a doubt he learned they were pregnant via Dr. Yvette Weatherly's office. Now she had to find out how many single, blonde, pregnant women were seeing the doctor. She got up, walked across the room and closed the door. Then she returned to the table and withdrew her cell phone from her purse. Keying in the numbers from her notes, she waited for the receptionist to answer.

"Dr. Yvette Weatherly's answering service, can I help you?"

Angel's eyes darted to the clock. 7:30. Was it really that late?

"Can I help you? If this is an emergency, or if you're in labor—"

"No, it isn't an emergency. I'll call the office in the morning."

"The office opens at eight."

"Thank you." Angel dropped the phone back in her purse. No, it wasn't an emergency, and no, she wasn't in labor, but she did need to see the doctor soon—and do her best to figure out how to keep Dr. Weatherly's blonde, single and pregnant patients...breathing.

Tucker hadn't planned on taking longer than an hour to determine where Lexie had headed. His impromptu meetings with the captain and the profiler put a slight wrench in his plan, as did the amount of time it took to persuade the good folks at Lexus that he was a homicide detective on the trail of a killer. But, as he'd predicted, he'd found her. Or at least he'd found her car, as good a starting point as any.

Last night, Lexie hadn't said anything about leaving town. In fact, she'd talked about interviewing the victims' families today and bringing their stories to the public. She'd been bound and determined to humanize each and every victim, until the public felt that every girl who'd been murdered had been a member of their family.

John had no doubt Lexie could do it. But she hadn't. She'd called in and requested a personal day, then headed to—he checked the address again—Valdosta.

Valdosta? A hundred and fifty miles from Macon. A hundred and fifty miles from the killer. Or so he thought.

The sun turned in for the day as he exited I-75, and his cell phone rang. "Tucker."

"Tucker, this is Pierce. How's your lead going?"

"Still working on it."

"Let me know if anything comes of it."

"Will do." John didn't know what he'd say if the captain pressed him for additional information. That he'd followed Lexie McCain to Valdosta on the possibility she had a lead on the killer? Or that he'd followed her to Valdosta on the possibility she might be in danger? *Or* that he'd followed her to Valdosta because he wanted to—period.

Captain Pierce had seen enough of John's work in the past to know he deserved full reign of his investigations, even this one, the only case that had ever yielded his own name as a potential suspect. That must have been enough reason to keep him from asking for additional details. "You'll be back in Macon tomorrow, right?"

"Planning on it."

"Good. I need you to use that warrant for Dr. Weatherly's office. Jackson determined both of the victims were patients there. What's more, the majority of single pregnant women in Macon go to Weatherly."

"She's the only female OB-GYN in town, isn't she?" Tucker followed the reasoning. "Why didn't we think of that before?"

"Maybe we needed a female's perspective. But the important thing is we've got a probable link in his MO, so I want to pursue it. Get everything you can on the patients who fit his criteria and bring it to the meeting tomorrow."

"Done."

"And if you learn anything else tonight, let me know. I'd rather go on the offensive with this thing, rather than sitting around waiting for his next attack. We've only got thirty-eight days until he kills again."

"If I get anything at all, you'll be the first to know."

"Good. I'll look for you in the morning." Pierce disconnected.

Tucker followed the directions he'd been given and turned down a side street off Mulberry. Within minutes, he entered a long driveway lined with towering magnolias. The branches met above him and formed a tunnel of leaves that absorbed every ounce of moonlight. At the end, however, the moon made up for lost time, illuminating a massive structure that resembled an elaborate dollhouse, complete with a wraparound porch and gingerbread trim at every peak. To the right of the entrance, a wrought iron sign identified the place as *Murrell's Assisted Living, An Exceptional Home for Exceptional Guests.*

Not what he'd expected, but he didn't question the information he'd been given when he saw Lexie's car, with its WGXA decal in the back window, parked nearby.

After pulling his Grand Cherokee in the next spot, he parked and got out.

Okay. He'd found her. Now what? What did an assisted living home have to do with the killer? Because John knew Lexie wouldn't have come down here the day after he struck without a tie-in.

When he'd first started this search, he expected to find Lexie on the trail of a prime suspect. However, he didn't foresee the killer hanging out in Valdosta, and he didn't anticipate finding him at an assisted living facility. But maybe Lexie had identified a victim's family member inside. There could be several tie-ins to the case, reasons causing her to change her plans today and head to Valdosta, but John saw none at all for her to put herself in danger or keep John out of the loop.

She *said* she trusted him. Then why didn't she tell him about her lead? He'd ask her, as soon as he found her.

He crossed the parking lot and started up the stone pathway leading to the porch.

"Who're you here to see?" The woman's voice echoed through the porch shadows.

John turned toward the sound and made out the petite figure of an elderly woman, her long gray braid hanging over one shoulder as she sat in a rocker on the far end of the porch. He couldn't make out her facial features. Even with the moonlight trimming the edge of the wooden planks on the porch, the majority of her face and body were hidden in the shadows of the gingerbread-embellished eaves. However, after blinking to focus, he saw the whites of her eyes, two circular pricks in the jet-black recesses of the porch.

"I asked you a question."

"Lexie McCain." He saw no reason to lie.

"Whatchu want with Miss Lexie?"

"I need to ask her some questions."

"She ain't broke no laws."

John glanced down to see the shield at his waist glistening

in the moonlight. "No, she hasn't. But I need to see her and make sure she's safe."

"Well, why didn't ya say so? She's inside, in Nicholas' room, but you better check with Jackie first. And you gotta ring the bell to get in. It's dark now, ya know."

"Will do." John nodded toward the tiny shadow, then turned to press the button beside the door. The familiar eight notes of the Westminster chime sounded from within the home, then footsteps echoed and the door creaked opened.

"Hello," The woman smoothed the front of her dress. "I'm Jacqueline Murrell. May I help you?"

"He's looking for Lexie!" the woman in the rocker yelled.

Ms. Murrell sighed, smiled then stepped forward. "Just a minute, please." She looked toward the tiny lady on the porch. "Agatha, aren't you ready to come in now? Your dessert is ready."

"Nope. The moon's bright, and I'm enjoying it. And don't call me that name."

"But that's your name. And it's a beautiful name, the name of one of my favorite authors, in fact."

"Is your name Jacqueline or Jackie?"

"Well, it's both. Jacqueline is my given name; Jackie is my nickname."

"Right. Well, I want to be Aggie today. I'll be Agatha again tomorrow."

"Okay, Aggie," Ms. Murrell sounded exasperated, "do you want to come in and have your dessert?"

"Not yet."

"Fine. Tell you what, I think Donovan wanted to come out and enjoy the moon too. How does that sound?"

"Sounds good. Sounds real good."

"Okay. I'll tell him you'd like for him to join you."

"All right."

Jacqueline Murrell turned back toward John, and her jaw dropped. She stared at his shield. "Is something wrong?"

"No, ma'am, I'm a detective with Macon's police department, and I'm working with Ms. McCain on one of her stories. I was concerned she may have put herself in danger by following one of her leads, so I came down to check things out."

Her brows lifted, head tilted to the side as she examined John. "Personally? Could've called her to see what she was doing, couldn't you?"

However, he did have an answer for her question. "She hasn't answered her cell phone today."

"Oh. Well, she's fine, I can assure you."

"No offense, Ms. Murrell, but I'd like to see that for myself."

"Yeah," she didn't hold back a knowing grin, "I kind of figured you did. Come on and follow me. I'll have to ask her if she wants to see you, though. If she says no, I'm afraid you'll have to leave."

John fought the urge to laugh. The woman weighed all of a hundred and twenty pounds, yet she had no qualms with informing a two hundred pound homicide detective that she was the boss under this roof. He liked her spunk.

"Hold on a minute." She put her palm against his chest, then stepped in a side room. "Donovan, Agatha's on the front porch and wanting company."

"On my way," a male voice responded. "Who was at the door?"

"A detective from Macon. He's here to see Lexie. Says he's helping her on a story."

Within two seconds, a tall elderly gentleman, his glasses pushed on top of his head to nestle within a sea of white waves, stood in front of John. "You're here to see Lexie?"

"I thought she might be chasing a lead on a story and was concerned for her safety." John wondered if the half-truth sounded more believable to the older man than it did to John.

Evidently not.

"Could've called the police down here to check on her, if you thought she was in trouble," Donovan pointed out. "I mean, it'd have saved you the trip, plus they could've gotten to her quicker, don't you think? *If* she was in trouble and all."

Why did John feel like this couple had him in the crosshairs and were ready to fire? "Yeah, I could have."

"But he wanted to see her himself, to make sure she was okay. Isn't that right?" Jackie fingered the silver bun on the back of her head, shot a knowing look to Donovan, and then turned her attention back to John.

"That's right."

Donovan's weathered face cracked into a smile. "Well, it's about time somebody watched out for that girl. She's done put herself in danger one time too many, if you ask me, chasing all those stories. I'm guessing she's after that killer they've been talking about in Macon, isn't she? Trying to solve the crime herself again, huh?"

"I'm hoping she's not trying to solve it on her own. That's why I'm here. But she is the lead news correspondent for the story."

"Don't surprise me." The old man pulled his glasses down and settled them on the bridge of his nose. "You gonna be able to keep her safe? She got too dang close to that killer in Atlanta. Ticked him off real good, if I remember right. He sure enough didn't like her interviews with that poor lady he hurt."

"Lexie doesn't realize we follow her stories." Jackie lowered her voice to a whisper. "But we can't help it. We care about her. She's a dear soul."

"She's not chasing any killer here, though," Donovan added.

"She's not?" If she wasn't working on the story, why had she come?

"No," Jackie shook her head, "But I'll let her tell you. Come on."

Donovan turned toward the door. "I'll head out to check on Agatha. Nice to meet you, Detective—"

"Tucker, John Tucker."

Donovan nodded, extended his hand and shook John's. "Nice to meet you, Detective Tucker, especially if you're going to watch out for Lexie." He turned and crossed the foyer then went outside to see Agatha.

"This way." Jackie started down the hall.

They passed a large room with a rock fireplace in its center. Three women and one man sat around a big screen television watching Wheel of Fortune and guessing the current puzzle. Then they passed several additional rooms, larger than college dorms but smaller than apartments, branching off both sides of the hall.

A few residents sat in their private domains reading newspapers, watching television or resting. Other rooms were vacant. He suspected those belonged to some of the Wheel of Fortune enthusiasts in the family room.

The home smelled of spiced apples, furniture polish and vanilla. John had visited quite a few assisted living homes before his grandparents passed away, but none as elegant as Murrell's.

"Nice place."

"We like it. Our residents are happy here." Jackie stopped by the only closed door in the hall. "Lexie's inside. I'll ask her if she'd like to see you."

"All right." John knew this would be—interesting. It wasn't as if he could say he'd been passing through. Two and a half hours from home wasn't a passing visit. Even so, he'd made the trip to see Lexie, and he wouldn't leave until he accomplished that goal.

Lexie's eyes burned, irritated and dry from lack of sleep. But she *had* slept last night. In fact, she'd achieved the most peaceful rest she'd had in a long time...with John Tucker outside her home.

But one good night's sleep wasn't enough to make up for the three nights she'd barely closed her eyes. The three nights since Cami Talton's body had been found, signaling the killer's return.

Her grandfather mumbled in his sleep, shifted in the covers and blew out a thick puff of air. She cringed. She hated that sound, those sudden exhalations of the elderly when they slept. The same sound she heard so many years ago, pronouncing death.

Lexie shook the memory away. How would she calm down enough to rest tonight if she kept remembering the pain? And she needed to sleep in order to think, to help the task force find the killer before he murdered again.

"No," Granddaddy whispered, frowning in his sleep.

Was he dreaming? Or remembering? As if she didn't know. How she wished she could tell him that they'd put the monster away for good.

But they hadn't.

He'd fallen asleep at 7:30 and would wake bright and early at 6:00 a.m. It'd been his schedule for as long as she could remember, early to bed, early to rise. Tonight the ritual would prove to her favor, because his pre-dawn awakening would allow her the chance to see him again in the morning before she drove back to Macon.

She looked at the clock. 8:15. Soon she'd leave and attempt to sleep in the guesthouse, a side cottage with four small rooms for those staying overnight to be near their family members. Lexie stayed there often. The cozy guesthouse provided everything she needed for a good night's rest. However, she knew it wouldn't. Not tonight, and not until they caught the killer.

But she *had* slept last night, which still baffled her. She'd gone so many years taking care of her fears on her own; she hadn't needed a man, hadn't needed anyone. But she'd be lying if she said she hadn't felt safer with John Tucker standing guard.

Had he felt the same? Had he experienced the connection that'd consumed her thoughts all day, making her wonder if perhaps she could feel safe enough to give her heart to a man again?

She'd tried with Phillip and had succeeded for a while. But then the old fears returned, and she turned away from her husband, hadn't been able to let him touch her because of the memories. The nightmares. The never-ending echoes of her screams.

But she hadn't thought of any of that last night with John.

Why did that realization make her feel so scared?

She decided to stop analyzing her response to the man until morning. Tonight she'd concentrate on learning how to sleep without him nearby.

Standing, she moved to the bed, kissed her grandfather's cheek, then turned to leave. She'd almost reached the door when she heard the faint tapping from the other side. Jackie's familiar soft knock.

Lexie opened the door and saw Jackie smiling. Then her gaze moved to the man who looked even bigger, even more invincible, when standing behind the petite older woman.

"You have a visitor. The detective said he's working with you on a story and wanted to make sure you were safe."

Lexie stepped into the hall and eased the door closed behind her, while her mind raced. How had he found her here? Angel wouldn't have given him this address unless something had happened. Unless something was very, very wrong. Plus, he didn't even know about their connection. He didn't know the man in the room behind her was her grandfather...and Angel's.

"John, what happened? Did they find him? Or did he find someone else? It isn't time yet." She rushed through the words in an effort to hear his response. "What happened?"

"Everything's fine. Ms. Murrell told the truth; I wanted to make sure you're okay. You didn't say anything about leaving today, and I knew how determined you were to get the story right, so I thought you might have followed a lead on your own."

Lexie blinked. "You followed me?"

"More like I found you."

"Why?"

"Like I said, I thought you were chasing this guy on your own and could be putting yourself in danger." He seemed to choose his words in Jackie's presence.

Lexie processed what he didn't say. "But why?"

Jackie cleared her throat. "Well, I need to go clean up a bit in the kitchen."

Lexie nodded, but never took her eyes from John's, not the usual brilliant blue tonight, but darker, more intense. "Why?"

"Because I wanted to."

She should be mad at the very least, but the honesty of his words settled deep in her chest then spiraled outward to every limb, making her feel warm all over. "Come on, we'll go outside where we can talk."

"You're okay then?" He stared at the closed door.

"Yes, this is my grandfather's room. He needed me today."

"Oh."

"Not what you thought?"

He smiled. "No, but I can't deny I'm pleased you weren't chasing the killer."

She returned the smile and chose not to tell him that visiting Nicholas Truman was close to the same thing; however, in this case, she wasn't chasing the killer. She needed to chase the killer away, from her grandfather's nightmares. And her own.

They walked down the hallway and out the foyer, then exited to the front porch, where Agatha and Donovan were coming back in.

"It's a bright moon," Agatha said. "Big and orange and round."

Lexie nodded at the lady. "Yes, it is."

"Donovan likes full moons too," the older woman added.

"That's right." Donovan opened the door for Agatha and waited for her to pass through. Then he turned to John. "We have two rooms open in the guest house. If you need a place to stay, you can have one of them. Lexie has a key to the building."

"Thank you."

Lexie waited until the door snapped closed, then turned to face him. "Well?"

"Well, what?"

"How did you find me?" She knew Angel wouldn't have told him, not now, not when they were so close to catching the killer, but Lexie couldn't fathom how he found her here.

"It wasn't that difficult, once I convinced the good folks at Lexus that I was a homicide detective tracking down a woman who could be in danger."

"Lexus?" Her gaze moved to her car, parked in the magnolia shadows.

"Yeah, thanks to your Lexus-Link, I connected to your personal advisor who, after I faxed a copy of my credentials, located your car and gave me this address." His straight, white teeth glimmered in the moonlight with his smile. "Guess I should applaud you for purchasing a state-of-the-art vehicle."

"Glad I could help." She smiled over her sarcasm. She couldn't get mad at him for tracking her down. He'd been concerned about her safety, but the look in his eyes said more. He'd told the truth. He came because he wanted to come, and her heart warmed at the realization.

"So, is your grandfather okay?"

"He's better now. He wandered off this weekend. We still don't know where he went, but he seems to be feeling all right, so I guess no harm was done."

"Does he leave often?"

"No, but every now and then he disappears for a while. Jackie told me he has a teenager visiting him now as part of a local church program. I'm thinking he may have gone looking for his new friend, or something like that. The boy may remind him of Phillip, Jr."

"Your son."

"Yeah. Phillip hasn't had a lot of time to come visit Granddaddy since college started last fall. So this teen may fill that void." She turned toward the porch railing, closed her eyes and inhaled the sweet scent of magnolia blossoms on the evening breeze. "I'm just glad he's doing okay." She hoped it wasn't too much of a lie. *Was* he doing okay? Or did he worry constantly over the killer's return?

"Lexie." He moved beside her at the edge of the porch.

"Yeah?"

"I did come because I was worried about you, but that wasn't all."

Lexie held her breath and waited for the rest.

"I came because I want to be with you."

She took another deep breath, let it out. "Are you going to take Donovan up on his offer to stay in the guesthouse?"

"I'm thinking I might."

Turning, she tilted her head to look up at the man touching her heart. "I slept last night, just knowing you were nearby."

"Maybe you can sleep again tonight, if I'm in the next room." When he smiled, the crinkle lines framing those intense blue eyes made her throat go dry.

It'd been so long since she'd felt true desire for a man, but she did now, with John. She moistened her lips, decided she needed to clarify last night's statement. "When I told you I wouldn't be with a man *that way* outside of marriage..." She hesitated.

He brought his face closer, so that Lexie caught the crisp scent of his aftershave mixed with the masculine scent of John Tucker. "Yes, Lexie?"

"I didn't mean that I didn't want *any* relationship. I just meant..." Her cheeks flamed, and she didn't know how to continue.

His eyes softened. Then he placed a finger beneath her chin and slowly, sweetly, lowered his mouth to hers.

It'd been a long time since Lexie had experienced a man's kiss, and she couldn't remember the last time she'd been kissed like this, if ever. He caressed her mouth, setting all of her hidden emotions free with the tender gesture and making her forget everything but the two of them. She forgot the loss. Forgot the pain. Forgot the nightmares. And, for a beautiful moment, forgot her fears.

# CHAPTER TEN

Two down, five to go, then this cycle would be complete. Anxious for it to be over, he realized that accomplishing his goal took time, and he wouldn't venture from the plan. He had to stay true to the pattern, true to the design for maintaining control. Capturing the power.

Monitoring the New Fellowship's website today had been beyond frustrating. They discussed a charity drive, the inner-city homeless shelter and other do-good projects. All safe subjects in their opinion, he supposed. The chat link that had discussed the killings had been extinguished, and PROTECT&SRV hadn't even logged on.

They were doing the same thing they'd done before, hiding from the truth, refusing to acknowledge the one among them committed to carrying out Brother Moses' plan. They were fools. Cowards. They didn't want to discuss what he'd done because they were ashamed that none of them had lifted a finger toward controlling the power; therefore, they were weak and powerless. And they respected the most pathetic one, the man who had been taught the truth from his father and still turned away. John Tucker. Well, when PROTECT&SRV logged on again, he'd get a real treat. He'd learn a little more about TRUTHLUVR, the one who followed through with the plan...and the one who killed Tucker's father.

His hands gripped the steering wheel as he eased the car past Cami Talton's tiny house. He took his time, slowing to a near standstill while he stared at the little home. When he'd located her house he'd known for sure that the Supreme One had selected her for his first kill. The white wooden siding, black shutters, even the swirling wrought iron railing on the porch made the house identical to Hannah's home. A firm sign that he'd chosen well.

He continued past her house, then started slowly across town. It wasn't a time for speeding. At 3:00 in the morning, no matter who you were, if you zipped through Macon, you drew attention. He didn't want attention. Besides, if anyone saw him at either location, they'd just think he was doing his job.

"The killer always returns to the scene of the crime." Most killers weren't able to do it under the guise that it was part of their job, but he could. And he had. In fact, this was his third trip to both sites.

Both other times, he'd gone inside, looked around and remembered the surge of power he'd experienced when he'd taken complete control. And all the while, the very people trying their hardest to stop his plan surrounded him while he gloated. They could try. Many had, and they'd all failed. They would again.

Unlike Cami's residence, Vickie Jones' duplex hadn't depicted the accuracy of his choice. However, he hadn't doubted his decision after his conversation with her on the park bench. Perfect, she had an angel's face surrounded by a halo of golden hair, both qualities disguising the sinner within. But he'd seen through her disguise. He'd known she, like Hannah, attempted to claim power for her own when it wasn't hers to claim. But he'd claimed it. He'd taken her life and conquered the child.

Until the cycle completed, he didn't experience the full impact of the power. He couldn't. He had only accumulated one part of the whole. As a result, he felt empty, unfulfilled and lost, which enraged him.

If it weren't for Hannah, for what she'd done so long ago, he wouldn't experience this void. He wouldn't feel so incomplete. He would have her and have her child—their child. But no, she lied. She sinned, and she betrayed the one who loved her most.

He pressed the accelerator to the floor and listened to the car peel out from the street. Forget creeping through town. He didn't want to creep; he wanted to roar. And he would roar at

Hannah.

During the long drive to the outskirts of Macon, he didn't meet a single car. No one saw him racing. No one saw the car swerve at every curve because he refused to slow down. No one saw...because the Supreme One protected him in his rite of passage. No one could stop him now.

So enthralled with the speed of his vehicle, he nearly missed his turn. The smell of rubber from his squealing tires penetrated his nostrils as he jerked the car in a hard right and tore through the underbrush, down the path, and to the place where he'd buried Hannah and her lover so many years ago.

He opened the car door and climbed out, then moved forward until he stood right above them. Over their bodies. Standing above the liars who didn't deserve to live.

Cool wind whipped through the trees, bringing the scent of pine and damp leaves. He closed his eyes and heard the songs. Voices amid the wind. Voices from the past. Those who sang in this very spot so many years ago. Songs of the powerful, songs of the chosen. He'd learned of fire and brimstone and power and supremacy. Right. Here.

And later, he'd taught Hannah what she refused to learn before—fire and brimstone, power and supremacy. Right. Here.

"He probably won't say anything." Lexie crossed the parking area with John in the pre-dawn haze. "But he'll know we're here."

"You sure you want me along? Because if you'd rather I not meet him yet—"

Lexie stopped walking, her feet crunching on the gravel as she twisted to look at him. "He's seen me alone for so many years. Whenever I come to visit, I'm either by myself, or I have Phillip, Jr. with me, but he hasn't seen me with another man since Phillip and I divorced. I think it would do him a world of good to see the two of us together, especially now."

"Why especially now?"

Lexie's stomach tightened. She'd begun to open her heart to John and felt closer to him than any man in a very long time. But she wasn't ready to tell him everything. Not yet.

Thankfully, Agatha's tendency to venture outside saved her from further explanation.

"Sun's coming." Agatha stared at the light filtering through the trees. "Coming now. Coming fast."

"Yes, it is." Lexie stepped up on the porch.

John followed her and didn't press the issue for an answer to his question.

If they were going to attempt some form of a real relationship, she wanted to be honest with him about her past. But since it wasn't merely *her* past, she needed to talk to the other person involved before divulging the secrets they'd kept guarded for so long.

She'd have to talk to Angel.

Jackie opened the front door before Lexie had a chance to knock. "I'm glad you're able to see him again this morning before you head back. Today's going to be a talking day."

Lexie grinned. "He's in a good mood?"

"I'll say. He's been chatting all morning, but that could be because Georgianne made biscuits and gravy."

Georgianne Holiday came to the residence each morning to prepare the day's meals. The main cook at three Valdosta assisted living homes, Georgianne visited Murrell's in the mornings, then two more before the day ended. She'd get everything in order for three meals, then head her way to do the same at the next home. And although she had to be in her late sixties, she had the energy of a teenager. She had already come and gone by the time Lexie arrived yesterday, so Lexie looked forward to seeing Georgianne this morning before she returned to Macon.

"Love biscuits and gravy." Agatha rocked on the front porch.

"Well then, you need to come in and eat while it's hot, Agatha."

"Aggie."

Jackie rolled her eyes, but grinned. "Yes, Aggie, you should come in and eat while it's hot."

"Coming." Agatha climbed from her rocker and bounded through the doorway, shoving her way past Lexie and John to get through.

"She gets a little excited," Jackie explained to John.

"I see that." He grinned. "Guess we have something to look forward to with those biscuits and gravy, don't we?"

"Oh yes, Georgianne makes the best." Jackie stepped aside so they could enter.

Lexie inhaled the peppery smell of Georgianne's fabulous white gravy and the yeasty smell of her fat, buttery biscuits. "You've never had biscuits like Georgianne's."

John inhaled, then nodded. "I'm looking forward to it."

"Is Granddaddy in his room?"

"Yes," Jackie answered, but her husband stepped forward and corrected her.

"He was, but he just moved down the hall to the dining room. He's already eating. I'd walk you down there, but I need to take breakfast in to Mrs. Johnson. She doesn't like to eat with the group, and if I don't grab some biscuits quick, your grandfather and his friends are liable not to leave her any."

"And I'm going to help Georgianne in the kitchen," Jackie added.

Lexie laughed. "Don't worry, I know my way around. We'll go sit with Granddaddy in the dining room."

They walked down the opposite hall from her grandfather's room. "I'm so glad he's doing better." She wanted to see him on a "good day." He didn't have many and to experience one with him was a rare treat. Plus, he might converse with John upon their first meeting.

Though only 6:30 in the morning, the dining room had already filled with elderly men and women at their most alert, and most chatty, stage of the day. A large television blared in one corner, and one of the men had commandeered the remote and increased the volume to a deafening pitch.

"Goodness, Mr. Vick, can you turn that down?" Georgianne winced as she crossed the room with two steamy plates of biscuits and gravy in her hands. She placed the plates on either side of Lexie's grandfather. "Looks like you've got some guests for breakfast." She indicated Lexie and John. "How ya doing, Lexie?"

"Great, Georgianne."

Doing a poor job of hiding her curiosity, Georgianne

surveyed Tucker. "Who's your friend?"

"Detective John Tucker." He extended his hand. "Nice to meet you."

Georgianne shook the proffered hand and grinned. "We're glad you're here." She winked at Lexie. "Really glad you're here." Then she twirled on her heel and returned to the kitchen, while Lexie fought the impulse to blush.

"Granddaddy, this is John Tucker." She kissed her grandfather's cheek before sitting down. "He's a friend of mine, and he's helping me with a story I'm working on. John, this is my grandfather, Nicholas Truman."

John's eyes widened, and Lexie knew he recognized the notable name. He shot a quick knowing look at Lexie, then extended his hand.

"Tuck-er?" Nicholas took John's hand and held it within both of his.

"Yes, sir." John sat at the table.

"He's a detective with the Macon Police Department." Lexie took a bite of her biscuit and gravy and let her taste buds enjoy Georgianne's talents, while she watched the exchange between the two men.

Her grandfather released John's hand, then leaned forward, tilting his head to examine Tucker's face.

"Everything okay, Granddaddy?"

"Yes."

John smiled, but looked a little disconcerted with Nicholas Truman's appraisal.

"The biscuits look good." John took a bite, then hummed his approval.

"Yes." Her grandfather picked up his fork and took a bite, but never took his gaze off Tucker's face. Then he continued eating, but didn't speak again. Instead, he kept darting his gaze from Lexie to John to the television.

Lexie had hoped he'd be more talkative today, as Jackie had indicated, but even though he'd already said more words than yesterday, she had a feeling the communication had already ended. She sighed and shrugged her shoulders at John, then ate her breakfast in silence.

She'd shared many meals like this with Nicholas Truman

throughout the past twenty-eight years, both of them eating and neither of them speaking, but with John present at the table, the silence seemed near unbearable. Her throat closed in, and although she knew the biscuits were heavenly, she couldn't taste them anymore. She continued eating and tried to keep the tears at bay.

When they finished their meal, Jackie took their plates. "I guess you'll be leaving soon."

"Yes." Lexie turned to her grandfather. "Granddaddy, I'll come back as soon as I can, okay?"

His gaze fixated on the television. Lexie turned to see that the local station aired her clip from Cami Talton's funeral.

"Turn. Up," Nicholas commanded, and Mr. Vick obeyed.

Within half a second, the television blared, the volume at its full capacity, while several residents held their ears and Lexie's own voice filled the screen as one of her pre-taped broadcasts aired.

*"Funeral services for Camille Evelyn Talton will be held today in Macon. Ms. Talton is believed to be a victim of the Sunrise Killer, a serial killer who has eluded the authorities for nearly three decades. A second victim, Victoria Arnez Jones, was found murdered in her home on Sunday. If you have any information involving either of these murders, please contact the Macon Police Department at—"*

Donovan claimed the remote from Mr. Vick and turned down the sound. "We watch you often, but not quite this loudly."

"He said turn it up." Mr. Vick pointed an accusing finger at Nicholas. "So I did."

"Well, it was nice of you to oblige him, but we're going to try to keep it to a low roar, if you don't mind."

Mr. Vick shrugged bony shoulders.

Nicholas pushed his plate to the center of the table then turned his attention to Lexie. "Get. Him."

"Yes." She turned toward Tucker. "I told him yesterday that I was helping the police find the killer."

John nodded, but Lexie knew the sharp detective sensed the truth. He'd studied the victimology and knew about Aunt Bev, but he didn't know the rest. Lexie would have to tell him.

Soon. *After* she talked to Angel.

"We're going to catch him, Mr. Truman." John said the words with conviction.

Nicholas nodded. "Good. Milton."

All color drained from John's face.

"Granddaddy, this is John. John Tucker."

"Milton."

And while she watched, Tucker's blue eyes widened once again. "Did you know Milton?"

Lexie waited. *Milton?*

Her grandfather nodded. "Milton. Tuck-er."

"You knew my father."

"Good. Man."

A tender smile covered John's face. "Yes. He was."

Milton Tucker. Why did that name sound familiar?

"Milton. Helped."

The memory clicked into place, and Lexie swallowed hard. Of course, she should've remembered that name. Milton Tucker, the Sheriff for Bibb County twenty-eight years ago, and the man who'd been so kind, who'd helped Lexie feel better, in spite of what had happened. He'd had a caring smile, jet-black hair and the bluest eyes...

She looked at John. No wonder she'd felt so safe around him. No wonder she'd been so drawn to him. Milton Tucker *was* a good man. And so was his son.

Nicholas Truman looked away from John to the television, where Lexie's footage ended and the local news anchor provided the updated profile on the Sunrise Killer. With his jaw set and his green eyes intent, Nicholas Truman demanded, "Get him. Tuck-er."

"I will. I promise."

Her grandfather bobbed his head, nodding in small jerks while frowning at the television. He didn't return his attention to the two people on either side of him; rather, he stared at the screen. His morning talk had ended.

Lexie didn't want to go, but if she and John were going to "get him," as her grandfather had requested, they needed to work on the case. "Granddaddy, we need to go to Macon now. I'll come back soon."

He bobbed his head, but didn't look her way.

Lexie tamped down her emotion and stood from her chair. "You ready?"

"Yes. It was nice to meet you, sir." John held out his hand, but this time, Nicholas ignored the gesture. Instead, he nodded and stared at the television. The newscast ended and a margarine commercial took center stage, but Nicholas Truman didn't seem to notice.

Lexie leaned toward him and kissed his cheek. "I love you."

Then she and John started to walk away, but her grandfather's words, spoken more clearly than any others this morning, made her stop and listen.

"Love. You. AJ."

Lexie stared at the back of John's truck as she followed him up I-75 from Valdosta to Macon. Peach orchards and pecan groves zoomed past as they progressed toward home, but she hardly noticed the exquisite Georgia scenery for remembering the look on John's face when he realized who she was.

He looked—betrayed. And that look stabbed her heart. He hadn't said a word when they left Murrell's, just climbed in his Grand Cherokee and led the way back to Macon.

She swallowed, preparing to say *something* when they got back, but she didn't know what to say. And before she could decide how best to explain, John Tucker jerked his truck to the right, then slammed on the brake when it hit the side of the road.

Lexie followed suit, relief flooding through her when she didn't run into the rear of his truck in the process. Her head banged against the back of the seat when her car stopped, then fear gripped her when the big gorgeous detective climbed from his truck, stormed to the passenger's side of her Lexus, got in and slammed the door.

"I thought you trusted me." The muscle in his jaw clenched between each word.

Her throat closed in. She shouldn't tell him everything, not until she spoke to Angel, but how could she tell him only half of the truth?

"When were you going to tell me your mother was one of

the victims? And why would you keep something that important from the task force?" Each word pronounced his frustration. "Why would you keep it from *me?*"

"I don't know."

"You thought it was me, didn't you? You thought I killed Abby and all the others? When did you change your mind? Tell me the truth."

"No. No, I didn't. Never did I think that, even before last night." Before the kiss that cemented how much she did trust this man.

His lips formed a flat, unconvinced line.

"I didn't." Lexie moved toward him, took her hand to his face and touched the firm jaw, felt the morning stubble that made him look even more intense, even more hurt. "I *never* thought it was you."

"Then why didn't you tell me your mother was a victim?" He still looked at her as though she were a stranger.

"Not my mother, my aunt. And I was going to tell you. I was, but there are more people involved."

"Like?"

Lexie felt sick. She did trust John, more than any man, but she couldn't tell him everything yet. She wouldn't do that to Angel. She couldn't.

"I need to talk to someone first." She slid her fingers up the side of his face to that beautiful sprinkle of silver at his temple. "But I promise, I'll tell you everything." She moved even closer and saw his features relax. "And I promise, I never, ever thought you were the killer. In fact," she leaned forward and brushed a soft kiss against his unyielding lips.

He growled low in his throat, pulled her close and accepted her kiss. His hands slid around her neck, then tunneled through her hair as he deepened the intimacy of the gesture.

Lexie moaned her approval. Her body tingled everywhere, surrendering to the pull, to the allure, of John Tucker.

After breaking the intoxicating kiss, he searched her eyes. "In fact...what, Lexie?"

"In fact, I trust you completely."

He smiled, and she welcomed the change. If he only knew, he'd done more for her in the past week than anybody else had managed to do in twenty-eight years. He'd taught her to trust men again, taught her to trust *him*. She enjoyed his touch, and desired, truly desired, his kiss.

"I'll give you time to talk to—whoever—but I want to know the story, Lexie, and soon. There's a killer out there, and like it or not, you're linked to him through your past. I'm assuming no one in Macon knows your family history?"

"One person."

"The one you need to talk to?"

She thought of Angel. "Yes."

"Okay. Talk to that person, but then, talk to me."

"I will. I promise." She kissed his cheek then scooted back to her side of the car, while John cleared his throat.

"She was your aunt?"

"Aunt Bev."

"I remember the articles said the senator lost two daughters. That's what they claimed caused the heart attack and the mental breakdown."

"My parents died in a car wreck the week before my aunt was murdered." She took a breath, then let it out. It had been a long time since she'd said it aloud. "Losing my mom and Aunt Bev so close together was too much for him to handle. My grandmother had died the year before, so I guess he felt like everyone he loved was being taken away. But—"

"But?"

"But it was the way Aunt Bev died, the way the killer murdered her and the fact that she was pregnant, that made him the way he is now, locked inside his head."

"Did he have any other kids?"

"Aunt Carol. She was the youngest of the sisters, and she's the one who raised me."

"Where is she now?"

"Died last year." Lexie didn't add that her aunt's death had been the second most horrible day in her life. And in Angel's.

He slid his hand across the seat and placed it on top of hers, sending a blissful warmth of understanding over her skin.

"Thank you." Emotion filled both words.

She didn't have to ask what for; she knew. This all-powerful male had been moved by her willingness to share, to trust.

"One more thing. AJ. What does it stand for?"

"Alexandra Jane."

"Alexandra Jane." He smiled. "I like that."

Angel stood outside Dr. Weatherly's office and watched the nurse unlock the door promptly at 8:00. Then she waited another fifteen minutes in order to survey the surrounding area before going in.

Pierce had a cop in an unmarked car watching the place; however, it didn't take Angel but a few seconds to realize it wouldn't do any good. Macon's biggest city park bordered one side of Yvette Weatherly's office, and in the short time Angel waited on the doctor to arrive she viewed no less than six men who visibly fit the profile. People enjoying the crisp spring weather packed the area. Joggers ran around an asphalt track. Elderly and young alike ambled through the park walking dogs, feeding birds and chatting.

The numbers in the area would go up as the day progressed, and it'd be impossible to spot their killer in the midst of the crowds. Even if a man returned periodically, that wouldn't produce a red flag. Most people who ventured to parks came often, which meant the cop in the car down the street was wasted effort. But it wasn't Angel's place to tell the police how to do their job. She didn't catch the criminals; she identified the type they were looking for then let the cops do the rest.

However, in the case of the Oklahoma City rapist, she'd taken an active role even though that wasn't included in a profiler's job description. But the task force in Oklahoma City had approved her idea, agreeing that she'd be most likely to recognize their perpetrator and capable of handling herself in a dangerous situation. That time, the local police were on hand at the restaurant and at the ready for anything to occur.

This time would be different. She couldn't inform the task force, because three men on the force were potential suspects. Lou Marker, Ryan Sims and John Tucker all fit the bill. Therefore, she'd called Leon Hawkins and relayed her idea, then Hawkins called Quantico. Now she needed to set everything in motion with the doctor. She'd tell Lexie later, after everything was set. No doubt her cousin wouldn't approve. Lexie didn't agree with lying or deception, regardless of whether it was necessary in the line of duty. Angel, however, hadn't grown up with the same moral compass as Lexie, and didn't have a problem with either. If God had wanted her to be good, He wouldn't have let her life begin with her mother's murder. And now she'd do whatever it took to catch a killer.

"Good morning." A woman, whose nametag read Nita, welcomed her to the office. "Come on in." Nita walked ahead of Angel through the airy entry.

"Morning." Angel followed her then watched her disappear through a side door. The waiting room had peach walls, teal chairs and a television centered on one wall. Within seconds, Nita reappeared behind the window of the reception area, slid the glass open then placed a large white clipboard and a pink pen advertising mammograms on the counter. "You can go ahead and sign in. You're a new patient, aren't you?" She grabbed a second clipboard from a side shelf. "I'll need you to fill out some paperwork regarding insurance, contact information, that kind of thing."

"Oh, I don't have an appointment this morning, but I do need to speak to the doctor for a few minutes."

"Are you having problems? Experiencing discomfort?" Nita raised the pen.

"No, I need to talk to her regarding two of her former patients." Angel displayed her credentials. "It'll only take a few minutes."

Nita frowned, put down the second clipboard. "Let me go ask if she can see you. Now would be a good time, since it looks as though our eight o'clock is going to be late." She gestured to the empty waiting room. "I'll be right back."

Angel waited at the window, while Nita retreated down the hall and a second woman entered. She smiled at Angel, then booted up her computer. "Do you need help?"

"Just need to ask Dr. Weatherly a couple of questions." Angel nodded toward the hallway Nita had entered. "I believe Nita's talking to her now." Might as well get on a first name basis with the nurses. Familiarity encourages conversation, and conversation equates to information. Angel needed all the information she could get.

"Okay." She opened a side drawer in her desk and dropped her purse inside, then yawned. "Definitely need coffee."

"Oh Mandy, if you're getting some, will you bring me a cup?" Nita re-entered the tiny reception room they shared.

Mandy smirked. "Sure, but the next cup is on you." She looked at Angel. "Want a cup? We have decaffeinated, if you're expecting."

Expecting? Angel fought the urge to laugh. Searching for serial killers didn't leave a lot of time for relationships, let alone a pregnancy. And her brief infatuation with Agent Stanley Carlton had last less than a week. "I've already had some this morning. Thanks."

"Okay. I'll be right back, Nita." Mandy headed out to get the coffee.

"Doctor Weatherly said she'll see you now." Nita dropped some files on her desk, then moved back to the side door to let Angel in. "Last door on the right."

"Thanks." Angel headed down the hall to find the doctor…and some answers.

After driving past Cami Talton's and Vickie Jones' homes, he spent a good portion of the night with Hannah and her lover. Telling them of his conquest. Informing them of what they had caused, what they still caused, so many years after their sin. He'd also spent a good portion of the night fuming at how the chatters on the Fellowship's website had dismissed him. He accomplished the true goal with every kill, yet they didn't care. Not even PROTECT&SRV. The Supreme One would be infuriated.

All in all, he had slept less than three hours, but he didn't need much sleep. During a killing year, his body pulsed with energy, with adrenaline produced from the challenge and with the bliss of accomplishing his goal, a high he only experienced in the midst of a seventh year, when he followed the pattern and claimed the power.

He'd gotten antsy last year with that girl he met in the park. She'd been blonde, pregnant and single. And so pretty, the kind of woman who could tempt a man and lead him to sin, convince him to give her what she needed to gain power. But he resisted the temptation, even when she smiled and flirted and laughed. She'd wanted him. He'd known it as sure as he'd known that if he met her this year, if her baby had come twelve months later, she'd be dead.

That woman had married a month before the baby came, proof she wasn't a chosen one. He'd been tested to see if he could restrain the impulse to kill before the right time. He'd been tempted, and he'd conquered the temptation. Another affirmation that he did the right thing.

His feet pushed against the asphalt, arms pumped and breath passed in and out of his lungs in a steady whoosh. As he did every day during his run through Central City Park, he counted his strides. Right, two, three, four, five, six, seven. Left, two, three, four, five, six, seven. Right...

The surge of excitement stirred in his veins. He pushed up the sleeve on his sweatshirt to look at his watch, but he knew what he'd see. He'd passed the thirty minute mark, and he began to experience that blessed runner's high, the euphoria when endorphin and serotonin release and everything becomes clearer. More focused. More real. He inhaled, pushed it out, inhaled, pushed it out, increased his stride and enjoyed the ability to remember every kill.

Starting with Hannah and her lover, the screams washed over his senses as he progressed through the park. He listened to her voice, begging him to stop, and felt that surge of power from feeling her body grow limp beneath his. Then he killed her lover. He'd whimpered and whined like a toddler, pathetic and weak and useless.

Right, two, three, four, five, six, seven. Another kill, two, three, four, five, six, seven. Claim the power, two, three, four, five, six, seven. Claim the child, two, three, four, five, six, seven.

By the time he'd progressed to his most recent kills and remembered Cami Talton's and Vickie Jones' futile struggles, he'd been running for an hour and felt ecstatic.

Then he saw the car.

He'd noticed it before, but the morning sun had cast a glare on the windshield and hidden the man from view. Now, though, he saw the sole individual perched inside drinking from a Racetrac sixty-four ounce cup, the same kind of cup the car's occupant drank from every morning.

He passed the vehicle and nodded to the guy inside, then continued around the track once more. On his next pass, he decided to let the runner's high slide in lieu of gaining information. Slowing, he approached the car and grinned.

Officer Richard Barnes rolled his window down. "Hey, you realize all that exercise ain't good for your heart." Then he reached across the seat and lifted a white and green paper bag. "This here's what you need to get you going. Cream-filled doughnuts. You want one?"

"Nah, I'll pass. The run gets me going." He jogged in place and felt his pulse skitter at the sudden change.

"Well, you ain't no spring chicken anymore. I heard about this fellow once who got so addicted to running and all that mind-numbing stuff it does, he had a stroke on the track and didn't even realize it. You're acting like you're trying to kill yourself out there. You might very well have one of those strokes like I read about."

Another grin. Nope, he wasn't trying to kill himself, but he did remember a few kills with every pass. "I think I'll risk it, and I'll still pass on the carbs and sugar."

"Suit yourself." The cop lifted his Krispy Kreme in mock salute. "But I like my way better."

"You watching the doctor's place?"

"Yeah, but half the men out here fit the description." He pointed to the surplus of individuals roving the park.

"I'll say."

Richard Barnes took a big bite of doughnut then used the back of his hand to wipe a dribble of cream from the corner of his mouth. "I told them this was a useless bit, but Pierce insisted. No sweat off my back, though. It's an easy deal."

"Yeah." A long blonde ponytail caught his eye, and he turned toward Dr. Weatherly's office. "Isn't that the profiler?"

Richard nodded. "Don't know what she's doing here. Nobody told me she was coming, but I figure those government guys have their own agenda, you know? Maybe she's asking questions, getting specifics about that other woman's pregnancy." He shrugged, then took another oversized bite of doughnut.

"I'm sure the Feds have their own plan." He eyed Agent Jackson.

"The Feds usually do."

"Well, if I see anybody looking suspicious, I'll let you know."

"Do that. But if you ask me, everybody out here looks suspicious. They're all exercising. That's crazy enough for me." He laughed, then grabbed another doughnut. "See ya around."

"Right." He jogged away from the cop's unmarked car, then progressed around the track, all the while keeping one eye on the blonde profiler climbing in her SUV. What was Angel Jackson doing at Dr. Weatherly's? Why would she need to, since she'd talked with Tucker about the answers he'd already obtained from the doctor. The notable detective would have given her copies of the files he collected and all information the doctor had provided on Vickie Jones.

He jogged around the track a couple more times to cool down and think about Angel Jackson. Sure, she reminded him of his victims, but he wondered if there wasn't more to it than that. Maybe her intelligence drew him to her, made him feel something of a kinship to the woman. In the four days since she'd arrived in Macon, she'd already produced a profile much more accurate than the last FBI guy's depiction. Listening to her, he'd have sworn she could see his face in the midst of her notes. But she'd looked right at him, several times. And had been clueless.

He smiled at that. She could come close, but she'd never get close enough. No harm could come to someone setting about to achieve justice. However, he couldn't deny that Special Agent Angel Jackson had caused the task force to look in the right direction.

A male, forties to mid-fifties. *Correct.*

Caucasian. *Correct again.*

Someone close to the case. He grinned. *Oh yeah.*

But she hadn't narrowed it down enough to exclude the remaining men involved with the case. And almost every one of them also fit the bill.

"Nice try, Jackson." He rounded another curve of the track. Squinting in the distance, he watched her black Tahoe pull out of the doctor's parking lot. She'd go to the police station, where she'd slave over her notes and figures for the remainder of the day, and the remainder of each day until he killed again.

He'd been impressed by her mind, though, when she linked the religious aspect to the crimes. Lexie McCain too, for that matter. It'd taken the two women to realize there had been another kill that first year, and it'd taken the two women to identify each kill occurred forty days apart and always started forty days before Easter. They'd understood the importance of the numbers and the semblance involved with each.

You would think they'd understand that he couldn't be stopped, that he served a purpose and had to reach his goal. But Angel Jackson and Lexie McCain weren't *that* smart.

Right, two, three, four, five, six, seven. Left, two, three, four, five, six, seven. *What's she doing?* two three, four, five, six, seven. *Need to know*, two, three, four, five, six, seven...

# CHAPTER ELEVEN

Angel pulled into the police station parking lot, cut the engine and sighed in frustration. Her trip to Dr. Weatherly's hadn't netted anything beyond what Tucker had already learned. The doctor had lots of patients, many of whom were blonde, single and pregnant.

Etta Green stepped outside the police station, lit a cigarette, then paced while she smoked. She nodded at Angel and darted occasional glances her way as though waiting for her to exit her vehicle and head toward the building. Angel would, but first she had to call the field office.

Fishing her cell phone out of her purse, she dialed Leon Hawkins and relayed the current status of the investigation, the same status as yesterday. She'd hoped that her visit with the doctor would at least provide a new lead to investigate, but her gut told her that past case history provided the best source of information they had now. Angel hated looking backward. True, studying the killer's signature and MO helped, but she despised feeling as though the task force was on the defensive. She wanted to take control, turn the case around so that they were the ones that were proactive, rather than the killer. That's the way cases were solved, like her previous case in Oklahoma City.

She finished her conversation with Leon, dropped the phone back in her bag then jumped when someone tapped on her window.

"You coming in?" Etta's voice echoed loud enough to be heard through the glass.

Angel nodded, grabbed her things and climbed out of the

Tahoe. Etta bristled with anxiety, and Angel assumed whatever the woman had to say had to do with the case. Maybe Angel would learn something new this morning after all. "What's going on?"

"You tell me." Etta squinted into the sunlight. Her breath had a hint of recent smoke, combined with peppermint. Angel saw the red and white striped candy pass from one side of Etta's mouth to the other as the woman dropped her bombshell. "Rumor has it you fit the profile. I figured the best way to find out was to ask. So. Do you?"

Angel blinked. *She* fit the profile? "Our killer is male." There were several other factors involved with the profile that would eliminate Angel and all other females from the scenario, but the obvious one seemed the best to relay in light of Angel's shock at the statement. What kind of crazy rumors had been started?

Etta tsked, smacked the candy then waved a bangle-clad hand. "Not the killer's profile. The profile for victims."

"I'm not pregnant." True, she hit two out of three of the killer's signature criteria, but two out of three—for this type of methodic killer—wasn't going to cut the mustard.

"That's what I told him," Etta shook her head with a frown, "but you're going to have to get in there and tell them all yourself. See, with the way you tossed your cookies at the crime scene, you know, and then you went to the doctor's office this morning. And we all know Tucker already checked out the doctor, so you wouldn't be asking her the same questions, right?"

Angel tried to make sense of the disjointed monologue, while Lou Marker entered the parking area. He parked his patrol car, got out and nodded at them as he strode toward the building. "Nothing new this morning, huh?"

Angel shook her head. "Not yet. Something will turn up."

He looked doubtful. "Any other news you want to share?"

"No."

He gave her one of those bobbing head moves that said he thought she was keeping something from him, but before she could say anything else, he walked past them and entered the building.

Etta waited until the station door closed behind Lou. "He's heard it too. News travels fast in a small town. So, it isn't true?"

"No." However, Angel had contemplated a way to start that very rumor and then serve herself up to the killer as bait. Had someone actually helped her accomplish the goal? "Who said I fit the profile?"

"Elijah Lewis." Etta's tone rang with distaste. "He pointed out that everyone saw you get sick at the crime scene and that FBI folks should be accustomed to things like that, so you shouldn't have gotten sick, which does make sense, you've gotta admit, though I hadn't thought about it before. And then he said he saw you this morning going into Dr. Weatherly's place, and we all know Tucker had checked out the doctor's information and that he'd already finished with that, so why would you go too...unless maybe you weren't going for the case?"

"I'm not pregnant." Angel wondered how many people she'd have to convince before the day ended, thanks to Elijah Lewis. Who had he already told? And in a town the size of Macon, how long until the entire county knew? Not very long. "And for the record, lots of 'FBI folks' toss their cookies. We're still human." Although Angel had never gotten sick before at a crime scene; however, she attributed her response to the fact that Vickie Jones had been murdered by the same man that killed Angel's mother.

"Oh well, you'd better get inside then and try to stop the wildfire."

"Wildfire?"

"Captain Pierce. He said if there's any way that you fit the victim criteria, he's demanding they take you off the case."

Angel's eyes widened. If the FBI wanted her on the case, she'd be on the case, whether the Captain agreed or not. However, she planned to set the record straight. "I'll talk to him now, and if you see that nosey photographer before I do, tell him to keep his theories to himself."

"I'll tell him, but I don't see that it'll do much good now," Etta said with an apologetic shrug. "The deed has been done. I mean, when people 'round here grab hold of something juicy, they've gotta tell it. And as far as most of them are concerned, a rumor is about the closest thing we get to the gospel truth. Think about it; no matter how many times Tucker tries to tell folks he couldn't have committed his wife's murder and how many times the police said he had an airtight alibi, people still whisper behind that sweet man's back. Ticks me off, but that's the way it is. If you say you ain't got a bun in the oven, I'll believe you, but if Captain Pierce and the other folks in there have already heard it—and they did see you run outside to lose your lunch at the crime scene—something they figure an FBI guy, or gal, wouldn't do..."

"I told you, FBI guys—and gals—are human. Some toss it at a crime scene." Though Angel typically didn't.

Etta held up her palms and her bangles jingled down her forearms. "Hey, don't shoot the messenger. I'm telling you the truth. There's a lot of people who won't believe you're not pregnant until several months pass." She frowned. "Maybe I shouldn't try so hard to fatten you up with my banana nut bread until all of this settles. Wouldn't want to fuel the fire."

"Until all of this settles? There's nothing to settle. I got sick after seeing a woman's dead body; I went to a doctor's office after learning her patients were at risk. I'm *not* pregnant. There's nothing to settle."

Etta nodded, but her big brown eyes said she didn't agree. "Well, we'll see."

"Just how many people could Elijah have told, anyway? I left the doctor's office less than an hour ago."

"Don't take no time to make a phone call or two, or ten." Etta laughed. "But like I said, we'll see. I just thought I should point out that it may not matter whether you talk to the captain; some folks are going to keep an eye on you, and your belly, for a while."

Angel pressed her flat stomach. Pregnant? She wouldn't know the first thing about caring for a baby.

They joined a couple of cops and crossed the parking lot, listening to the two men discuss their theories regarding the recent murder. One thought the killer knew both victims; the other wagered he didn't, that he picked them because they fit the criteria. Angel didn't comment. One held a door open for

Angel and Etta, then the two men continued down the hallway while still discussing their theories. Etta brushed her hands together, muttered "Good luck," and headed toward the dispatch desk, while Angel turned her thoughts from the killer to her so-called pregnancy. Then she made a beeline for Pierce's office.

With the door open, Angel stepped inside assuming he'd sense her presence and ask her to sit down.

He didn't even notice he had a guest. Instead he banged at his keyboard, his face drawn together as though he stared at a killer on the screen.

"Captain Pierce." She stood her ground when he turned to glare.

"I'm emailing Hawkins. If the rumor is true, there's no way you should be working on this case." He stopped typing to look at her. "Well?"

"I'm not pregnant, and I'm surprised you'd even consider emailing Leon before talking to me."

His mouth dipped at one corner, and he ran a hand across the back of his neck while he grimaced. Then he closed the email window and turned toward Angel. "You didn't say anything about going to Weatherly's office this morning, and you said you'd keep us informed of all case proceedings."

"I decided to follow up with Weatherly on my own. No offense, Captain, but the FBI doesn't have to inform you of our every move. I tell you what I do as a courtesy, not a requirement. And, for the record, I am not pregnant."

He sighed. "This case is taking a lot out of all of us. We don't want five more lives on our hands at the end of this year."

"It's ten lives when you count the babies." Angel knew those babies counted. She *was* one of those babies, after all. The only one that survived his attack. "And trust me, the FBI feels the same way; however, even if I were pregnant they wouldn't remove me from the case. I've done too much work and researched this killer too thoroughly to walk away now, for any reason."

"But you're not pregnant. That is what you said."

"Right, I'm not. No way, no how." However, in the back of

her mind Angel remembered her brief fling with Stan Carlton and realized that there was a slight chance…

"Hold on while I call Marker. All we need is for the paper to get wind that we have a blonde, single and pregnant female working the case." He twisted in his chair and snatched his phone, then proceeded to tell Lou Marker that their profiler didn't, as Etta said, have a bun in the oven.

Angel sat in Pierce's guest chair and waited. Elijah Lewis had wasted no time spreading the word, if Lou Marker had been the one who told the captain. How far had this thing already gone? And would Marker even believe the captain when he told him the truth? She'd seen the way he looked at her in the parking lot, like she had a big, juicy secret. Chances were that some people wouldn't believe that Angel didn't fit the killer's criteria until several months passed and her stomach didn't hit a full bloom.

Then again…if they did believe the rumor, couldn't she use that to her advantage? Sure, she could deny it, but even so, some people would still believe it as fact until proven otherwise. Why couldn't she use their natural instinct to turn this case around? She'd wanted to be proactive. You couldn't get more proactive than becoming what the killer wants in a victim.

And what if she actually was? No, surely not. She'd only been with Stan once.

Aunt Carol's words of warning when Angel had been a wild and rebellious teen whispered through her mind once more.

*It only takes once, Angel.*

Angel had told her aunt the truth back then; she wouldn't do anything to get pregnant, because she wouldn't bring a baby into a world like this. She'd said she never wanted to have kids, and she wouldn't.

But what if she was now? What if she'd inadvertently become the exact thing their killer wanted? A blonde, single and pregnant female.

She hadn't told Pierce how the FBI caught the Oklahoma City killer. Her skin still tingled when she recalled entering the restaurant then getting the call that she'd left her lights on. It'd almost been too easy. She called her backup, waited until they were at the ready, then walked outside.

For a split second, she thought she'd messed up. From the previous attacks, she believed he wouldn't strike until she reached her car. Wrong. She'd barely cleared the entry of the restaurant and started down the tiny tree-covered path leading to the parking area when his body cinched hers against his, the lower arm squeezing her chest so tight she couldn't breathe, while the other hand clasped over mouth and nose.

Thankfully her FBI training kicked in full force. By the time her backup got there, less than five seconds flat, the guy was already sucking wind from her heel to his groin. So much for her fellow profilers saying her flexibility wouldn't come in handy. She'd bet a year's salary he hadn't seen *that* move coming. And because she'd been willing to play bait, Bennie Buzan had established permanent residence in the H Unit of the Oklahoma State Penitentiary.

Angel hoped by the end of this case, the Sunrise Killer found himself in an equally fitting residence. Oklahoma's H Unit housed the "worst of the worst" inmates in an underground concrete bunker, making the prison escape-proof. Inmates were locked down twenty-three hours of every day with only an hour's exercise provided in a caged yard. Most H Unit prisoners had minimal contact with other human beings for the duration of their term, which Angel thought perfect for a man like Bennie Buzan, who'd raped and tortured eight women before he'd been caught.

The Sunrise Killer deserved an equally severe punishment. In fact, he deserved worse, much worse. And Angel would love to deliver it. Although she wouldn't take the law into her own hands, she could help in his capture, in much the same way she'd done with Bennie Buzan's fate.

As bait.

"Lexie, good to see you back." Paul Kingsley's loud voice made Lexie jump. "No need to be nervous. It's just me. That killer has everybody jittery, doesn't he?"

She nodded. "I guess so. Dinah told me to wait in your office. She said you'd be here soon."

"I know." He picked up the remote, flipped on the

televisions then dropped his duffle bag on the floor. A health fanatic, Paul looked like he always did when he came into work, like he'd just finished a morning workout. Except on a typical day he made it into work well before—she glanced at her watch—9:30. "I called her on my way in. She mentioned you wanted to see me. Did you learn anything new about our guy yesterday? Got anything for the lead story?"

"No, I really took a personal day."

He glanced at his computer and wiped a drop of sweat from his temple. Or a drop of water. Maybe he showered after he came in. It amazed Lexie how he could show up in the middle of the night to verify the early news progressed on schedule and still managed to exercise every morning. Lexie suspected his work schedule had been a major reason why his marriage had failed, not that she'd ever point that out to her boss.

"Tucker was supposed to call and fill me in, but he must've forgotten. We were afraid you'd gone off chasing that madman on your own." He cut his gaze at her and grinned. "Wouldn't be unlike you to put yourself in danger for a story, would it? I'm guessing John did find you, right?"

"He found me." No need telling Paul they'd followed each other back to Macon, after she'd introduced him to her grandfather this morning, then told him a portion of her past. Not everything—yet—but enough that he believed her and believed that she trusted him.

"Good. So, what did you want to talk to me about? The story?"

"Yes. I have an idea about a way to bring the public closer to it, make them care about the victims and get more people out there to be on the lookout for the killer."

He leaned forward in his chair. "Go on, I'm listening."

"You may remember in my films from the Atlanta station how I profiled each victim of the I-20 rapist. I covered those he'd killed, as well as the sole survivor."

"Of course I remember. That was some of your best work, and it convinced me we had to have you here. You're thinking about doing that again for the Talton and Jones women?"

"I'm thinking about starting with them and working my way back, through each woman he murdered throughout the past four cycles."

"I like it." He nodded. "It will humanize them and remind the public that these aren't just names. They're people whose lives have been taken. People, like our viewers. And like their mothers, sisters or daughters. Yeah, I like it a lot." He jotted something down on a yellow pad. "But why not start with the first victim and work your way forward? Seems that'd make more sense."

"Two reasons. One, I have more information about the most recent victims, so it'd be easier to portray their stories and will give me time to accumulate details about the prior victims. And two, because the police still don't believe the first victim has been identified yet."

"Right. The missing persons info." He glanced back at CNN. "Nothing come of that yet?"

"According to Captain Pierce, the names should be available today, but I'll need time to find out as much as I can about that first victim, since right now we don't even know her name. Or what he did with her body."

"Sounds like you've got it all worked out, McCain. As usual."

"Then I can run with the stories?"

"Of course. And I want you to continue a separate piece regarding the updates on what's happening with the task force. The more the public is informed, the better. You're going to spotlight one victim per day?"

She nodded. "That's the plan."

"Perfect. Starting today or tomorrow?"

"Tomorrow. I have to attend the task force meeting in an hour, then I'll start working on Vickie Jones' story. Problem is, there isn't any family to interview, and her ex-husband isn't talking to anyone."

"You spoke to him?"

"Called him this morning on my way in. Got a 'no comment.'"

"What about the waitress that found her? She should be able to give you some insight."

"I reached her this morning at the Waffle House, and she agreed to meet with me this afternoon. She's determined to help the police find the man who hurt Vickie."

"Great. We'll run her story tomorrow and promise Cami Talton's for the next day." He tapped his pen against the paper. "This is quite an ordeal you're taking on, McCain. Sure you'll be able to produce one a day?"

"I have to. We don't have that many days before he strikes again. I believe humanizing his victims and outlining how horrendous his acts have been will increase public awareness. Maybe even convince someone who knows something to come forward." Her skin tingled the way it always did when she worked on a breaking news story.

"Let me know if you need help. And keep me aware of whatever you find out, whether it makes the broadcast or not. I can pull another reporter to aid with research if you need it."

"I've got everything I need in those police files. If I can interview a family member or two for each victim as well, that should give me what I'm looking for." A method of presenting the information in a way that will make people stop, listen and heed her warning.

"All right. But if you change your mind about needing help, let me know." He pushed the pen and paper aside, stretched his arms, then clasped his fingers behind his head. "I don't say it very often, but you do a great job around here. We're glad you're on board."

"Thanks."

"You're going to the police department, then?"

"Yeah."

"Let me know if they come up with any new angles on the killer."

"I will." She left his office, stopped by her cubicle and grabbed her notes, then turned and nearly ran right into Melody Harper, her granny glasses balancing on the tip of her nose.

"Sorry, Lexie. I was wondering if you'd heard anything else about that killer. Delia's been a wreck knowing he's out there and all. I know she's married, but what if he doesn't know that? Kevin travels all the time, and Delia's often by herself. What if the killer thinks she's single? I've been trying to talk her into moving in with me until the guy is found, but she doesn't want to leave their home."

"I don't have any new information other than what's been aired, but I'm working on learning more. In any case, this guy is smart. If she's married, he knows it. And he's very specific about his criteria."

Melody forced a smile. "Yeah, you're right, I'm sure. But I'll feel better when the police get the lunatic."

"You and me both."

"You'll let me know, though, if you learn anything new?"

"I'll let everyone know. I promise."

Melody nodded, then returned to her cubicle.

Lexie had fifteen minutes before the task force meeting. The police station was only five minutes away, so she maneuvered through the maze of cubicles in the office and sprinted across the parking lot to her car.

She jumped in and started to turn the key when her cell phone rang, the caller id displaying *RESTRICTED*. Even so, she hit the talk button. "Hello."

"I need to tell you something."

Lexie's hand pressed the phone closer to her ear. "Angel? Where are you calling from?"

"The line is secure. And I need to let you know something. I went to Dr. Weatherly's this morning to talk to her about the case."

"But John already talked to her."

"I know, but I thought she might have remembered something."

"Had she?"

"No, but Elijah Lewis saw me at her office and assumed that I must be pregnant, since he'd seen me getting sick outside of Vickie Jones' home."

"That's crazy." Lexie thought of the sleazy photographer. "And I'm guessing that he spread the news."

"Made it to Pierce in less than an hour."

"Gotta love small town gossip. But you're telling them it's not true, right?"

"I'm *telling* them." Angel drew out the verb.

"What does that mean?" Then Lexie made an *ahh* sound. "They don't believe you, do they?"

"No, but there's more to this, Lexie. I told Pierce I wasn't, insisted I couldn't be, but then I realized that wasn't true."

"That *what* wasn't true?"

"I told him there was no way I could be pregnant, but the truth is, there is."

"Angel, you haven't even been seeing anyone. You've told me that every time we've talked."

"I know, but it wasn't a relationship. Just a brief infatuation. And when I got to thinking about me getting sick at the crime scene, something I never do, and then I started counting the days, I realized that I might actually be pregnant."

"You're pregnant?" Fear pulsed through Lexie at the mere thought. She pinched her eyes closed, said a quick prayer to say the right thing. "Angel, that isn't right, to bring a child into the world without love between..."

"Don't preach to me, Lexie. I can't take it. I've got to decide what to do."

"What to do?" Angel had always been against harming an unborn child, especially because of the Sunrise Killer. He'd killed her mother, twenty-eight other women and all of their babies. Surely Angel hadn't changed her feelings toward anyone who took the life of a child. "What do you mean? You—you aren't thinking about having an..." She couldn't make herself say the word.

"No, no, I'd never do that. You know that, Lexie. I'd never do anything to hurt a child, even if it's one I hadn't planned. But if I am pregnant, then I know the truth. I'll be the killer's next target."

Lexie's head fell back against the seat. "Angel, you can't do it again. That killer in Oklahoma nearly got you last time, remember? You're *not* going to use yourself as bait. And it wouldn't be just you either. If you're pregnant, you're risking the baby too. I won't let you."

"Listen. I've already got it approved with my team. I called Quantico and they agreed with my plan, but they didn't realize I might actually be pregnant. However, that won't change anything for them. Pregnant or not, this is my case. And pregnant or not, they agreed for me to act as bait. They're sending plenty of backup. It'll work. We can get him this way. The thing is, since three members of the task force fit the profile, I'm not going to tell any of them that I've become the target."

Lexie couldn't fathom that Angel might be pregnant. "Have you told the baby's father?"

"No."

"Who is it, Angel?"

"You don't know him, Lexie, and who he is isn't what's important now. Whether the killer sees me as the perfect target, that's what's important."

"How do you know he'll even come after you?"

"I fit the criteria. I haven't taken the pregnancy test yet, but I just picked one up, and I'm fairly certain it's going to tell me that I'm about eight months away from a baby. If I am, he won't pass up the opportunity. I'm a thorn in his side, for sure."

"If you are pregnant, you need to tell the task force. They could help." Lexie closed her eyes again. *God, please, don't let Angel be pregnant. But if she is, Lord, as in all things, let Your will be done. But protect her please, Lord. Protect her, and protect the baby.*

"I'm not telling the task force anything. I've told Pierce and Etta the rumor isn't true. I'll let them relay the information. Then I'll start showing signs of pregnancy. That will get their attention. Any way I look at this thing, the killer would be close to the case. If it appears I lied to them about the pregnancy, that'll only pique the killer's interest. He may not be a task force member, but he could be."

"You said three of them. Who are you counting?" Lexie asked, realized—feared—the reasoning behind the given number.

"Lou, Ryan and John."

Lexie's attention quickly turned from Angel's potential pregnancy to John's innocence. "John didn't do it. You *can't* still suspect him."

"Hey, I've seen the way you look at him, and I admit I trust your judgment, but he does fit the profile."

"I think I may love him." Lexie waited for a response, or the sound of Angel's breathing. She heard nothing. "Angel?"

"I told you not to get involved. Not until we know for sure."

"He's innocent, Angel. I can see it in his eyes, and I feel it. Plus, I realized this morning why I trusted him so soon. He looks like his father."

"His father?"

"Milton Tucker, the Bibb County Sheriff back then, when it happened. He's the one who came to talk to me after everything; he's the one who made me feel safe. And he was a friend of Granddaddy's."

"How do you know this?"

"Granddaddy said so, this morning."

"He talked to you? In sentences?"

"Broken sentences, but yeah, he did. And he looked at John and saw Milton Tucker's son."

Another silence echoed through the line.

"Angel?"

"You took John Tucker to meet our grandfather?"

"He followed me down there. He thought I might be chasing a lead on my own."

"For Granddaddy to remember, and to speak it aloud, that's huge, Lexie."

"I know. I couldn't believe it. And there's something else I should tell you." She hoped Angel took the next news well, especially since Angel seemed to be getting a lot of unexpected news today.

"What else?"

"He called me by name, in front of John."

"Your full name?"

"He called me AJ. But John asked what the initials stood for."

"And you told him?"

"I trust him."

"You told him." Angel's disbelief filtered through her words.

"Yes, I did." Lexie wouldn't feel bad for what she'd done. John wasn't the killer, and the sooner Angel realized that, the better.

"Has he put it together yet? Has he put *us* together?"

"No. He knows about my parents and Aunt Bev. But I plan to tell him everything. I just wanted to let you know first."

"Lexie, if you've misjudged him—"

"I haven't." Lexie would stake her life, and her love, on it.

"Okay. Then we'll deal with that as it comes. And if we *can* trust him, that may help me with my plan."

"How's that?"

"If I convince the killer to come after me, and if we haven't caught him within the forty day period, then I could use a guy like John Tucker around to help me catch him before he kills me."

Lexie's throat went dry, and she forced a swallow. "Don't even say that."

"He won't," Angel assured. "I'm not going to let him hurt our family again. I'm saying it wouldn't hurt for me to have another gun along for the confrontation."

"When are you going to take the pregnancy test?"

"When I get back to my hotel, after our meeting. And you should head over here. The meeting starts in five."

"On my way." Lexie disconnected and said a prayer that Angel would trust John, especially if she had a baby to protect. Because *she* trusted him, more than to protect her from a killer. She trusted him with her heart.

John stared at the computer monitor in disbelief. He'd only had an hour before the task force meeting, long enough, thanks to the State's birth records being more up to date than the missing persons' info. The detective in him refused to wait to learn more about Lexie's past. Or maybe the incredible urge to protect her from the killer caused him to forge ahead. In any case, John had started searching, and the State's database didn't disappoint.

According to the Georgia birth records, Nicholas Rydell Truman and Lauren Wilson Truman had three daughters: Sophia Clair, Carol Lynn and Beverly Diane. He selected Lexie's mother's record first. Sophia Clair Truman married Joseph Wilkins and had one daughter, Alexandra Jane Wilkins, on January 22, 1977.

January 22, Lexie's birthday. He made a mental note.

He next selected Carol Lynn's record. Aunt Carol, as Lexie had called her, never married and had no children. Caring for her mentally-challenged father as well as her orphaned niece filled the woman's life until she died last year.

John clicked on the daughter murdered by the Sunrise Killer. Beverly Diane. Lexie's aunt had been either separated or divorced when she became the killer's target, since her married name displayed on the screen. The death acknowledgement at the bottom of the screen identified Beverly Diane Truman Jackson. Odd, since all of the articles had listed Beverly Truman as the victim. There were no details about the cause of death. John hadn't expected any, but he thought he might find *something*.

He collapsed the window on the computer, turned to the stack of victimology on his desk and opened the file of 1985 victims. Flipping to the third page, he viewed the pretty, smiling blonde in a whole new light. Beverly Truman, prominent senator's daughter...and Lexie's aunt.

A knock sounded on John's door, then Ed Pierce poked his head in. "You're coming down, right? We've got the missing persons' names from the State."

"Be right there."

Pierce nodded, then left, while John continued to scan the information. What had he missed? He read through Beverly's file again. Lexie—or AJ—hadn't been mentioned as a surviving relative. But then again, none of the victimology reports included children.

Children. John turned back to the computer and opened the window displaying Beverly's information and then noticed a name listed in the *children* field.

*Olivia Danielle, female, born May 17, 1985.*

He moved his attention back to the death acknowledgement field at the bottom of the page, to the date of death.

*May 17, 1985.*

His phone buzzed, and he slapped the speaker button. "Tucker."

"We're ready in the conference room," Pierce said. "Need you down here."

"On my way." He closed the State's database on his computer and grabbed the victimology file. The impact of the information he'd obtained today, from Lexie and from the database, made his head pound. Lexie's aunt had been the killer's second victim, or rather, his third victim, if their theory was correct, and he'd murdered seven women that first year.

Not only that, but her aunt appeared to have been the only woman who delivered her child after the attack. She hadn't survived, but her baby did. A baby girl named Olivia. Why hadn't Lexie told him about the surviving baby, a baby who would be Lexie's cousin? Surely the killer didn't realize one of the children had survived. If he did, wouldn't he have felt compelled to go after that child, to complete his sick plan?

John needed answers, answers that Lexie could supply, but he couldn't get them with an audience, particularly not the task force trying to nail the man who'd murdered her aunt.

Leaving his office, he started toward the conference room. During their meeting, he'd keep his newfound knowledge to himself, but afterwards, he and Lexie were going to have a serious heart-to-heart. And find out how much she knew about the Sunrise Killer.

John entered the conference room, where she had joined the profiler, Pierce, Marker, Sims and Naylor to reevaluate their plan of action for the case. He nodded a hello to Lexie. For the time being they'd decided to keep their personal interests private, at least in regards to the task force.

Taking his seat, he turned his attention to his information file and kept his eyes away from the woman who had a bigger agenda to solving these murders than she'd first admitted.

Why hadn't she told him the truth?

Before he could think about it further, Pierce spoke up with two bombshells of information and threw John Tucker's world even more off-kilter.

"A couple of things we need to cover now that everyone is here. First, Special Agent Jackson has an announcement. Go ahead." Pierce nodded to the profiler.

She stood and cleared her throat. "I'm sure several of you have heard the bizarre rumor that I now fit all parts of the killer's criteria. I want to set the record straight. I tossed it at the crime scene because, believe it or not, even FBI agents can have a weak stomach. And I went to Dr. Weatherly's office this morning to see if she had any additional info to help the case, *not* because I thought I was pregnant." She looked at Lexie, the only other female in the room, then returned to her seat.

"Okay," Pierce said. "If any of you hear anything at all about Agent Jackson's so-called pregnancy, I'll expect you to dispel the rumor. We do not need our profiler on the killer's hit list. Agreed?"

John hadn't heard the rumor, but judging from the responding nods at the table, several of the others had. Great. Who else in Macon thought Special Agent Jackson was pregnant? Did the killer? Before John could process all of the problems associated with the pregnancy rumor, the captain dropped the second bombshell.

"Hannah Sharp and Logan Finley." Pierce handed copies of the missing persons data sheets to Agent Jackson and directed her to pass them around the table.

John accepted his, then passed them on, staring in bewilderment at the two names and their corresponding information.

Hannah Elizabeth Sharp, 16, reported missing February 27, 1985, the day after the first kill should have occurred. Logan Wyatt Finley, 18, reported missing the same day.

Tucker closed his eyes and remembered Hannah, her long blonde hair, deep blue eyes. He could almost see her, laughing with him, flirting with him, wanting him. She'd been mature beyond her years and captivated all of the teen boys in the Fellowship. He opened his eyes, saw Ryan and Lou's expressions, and knew they were thinking the same thing. If the three of them weren't suspects before, they sure were now. For the time being, all attention moved off of Agent Jackson's rumored pregnancy to the two names on the page. Hannah and Logan.

"But she and Logan left." Ryan answered the silent question passing between them. "They ran away and got married. Everyone knew it. They weren't missing. They just left town."

"You knew them?" Pierce asked.

Lou stared at the file. "We all knew them. Me, Ryan, John."

"I knew her." Zed's confession wasn't as condemning as the others. Angel Jackson had already pointed out he didn't fit the profile. But the three at the table who were teens in 1985, teens who knew Hannah Sharp in 1985, did.

"It wouldn't have been Hannah." John couldn't believe it. "She wasn't his first victim."

"How do you know?" The profiler turned her full attention to John. "How can you be so sure, Tucker?"

"She left with Logan. She told everyone they were running off, and then they did."

"We were all friends back then. All of us." Ryan indicated John and Lou. "Not just us, but lots of other guys and girls from Macon. We hung out, had a good time, you know, the way guys and girls do as teens. But Hannah stood out from the other girls in school."

"You think Hannah Sharp was the first victim?" Zed asked the captain.

John spoke first. "Nobody killed Hannah. She eloped with Logan to get away from her family. The whole town knew it. That's why they both disappeared. If she was the first victim, why would her boyfriend have disappeared too? It wouldn't make sense. They ran off together."

Pierce lifted the information sheets and stated the obvious. "There's no record of recovery on either of them."

"I'm sure she eventually got in touch with her family and let them know she was okay." John didn't want to think about Hannah as a victim. "She may have been a little wild, but she loved her folks. She'd have called them."

"Her parents *were* odd," Zed said.

"They may have had different ideas about things, but they came around, along with the rest of us." John hoped Ryan and Lou wouldn't find it necessary to elaborate. "We need to talk to them and verify that they've heard from her since she left back then. I'm sure they have. She's somewhere raising her own teenagers by now."

"Her family won't talk to us." Zed looked toward Tucker. "They don't do government. You remember that, John."

"What do you mean, they don't do government?" Angel asked.

Zed Naylor rubbed his hand down his face, then shook his head, battling with how much to tell. John knew it, as sure as

Ryan and Lou knew it, judging from the looks on their faces. Why did it have to come back to haunt them now?

Because, whether he admitted it aloud or not, John knew the truth. Hannah Sharp, the woman who'd smitten them all with her flirtatious smile and golden hair, John Tucker's first love, *had* been the killer's first victim. They should've thought of Hannah before, but they hadn't. Everyone thought she and Logan eloped.

"Was she pregnant?" Lexie's question silenced the room.

Lou straightened in his chair then looked at John. "Well, was she?"

"Why are you asking me, Lou?"

"Just thought you might know, that's all."

"Well, I don't."

Lexie's green eyes sought John's.

He looked away. Yeah, he'd tell her, but not now, and not with the remainder of the task force scrutinizing his every move.

Hannah. How could he have forgotten Hannah?

"We need to find out if her family has heard from her and if Logan Finley's family has heard from him." Angel continued scanning the new information. "If she was the first victim, and if he went missing at the same time, that tells us one of two things."

"That he killed Logan too?" Zed guessed.

"That's one thing, but the other possibility is that our killer *is* Logan Finley."

All eyes moved to Angel.

She continued the scenario. "Maybe she was pregnant. Maybe he found out the baby wasn't his, and he blew a fuse. Or maybe it was his, and he didn't want a child. I just want to make sure we cover all possibilities."

"But that'd mean Logan Finley is living in Macon now. We all know Logan. We would see him in town," Ryan said.

"Probably." Angel squeezed her eyes shut, then popped them back open. "Yeah, you're right. The killer is living here, and if everyone knew Logan Finley, someone would've seen him after that date. *But* if our killer murdered both of them, then he killed eight people that first year. That'd venture from his plan."

Lou spoke up. "Not if he's only counting the pregnant females. Maybe the guy was a problem he had to eliminate."

"Spoken like a profiler." Angel pointed to Lou. "You could be right. Either way, we need to talk to their families and see if they ever heard from them."

"I still see Logan's folks from time to time," Zed said. "They never heard from him again, but they assumed he and Hannah started their life away from the situations they faced here." He quirked his lip to the side, producing two thick paths of wrinkles down one cheek. "As far as her family, I haven't seen them in years. They still live out from the city, and they don't take to strangers. Any of y'all seen them around?" He looked at John, Ryan and Lou, and all three men shook their heads.

"Well, if Hannah and Logan were killed by this guy, then their past factors in. Plus, it'd make sense that he picked symbolic numbers," Zed said. "And that he picked pregnant women."

"Why? Why would that make sense? What is it about their past that tells you that?" Angel thumbed through her information packet searching for anything that would corroborate his statement, then looked back at Zed. "What is it?"

He looked at the others around the table, then shrugged. "Most everyone here knows about it. I was one of the main ones practicing back then, but I learned better. Some folks didn't. Hannah's family still practices."

"Practices what?" Lexie asked.

"It was an old cult." Lou shifted in his seat. "The Fellowship, that's what Brother Moses called it."

"We didn't call it a cult, though I guess that's what it was." Zed continued looking at Hannah and Logan's information sheets as he spoke. "I was a deacon, after all. So was Sheriff Tucker, right up until the day he died." He looked at John. "We thought we were doing the right thing, didn't we?"

John nodded. He'd wanted to forget how foolish they all were back then, but his parents had been sucked in by the lies, and so had he.

"Who is Brother Moses?" Angel jotted notes on the outside of her information packet.

"His real name was Horace Waters." John hated all of this coming out now.

"Horace Waters?" Angel added the name.

Zed nodded. "Yeah, he was a preacher at a church downtown, but then he started telling his congregation that God had visited him personally and told him what people were doing wrong and how they had to stop the sin."

"It wasn't God that had visited him," John corrected. "It was the Supreme One."

"I thought the Supreme One *was* God." Lou's face displayed his confusion.

"You weren't paying attention in Sheriff Tucker's classes." Zed chuckled, but no one joined in.

"The sheriff was involved in this—Fellowship?" Angel scribbled as she tried to keep up.

Lou leaned forward. "Yeah, John's father was a deacon."

"Your father?" Angel turned her attention to John.

John nodded, but didn't speak.

Angel stopped writing, then frowned as she reread the words now filling the outside of her manila file. "Zed, you said it would make sense that the women he picked were pregnant. Why would it make sense?"

"The Fellowship saw children as a symbol of power. The more children you had, the more powerful you were within the Fellowship. Women who couldn't conceive were outcasts. Men who couldn't impregnate their wives were too. Those were signs that they'd been disinherited from the Supreme One, so they were also excommunicated from the group."

"How many members did the Fellowship have?"

He shrugged. "Hundreds, I suppose. We didn't keep a roster. You knew those who were members and those who weren't. But you're talking about it in the past tense. Like I said, Hannah's family still practices. I think plenty of folks do; they just don't meet in person anymore. Everything is done on the Internet, from what I hear."

"Do you know the web address?" Angel flipped the page and kept writing. "Or do any of you know it?"

Lou, John, Ryan and Zed shook their heads in denial.

"I'm sure it won't be easy to find, but the techies at the field office should be able to track it down, if I can't find it with a bit of Google and Yahoo." She cleared her throat. "And *all* of you were members?" She pointed to Ryan, Lou, John and Zed.

This time, they nodded.

Lexie's chair scraped against the floor as she scooted closer to the table. "In this Fellowship, what did they think of a single, pregnant woman?"

Zed frowned, but Lou didn't hesitate. "She'd sinned, and she didn't deserve to live."

Ryan joined in. "Any single woman. Never married, or divorced, or even separated. If she wasn't with her husband, or if she hadn't become pregnant by her husband, they wanted no part of her. We were to disassociate from her and wish evil on her."

"What happened to Brother Moses, or Horace Waters?" Pierce asked.

John answered, "He up and left town in the early eighties. I thought the group busted up at the same time. I didn't even know they still practiced."

Lou cleared his throat. "They do, but it's only a few, those over-the-top ones like Hannah's folks."

"Sounds like our guy could be included in that over-the-top number. Any idea where they meet? Or when?" Angel asked.

"They don't meet," Zed said. "After Brother Moses left, they decided to preserve the sanctity of the Fellowship, they'd have to conduct everything in private. From what I understand, even the ones still practicing aren't sure which other members still feel the same way. Kind of a don't-let-your-right-hand-know-what-the-left-one-is-doing mentality. I think there are still some of that number Lou referred to as 'over-the-top,' but I believe there are others who are members for other reasons. They don't follow all of Brother Moses' teachings, but they like being a part of the charity arm of the group."

"Charity arm?" Lexie questioned.

"Brother Moses may have had some warped ideas," Zed explained, "but he also had some good ones. He started the majority of Macon's charity groups, a homeless shelter and a soup kitchen while he ran the Fellowship."

"Even though many of the folks who managed his charities left the Fellowship, they remained connected, in a sense. They still wanted to help others, just on their own instead of under the Fellowship's guidance," Lou added.

"Would Hannah's parents work at one of those charities?" Lexie took notes frantically as the abundance of new information increased.

Zed shook his head. "Nah, they live out from the city, like I said before. They're the type that believes in living off the land. You know, a garden, farm, the whole nine yards. They don't come into town."

"Do you think Hannah's parents would tell us if they ever heard from her after she left?" Angel asked.

"Nope. They disowned her," Ryan said. "Excommunicated, that's what the Fellowship called it. They didn't want to acknowledge they'd borne a sinner."

"Well, *someone* reported her missing." Pierce waved the form. "Mable Sharp."

John knew Mable well. "Mable is her grandmother. She never agreed with the Fellowship, so she doesn't have much to do with the family. I see Mable around town every now and then."

"You know her?" Angel asked.

"Yeah, I know her."

"She hasn't ever mentioned her granddaughter to you? Said whether they ever heard from her? Found her? Anything?" Pierce sounded as though he doubted the woman wouldn't have mentioned Hannah.

John shook his head. "Like I said, she didn't have anything to do with the Fellowship, so for most of those years she barely even saw her grandchildren. And if Hannah's folks are still practicing, they wouldn't have anything to do with her."

"Well, somehow she knew her granddaughter was missing. She reported it." Pierce tapped the form.

"Do you want us to see if Mable knows anything, captain?" Zed started to stand. "I know where her place is and could head over there now."

"Do that. Then let us know what you find out as soon as

possible."

Zed gathered his things and headed out.

Pierce stared at the missing persons sheets for Hannah Sharp and Logan Finley. "I'm betting, from everything we've stated, that we now have the name of our first victim. Hannah Elizabeth Sharp."

"Which means we can narrow our profile even more." Angel continued writing notes as she spoke.

"Our killer knew Hannah Sharp," Lexie said.

Angel looked at Lexie. "Not only did he know her, but he knew her well. Either he had a relationship with her, or he tried to. Nothing stings a male teen more than being on the short side of a love triangle."

"So, do we know who, other than Logan Finley, had relationships with Hannah Sharp?" Pierce asked.

Ryan and Lou remained silent, but John knew they couldn't hide the truth. "We all did."

# CHAPTER TWELVE

After meeting with the task force for the majority of the day, Lexie conducted an hour-long interview with Sylvia Rawlins to portray an accurate picture of Vickie Jones, then headed for her office to prepare her segment for tonight's broadcast. She kept waiting on a call from Angel to let her know the results of the pregnancy test, but so far, she'd heard nothing. Knowing Angel, she was working late with the task force and putting off the test that could pinpoint her as the perfect victim.

To keep her attention off Angel, Lexie concentrated on Sylvia's depiction of her friend. She described Vickie as a beautiful girl with typical hopes and dreams. She wanted a nice home, a husband who loved her and a house full of children. By all indications, Vickie would've been a great mother.

"She loved kids. Whenever a family came in the restaurant and had a baby with them, Vickie directed them to her section. She wanted to be near those babies." Sylvia sniffed and cried through the interview, missing her friend and distressed by the unnecessary loss of life.

Lexie was distressed too, both by what the killer had accomplished and by everything she learned at the task force meeting. She had known by the look on John Tucker's face that he'd had a relationship with Hannah Sharp. She'd also recognized the same look on Ryan Sims and Lou Marker's faces. That had been disconcerting, and hadn't boded well for their innocence even though she knew in her heart John wasn't guilty.

"I knew her, you know." Paul Kingsley leaned against the opening of Lexie's cubicle and held the printed text of her broadcast in his hand.

"Vickie?" She squinted to see the copy. It'd been a long day, and her eyes burned from staring at her computer monitor. Paul must have been waiting for the text, since he responded within five minutes of her hitting the send key.

"No, I haven't printed that one out yet. I was talking about Hannah Sharp. I knew her back then. She was like all of his victims, a pretty girl, full of life and excitement. She was one of my closest friends." He shrugged. "I thought she eloped with that Finley guy. Never dreamed she could've been the killer's first victim, but she does fit the criteria for blonde hair and single. If she was pregnant, though, I never heard anything about it."

"They're still checking things out. We should have a clearer picture tomorrow." She pressed her fingers to her forehead. Her head throbbed. "Zed is meeting with her grandmother tonight. The police think the killer may have known Hannah Sharp and that he may have been a part of the group called the Fellowship. I realize it's jumping the gun a bit, as far as fiction versus fact, but it won't hurt for our viewers to see how we're thinking."

"You realize this broadcast is going to cause a lot of people to talk about the Fellowship."

"And?"

"And I like that. They'll want to keep watching to learn more, which equals more viewers, which equals higher ratings." He winked. "Folks 'round here have been too scared to mention the Fellowship. Far as I know, it's never been covered in any media. But when you put this as our lead story, you can guarantee every one of the affiliates will pick it up. Religious fanatics tend to have that effect on inquiring minds, you know. Great job, McCain."

"Thanks." She finished keying in her notes on Cami Talton. She'd started gathering her data tonight to get a head start for the next victim's segment. Then she processed Paul's words, and what he hadn't said. She stopped typing and turned toward him. "What do you know about the Fellowship?"

"What do you want to know?"

"Were you part of the group?"

"We all were. It was the cool thing to do back then. You know, head out to the woods, start a big fire, chant and pray and sing. I had five brothers and two sisters. My family was royalty in their book of 'children equal power.'" He laughed out loud.

"Didn't you ever think the killer could've had something to do with the Fellowship?" She knew Paul was on top of things when it came to the news. "I mean, all of the Easter kills, and the seven years apart, and seven women. Even the forty days between murders. Seems like if so many people were involved in that cult, then somebody would've picked up on his clues."

"Don't call it a cult." His voice lost all pretense of humor. "We may have had our ideas muddled, but we were trying to accomplish something right. A lot of good came from the Fellowship too. It wasn't all negative. Don't forget that."

"Okay." Lexie felt uncomfortable with the direction of this conversation and suddenly became quite aware that only she and Paul remained in this portion of the building. Or were there others here? She strained to hear the sound of keyboards clicking, but heard nothing.

He cleared his throat, regained his composure, and produced another smile. The grin didn't make it to his eyes.

"Sorry. I wasn't thinking about how close people are to their religion." She loved God and had no doubt that He'd seen her through the tough times of life. She knew for certain He had been with her the day she helped save Angel. But Lexie found the type of twisted "religion" of the Fellowship foreign. As well as how sensitive the cult's former members might be about the group's practices.

He didn't accept her apology, but he also didn't look as aggravated. "Back to your question. No, I never thought the killer had anything to do with the Fellowship, because the members of the group celebrate life, thus the reason for children, particularly newborns, to be a symbol of power. Why would they kill? Life brings power."

"But maybe one of the members began to believe you gained more power by taking life."

Paul mulled that over. "Maybe. Or maybe he thought that by taking a child from an unworthy parent, he controlled the power that wasn't meant to be bestowed."

Lexie opened her mouth, then snapped it shut. Instinct would have her tell him that the killer would think the same thing, but given how he'd seemed so bothered by her earlier comment, she decided to keep that one to herself. "I'll try to include some of that theory in tomorrow's profile update for the killer."

"Sounds good. So, you done for the day?"

"Yeah, but I can see myself out."

"Nonsense. I'm leaving anyway, and there's a killer out there, remember?"

She nodded. Oh yeah, she remembered. She grabbed her things, said a prayer she wouldn't say anything else to offend her boss before she made it to her car, then followed him out.

"You realize I don't expect you to work until ten every night. That's why you tape your segments in advance. You're putting in way too many eighty-hour weeks, McCain." He opened the door for her as they exited the building.

She glanced at the time on her phone. "I didn't realize it was so late."

"Your interview with Sylvia Rawlins must've taken some time."

"Longer than I realized." She walked through the crisp night air until she neared her car. "Thanks for seeing me out."

"You're welcome."

"I assume John will be waiting in my driveway when I arrive." She had become quite accustomed to their tag-team ritual of watching over her.

"I'm supposed to call him once you're on your way." He laughed. "You're good."

"I'm a reporter, but the two of you don't hide your plans very well, either."

"That's what our mothers always said when we were in high school. Go figure."

Grinning, she climbed in her car and started home, looking forward to seeing John in a few minutes and also grateful Paul had started behaving like her friend again before she left. Whatever she'd said or done to bother him, she must've rectified her mistake. Thank goodness. She had no intention of making an enemy out of her boss.

Lexie drove through town with her window down so she could inhale the scent of Magnolia blossoms filling the city. Her Magnolia trees were in full bloom, and the big white clusters dotting the branches stood out beneath the moonlight. She knew the large azalea bushes surrounding her porch were also in bloom; however, her work schedule had kept her from home during daylight hours, so she hadn't been able to appreciate the abundant red and white blossoms the realtor had promised her when she bought the house. Maybe she'd see them soon. After they caught the killer.

Right now, the mountain of a man sitting on her front porch swing formed the best view provided by her home. His black hair blended with the night, but those two sexy patches of silver at his temples glistened in the moonlight.

"I forgot to leave the porch light on." She stepped toward him.

"Yeah, you did. Wouldn't be too safe walking in, if you didn't have a cop waiting at your door."

"But I knew I would."

He lifted a thick, black brow. "Getting confident in this relationship already?"

Lexie grinned. "Maybe."

"Works for me." He smiled back, then indicated the spot beside him. "Wanna enjoy the night a while?"

"Sure." She placed her purse and briefcase on the porch and sat beside him on the swing.

John wrapped a strong arm around her, pulled her against his side. Then she closed her eyes and sighed as he gently pushed the swing back and forth.

They enjoyed the quiet for a while, then he cleared his throat and asked, "So when were you going to tell me about your cousin?"

Lexie wasn't that surprised by the question. She'd known any detective worth his salt would have investigated her background after learning the tiny tidbits she'd provided. Then again, any reporter worth her salt would have checked out a few things about him too, and she had. "Tonight. Or tomorrow. When were you going to tell me about the Fellowship?"

He laughed. "Tonight. Or tomorrow."

"Sure you were. You want to go first, or you want me to?"

"You go ahead. And just so you know, I also learned who she is. Should've seen the resemblance."

Lexie figured that, so she didn't flinch. "We don't look that much alike, other than the eyes. We both have Truman green eyes."

"A shame she never got to meet her mother."

"I know."

"I'm assuming the name change was to keep the killer from knowing everything that happened after he left the scene?"

Lexie nodded. She'd anticipated this conversation all afternoon, but the emotions involved with remembering the past, that awful day, still caused her throat to pinch closed, her chest to tighten, and her heartbeat to pick up a notch.

"You know, we don't have to talk about it if you don't want to."

"No, I want to." She felt a little more secure revisiting the past when she had John at her side, the comfort of his strong arm wrapped around her, holding her close and protecting her from the pain of remembering.

"You were there, weren't you? The reports didn't say anything about it, but that's the only thing I can figure that would've gotten the medical personnel to your aunt in time to save the baby. Someone was with her. It was you, wasn't it? You got help for her?"

"Yeah, I did."

"But he didn't know you were there?"

"No. We were leaving Macon that morning. Aunt Bev had taken me back to get my things. I was mad about everything— losing my parents, leaving my home to go live with Granddaddy—everything. I mean, I loved him, but he hadn't been the same after Grandma died. Aunt Carol was there, and I knew she'd take care of me." Lexie frowned. "But I was still mad, sad, whatever."

He rubbed his hand up and down her arm and pulled her closer. "You were what, eight? That's so young, Lexie. Don't blame yourself for being upset that day. I'm sure your aunt understood."

She took a deep breath. "Aunt Bev let me bring some of Mama and Daddy's clothing in the car, with lots of it in the floorboard of the backseat. I talked her into letting me rest on the floor, beneath the clothes, while she drove. She'd have never let me out of my seat buckle on a regular day, but I guess she felt sorry for me, because I was so upset."

"You were hidden beneath the clothes?"

"Yeah. I think I must've drifted off to sleep, then the car started slowing, and I couldn't figure out why we were stopping already. I knew we hadn't been far enough to get to Granddaddy Truman's. Then I heard Aunt Bev ask someone if they were okay, and if they needed help."

"Back then people still stopped to help folks out around here. Southern hospitality and all."

"Yeah, but I heard her voice change. She realized she'd made a mistake, but it was too late."

"And he never saw you?"

"No. He slammed her head against the front seat, and she looked at me, and I knew I had to stay quiet, stay hidden. So I did. Then I heard...everything. I remember praying, begging God to make it stop—to make *him* stop—and then he did. And then I started praying for Him to let me get help in time." She swallowed. "It was too late to save Aunt Bev, but I helped save Angel. God let me save her."

John looked like he wanted to say something, but then his mouth flattened and he pulled her even closer.

"Go ahead. Say it."

His head shook. "I'm just wondering what makes you see the positive in what God did, the fact that He helped you save Angel, instead of focusing on the fact that He didn't save your aunt."

Lexie heard what he didn't say. "You blamed Him for what happened to Abby."

"Yeah." He inhaled, like he planned to say more, but then left it at that.

"Do you still?"

"I'm working on it." He sighed. "Lexie, I'm so sorry for what you went through back then. No child should have to go through anything like that. It's hard enough on adults. I can't imagine how hard it was for you to deal with losing your parents and then witnessing your aunt's murder."

"According to the doctors—therapists—who saw me after it was over, I probably saw his face."

"But you don't remember?"

"No. I remember Aunt Bev's screams, and then the silence after, the sound of his car leaving, and then trying to find help in time. But I can't remember his face. Maybe I kept my eyes shut, but it seems like I would've tried to see him, so I could tell someone who hurt her." Lexie turned toward him. "Angel believes that's why I got into the media, because I'm determined to tell people everything they need to know when it involves finding criminals. I guess the profiler in her is always trying to classify people."

"Makes sense." He kissed her forehead. "Tell me about Angel, or Olivia."

"Aunt Bev and I had picked names for the baby that morning. I guess she thought that would cheer me up. We decided on Olivia for a girl, Jameson for a boy. When Aunt Carol told me I'd helped save my cousin, I told her she had to be called Olivia. She said we'd name her Olivia, but she thought we should call her Angel, because she lived in spite of his attempt to kill her."

"Sounds like a wise lady."

"The Trumans were known for being wise. Aunt Carol was only twenty-two, but she had to take over with all decisions that day. Granddaddy had a heart attack when they told him what had happened. And later, he had a complete breakdown."

"Most people knew the senator had a heart attack when he learned his daughter had been killed. But it wasn't common knowledge that his granddaughter witnessed the crime, or that his newest grandchild had survived in spite of the attack."

"The police thought the killer would come after us if he knew I might have seen him, or that Angel had survived. They recommended we leave. So Aunt Carol moved away from Macon. She decided on Valdosta, since it had the nicest home for Granddaddy, and she raised us there while doing her best not to broadcast our Truman family tree."

"Her decisions saved your lives."

"And gave us the chance to plan how we could stop him."

He straightened. "I seriously hope the two of you aren't planning to go after him alone. That's what the task force is for, what the police is for—and that's what *I'm* for."

Lexie thought about her words before responding. She didn't want any false pretenses between them. "He killed my aunt. He ruined our lives, kept Angel from ever knowing her mother and caused my grandfather to have a mental breakdown. I turned to God to get me through everything, but Angel never gave Him a chance to help. In fact, I'm pretty sure she blames Him too. And then there's the fact that I've never been 'normal' around men. You should know that I stopped letting Phillip even touch me after we had Phillip, Jr. I tolerated it for the first few years of marriage, but I *never* liked being touched. I believe I still think of that man hurting Aunt Bev whenever a man has physical contact with me."

John's jaw flexed. "But I've touched you, Lexie. Maybe not sexually, but emotionally…and physically. You didn't pull away from my kiss. And you aren't pulling away from me now."

"I know. And I think it's because my fears are nearly gone, and that we are about to catch him, stop him."

"You believe if we stop him, you'll be okay."

Lexie nodded.

"And you—and Angel—want to have an active role in stopping him. *That's* the reason you both chose your professions, isn't it?"

She wouldn't deny the truth. "Yes."

John realized that, if given the opportunity, Lexie and Angel might not be content to *help* find the killer. He'd heard the intensity in her tone, the emotion, many times before from victims set on revenge. And more times than not, that emotion affected judgment, affected rationality. What would either of the women do if they did find the killer? He couldn't condone Lexie, or Angel, or anyone else taking the law in their own hands. And he didn't want to think about the possibility of Lexie face-to-face with the killer…again.

"You have a gun?"

"Oh yeah."

"Know how to use it?"

"Angel taught me."

"Have mercy," he mumbled, then smiled when he heard her laugh. "Lexie, you need to let the authorities handle him."

"If they handle him, that's fine, but if I get the chance, I'll pull the trigger."

"In self-defense, you mean, right?"

"If you say so."

He took a deep breath, wondering how far they needed to go into this subject. He didn't want to upset her, but he had to make sure she wouldn't try to stop this killer on her own. For the past week, he'd guarded her while she slept because he never wanted her to come face-to-face with a killer. What if, deep down, she *wanted* to find the killer herself?

Trying to focus on the best means possible to remove that notion from her thoughts, he turned to the one thing he knew might make a difference.

Her religion.

"You said you turned to God to get through the past."

"I did."

"Still turn to Him?" He slid back into the ways of his youth, when every conversation had an underlying religious thread.

"Yes, I do."

He felt her back stiffen as she sensed the direction of this conversation.

She shifted on the swing to face him. "Eye for eye, tooth for tooth, hand for hand, foot for foot, burn for burn, wound for wound, stripe for stripe."

He cleared his throat. "Never avenge yourselves, but leave it to the wrath of God, for it is written, 'Vengeance is mine, *I* will repay, says the Lord.'" He swallowed. "*He* will make him pay."

"But He hasn't yet, and women are still dying."

Occasionally, John's upbringing and the required daily scripture memorization that consumed it came back to haunt him in the night, where verses condemning his choices in life doomed him to hell. Now, that memory of scripture provided what he needed. "At the time *I* have planned, *I* will bring justice against the wicked." He paused. "God *will* judge him, in His time."

"You said that you blamed God for what happened to Abby."

"I do, sometimes."

"But you're trying to convince me He is in control?"

"I don't want you getting hurt."

"I believe you," she said, "but there's more to it than that, isn't there?"

"What do you mean?"

"You believe those verses too, don't you? You think God will make him pay, and you think it's about to happen, don't you?" Her green eyes caught the moonlight and displayed the intensity of her emotion.

"I—yeah, maybe I do." He found it hard to admit, since he hadn't turned to God for anything but hatred over the past fourteen years. But deep down, he realized that he still hoped—prayed—that God did care and would somehow make things right again in his life...and in Lexie's.

"You learned a lot about God in the Fellowship, didn't you? Even though their practices were off, you still learned a lot?"

"You have no idea." John recalled endless hours of listening to Brother Moses, of studying his bible and reciting not only verses but chapters of scripture.

"Tell me about the Fellowship. And Hannah."

Bringing up religion—and his knowledge of scripture—had opened the door wide for Lexie to bring up the subject of the old cult. But John had expected this conversation. Might as well get it over with. "What do you want to know?"

"How did you get involved with the group? How many guys in the Fellowship could be our killer? Is there anyone who stands out more than everyone else as the most likely suspect? And what kind of role do you think Hannah Sharp had with starting this guy's killing spree?"

John grinned, glad she didn't condemn him for hitting her over the head with a bit of scripture. And also glad to see the journalist, rather than the woman who'd been hurt by the killer, resurface. "You ever slip out of reporter mode?"

She pinched his arm. "No, and you haven't answered any of

my questions."

He feigned pain and rubbed his arm, but she shook her pretty head, not falling for it. "Hey, I'm going for sympathy here."

"Not buying it. And I'm waiting for your answers." Then she kissed his cheek and squirmed her way out of his embrace. "Wait a minute. I'll be right back." She grabbed her purse and briefcase from where she'd plopped them on the porch, unlocked the door and entered the house.

He touched his cheek where she'd kissed him. He now realized how huge a breakthrough Lexie had made to let him hold her, kiss her, care for her. John slid his eyes closed. *God, let her trust me.*

The lights from inside beamed through the windows and illuminated her, walking through her living room and grabbing an afghan from the back of her couch. He watched her cross the room, flip the lights off, turn the porch light on and head back toward him.

"I'm a little chilled." She held up the blanket, then crawled back in his embrace on the swing.

John tucked the afghan, decorated with embroidered peaches, around her shoulders, then snuggled her close. "Better?"

"Yeah."

"We could go inside, where it's warmer."

"No, I like sitting out here with you."

"And the thought of being *that* alone with a man isn't appealing to you."

"I still have issues, but…"

"But?"

"But I'm getting better." She gave him a soft smile.

"Because of me?"

"Because of you." She shivered and then pulled the afghan tighter around her shoulders. John didn't know if the cold or the topic of conversation had her trembling, but he pulled her even closer and kissed the top of her head. "I won't give up on you."

She looked at him, eyes filled with tenderness. "Thank you." Then she inhaled, exhaled and said, "So, tell me about the Fellowship."

"Right. Back to business."

"If that's okay with you."

"It'll do for now." He grinned, squeezed her shoulders, then told her what she wanted to know. "I'm not sure when the Fellowship started, but I know it existed as far back as my grandfather. He'd been Horace Waters' friend before Horace became Brother Moses. My grandfather was a deacon, then my father as well."

"That didn't cause a problem when your dad ran for Sheriff?"

"You'd think it would, but no, it didn't. There were too many people with too much power involved in the group, and they were behind him one hundred percent. Matter of fact, Dad's opponent never stood a chance without the backing of the Fellowship."

"How did someone become a member?"

"You were either born into it, or you were invited by a member. It wasn't the kind of group where you could show up and try to get in."

"But a lot of teenagers were members back then? When you were a teen?"

"Practically everyone I knew. The Fellowship promoted kids and youth in general, since children were considered the lifeblood of the universe, so they encouraged us to convince our friends to come. I brought tons of people in."

"Like who?"

"Of people you know, Paul and Ryan."

"Not Lou?"

"Lou was already a member. His father was part of the eldership, one step up from a deacon and part of the decision-making team, defining what the group stood for."

"What about Logan Finley?"

"Logan was one of the few guys I knew that wasn't involved with the Fellowship. He was a few years older than the rest of us. We all knew him, though, as Central High's quarterback when we were in junior high."

"He and Hannah dated?"

"Not to start with. We were juniors in high school before

they got together, and I still don't know where they met. She spent most of her time away from school with the Fellowship, so it kind of surprised all of us and her family when she all of a sudden had an interest in Finley."

"Her family was upset?"

"Upset is a major understatement. Hannah flipped over Logan from the get-go, but her folks wouldn't allow her to date anyone who wasn't part of the Fellowship. Logan's father preached at one of the small community churches downtown, so that didn't go over well. Preachers from other denominations were considered false teachers."

"What about the members of the Fellowship? What'd they think about her seeing someone outside of the group?"

"According to the group laws, she should've been excommunicated."

"But she wasn't?"

"No. Her father appealed to the eldership to allow her to stay and promised she'd stopped seeing the non-believer."

"But she didn't." Lexie felt sorry for the two young lovers who dared defy a cult.

"No. Hannah snuck around with Logan. Everyone at school knew about it, because she didn't keep secrets from her friends, but her family and the rest of the Fellowship were in the dark. Or at least we thought they were."

"How about the other kids she hung around with, other members of the group? Did any of them get upset with her for dating Logan?"

John nodded, remembering the heated discussions they'd had with Hannah at that time. "Everyone did, me included." Then he thought more about the conversations around the lunch table at school. "No, that's not true. The guys were all upset with her. The girls were proud of her for sticking up to her folks and getting the guy she wanted."

"Makes sense. The girls were thrilled she went after the happily ever after, while the guys were ticked she wasn't vying for their attention anymore."

He nodded. "That pretty much sums it up."

"I've seen Hannah's picture. She was supermodel pretty."

"Yeah, the prettiest girl in Macon at the time, without a

doubt."

"And she had the boys hooked."

"Every guy around wanted to be with Hannah Sharp."

Lexie wrapped the afghan around her like a cocoon. "You're included in that number, right?"

"Yeah, but Hannah dated all the guys in the Fellowship at one time or another. She liked boys, got along well with them. You know, she was the kind of girl who could be your best friend, but also—"

"Make you think about being more than friends," Lexie finished. "But did she think about it, or did she do more, with the guys from the Fellowship? To fit the criteria, she'd have been pregnant."

John felt odd talking about Hannah when he believed she'd experienced a horrible death way back then instead of running off with the guy she loved, as everyone believed. But to get to the truth of the present, they had to unearth the truth of the past. "She was extremely sexual, especially to be so young. And although we never discussed it, for fear of getting cast out of the Fellowship, I'd venture to say that every one of the guys she hung around with slept with her. She'd hang around after school, then ask someone to drive her home."

"And more than driving happened?"

"Yeah."

"I think she didn't feel loved at home, so she looked to find it elsewhere, you know."

"What I'm wondering is whether her sexuality killed her. What if some guy she slept with wanted more, or if he thought that when she decided to elope with Logan Finley, she chose Logan over him. Jealousy has caused its share of murders, and if it were someone in the Fellowship, the religious tie-ins would make sense. The symbolic numbers, the Easter kills, all of it. But we still don't know whether she was pregnant."

"She was."

Lexie's eyes widened. "How do you know?"

"Zed called me after he met with Mable. Seems Hannah told her grandmother, and a few trusted friends, about her pregnancy. She didn't want her parents to find out, and she wanted to marry Logan, so they planned to elope. Mable said

Hannah visited her to tell her goodbye, and that Mable thought she'd talked her into staying. She said Hannah promised she'd stay if her family would allow her to marry Logan, which Mable believed they'd do rather than lose their daughter."

"Then Hannah went missing."

"And Logan did too. We all heard the rumors that they were eloping, so everyone thought they'd followed through with their plan. But according to Mable, she never heard from her again, and Hannah's family assumed she was 'taken from this earth' because she'd sinned."

"That's terrible."

"Terrible, but befitting a diehard member of the Fellowship."

"You said she told a few trusted friends, but you didn't know. Weren't the two of you still friends then?"

"We were friends, like all of the Fellowship teens were friends, but we'd stopped talking as much by that time."

"Why?"

"Before she met Logan, Hannah and I had gotten pretty close. Matter of fact, even though we were just kids, she talked about marriage and babies, the whole nine yards. I guess I kind of got spooked by the whole thought of growing up so fast. I told her we were too young. We were only sixteen, after all."

"That didn't go over well?"

"She didn't speak to me for three months, until she started dating Logan and forgot about those old feelings. He wanted the kind of relationship she wanted. Like I said, she wanted to be loved, and he loved her. You could see it all over him whenever they were together."

"But when were they together? He couldn't go to the Fellowship's gatherings, right?"

"Right, but they managed. Hannah would skip school every couple of weeks and spend a day with him, and he'd come to Central High to see her in the afternoons. Her folks figured she had track practice, or whatever other excuse she fed them. When Hannah made her mind up about something, she did whatever it took to make it happen."

"And she'd made her mind up about Logan."

"Yeah."

"Can you remember any of her old boyfriends, or guys she'd been with, getting overly upset about her feelings for him?"

"None come to mind. But like I said, none of the folks in the Fellowship were all that thrilled."

"The killer was a part of that group. You don't happen to have a list of all the members, do you? Where we could determine which members of the Fellowship fit our profile?"

He shook his head. "I didn't keep any reminders. Didn't want any."

"Tell me something, why did the group break up?"

"Horace Waters—Brother Moses—left in '88. No one knew why, but we figured it had something to do with the Fellowship. It had to. He lived for that group. But the authorities didn't do any real investigating. I believe the State had become concerned at the numbers of the group and at the power they had over local government. I mean, my father was the sheriff and a Fellowship deacon."

"You think someone had Horace Waters killed?"

"Or forced him to leave and never come back. And I know from listening to my father's conversations that no one wanted to take Horace's place for fear of the same thing."

"Whoever led the group was going to die."

"That's the message they got."

"So they split up when? In '88?"

"I think that's the year it ended, but some folks still follow the group's laws, according to Zed. He said the Sharp family is still practicing."

"And the killer is too."

"Seems that way."

Lexie squinted as bright lights pierced the darkness while a vehicle crept down the street toward her home. "Kind of late to be taking a leisure drive. Goodness, those lights are bright."

"Yeah, they are." The car rattled as it edged down the street. The hair on the back of John's neck stood up, and he moved his hand to rest beside his gun. Ready and waiting.

"Something wrong?" Lexie straightened and followed his gaze to the car, now nearly even with her house.

"I don't know." He wasn't the type to overreact. Maybe his

gut tensed because they had been discussing the killer, but in any case, he didn't like the look of the car, and he didn't feel safe sitting out in the open like big, easy targets.

The vehicle slowed to a near stop, and the driver lifted his hand.

John already had his finger on the trigger when he recognized the driver. "Elijah."

Lexie waved at the photographer, then watched him pass. "Late for him to be out cruising, don't you think?"

"Yeah, I do think."

"He's all the time talking about scooping out the best leads, though. Maybe he drives around at night trying to catch something on film. Maybe he's trying to catch the killer." She sounded impressed with the photographer's ingenuity.

"He's close to the cases," he thought aloud. "And he's the right age."

Lexie's mouth dropped open. "Was Elijah Lewis part of the Fellowship? Part of your group back then?"

John nodded. "His grandfather was an elder and Reverend Waters' right hand man, but Elijah never quite fit in. Always odd, like he is now, and way too nosey. We didn't hang around with him. No one did."

She shook her head. "I don't think it's him."

"How can you be sure?"

"I saw the killer."

"You said you couldn't remember his face. Have you remembered something else?"

"No, but I can't help but think—hope—that I'd sense something whenever I meet him. Don't you think I'd know, somehow, if I ever saw him again? However, Elijah is the one who started the rumor that Angel was pregnant. He said he saw her at Dr. Weatherly's office, then told Etta—and a few other people—that he thought she might be pregnant." Lexie pulled her phone from her pocket, glanced at the display. "She was supposed to call me tonight."

"You want to call her?"

She shook her head. "No, she could still be at the police station. And we're not supposed to be all that close, you know. Just members of the task force."

"Females are always a little closer than average coworkers, aren't they?"

She smiled. "Yeah, but I'm sure she'll call later."

John thought about the man who'd so quickly started the rumor that Angel was pregnant. "I wonder why Lewis went by Dr. Weatherly's place."

"Probably taking photos at the park. The paper is always reporting the park activities in the Life section."

"Maybe." John decided to keep a closer eye on the odd photographer.

"Elijah may seem a bit quirky, but he hasn't ever made me feel uncomfortable. I think that means something."

"I hope you're right." The thought of Lexie being face-to-face with the killer and not recognizing him bothered John. Then again, the thought of her being face-to-face with the killer at all bothered him just as much.

"There's one more thing about his signature that I don't get. I'm sure it must have something to do with the Fellowship, but no one has mentioned it, so I can't be sure. Then again, it could be because of Hannah."

"What?"

"The blonde hair. Why do all of his victims have blonde hair?"

"It's a sign of purity, particularly if it's so blonde it's nearly white. Angelic is the way it's described in the Fellowship's creeds. A woman with hair of an angel is an angel on earth. If she doesn't live up to that statute of purity, that is, if she doesn't remain a virgin until marriage, or stay true to her husband after marriage, then she equates to a fallen angel and should therefore be condemned."

"Condemned, as in killed?"

"They never specified, but I always assumed that's what it meant."

"Hannah didn't have a chance. And neither did those women he singled out. They had every bit of the criteria he wanted, and he made it his mission to kill them." She paused, swallowed. "Including Aunt Bev."

He pulled her closer. "You're still shivering. You should go inside."

"It's okay. I want to understand why he picked her, and even though it still doesn't make sense to me, at least now I see how she fit his criteria."

"We will get him, you know." John hoped she believed him and prayed he told the truth.

"I know."

"And the police will pull it off without you having to pull the trigger." He tried to lighten her mood, uncertain whether anything would succeed.

She looked up at him and smiled. "If they find him first, that's fine. But if I find him, or if he finds me, I won't let him win again."

"No, I don't expect you will. But I pray to God that doesn't happen." John stood from the swing, then he walked her to the door, watched her go inside, and prayed that very thing.

Lexie got ready for bed then glanced out the window to verify that her personal protector hadn't left. Sure enough, John's Grand Cherokee held its usual spot in her driveway. She couldn't see inside, but she knew he was watching, so she lifted a hand, then turned to crawl into bed.

Her cell phone buzzed from the nightstand with a text. Expecting it to be from John, she picked up the phone, saw the caller listed as RESTRICTED and opened Angel's message to confirm her fear.

*Positive.*

# CHAPTER THIRTEEN

Dr. Weatherly's first available appointment for a new patient was twelve days after the EPT confirmed Angel's suspicion that she was indeed pregnant, which meant twenty-five days remained until the killer struck again. Unless they stopped him first.

In case they didn't, she planned to be the most blatant, obvious choice for his target. Lexie's nightly broadcasts had conveyed what he looked for in a victim. If they got the point across, in twenty-five days all blonde, single and pregnant women will have gotten away from Macon. Far, far away. While Angel would be here. A blonde, single and pregnant thorn in his side. She'd already had two vomit-induced sprints to the restroom during task force meetings and had confessed the truth to Captain Pierce. No, she hadn't thought she was pregnant when he asked her before, but she'd been wrong. The FBI, in spite of Pierce's objections, had no problem with her current state and agreed with her newfound condition providing the perfect scenario for Angel to serve herself up to the killer as prime bait.

Pierce refused to share her pregnancy with the task force and provided a viable rationale to Leon Hawkins and the guys at Quantico for keeping quiet, since three members of the task force were potential suspects. The powers that be agreed, and Angel went along with their assessment, but she made no effort to hide her slowly growing stomach from the group, or the fact that she had this doctor appointment.

She climbed out of her Tahoe, tossed her hair, then strolled across the parking lot to Dr. Weatherly's office. Before entering, she turned toward Richard Barnes, the cop watching the place, and smiled. He thought she felt protected as long as he stood guard, which couldn't be further from the truth.

Somewhere in the crowded park, or at one of the offices across the street, or perhaps even in the form of a hidden camera, the killer watched her now. Angel sensed his presence, and she knew better than to doubt her agent's intuition.

Throughout the past week, she'd perfected her profile for the man. She'd added above average intelligence to the criteria she'd listed. This came through when she analyzed the autopsy protocols for all victims. Even the most careful criminals slipped up every now and then when their murders were so similar. They'd forget a tiny detail, overlook a clue they left behind, or do something that told a little too much about their personality.

This killer didn't make that mistake.

Throughout all of the murder series, not one piece of DNA remained at the scene. No fibers, no hair, no semen, no anything. Their killer had perfected clean-up, which made Angel look at the police, and those members of the task force, even more closely.

But even with John Tucker's name eliminated from the list, she still had Ryan Sims and Lou Marker. Two suspects, rather than one. And two, any way you look at it, is one too many.

She didn't want to follow in Stanley Carlton's footsteps and accuse an innocent man. She pressed a hand to her stomach and thought of her fellow profiler, the father of her baby. After this case was over, she'd have to tell him about the pregnancy. But she'd worry about that after she, Lexie and John caught the killer.

Like Lexie, Angel believed in John Tucker's innocence. The three of them discussed the case daily via Angel's secure line and Lexie's speakerphone at her home, and they'd finally agreed with Angel's theory: they could only catch the killer by forcing him to pick a certain woman, then have the tables turned. The method had worked time and time again with the profilers in Angel's unit. Though primarily used in robberies, the system had also been applied to other criminal offenses as well. The profilers determined what the killer looked for, then eliminated that scenario from all areas but one.

And, in this case, the "one" was Angel.

When Angel had to solve a series of bank robberies in Memphis, she determined what type of situation the criminal preferred. In that case, he'd wanted a bank with no windows so he couldn't be viewed from the street, a place where the alarm had been tripped a few times during the week prior, and a location with a majority of female employees. An armed guard as a regular presence in the lobby also deterred the robber.

Therefore, Angel and her colleagues selected one bank as the premier target for their criminal and gave him everything he wanted. All women tellers and loan officers, no guard in the lobby, no windows, and an alarm that had been tripped three times the week before, meaning police would respond more slowly, in a criminal's point of view. Then they placed police officers and guards in plain sight at all other branches, while keeping the federal agents in plain clothes at the site of choice.

Sure enough, the robber struck the selected bank, and Angel attributed another arrest to her credit.

For the Sunrise Killer, however, she'd use an approach similar to the tactic she'd used with the Oklahoma City rapist. With the news media on top of his criteria, and with Lexie's broadcasts humanizing his victims, Angel believed most women fitting his criteria would leave town before the next strike. She, on the other hand, would stay. And to further ensure he selected her, she taunted him daily.

Though, at Pierce's insistence, she hadn't formally announced her pregnancy, Angel could tell that most of the task force suspected the truth. She'd had a pack of crackers in her purse at all times in case she had a sudden urge for a snack, had started wearing blousy shirts, and had been "craving" spinach-artichoke dip. Her pregnancy would draw the killer to her like a bear to honey, and she knew it. But little did he know, this honey was good with her Glock.

She entered the office, signed in, then watched three graphic births on the television before a nurse called her back. Within minutes, she'd provided a urine specimen, given blood and awaited the doctor's arrival in her designated examination room.

Angel's pulse skittered as the knob turned and Yvette Weatherly, her belly swollen with her own child, entered.

"Good morning, Ms. Jackson." Dr. Weatherly closed the door.

"Good morning."

Yvette sat down on the rolling stool near the exam table, shook her head, then lowered her voice to a whisper. "I must say, your phone call and your request caught me off guard. I realize you're FBI and all. But are you sure you want to do this?"

"Yes." She'd never been more certain of anything. This would help her catch the man who'd killed her mother.

"All right, then." The doctor frowned as she annotated the information on Angel's chart. "You were correct. You're pregnant. Nearly eight weeks along. And I'll have your chart notated as such, as well as my computer files."

"Perfect."

"I can't believe I'm doing this, treating you instead of referring you to a doctor away from Macon; that's what I've been doing with all of my blonde, single and pregnant patients. But I can't argue with the points you made. From what you said, you've done this kind of thing before to catch killers, and I agree that we need to catch this guy, particularly now that I know he's targeting my patients."

"Don't worry. We'll catch him." Angel hopped off the table and picked up her purse. "So, when is my next appointment?"

"With a normal pregnancy, you won't return for four weeks."

"I can't wait that long. He needs to see me here. Is there any reason you'd see patients more often?"

"If it were a high risk pregnancy. For older women who are pregnant, I'd see you more often. At your age, if you were hemorrhaging or something of that nature, then I'd also see you more often."

"What would cause a woman to hemorrhage at this stage in the pregnancy?"

"At eight weeks, it's very early yet, so it'd most likely be stress-related."

"Can't get more stressful than hunting a serial killer." Angel grinned.

"No, I dare say you can't. So you're wanting to come back in, say, two weeks? In case you have any stress-related problems?"

"Yes, and so he can see me here again."

The doctor annotated the information on Angel's chart. "You're sure this is the only way to catch him?"

"It isn't the only way, but I believe it's the best way."

"Well, Ms. Jackson, take care of yourself." She raised her voice so the nurses and additional patients outside could hear. Then she headed for the door. With her hand on the knob, she lowered her voice again. "I mean that. Be careful."

Angel nodded, waited for her to leave then got her things.

Lexie carried a copy of her questions for tomorrow's interview to the conference room. It would be the most difficult one to air, until the one for Aunt Bev. But tomorrow the segment would feature Abigail Lynette Tucker, and Lexie didn't relish having to remind John how his wife had died.

Although the task force had picked up on their relationship—Elijah Lewis had announced to the world that he'd seen the two of them cozy on Lexie's porch and that he suspected John spent his nights there—they were determined to convince the group that their personal relationship stayed separate and apart from their professional one.

In order to do that, Lexie couldn't treat him differently than any of the other family members she'd interviewed. But to let the public see the victim as a real person, she had to ask very personal questions. Questions that sparked memories. Questions that hurt.

And she didn't want to hurt John.

After Elijah's gossip made its way through the police department, every office at the television station and the majority of the city, they hadn't made a secret of their relationship. But Lexie had done her best to let everyone know John guarded her each night from his car. She thought, and hoped, that most believed the truth. The majority of Macon had hoped the notable homicide detective would find love again. They'd known how he'd been hurt following his wife's murder; moreover, they'd watched him face accusations from the former profiler and had seen his stellar reputation questioned by the media. In other words, they wanted to see John Tucker happy.

So did Lexie.

For the past two weeks, they'd spent every night and much of every day together working on the case, working with the task force and becoming closer than she'd believed possible. Maybe because they shared a history with the killer, John losing Abby and Lexie losing Aunt Bev. Or maybe because a part of her knew John's father had helped her so long ago on that horrible day, and the actions of the father drew her even closer to the son. Or perhaps because ever since that night on the porch, they'd discussed religion together almost daily, as well as how their backgrounds affected their beliefs and their faith. Lexie had discussed her concern for Angel's lack of faith and how she prayed her cousin would find God.

With all of their talks, she and John connected on a deep, emotional level. They understood each other, so much that they could communicate without words. John looked at her, and she knew what he thought, felt, needed. Sometimes the strength behind that emotion sent a shiver down Lexie's spine.

Like right now.

She entered the conference room and looked at him, seated on the other side of the table by Ryan Sims. Those penetrating blue eyes connected with hers, and she knew what consumed his thoughts. In a little while, the two of them would have to discuss Abby, what his wife meant to him, and the killer that took her life.

Talking about his deceased wife wouldn't hurt their own relationship, Lexie knew. Far from it. She suspected it would make them even closer, because they would have tackled a difficult situation and survived it together. But that didn't make either of them more eager to perform the task.

"How are things going?" She placed her folders across from him at the table. "Anything new?"

He gave her a slight smile and Lexie's heart melted. Everything would be okay. They'd do the article on Abby, then on the previous victims, and they'd catch the killer in time.

They had to. But they had no leads yet, and everyone at the table knew it. Lexie prayed for a new lead, because she couldn't stand the thought of offering up Angel and her unborn baby as bait. Deep down, she knew she couldn't let that happen, though she had no idea how to stop it.

"Nothing new." Ryan dropped his pen on the table next to his notes. "No one's come forward with any new information, and if nothing surfaces we're going to be sitting here just like last time, waiting and watching while he kills someone else. If you ask me, we're not doing enough to catch this guy. Seems like our profiler should be able to give us something to work with. That *is* the FBI's job here, isn't it? Come in and tell us what the problem is, then tell us how to fix it. Seems she owes us a bit more in that department."

As if on cue Angel made her entrance, and by the fire in her emerald eyes, she'd heard the lieutenant's comment. "I have a new avenue I want to recommend to the team, one that I believe will shake our killer up a bit. I'll explain as soon as the others arrive."

Lexie knew Angel's recommendation had nothing to do with her pregnancy. She'd agreed to keep her condition to herself for the time being, though Lexie hadn't missed the knowing glances from the other task force members any time Angel left the room with an upset stomach.

Lou Marker and Zed Naylor entered the conference room at precisely 11:00, followed by Captain Pierce, and Lexie tried to control her worries for her younger cousin so she could find out about the "new avenue" Angel planned to pursue.

"You said you have an announcement, Jackson?" the captain asked.

Angel shuffled her notes in place. "I do."

"Go ahead." Pierce looked as though he wanted to hit something. Lexie knew the man hated the fact that he didn't have the authority to remove Angel from the case, but the FBI trumped him, and that was all there was to it. In fact, Lexie figured he was lucky she hadn't bought a billboard in the middle of Macon announcing her pregnancy.

"I've studied prior cases, and with this kind of killer, one who thrives on perfection and a systematic approach to his murders, our best chance to force him out of his cycle is to make him mad, goad him into doing something atypical."

"What do you have in mind?" John asked.

Lexie looked at John, then Angel. Angel had already told both of them that she attempted to do that very thing with her pregnancy. That hadn't been enough for Angel, and Lexie wondered how far her cousin would go to pull this killer out of hiding. Of course, if they really wanted to force him out, they could announce that Lexie had witnessed one of his murders and that Aunt Beverly's baby had survived and now profiled the killer who murdered her mother.

But although that tactic had the potential to oust the killer, since he'd want to eliminate both of them as soon as possible, it'd also oust the only known witness to his crime. And since Lexie didn't remember seeing the man's face, letting him know would issue her own death sentence—which meant Angel had come up with another approach for forcing his hand.

But what? And why hadn't she forewarned Lexie and John?

"We've been looking at victimoloy to tell us about our killer." Angel indicated her thick victimology file. "And that's, of course, a viable means of learning more about him, about what kind of victim he's looking for and how he makes his selection. However, I realized today that I overlooked a key aspect to the criminology of this case."

"How's that?" Lou asked.

"The first victim. Zed has been working hard to get information on Hannah Sharp, and from his meetings with her family and friends, we know she was pregnant with Logan Finley's baby, that she'd planned to run off and get married to avoid her family's disapproval, and that she never made it, since no one has heard from Hannah or Logan again."

Zed cleared his throat. "That's right."

"So, let's assume that Hannah Sharp was his first victim, or rather, that Hannah Sharp and Logan Finley were his first victims. What's different about that case than all the others?"

"There were two victims," Lou said.

"And no bodies," John added.

"Exactly. That's the part that I'm focusing on. No bodies. With every other kill that first year, he left the bodies out in the open, ready to be found. Seven years later, with the second series, he'd developed remorse of some type, either from a marriage or a relationship, or maybe even the end of his leader, since Brother Moses left in '88 and some presumed him dead. In any case, with that second series, he started leaving the bodies almost ceremoniously atop their own beds and within their own homes."

Ryan Sims leaned forward in his seat and glared at Angel. He'd grown weary of the profiler and her assessments, and even though he didn't voice his displeasure, he didn't try to hide it, either. "So what are you saying?"

"I think he semi-planned his first kill. He picked the date, based on his religious numerology preferences, and he knew his victim, Hannah. I don't know that he meant to kill Logan Finley at that time, but perhaps they were together on the specified date, and he had to kill him in order to kill Hannah as well. But in either case, I believe at that time, he hadn't yet decided this would be a recurring act."

"He didn't realize he would kill more people?" Lexie asked.

Angel nodded. "That's what I'm thinking. And I don't know what changed after that point, but I'd venture to say it had something to do with a twisted interpretation of the rules and regulations of the Fellowship, with their take on children equaling power and those expecting a child out of wedlock gaining that power illegally."

"Unbestowed," John corrected. "That's what we called it. Having a child out of wedlock gained power that hadn't been bestowed on that person. You weren't allowed to have a child without the bond of marriage, and those that did were excommunicated from the congregation. Right, Zed?"

"That's right."

Angel perked up at that, pointed a finger in the air, and continued, "Which fits. He dealt the punishment to the girl who'd committed the crime, and perhaps he dealt it to her boyfriend as well, but at that time, he didn't want anyone to know what he'd done. Maybe he hadn't decided if the act could be justified yet, and then after thinking about it, he convinced himself that it was not only justified, but required."

Throughout the course of the case, Lexie had watched

Angel work, but she'd never seen the inner reasonings of her cousin's mind in progress, not the way she did right now. Listening to Angel's thought process and watching the way she put it all together, the entire room absorbed her analysis of a killer's psyche, with her description flowing as if she were discussing the weather.

"All right," Pierce said, "I can see where you might be onto something here, but what are you suggesting?"

"I'm suggesting that when he killed the first time, he not only wanted retribution for Hannah Sharp; he also wanted to cover up his crime. Literally."

"You think he buried her," John said. "He didn't want anyone to know what he did, so he buried her."

"I do." Angel seemed impressed that he followed her perception. "And because he is such a perfectionist, I don't believe he'd have buried her anywhere. I think he put her body somewhere symbolic of the crime she committed, a place that would remind him of what she'd done when he returned to the body dump site." She paused, took a moment to scan everyone in the room. "And he *does* return to that original site. Every killer does. I'd venture to say he's been there a few times this year, when his newest series started."

"Why?" Lexie asked.

"To remind him how and why it all began."

"Where do you think he buried her?" Lou Marker's accusing glare changed to a look of acute interest.

"I believe he'd want to put her close to the Fellowship, somewhere that would emphasize the rules she'd broken." She looked at Zed. "You said the Fellowship met outdoors, in the woods, right?"

Zed nodded. "Outside of town, with a narrow access off one of the county roads."

"Probably not even utilized by people who weren't in the group, right? At least at that time?"

"Right. You think that's where her body is?"

"Don't you?"

The older man's eyes widened, his face searched out the former members of their group. Lou, Ryan and John. "What if she's there? Back then, everyone refused to mention that she'd gone, refused to acknowledge she'd ever existed, because of her family and because of our rules. What if the girl had been murdered and buried right there where we gathered? What if the killer stood right above her and, knowing that, somehow found satisfaction that the group had disowned her? And no one even looked for her." He shook his head. "It ain't right. No one even tried to find her."

"You think she's there too, don't you?" Angel looked as though she already knew the answer.

Zed, his wrinkled face full of disgust, nodded.

"If we find Hannah's body, and Logan's too, assuming he buried them near each other, then we'll upset his pattern. He undoubtedly returns to Hannah to remind him of his purpose. If we remove that ability, we'll remove his original point of contact with his crime." Angel turned to Zed. "All of you who were former members still remember where the group met back then?"

Still dazed, Zed nodded, while Lou answered, "Yeah, we remember."

"Then let's get on it." Pierce sounded eager to make headway in the case and to have an impact in the killer's plan. "Give us the directions and let's get the crime scene van out there. If he did bury Hannah Sharp and Logan Finley at that place, we should be able to find them."

# CHAPTER FOURTEEN

Lexie spent the majority of her time at WGXA in the evening, after her interview with a victim's family had aired, constructing the questions for the next day's broadcast. When the remainder of the task force headed to the Fellowship's former meeting location, she had John drop her off at her office to prepare for the first of tomorrow's two interviews.

She'd been informed that the excavation of the bodies, if they were indeed buried at that location, could take several hours or even days, and she hadn't wanted her segments for tomorrow's news missing in action while she watched and waited for something that might not turn up.

But deep down, Lexie knew Angel had the right idea, and she expected to hear that Hannah Sharp had been buried on what was once considered sacred ground by the fanatical group.

It still amazed her that John, Lou, Ryan, Zed and Paul had all been so obsessed with the cult-like assemblage. And, from what John had told her, so had a large portion of the town. Even now that the group had been disbanded for over twenty years, the Fellowship still dominated Macon's gossip frenzy.

Everywhere Lexie went, people asked if she'd heard any additional names that had surfaced regarding the group. She wasn't sure whether they were trying to find out who had been involved, or whether they were hoping their own affiliation hadn't been unearthed. Either way, she told them the truth. If she learned anything, they'd hear about it on the news. She had hoped the profound interest in the Fellowship's relationship with the killer would remain outside of her office. With

Melody Harper in the next cubicle, however, that wasn't a possibility.

"Lexie, you got a minute?" Melody popped her head around the wall at knee-level, still sitting in her chair while she asked. Her gray bun drooped from the top of her sideways head and her granny glasses dangled from a beaded strap around her neck.

Lexie gave the lady a smile that she assumed the woman needed. "I finished updating the information from the profiler and sent it to Paul for approval. And since I've got to wait a while before I'll be able to do my interview, I've got a minute."

Melody's eyes looked tiny without her glasses, and she squinted a bit as she rolled her chair across the floor to fill the opening to Lexie's cubicle. "You've got to interview John Tucker about his wife, don't you?"

Lexie nodded. "She's the next victim to be featured."

"That'll be tough, don't you think? Since the two of you have been seeing each other and all."

"It's tough with any victim's family. They've all lost someone they love, and it hurts to hear about their pain. But I still think it's the best way of getting our readers to relate to the victims and to care whether or not we get this guy before he kills someone else. Plus, it lets them know what to watch for."

Melody bobbed her head, her gray bun threatening to topple. "I know. I found Delia crying her eyes out last night over that lady's story. Of course, Delia's getting close to her due date, so those hormones are messing with her emotions. About to drive my boy over the edge, not knowing how to help her when he calls to check in. She went ahead and moved in with me, by the way. I know she doesn't fit what the guy's looking for, since she's married and all, but since Kevin is gone so much, we were afraid the killer might not catch on that she's got a husband."

"This killer would know, but the police are hoping to stop him before he strikes again, anyway." Lexie prayed they did, since she had no doubt Angel would be his number one target if they didn't.

"I hope they do. So, have you heard anything? The talk radio station announced the police had a lead on where the first body is buried. Is that true?"

"I've got it in the copy I sent to Paul for tonight's broadcast, but yeah, that's true."

"And is it that girl you've been talking about in your stories? Hannah Sharp? I don't know any Sharps, but I heard some folks talking at church Sunday morning who knew a thing or two about them. Said they're, well, kind of odd. You know, some of those folks who keep to themselves, stay a ways out from town and kind of live off the land. Used to be a lot of that type around here, when that Fellowship was so popular, but you don't hear much about them anymore."

Her mention of the cult piqued Lexie's interest. "Melody, did you know anyone who belonged to the Fellowship?"

"Nah, Charles and I moved here in the early 90's. It was all pretty much a done deal by then, but I've heard folks talk about it." She pulled her glasses up and settled them on her nose. "Kind of glad I wasn't around for all of that. Pretty spooky stuff, if you ask me. To think, you'd cast a teenager out if they got pregnant? What good does that do? That's the time they need family the most. That just ain't fitting. And it ain't very religious-like either, if they kept saying they were into religion and all."

"I agree."

"Mrs. Harper, I need to speak to Ms. McCain for a moment." Paul Kingsley towered above Melody in her chair. "And have you already finished your pieces for the day?"

Melody's face turned a brilliant purplish-red. "I was just leaving." She pressed her heels down, then turned her head before backing up. "Sorry. Excuse me."

He stepped out of her way, then frowned at her as she rolled back to her cubicle.

Lexie looked up at her boss. "You got the copy for tonight's story?"

"Yes. It's fine, unless they find those bodies. If they do, then we'll want to do a quick update, but you can email that from home and let the anchors provide the update on your behalf. I want you to stay in touch with the authorities until the last minute for submission, so we can have the jump on the other stations with the story if it breaks."

"I plan on it."

"And what about the segment on Abby Tucker?"

"I'm supposed to interview John later today. We were about to go over it earlier, but he went with the other task force members to the place where they believe the bodies may be buried."

His brows lifted. "Tucker went back to the gathering grounds?"

Lexie nodded. "Captain Pierce wanted all of them to go and be involved in the search. Why wouldn't he go?"

"He never returned. After the group disintegrated and then his father died, he didn't want any reminders. I guess I figured he'd still be determined to stay away."

"Did anyone go back there after they stopped meeting?"

"A few people who weren't ready for it to end. They met a few times, but they were pretty disappointed in the numbers that showed, so they gave up. I guess you could call them the true diehard Fellowshippers." He crossed his arms, leaned against her cubicle wall. "But John wasn't one of them. He swore he'd never go back. Guess it seems odd he's going now. But then again, that's his job, isn't it?"

"The killer would have been one of those people who went back. Can you remember who tried to keep the group going?"

"No. I wasn't a part of it." The reporter in Lexie said he knew more, but his face remained set, so he'd decided the topic wasn't up for additional discussion. She made a mental note to ask John about it later. The names of those "diehard Fellowshippers" as Paul called them would be of interest to the task force.

"You know, if John is too involved with finding those bodies and you need to talk to someone who knew Abby, you could interview me. We were all friends in high school, and then we hung out together when we were married as well. Kathleen, my ex-wife, and Abby were good friends. And I believe I knew Abby well enough to give our viewers a true depiction of her. She was a special lady, and we want to portray her that way."

"Yeah, we do." John walked up to stand beside Paul, "But I'm here now, and I'll be able to help you with the story, Lexie.

Thanks for offering to help, though," he said to Paul. "You're right. You did know her well, and she thought a lot of you."

Paul smiled. "I didn't hear you come in."

"I didn't expect you back so soon." Lexie noticed John looked stressed and suspected why. "Did they find anything?"

"Yeah, they did."

"They found them?" Paul asked. "Hannah and Logan?"

"The team has uncovered two bodies, and they appear to be Hannah and Logan. I didn't realize you knew we were looking for both of them."

Paul lifted a sheet of paper in his hand. "Lexie's copy for tonight said you believed they would be together."

John nodded. "Right. Well, they were. Or at least Hannah. We believe it's Logan Finley's body buried with her, but they're still verifying that."

"Where were they? Exactly?" Paul's head shook as he asked the question.

"Buried deep, right in the center of the meeting grounds."

"Beneath the altar?"

"Where the altar used to be. Now it's just a flat patch of earth. But that's where they were."

"How do you know it's Hannah?" Lexie asked.

"Her locket, it was still intact. They'll have to do the typical autopsy tests for verification, but I'm betting that locket says it all."

"The one with her initials? H.E.S., right, for Hannah Elizabeth Sharp?"

"Right." John looked surprised. "You have a good memory. I didn't remember it at first."

"She loved that locket. Her parents didn't give her a lot of nice things, so she took care of the necklace. One of her boyfriends gave it to her, I think. But I can't remember which one."

John ran a hand through his thick black waves. "I can't either." He turned to Lexie. "Hey, it's been quite a day, but I know you need to get that interview on Abby. I'm ready if you are."

"Sure."

"Listen, why don't you two head on out and do the

interview somewhere private." Paul pointed to the next cubicle, where Melody Harper had stopped typing and no doubt hung on every word and prepared to call everyone she knew to tell them Hannah Sharp had been found. Paul didn't want her also privy to the information regarding John's deceased wife.

Lexie agreed with his suggestion. "That sounds good. I'll email the updated profile info, as well as the copy for tomorrow's broadcast on Abby Tucker, before 10:00."

"Take as much time as you need. I'm working another late one. And I know you'll do a great job."

"I'll try." She gathered her things, said goodbye to Paul and left the station with John, who looked as if the finding of Hannah Sharp and Logan Finley had been less of a triumph for the task force and more of a heart-wrenching blow. This afternoon, he'd learned two of his friends from high school were murdered. Now he'd have to talk about the emotions surrounding his wife's death.

The day wasn't getting any better.

John escorted Lexie from the building, helped her in his Grand Cherokee, then climbed in the driver's side. He sat there for a moment, the events of the past few hours weighing over him like granite, or rather a granite tombstone, the kind of monument that should've marked Hannah and Logan's grave throughout the years, instead of the filthy mulch and dirt and nothingness that hid what had been two vibrant lives. One of which had been a dear friend, and for a short time long ago, she had been more.

With each careful pass of the shovels, the group had become antsy. Although the Fellowship's grounds should've been overgrown and dense like the surrounding forest, it wasn't. The brush had been recently disturbed, broken branches identified someone had driven into and through the barriers, and though there were no footprints to be found due to the blanket of pine straw and damp leaves on the ground, John had no doubt the killer had visited the site.

He'd been impressed with Angel's assessment of the killer. She'd seen into his head and followed his thoughts, and because of her ability, they'd found Hannah and Logan. The two would receive the mourning they deserved and closure for the families. Well, Logan's family at least. Hannah's had written her off long ago, which made Tucker livid. She'd been a vibrant, energetic, typical teenage girl who loved life and wanted to experience every aspect. Because of that, hers had been snatched away, and her family hadn't cared.

Throughout the excavation, Angel had been the only female at the site. She'd encouraged Lexie to return to work for the afternoon rather than participate in the search for Hannah and Logan's remains, and Tucker had seconded her proposal. Lexie didn't need to see what they found, but in his opinion, neither did Angel. However, the profiler wasn't concerned with his opinion. She held her emotions intact and didn't let on that this case ranked more important to her than any other.

Until they found the bodies.

He'd seen her then. She stood across from him with her face void of color, then she turned from the group and entered the recesses of the forest. John followed her and held her long blonde hair while she vomited. Then he held her, until she gained her composure and prepared to face the frantic group.

"He's the worst I've seen. They're saying they found two bodies, but there were three people buried in that tomb. Hannah, Logan and their baby." She touched her stomach, her green eyes redlined and intense with the realization that so many not only lost their lives, but also their unborn children. "And he killed my mother."

"We'll get him." John meant the promise. She and Lexie had suffered throughout their lives because of this monster, and they still suffered now. John had also suffered, losing Abby and now watching Lexie endure the knowledge that the killer still hurt and murdered women, the way he'd hurt and killed her aunt. They had to stop him. John had to stop him. But first, he had to find him.

"If you don't want to do this interview, we don't have to," Lexie said from the passenger's seat. "I could talk to Paul and use his background with Abby to gain the personal information I need. I don't want to make your day any worse."

How long had he been sitting here, the keys in his hand while Lexie waited for him to make a move? The killer consumed his thoughts, gaining control, and John wouldn't let him win. He turned in the seat and looked at Lexie, beautiful, caring and loving Lexie. Reaching out, he touched her cheek, then he leaned over and brushed a soft kiss on her lips. "I appreciate your offer, but you and I both know it'll mean more and produce a better image of Abby if I answer your questions personally."

"It will, but—"

"No. No buts. I want to do this. Yeah, it's been a rough day, but it's been a rough day for you too." He paused, then decided to go ahead and tell her what he knew she'd want to know. "Angel didn't take it well."

The sunlight of late afternoon filtered through the car and seemed to focus on her face, etched with concern. "Is she okay? Did—did anyone wonder why she didn't take it well?"

"No. It was hard on all of us, and we tried to handle it like men, but we all knew Hannah and Logan. I've never been to a drop site when I've known the individual, and it's different. Angel held it together throughout the excavation, but when they found the first body, then the second, she couldn't."

"I should've gone with her. I shouldn't have come back to work."

"No, I think she did the right thing telling you to work on the article. Going to the site is part of what she does in her job, to give her a better interpretation of the killer's actions. And she knew the emotions involved with finding those bodies and knowing the same guy that put them there killed Beverly Truman would be too traumatic for the two of you to endure together. You may have inadvertently let your relationship be known, and we can't afford for the killer to learn that the two of you are related, and that you saw him back then."

"But Angel needed me, and I wasn't there."

"No, but I was."

"You helped her?" Her eyes glistened, on the verge of tears.

"Yeah, I did. She only lost it for a few minutes. She also mentioned that tossing her lunch once again would help fuel the pregnancy suspicions and help her plan."

"That's Angel, ready to fight the world with a vengeance." She gave him a slight smile. "I'm glad you were there."

"Me too." He waited a beat then, because he'd promised Angel he would and because he couldn't keep anything from Lexie, he told her what he'd been dreading most throughout the drive from the Fellowship grounds to WGXA. "And there's something else, something Angel wanted you to know, but she didn't want to risk calling you at work."

"What is it?"

"The location of the Fellowship gathering place. We never mentioned it in our meeting this morning, since most everyone there already knew. But after Angel saw where we went, she said you'd want to know."

"Where is it?"

"About twelve miles outside of town, down County Road 42."

She put a hand over her mouth then eased it away. "I thought it wasn't on a main road. I'd assumed the woods, from what you described." She paused, leaned her head back and whispered, "I never imagined it could've been the same place."

"It is off the main road, or at least off of the county road. But Angel told me that your aunt took that road that day, when he stopped her and attacked her. We're thinking he may have been there, at the place where he'd buried Hannah and Logan, before you and your aunt arrived."

"It was a dirt road, covered in loose gravel." She remembered the crunching sound of rocks beneath his shoes when he neared the car. Then, because she couldn't control the force of the memory, she remembered the look in her aunt's eyes. Her screams. Lexie gasped. "We drove right to him. On the day he'd already decided to commit a murder." Then she shook her head. "But he couldn't have known we would, and he had no idea about her pregnancy until he got to the car."

"Which was what Angel said today when she spoke to me about it. She believes, after viewing the Fellowship grounds and trying to determine how the man thinks, that he believed some spiritual force would show him the next victim he should claim. Then he left the gathering grounds and pretended his car had broken down on the road and waited for someone to stop."

"The police said other people had seen a teenage boy broken down on that road earlier that morning," Lexie said. "Some had even stopped to help, but he'd claimed he was okay."

"I know. After Angel and I talked, I pulled the information out of our files and reviewed it again. If they could have identified the guy, the killer would've been stopped long ago, but I think the police didn't believe a teen could've done what was done to your aunt, and they didn't follow up with the witnesses like they should have." He shrugged. "In 1985, I'm afraid the cops didn't realize the killing instinct could occur prior to adulthood, or they didn't realize someone could be that brutal if they were so young. But evil isn't age-specific."

"Or maybe he wasn't a teen. Maybe he just looked young."

"That's a possibility too. But in any case, the police didn't follow through, and the guy got away."

Lexie turned, grabbed her seat buckle and snapped it on. "I want to go there."

He didn't have to ask where. Angel had told him Lexie would want to know for sure whether he'd attacked Beverly near Hannah's body. As an investigative reporter, she wanted to know as much as possible about everything. But John dreaded taking her, because he suspected it had been twenty-eight years since the little girl called AJ had been on County Road 42. "Are you sure?"

"Yes."

He blew out a breath. "Okay. But go ahead and get out your tape recorder."

She looked confused, but she followed his instruction and withdrew the tiny recorder from her purse. "Why?"

"If we're going to confront the pain from your past, we're going to confront mine, too. And we'll do the two together, so I can help you deal with yours," he leaned across the seat, touched a finger to her chin, "and you can help me deal with mine."

Lexie bit her lower lip. "You're ready to talk about Abby?"

"No, I don't guess I'll ever be ready, but I need to. Even though most of the town remembers her, or at least remembers her death. But they didn't know her, and in order for them to care about each and every victim, they need to know them. You've stirred the emotions of everyone in Macon with these stories, let them know what the world lost when these women were killed. They deserve to know about Abby too."

"Okay." She pulled a notebook from her briefcase and flipped to the questions she'd asked each family member in the earlier interviews. She kept the questions the same to keep each consistent; however, the amount of information within the stories varied, dependent on what aspect of the victim had most touched the family member. Therefore, although each interview conformed to the rest, they were also unique, like the individuals described.

Since John had seen each of Lexie's previous interviews, he knew what she'd ask, which helped. Some. However, he still prepared for the emotional onslaught of remembering how much Abigail Tucker meant to him fourteen years ago.

Cranking the truck, he backed up, then started out of the parking lot. "Go ahead."

# CHAPTER FIFTEEN

Lexie's interviews were done privately, with only the victim's family member and her tape recorder present for the event. After they completed the interview, she composed the copy, submitted it for Paul's approval then taped the segment. She'd never been more grateful for the procedure than right now. Lexie didn't want to interview John on live TV. Too much emotion involved, on his part and her own.

She pressed the record button and scanned the basic list of questions that had proven effective with her former interviews. When she questioned family members about their loved ones, the list hadn't seemed invasive. However, with Detective John Tucker on the responding end, it did.

She cleared her throat. "You're sure?"

"Yeah."

Gaining her composure, she asked the first question. "How did you know Abigail Tucker?"

"Abby was my wife." He seemed to relax in his seat and prepare for the round of questions.

"Can you tell me how the two of you first met?"

"Originally? Or when we started dating?"

"Originally." The more she could tell her viewers, the better. They'd see the relationship Abby and John had developed and shared, and would care even more about the fact that she'd been taken from this world, along with her child.

"I met her the first day of seventh grade. Abby's family had moved to Macon over the summer, because her father had taken a job teaching Social Studies at Central. She was kind of nervous about starting at a new school, and at that awkward age, twelve, where you want to be popular, but you don't know how. I'd been elected the class representative for the Junior SGA, and one of my jobs was to make the new kids feel welcomed."

"How did you do that?"

"I introduced her to folks, took her around the school and helped her learn the ropes. I tried to help her blend, but she was still pretty shy until lunch that first day, when I thought I'd help her out by carrying her tray."

"You were flirting."

"Hey, I was thirteen. It was in my nature to flirt." He gave her a sly smile and Lexie found herself wishing she could've seen him back then trying to impress the pretty girl.

"What happened when you carried her tray?"

"So, I'm walking across the lunchroom with these two trays filled with hard tacos, limp salads and fat cinnamon rolls, and sure enough, someone had spilled taco grease on the floor."

"Taco grease?"

"Yeah, that red stuff they try to make you think is taco sauce, but you know it's just the grease they didn't drain." He laughed. "We didn't mind, though. If you ask me, that's what made them taste good."

She could picture him, the confident teenaged SGA rep determined to impress every girl at school with his suave, debonair style. And falling up short. "So, what happened when you and your two trays of food had a run-in with the taco grease?"

"Kaboom."

She laughed. "And Abby suddenly didn't feel so bad about the first day of school?"

"How could she? This guy trying his best to impress her had ended up sprawled on the lunchroom floor covered in limp salad and taco grease. She felt pretty near perfect after that."

Lexie realized they'd ventured off the original question, but her viewers would like the personal story, and she planned to include the entire taco grease scene in her report.

"Tell me about your time later, when the two of you began a more personal relationship."

"From that day on, we were always friends. Every now and

then, we'd take a turn at trying out the boyfriend-girlfriend thing, but throughout high school, we were more friends than anything. She dated other guys. I dated other girls. But we always seemed to come back to each other when things didn't turn out so great with other people."

"Was she a member of the Fellowship?" This question had been added to the past few interviews, the ones conducted after they learned the killer had been a member of the group.

"No, which had a lot to do with why we didn't pursue a more intense relationship back then. As a deacon, my father had no intention of me dating someone from outside the Fellowship."

"But later that changed?"

"He was killed in '88, around the same time that Brother Moses left and the group fell apart. After that, mine and Abby's relationship grew into something more than friendship. Before long, we started seeing each other exclusively."

Lexie honed in on the detail she hadn't heard before. "You said your father was killed. How did he die?"

John's mouth dipped down on one side, then he took a deep breath and answered, "A friend of his called him to his home, said he and his wife were arguing and that she had a gun. He asked Dad to come over and try to talk to her."

"So he died answering a domestic disturbance call?" Lexie found herself amazed at the many layers of this man and at all of the heartache in his past.

"Yeah, but the call didn't go to the station. The guy called my father at home."

"What happened?"

"By the time he showed up, she'd shot her husband and waited on Dad. The minute he got out of the car, she shot him, then she turned the gun on herself.

"Oh, John, I'm so sorry."

He swallowed, then cleared his throat. "After his death, Abby and I grew closer."

"And the two of you married—when?" Lexie's heart still ached from John's loss of his father, but her mind realized he wanted the interview to move past that particular pain.

"We married in 1991."

"So you'd been married eight years when she died?"

"Yes." His jaw twitched, and his hand tightened on the wheel.

"And the child she carried, it was your first?"

"We tried to get pregnant before. Both of us wanted to have kids the minute we got married. We wanted to be young parents, but it just didn't happen. We figured it was because of our stressful jobs, or that's what we heard, that stress could cause things not to happen as easily. I worked homicide and Abby worked fulltime as a court reporter. Both are stressful jobs, of course."

"But then she did get pregnant."

His hand opened on the steering wheel, then gripped it again. "We considered going to a fertility specialist, but then she got pregnant."

"And the two of you were anxious to have that child. Elated that your dream had come true, right?" She knew his response would touch her viewers' hearts, as it would touch hers.

But she wasn't prepared for his answer.

John reached over and pressed the stop button on the recorder. "This can't go on the air, okay?"

"All right." She wondered what could be worse than discussing what happened to his father and his wife. "What is it?"

"I'd have loved that child, no matter what. And if things had worked out between us, we'd have raised him or her as our own, but you know from the reports that Abby and I had separated. The stresses of our jobs had taken over, and she didn't understand why I had to spend so many hours away from home working on the Sunrise Killer case. She—turned to someone else." He inhaled, exhaled. "The baby was his."

Lexie's chest clenched. She hadn't known. If she had, she'd have never put him through this interview, through having to relive not only the pain of losing his wife to a killer, but also the pain of losing her to another man. "I'm sorry." She hated how weak the two words sounded in comparison to the heartfelt emotion behind them.

"Don't be. I loved her, even after I found out. But the truth is, I didn't even know about the baby until after she died. She never told me, and it'd been too long since the two of us had been together for the baby to have been mine."

"Do you know who—"

"A cop, he worked with me on the case. We were friends. He left Macon though, after he confessed the affair to me. I haven't spoken to him since."

She nodded, not knowing what else to say.

"Do you have enough for the story?"

"Yes." She did, more than enough.

"I didn't mean to keep that from you, but I don't like to talk about the problems Abby and I had, or the fact that she cheated. And if I hadn't been so involved in that case, and spent so much time away—"

Lexie leaned across the seat. Starting at the tiny crinkles beside his eye, she brushed the backs of her fingertips down the side of his face, then moved closer to press her lips against his neck. "You can't blame yourself for that. You were doing your job."

His throat pulsed against her lips. She stayed there, close to him, giving him her warmth, showing him compassion for what he'd experienced by showing him she cared.

She had plenty of information to provide an accurate picture of Abby Tucker without sacrificing the private aspects that would remain solely with John. She closed her eyes, rested her head against his shoulder.

"Lexie."

She opened her eyes, eased away from him…and viewed the very place that had been the backdrop of her nightmares for the past twenty-eight years.

"Pull over." Her words came out scratchy and raw, and she swallowed past the instant fear that rippled down her spine. After all these years, *she'd* returned to the scene of the crime.

John steered to the side of the road and parked. The red and blue lights from the cops still on the Fellowship grounds flashed a constant reminder that hours ago, Hannah Sharp and Logan Finley had been found in the woods less than a quarter of a mile from where he now parked. "What do you want to do?"

"I'm not sure, but I need to get out, and I need to get closer to where we were."

He nodded. He'd been around survivors before when they returned to a crime scene where a loved one died. Although detectives brought them back to the scene to learn whether they remembered any details of the crime, he knew why they hadn't brought Lexie back to the scene so long ago. No way should an eight-year-old have to endure a forced memory of her aunt being murdered. Plus, she had already blocked the images from her memory. Even if the cops thought it might help solve the crime, they wouldn't have been willing to sacrifice her sanity to do it, and one of those cops had been his father, a good man who would never do anything to harm a child.

Now, however, Lexie had matured into a knowledgeable woman ready to face the demons of her past. One demon in particular, the one who'd killed her aunt on this road.

"I'll need to go clear this with the guys on the scene. They should recognize my vehicle, but just in case, I need to let them know I'm here."

"All right."

"Wait for me before you start trying to remember more. Stay in the truck until I get everything cleared. I don't want you to do this alone."

She chewed her lower lip, frowned at the road before her, and nodded.

John climbed out of the truck and hadn't breached the boundary of the woods before running into Pierce. "I thought they were done. What are they looking for?" He indicated the CSI team, still scouring the ground they'd covered earlier.

"Agent Jackson wanted them to search again for anything the killer could've left behind. She has no doubt, and neither do I, that he's been here. Someone cleared that brush. But I believe if he left any clues behind, they were destroyed when the team started digging. I thought she might be onto something, but I never dreamed we'd find them so quickly."

"We wouldn't have, if we hadn't had so many members on the task force who'd once belonged to the Fellowship. It only made sense if he buried them here, they'd be at the spot for the altar."

"Yeah, well, CSI came back to look, but I think we're about to call it a day. We haven't found anything new."

"No one called me."

"You'd have been called if anything turned up. But I knew you were working on the interview for the TV station, and that's important as well, in light of the new bodies being found. I can't help but think someone out there knows something."

John nodded. He suspected no one knew anything at all about the killer except the woman sitting in his truck. However, although she may have seen him in the past, she couldn't remember him now. And until she did, the fact that she'd witnessed one of the murders wouldn't help the case.

"We'll be out of here soon. Were you wanting to take another look around as well?"

"Yeah. I've got Lexie with me. She wanted an accurate depiction of the scene to describe for her story." A half-lie, but he couldn't tell the captain the truth, not until they caught the killer.

"Good idea. Elijah came earlier snapping photos of the area for the Telegraph. The newspaper will depict the scene; it'd be good for her to see everything herself too, though. You know, I don't like to feed the media, but in this case, I agree with Jackson. The best way to oust this guy is to put his actions out there for the world to see. And this place, I've gotta tell you, gives me the creeps."

John remembered traveling down this hidden path several times each week as a kid. He'd listened to countless sermons, learned endless rules, and experienced the fear of "all powers unknown" from Brother Moses upon this land. It'd been a combination of horrible and awe-inspiring at the same time. Right now, horrible claimed control. "It does the same for me."

"I'll go back and make sure they haven't found anything else. It'll be dark soon. Guess if Ms. McCain wants to take a look around, you guys should get started. If the CSI group finds anything of interest, I'll give you a yell. If not, we'll be out of here soon." He slapped John on the back. "We're getting close, Detective. I can feel it."

"Good, because we're running out of time." John returned to the truck, where Lexie sat, her arms wrapped around her middle while she stared at the road ahead. He opened the door. "You sure you want to do this?"

Less than an hour ago, she'd asked him the same question, regarding his interview about Abby. Both of them understood the difficulties involved with this case, with this killer, and with the memories haunting them as a result of the murders.

He wouldn't have thought less of her if she chose to leave, to flee the scene of so much pain. But he knew Lexie McCain, so he understood that she wouldn't be satisfied until she faced the demons. And part of him wanted her to find a means to close this door from her past, so that perhaps she could find the will to open a door for her future with him.

"I have to do this." She climbed from the truck.

John wrapped an arm around her. "Okay. Where were you?"

She pointed ahead. "Over that hill."

They started walking, while thick clouds covered the last bits of sun, and the temperature dropped. It didn't look very far at first, but as they walked, John realized that he should've offered to drive. "I didn't realize it was this far."

"I did. I remember looking out from the top. It wasn't paved back then."

"No, it wasn't. They didn't pave the county roads until the early nineties."

"I slipped and fell, busted my lip and chipped this tooth." She indicted her front right incisor, shaped odd along one side. "I didn't want to get it fixed. It reminds me of Aunt Bev."

John's throat closed at the sound of emotion in her quivering voice. So much pain for an eight-year-old to endure. So much pain for a grown woman to remember.

They reached the top of the hill, and Lexie stopped walking, then turned to view the road behind her. The police cars were leaving, the red and blue pulsing lights fading as they returned to Macon.

"There was a house." She pointed to the lower left, to a flat meadow that buffered the edge of the woods.

"I believe I remember a house being there. I guess they tore it down at some point."

"The man who lived there—I can't remember his name— but he was out in his garden. He wiped his head with a red handkerchief, and that's when I saw him. I remember wondering if I should yell at him or not." She sucked in a small gulp of air. "I thought maybe he was the killer and trying to act busy to trick me." A glaze of tears covered her dark green eyes. "Strange, isn't it? I mean, I'd heard the killer drive away, but in my head, I still believed he could be anywhere, even standing in the middle of that field."

"What did you do?"

"I had to decide whether to scream, to try to get his attention and get help for Aunt Bev, or to be quiet, to keep the killer from coming back and hurting her again, or from hurting me." She wrapped her hands around her stomach and shook her head, remembering the terror of the decision.

"And you yelled for him to come help."

"I yelled as loud as I could, and I prayed he got there in time." She continued shaking her head as she spoke. "He saw me, and he yelled back toward his house, and a woman came out on the porch, then she ran back inside. I guess she's the one who called the police. It must have been his wife, but I never saw her again. I just turned around and started running back to the car, back to Aunt Bev, while he followed."

"Was she still alive when you got there?"

"Yeah, but her breathing sounded strange. I think the killer knocked her unconscious, because I thought she might already be dead when I left the car, but then she kind of gurgled, and the blood was everywhere."

"Then what happened?"

Lexie turned and started down the backside of the hill. He caught up to her and wrapped his arm around her while she moved. She didn't speak for a while, but continued to walk, while a soft mist fell from the darkening sky. "Over this next hill."

They topped the hill. Lexie moved even closer to John. "Right there. That's where we were. The ambulance came, and the police came—and your father—and they all tried to save her. They took us to the hospital in Atlanta, because they thought the doctors there might be able to save her, but they couldn't."

"They saved the baby, though."

"Yes. When they realized Aunt Bev had died, they took Angel—Olivia. Aunt Carol held me tight and kept my head buried in the crook of her neck. Then she told me Aunt Bev had gone to heaven, but that the baby was okay. I don't even remember when she told me. I can't remember if we were here, or if we were at the hospital in Atlanta." Lexie paused. "At the hospital. That's right, because Granddaddy got there while she held me. He came in frantic, his face all creased with worry and he asked about Aunt Bev. Someone, I guess a doctor, told him they couldn't save her. I remember his scream; it made my heart clench. They were trying to tell him about Angel, but he couldn't hear the words. He grabbed his chest." Her jaw twitched at the painful memory, throat visibly tightened, as though she struggled to keep emotions at bay. "The rest of the day is a blur."

He pulled her close and held her as the mist turned to rain. "Do you remember anything else? About the killer?"

She sobbed against his chest. "No. I can't remember anything."

"It's okay, Lexie. Come on, honey, let's go home." She nodded, then let him lead her away from the memories, away from the past and, although they didn't realize it at the time, away from the killer.

# CHAPTER SIXTEEN

"The rumors are still going around. They're not true?" Etta Green stood in the hallway outside the dispatch office and watched Angel progress toward the lobby.

"Depends on the rumors, I suppose." Angel brushed her hair from her face. She'd spent another day staring at victimology records, autopsy reports and anything else she could find trying to locate a detail they'd overlooked.

She'd found nothing.

"It's hard to keep secrets around here, especially from me." She eyed Angel's oversized top.

"We did get positive identification for the bodies today. Hannah Sharp and Logan Finley. Is that what you're talking about?"

Etta's bracelets jangled as she waved. "I heard about that from the deputies in the break room and on the news. Oh, and the radio. That guy on the news talk radio channel is covering the murders twenty-four hours a day. Matter of fact, starting tomorrow, he's going to be taking calls from women who fit what the killer goes after, since we'll be down to the last three days."

The last three days. They'd worked the case solid and had a profile of the killer, but too many people fit the profile, and not one soul had come forward with information on his identity. And now the radio station publicized that there were women out there fitting his criteria?

Angel only wanted him to have one woman to choose from. "Get me the number of that radio station, Etta."

Etta waved her bangle-clad arms. "Oh, I didn't mean talking

to women in Macon. He's got an 800 number, and he's asking women from other cities to call in and tell how they'd feel if they lived in Macon. He made no bones about telling all women who fit the killer's type in Macon to get out of Dodge."

"Thank heaven for small favors."

"The rumor is the one saying you've got a little one on the way. It's still going around."

Angel didn't miss a beat. She hadn't announced her pregnancy, because Pierce had told her to keep the facts to herself and let the department determine the truth on their own. But she wouldn't lie to her new friend. "Etta, I'll tell you the truth. I've promised Captain Pierce I won't say anything else about it." She glanced at her stomach, a little rounder than it'd been the first time she'd met the sweet lady, and not merely because of Etta's delicious banana nut bread. "So I am not going to say anything else about it."

Etta's mouth flattened, and she nodded, as if she'd known the truth already. "Well, I'm certainly not going to broadcast it, or anything, or feed the rumors." She audibly sighed. "You can take care of yourself, though, I assume, with all of your FBI training and all, right?" Her look of hope touched Angel's heart.

"Right." Angel certainly planned to take care of herself, as well as the tiny person growing inside of her. For the past few weeks, since learning about the pregnancy, she'd felt different. An appreciation for life, and a desire to protect this baby.

"I know it ain't the ideal situation, raising a child without a husband in the house, but my girls have turned out okay, even though their father didn't stick around long enough for the ink to dry on the marriage license."

"You're still married to him?"

"I reckon I am. I ain't got nothing that tells me any different."

Angel leaned against the wall, eyed the sweet woman who'd grown dear to her heart. "You still love him?"

Etta blushed. "I guess it's true what they say. You can't teach an old dog new tricks. I come from a family that marries for life. I married. He left."

"And you still love him."

"Yeah, I reckon I do."

"Then I hope everything works out the way you want."

"Well, thanks. You know, there's only three days until the killer tries to strike again. Why don't you come over and spend the night with me and my girls that night, just to be on the safe side? We'd love to have you, and I'll make you a home-cooked meal like you ain't ever had before, complete with my special recipe banana nut bread."

"I'll be fine on my own, but I'd love to take a rain check for the meal, if you don't mind. And speaking of your banana nut bread," she dug around in her purse, then withdrew an index card. "I wrote the information down for the jacket. They've got them on sale now, and they still have them in yellow, so you should go ahead and place your order."

"Thanks!" Etta snatched the card and grinned enough to display gold tooth. "Guess that means I'll have to give you my recipe, huh?"

"That's what it means."

"Tell you what, I'll call you with it. I could try to recite it from memory, and I might get it right, but I don't want to leave anything out, since you've been so sweet to give me the jacket information. You've even got the item number on here." She tapped the card. "This should be a cinch to order."

"Well, if it isn't, let me know. I'm a savvy Internet shopper."

"I think I'll manage. Hang on a second." She disappeared into her office, then returned with a notepad and a pen. "Jot your cell number, and I'll call you with the recipe from home."

Angel wrote the number and handed the pad back to the sweet lady. "Thanks."

"No, thank you. CiCi is gonna love the new coat."

"I'm sure she will. I'll see you tomorrow, Etta." Angel headed toward the lobby.

"See you in the morning." Etta jangled back to her room.

Angel stepped outside, and the heat enveloped her completely. Three days until May 10th, the date the killer would strike again. She'd done everything she could to stop it, but he'd still try to accomplish his goal this Friday. She hoped he tried to accomplish it with her. FBI special agents weren't trained to merely shoot. If she withdrew her weapon, she'd shoot to kill, and she wouldn't lose one minute's sleep over it.

"Angel," Lexie neared the building with John by her side, "Where are you going?"

"Back to Cami Talton's and Vickie Jones' houses. And I know, we've gone over both with a fine-toothed comb, but I don't think it'll hurt to give it another go. How did Hannah's family take the news?"

John had offered to deliver the news that one of the bodies they found had been verified as Hannah's. He'd known the Sharps in the past and had felt the news would come easier from him. Lexie had gone along to provide a female counterpart. Angel's team used the same procedure to deliver bad news, and she'd been impressed with John for suggesting Lexie accompany him for the trip.

Lexie frowned. "It didn't go very well."

"They claimed she died the moment she slept with Finley without the bond of marriage, rather than on the day when she was brutally murdered." John's anger at their response bristled through his words.

"They acted like they didn't care. But I believe I did see a tear in her mother's eye." Lexie's eyes were tear-stained, and Angel suspected her cousin had shed more tears for Hannah than her own parents.

"Well I hope so." Angel had never understood parents that didn't give their children unconditional love. She may not have had her parents growing up, but she'd received that from Aunt Carol, and from her cousin. "So what are you doing now?"

"Meeting with Pierce." Lexie pushed the strap of her computer bag up on her shoulder. "He wants to get another detailed round of information out to the public before Friday. We're doing a major media blitz requesting all women who fit the criteria to leave town."

"According to Etta, the DJ on the talk radio station has jumped on it."

John nodded. "Yeah, that's what we heard."

Lexie stepped closer to Angel. They'd started spending more time talking one-on-one, since everyone assumed they were discussing the case. Both of them looked forward to the day they could announce their relationship to the city, and announce that they'd defeated the man who killed Angel's mother. "Did you go see Granddaddy yesterday?"

"Yeah. He's doing okay, but still watching the news nonstop. He knows it's about time for something to happen."

"I've decided to head to Valdosta on Thursday, while John stays here to watch after you."

"I think I can manage on my own," Angel shook her head when Lexie tried to interject, "but I'm not going to turn down your offer. Even though I caught the Oklahoma City guy by playing bait, it didn't go as smoothly as I'd have liked, and I think having an extra gun hiding out in my hotel room wouldn't hurt at all."

"That's the smartest thing I've heard you say in years."

Angel snorted. "Well, I'm glad I've impressed you. Now, I'm going to check out the last two crime scenes again, just in case we missed something."

"We didn't," John said. "But go ahead."

Angel tossed her hair in mock defiance, then stalked toward her Tahoe.

He watched her, the confident gait, the long blonde hair, the air of control. Little did she know, he still mastered his domain. And hers. FBI agent or not, Angel Jackson had sinned, and she'd pay for her crime. He knew she carried a child, no matter that she hadn't confessed the fact.

She passed his car in the parking area.

He smiled and waved.

She waved back.

Foolish woman, trying to claim power that wasn't hers and believing she could save herself from her destiny. She couldn't. No one could. And no one could stop him, no matter how hard they tried or how close they came to the truth.

John Tucker and Lexie McCain stopped shy of the entry to the police station. The detective turned toward her and leaned in, said something close to her face, and she smiled. Then he tucked a blonde curl behind her ear and stroked his finger down the column of her throat.

They were disgusting. He held his breath as Tucker said

something else to her, then brushed a kiss on her forehead before they entered the station. He knew Tucker had been staying at Lexie's house, knew they sinned. If only Lexie McCain were the chosen one, he wouldn't have any question about who his next victim would be. Angel Jackson intrigued, but Lexie mesmerized. She'd create riveting power. He felt it when he watched her speak, sensed it in the way she moved. Her child would hold great power.

If only the rules were different, he'd remove John Tucker from the picture. But rules were rules, and in his case, they weren't made to be broken.

*Logan Finley. Logan. Finley.*

"That didn't count." Finley refused to hand Hannah over, even when the idiot knew what had to happen. Logan became an obstacle, and he had to be removed. Since then, it hadn't happened again. Every sacrifice had been provided without interference.

*What about the other two?*

He wiped a drop of sweat from his temple and swore aloud. He wouldn't feel guilty over Finley. His death didn't break the rules. Killing him had been removal of a necessary evil. He wouldn't think about the others. How could he have completed his plan if they told what they knew? Both of them would have told; they said so. He'd been so certain they—of all people—would understand. But they didn't, and he had no choice.

He cranked his vehicle, started from the lot, and headed out of Macon. Within fifteen minutes, he'd returned to the place where he'd spent so much time as a child. Police tape curled around the trees, forming a thin plastic yellow barricade that kept vehicles from the path.

Parking the car, he got out and inhaled the scent of the forest, of damp leaves and mulch and earth and death. Oh, he knew the scent of death, strong and powerful and sweet. Sweet victory. He'd claimed it first right here, with Hannah and Logan, so long ago. It'd been so easy. He asked them to meet him, so he could wish them well on their journey and show there were no hard feelings. He even told them he wanted to give them some cash to help them get on their feet when they began a new life for themselves and for the baby Hannah carried.

And they'd come, with Hannah even daring to wear the locket *he'd* given her, the symbol of what should have been, of what they'd shared before she betrayed him with Logan Finley.

Stupid. They were so naïve, so trusting. Didn't they realize they'd sinned? Didn't they know they had to pay for that sin? Retribution.

A soft rain started to fall. He turned his head toward the sky and let it bathe his flesh. He'd been so hot, heated by the thoughts of evil, and the cool kiss of Heaven rewarded him, washed the filth away. He'd always loved rain.

Blinking through the water, he looked toward the hill where John Tucker and Lexie McCain had huddled, caressing each other as they stood and viewed the expanse of the Fellowship's lands. Had they been awestruck by the power here? Had they even realized the magnitude? And of what had occurred on this very land?

"Hey, you're back?"

He swallowed hard, then turned on his heel to view Richard Barnes walking up the pathway toward the street. Barnes ducked beneath the yellow tape, popped back up on this side, and grinned. "Nasty weather, huh?"

"Yeah. Nasty."

"Seems everywhere I go, you're right behind me." Barnes stretched his grin into round cheeks as though he found something funny about surveying the place where believers had rejoiced, and sinners had died.

"I didn't see your car."

"Parked over the hill there." Barnes jerked his head to the right. "We decided to look a little farther out, see if we saw anything the others may have missed. I'm wanting a promotion, you know, and I figured finding something extra to help them solve this case wouldn't hurt." Richard stepped closer, chuckled, then slapped his arm. "I didn't realize you were so buff. You work out, huh?"

"Yeah, I do. You said 'we.' Who else is here?"

"Just Omar and Sal. Omar is over there in the meadow. See?" Richard pointed toward the flat field bordering the forest, where a cop wandered around the edge of the trees looking more like he wanted to stay out of the rain rather than solve a crime. "Sal is checking out the area surrounding the old altar, where the bodies were found."

"Oh."

"You going back in to view the scene? I'll go with you. We can see if Sal has found anything worth noting."

"Nah, that's okay. I'd rather take a look on my own. Guess I'm like you, trying to find additional clues. I'll steer clear of Sal and let him do the same."

"Right, get more clues. I knew that's what you were doing. That's your thing, after all, right? Getting information."

"Right."

"Richard, I haven't found anything, and it's coming down like a Bible plague! I say we head out!" Omar yelled.

Like a Bible plague. What a unique reference. Perhaps Omar knew the law of the land, this land in particular.

"All right!" Richard grinned again. "Guess we're heading out. He's right. This rain is working up." He slung water off the side of his face to emphasize his point. "You still going in? Wanna tell Sal we're in the car, where it's dry?" His eyes squinted through the water.

"Yeah, I'll tell Sal."

"Okay."

"Hey, Barnes?"

The cop stopped walking. "Yeah?"

"I thought you were watching the doctor's place."

"I was, but there's no reason to anymore."

"Why's that?"

"All the females fitting the description have left town." Richard laughed. "Can't say as I blame them, but for the past two weeks, there haven't been any patients who aren't brunette, black-haired or redheaded. Well, except for the profiler, and we know he's not gonna touch her."

"Why is that?"

"Everyone knows those FBI agents know their way with a gun. And besides, she flat out said she wants to do him in." He winked, made a clicking sound with his tongue. "I think the only way he'll go for Angel Jackson is if she's the last blonde, single, pregnant lady in Macon." He laughed out loud. "Then again, with all of them jumping ship, she may be."

Thunder boomed in the distance, and the rain grew as thick as a water wall.

"I'm outta here. Tell Sal to get to the car. If I were you, I wouldn't wait too long about heading out too. But do whatever ya want."

"Thanks." He watched Richard jitter away in the rain like a nervous little kid. "I will. In fact, I'll do exactly what I want."

But he wasn't going to do what he wanted today. He *wanted* to go back to the now open grave and remember the day so long ago when he put Hannah and Logan Finley inside. But that desire died when Sal's scream echoed through the woods and rain.

"Barnes! Get over here! We've got another body!"

# CHAPTER SEVENTEEN

Angel stormed into Ed Pierce's office without the common courtesy of knocking. He didn't deserve courtesy today; he deserved a throttling. What had he been thinking?

His head jerked to attention, and he stopped typing on his computer keyboard. "Jackson. You may be FBI, but this had better be important for you to barge in uninvit—"

"What were you thinking?" Her voice sounded calm in comparison to her anger. "And tell me you're not communicating with him now."

"With who?" He didn't sound convincing. He knew, and he'd give her the truth about it soon, before he blew their case—correction, *her* case—out of the water. "Want to tell me what you're talking about, Agent Jackson?"

"I'm talking about this." She held emails from the techies at the field office. Emails that identified the website of the "New Fellowship," as well as the transcript of this morning's heated chat session, a session between TRUTHLUVR and PROTECT&SRV.

He took the paper, scanned the text. "So your guys found the website they use."

"Yes." She sat in the closest chair, scooted up to his desk to face him head on. "And they also learned the identity of most of the users, courtesy of their home computers."

"Most of the users?" He frowned at the confrontational text between the two screen names on the page.

"Yeah. See, the techies explained it to me today. It didn't take a whole lot of searching online to find those who called themselves the 'New Fellowship of Macon,' or NFOM, for short. Then they set about defining the users who had logged on over the past four months, assuming the killer would want to stay aware of the group as he planned—and committed—his murders."

"I see."

"It didn't take a lot of effort to get the Internet Protocol addresses for the computers, but identifying their MAC addresses, the Media Access Control for each individual computer, proved a little more difficult. In fact, one of the computers had its MAC address so encrypted, the guys in Atlanta still haven't identified the machine's location. But they will."

"Which user?" Ed's tense jaw line said he knew.

"TRUTHLUVR. Our killer. But the guys had no trouble identifying his online nemesis, PROTECT&SRV. The computer is registered to Edward Allen Pierce. Sound familiar?"

"I wasn't a member of the original Fellowship. I'm not the man you're after; he is." He pointed to TRUTHLUVR's text on the page and let the pad of his first finger thump it. "And the New Fellowship isn't anything like the old. We're focused on serving Macon, providing help to charities and promoting a unified glorification to God. That's it. No 'power in children' and no condemnation for marriage outside of the Fellowship body. Those things have changed. It's a very positive, very private organization, and I've been blessed to be a part of it. I don't want this lunatic ruining what we have."

"But he is ruining it, whether you like it or not. And he'll continue to do so, unless we stop him. By keeping your communications with him from the task force, you're withholding evidence, Captain, any way you look at it."

"I didn't want to betray the Fellowship. I couldn't. Judith and I hadn't ever gotten into religion before, but we had always felt we wanted something. Our neighbor is a member and introduced us to it. The Fellowship is online now, but we know each other and help to communicate the strong values of the organization throughout the city by supporting charities, formulating neighborhood peacekeeping organizations, you know, the things behind the scene that keep Macon safe, but don't involve the police force. Let's face it; cops can only do so much. It's people who get the job done and give the community the face of peace or violence. But I never realized *he* was online until this morning. In fact, I planned to tell the task force about the interaction, even if I hadn't determined when or how."

"Well, I'm here now." She pointed to herself. "Tell away. And you can start by explaining who this 'Tiny Tina' person is."

"That's the thing. I have no idea."

Angel took the pages from him and read aloud, "TRUTHLUVR: I know who you are, and you can't stop me." She peered at Pierce over the top of the paper. "*Does* he know who you are?"

The captain shook his head. "He thinks he does, but his comments say he doesn't. I have no idea who he thinks he's talking to."

"Well, it's a cop, and a cop who would know this 'tiny Tina' person."

"I gathered that much, but I've never heard of anyone called 'Tiny Tina' in Macon, or anywhere else, for that matter. I planned to ask the task force if anyone knew."

"When you decided to tell the task force of your involvement, you mean?"

"I *was* going to tell them."

"He says that he can hurt you again, if you don't get out of his way. Then he asks if you think Tiny Tina pulled that trigger. And you have no idea who this Tina person is?"

"None whatsoever."

"Well, someone around here does, and I'd say it's about high time we find out who that someone is."

After John received the Captain's call that there had been a new development in the case, he and Lexie wasted no time returning to the station. He held a large, black umbrella over the two of them as they hurried toward the main entrance, where Etta Green opened the door and urged them inside. Her thick ringlets whipped around her face as she pulled the door closed against the heavy rain. "Well?" She grabbed the umbrella, gave it a good shake to remove the excess water, then plopped it in a plastic stand by the door.

"Well, what?" Though John knew Etta could spot a break in a case as well as the greenest field cop.

"Well, what's going on down the hall?" She raised her dark penciled brows while she waited for his response. "And don't you dare say it's nothing, because I've never seen Captain Pierce looking so tense before in my life, and that includes the day one of the guys arrested his nephew for drugs."

"We don't know," Lexie said.

John added, "But we will find out."

"Do that. And when you find out, tell me."

"We will." John led Lexie down the hall toward the conference room. "You sure you're ready to deal with whatever they've found out, after everything you've gone through this afternoon?"

Her eyes narrowed. "If you're sure you're ready to deal with whatever they've found out, after everything *you've* been through this afternoon."

He smirked. "Is there anything you're afraid of, Ms. McCain?"

"Yes, there is. But the one thing I'm not afraid of...is facing that fear head on."

He turned the knob on the conference room door. "Then I'd say we're ready for anything." But upon entering, and hearing the name that had haunted him for years, John wondered if he'd spoken too soon.

"So, we need to know who she is." Angel directed the question to Zed. "This 'Tiny Tina' he refers to."

Zed Naylor and Ed Pierce, the only other task force members in the room, turned toward John and Lexie.

Angel acknowledged their arrival with a brief nod. "We're discussing an update in our information on the killer. We've called and left messages for Sims and Marker to get here too, but we're not going to wait for the whole task force. This needs our immediate attention."

"I told you," Pierce answered, "I haven't heard that name before today."

"No." Zed looked at John as he spoke. "No, you haven't, but

I have. Tucker, you better sit down for this one."

The room seemed to close in around John as he moved toward Angel and the paper she held. "What is that?"

"It's a long story, but the meat of it is that Captain Pierce is a member of the 'New Fellowship,' which is an off-shoot of the original, but without the outlandish notions. Is that fair enough to say?"

"Fair enough." Pierce didn't seem happy.

"And this New Fellowship has a website where members can share news, inspiration and all, as well as chat with each other in online chat rooms." She lifted several sheets of paper. "This transcript, taken from one of those chat rooms this morning, shows where Captain Pierce talked to someone with the screen name of TRUTHLUVR. It appears this TRUTHLUVR is our killer."

"We've found him?" Lexie whispered.

"No, not yet. The techies are working on it, but he used a public computer at an Internet Café on the south side of Macon this morning, so the trace didn't do us any good. At previous times, however, he logged on from a computer system encrypted well. The guys at Quantico believe it's his home system, but it's going to take a bit of time to break through the encrypted information." She crossed her arms and looked resolute. "But they'll get the job done, I have no doubt. However, right now what we need to figure out is who our killer *thought* he talked to. He believed Pierce, or rather PROTECT&SRV, was someone else."

"Protect and serve?" John looked at the captain.

"My screen name. I didn't think it'd hurt for them to realize they had a cop who believed in the Fellowship."

"Until today, TRUTHLUVR had never participated in an active chat session, though he had several recorded sessions where he'd logged into various chat rooms on the site," Angel confirmed.

"He lurked, but we have a lot of lurkers in the Fellowship." Pierce shrugged. "So we never questioned when he entered the chat room. Lots of folks enter and merely observe."

Angel huffed out a breath. "Okay, in any case, he started chatting today with Pierce about the previous murders. He stated he followed the Supreme One's plan. But when Pierce told him his interpretation of the plan was skewed, TRUTHLUVR sent a message of pure venom, blasting the entire New Fellowship as"—she read from the page—"hypocritical whoremongers, and then he ended with a single sentence about this name."

John's throat tightened. "Read the sentence."

"Wait. Agent Jackson needs to know who Tina was, so she can—"

"No," John said. "Don't sugarcoat anything for me, Zed. I want to know what he said about that day."

"What day?" Lexie asked, but John remained firm in his decision to stay quiet until he heard what the killer knew about the day his father died.

"It says," Angel held the page out as she read, "Stay out of my way, officer, or I may have to hurt you again. Did you really think it was Tiny Tina who pulled that trigger?"

"No way." Ryan Sims entered the room. "Where did you get that? And what do you think it means?"

"It's from an online chat session I had this morning," Pierce informed the last two members of the task force, as Lou Marker took his seat. "A chat with our killer."

"How did you manage that?" Marker asked. "And why are we just finding out?"

"I—" Pierce started, but Angel intervened.

"We don't have time for all of that now. What we have to concentrate on is dealing with the situation and determining what this means. You all know more about this Tiny Tina person than I do, and I'd appreciate it if you would clue me in."

John cleared his throat then spoke with a voice that sounded strong and secure, betraying the fury pulsating through his veins. "She's the woman who killed my father."

The entire room fell silent. Angel read the sentence again in little more than a whisper. "Did you really think it was Tiny Tina who pulled that trigger?"

"I never thought she did it. It was too bizarre, but then all of the evidence said that's what happened." John's words were steady but filled with the emotion, with the memory of losing his father. He'd been with Abby and several of their friends at a local drive-in watching the movie *An Officer and a Gentleman*. He'd been nineteen, and none of the guys their age wanted to go, claiming it too girly, but the females in the group had prevailed. Odd that he remembered what movie played when the cop car pulled into the drive-in and Zed Naylor delivered the news that his father wasn't coming home. Then again, why wouldn't he remember the movie's title? It summed up the man who died that night. An officer and a gentleman...Milton Tucker.

"What happened?" Angel asked. "Or what did the evidence show?"

Zed's face looked grim. "Want me to tell her?"

"No, I will." John couldn't recall sitting down, but he had, and everyone's attention focused on him at the table. He sensed Lexie's presence in the next chair. She'd moved closer but hadn't said a word. No one did. In fact, the room fell silent as he began to speak.

"On July 15th, 1988, like I said, I was at the drive-in with Abby and some of our friends. Dad wasn't on duty, and Aaron Rainwater called him at home. Aaron and Dad were fishing buddies and Fellowship deacons, so when Aaron called him over saying he and Ernestine, his wife, were having trouble, Dad went. Aaron and Ernestine were known for their heated disagreements, but they always worked things out until that night. Anyway, Dad left me a note saying where he'd gone then drove to their home on his own.

From what the crime scene guys put together, Ernestine shot Aaron, then waited for Dad. When he got there, she fired at him, killing him with a single bullet to the chest, then she turned the gun on herself." John paused, his throat tense at how vivid the memory replayed in his brain. "It didn't make sense to anyone. They were always fighting, but Aaron and Ernestine had never taken it that far, never had any weapons involved before. But the evidence showed a triple homicide and suicide case."

"Tiny Tina?" Angel questioned.

"It was Aaron's nickname for Ernestine." He couldn't believe it. If this guy—TRUTHLUVR—had told the truth, then the same man who killed Abby killed his father. John's

stomach knotted at the realization. He'd always known that
Ernestine hadn't pulled that trigger, had sensed it deep in his
gut. The killer had forced Aaron to call his friend over—had
Aaron at gunpoint during that call, or worse, had Tina at the
end of the gun—then he shot Aaron, Milton Tucker and then
Ernestine Rainwater had fallen victim...and accused. John
slammed his fist against the table.

"We'll get him." Angel's eyes blazed with certainty. "We're
close, and he's slipping up. The fact that he posted to an online
chat group says he's got a few chinks in his armor. The fact
that he's talking about previous murders, and providing new
information to help us in our investigation, says that those
chinks can become gaping holes. We're going to get him this
time.

"We will—" John started, but stopped when Etta Green
entered without knocking.

"Barnes just reported in." Her voice quaked with the
eagerness to share her news. "They found another body, not far
from where Hannah Sharp and Logan Finley were buried. And
they think it's"—she paused to catch her breath—"Brother
Moses."

He needed to vomit, needed it so much that he could taste
the bitter bile working up his throat, but he couldn't let the
impulse have its way. Not now. He had to pull it together and
act as interested and as intent as everyone else combing the old
gathering grounds.

Why had he put Moses here?

Because that's where he belonged, in the location where his
pulpit used to stand, feet from the altar, and feet from where
Hannah Sharp and Logan Finley had been buried. It'd seemed
so right back then, so symbolic. Brother Moses had preached a
fire and brimstone sermon that said everyone outside of the
Fellowship was going to hell and would be punished if they
didn't "see the way and follow the plan." That sermon had
prompted him to stay after the remaining members left the
gathering grounds.

He'd decided that Brother Moses deserved to know what a
good and faithful servant he'd been and told him in detail about

the two sinners that he'd buried beneath the Fellowship's altar. Then he'd gone on to describe how he'd killed the other women as well and how he believed his plan had come from the Supreme One. He wanted Moses to know that he also believed that the Fellowship needed to show Macon that they meant business and that sinners would pay the price.

He'd expected Brother Moses to praise him, to honor him and bestow upon him a title such as his own. A new name for the most faithful of the entire Fellowship. Nothing as grand as Moses or Supreme One, but something along the line of deacon, perhaps. A deacon at twenty years old; he could handle the notoriety and responsibility of that.

It didn't happen. Moses said he'd taken God's vengeance into his own hands and said he wanted to discuss the "revelation," as he called it, later at his home. But he'd planned an ambush. Moses had called Deacon Tucker, but Milton Tucker was on the job and couldn't talk about the "unique situation" until later.

It'd taken less than two minutes to decide to kill Brother Moses and send him to his maker. The true Supreme One would understand a necessary means to achieve the appropriate end.

But now, as he watched the crime scene unit excavating Brother Moses' body from the muddy grave in the midst of a torrent of rain, he began to wonder why he had given Moses the courtesy of having his personal cross, an ivory piece trimmed in gold that he always carried and displayed throughout his sermons, on his chest. It'd taken Barnes less than a second to recognize the piece and predict that the body belonged to the Fellowship's former leader.

He blinked, wiped the rain from his face. No. There was a reason all of this happened. A test to verify his worthiness of the monumental responsibility that had been bestowed upon him by the Supreme One. In order to pass the test, he had to convince this group scanning his personal burial ground that he also wanted to find the killer and make him pay.

Another trickle of bile trudged up his throat. He swallowed it. Yes, he needed to vomit, but he needed something else even more. He needed to play the part of a concerned citizen of the community. And then, he needed to kill.

Lexie focused to read the last line she'd typed on her screen, but the words blurred together and made her head throb in agony. The most important story she'd ever covered, the one that would be seen more than any other since every news station in the south waited to pick it up, and she couldn't tamp back on her nerves enough to finish the piece.

The lead line of her story screamed at her.

*One. More. Day.*

Why couldn't they have caught him before now? And why did she feel so sick? She'd tossed her breakfast at the police station. The task force had reconvened a final time to go over all of the new information. Now it appeared that the Sunrise Killer had murdered Brother Moses and that he, not Ernestine Rainwater, murdered John's father. The question regarding those two murders was—why? Had Brother Moses and Milton Tucker been on the verge of learning the truth about the killer? Or did they know and threaten to tell the authorities? What had happened way back then?

*That* was what the task force, particularly John Tucker, wanted most to know. But they couldn't investigate to learn the answers; they didn't have time. Angel had directed their primary objective remain the same—pinpoint where the killer would strike next and stop the murder.

The mingled combination of fierce determination, anger and pain on John's face had caused Lexie's chest and stomach to clench tight, which hadn't been a good thing. She ran from the room with her hand over her mouth, barely making it to the bathroom in time, then threw up with a vengeance, while Etta Green offered soothing words and cool cloths.

Had she ever gotten so upset she'd vomited? No, never. In fact, she'd always been a real trouper when it came to holding it all together. But this morning, not only had she not held it all together, she couldn't even hold her head upright. How pathetic. And now that she had every bit of information for the final piece, the segment that summarized each of the killer's victims, she couldn't make her stomach settle down enough to type the words.

# PROFILED

She knew the truth; her worry for Angel and her baby consumed her now. What if the killer took another person she loved? How could she live if something happened to Angel? The extent of her worry was actually making her sick, and she couldn't control it. She closed her eyes. *God, you let me save her on the day she was born. Don't let anything happen to her now.*

"You sure you're okay?" Melody Harper's head poked around the side of the cubicle like a turtle peeking from its shell.

Saliva pooled in Lexie's mouth. She did *not* need to think about turtles. But she did. "Excuse me." She darted past Melody and shot toward the bathroom. Since she had no food left to lose, she spent five minutes dry heaving, then splashed her face, rinsed her mouth and headed back to her desk determined to finish her piece.

"McCain, you gonna make it?" Paul entered the tiny cubicle behind her wearing aftershave, something strong. Did he always wear that much? Did he *have* to wear that much?

Lexie's eyes burned, throat convulsed, and she started running again. This time, when she returned, he sat in her chair. He stood, motioned for her to sit. "How much more do you have to go on the story?"

"A lot, but today's the last day to get the information to them, and I've got to finish."

"I know. There's no way I would suggest you quit now, nor is there any way I'd suggest you passing off to another reporter; however, if you don't go to a doctor and get something to help, right now, I'm going to find it necessary to fire you." He jerked his head in a single nod, then pointed to the mock doorway in her cubicle. "And after you get something to help, go home, take the meds, then call Henry when you're ready to tape the segment." He crossed his arms beneath his chest, leaned against her wall and waited.

"The doctor, huh?" She grabbed her purse. "I'm guessing I look as bad as I feel?"

His head tilted, steel gray eyes studied her. "I'm going to ask you something, and I want the truth."

Lexie had no idea what Paul would ask, but his tone told her to prepare for the worst. Melody heard it too, because her typing came to a screeching halt. "What do you want to know?"

Paul cleared his throat. "I pass your house on my way home each night and again each morning. I've seen Tucker's truck."

"You know that he's been seeing me home."

"Listen, what you do away from here is your business. But if you now fit all of the killer's criteria." When Lexie gasped, he continued, "If you're pregnant, McCain..."

"I'm not. He guards the house, in his truck, in the driveway."

"How many times have you tossed it since you got here today?"

"Three, but I must have some kind of bug."

"Actually four," Melody piped in from her cubicle.

"Ms. Harper, don't you have work to do?"

"Yes, sir," she mumbled, but Lexie didn't hear her typing.

"Lexie, if you're pregnant..."

"I'm not. I can't be."

"Are you telling me that Tucker hasn't been spending his nights at your place?"

"He has, but like I said..."

"No." Paul stopped her explanation and pointed toward Melody's cubicle. "We don't need to discuss this further. Go to the doctor. See what's going on. And, if I'm right, you'd better leave town. Today."

"I'm telling the truth." She powered down her computer then left the office walking slowly so she wouldn't upset her nervous stomach.

Climbing in her car, she made a decision that would change her life, change all of their lives. Grateful John was busy making preparations with Angel for tonight's attack, Lexie didn't tell either of them what she planned, but she knew in her heart that she'd made the right decision, the only decision. They expected the killer to go for Angel since she was the only female in town that fit his criteria. They also thought Lexie would leave this afternoon to spend time with her grandfather until they caught the killer.

Yes, she'd go see Granddaddy, since Jackie called saying

he'd asked for her, but she wouldn't stay all day. She'd visit, then return to Macon. Because, Lexie now suspected that the killer would hear that Angel wasn't the only blonde, single and pregnant female in town. She didn't believe in sex outside of marriage, and she hadn't had sex with John. She also didn't believe in lying or deceiving, and she wondered what God would think of what she was about to do.

*Stay with me, God. I'm going to need you today more than ever. Please understand. Please be with me. Don't leave me, Lord.*

She left the parking area and drove the short distance to the doctor's office, not the office Paul had meant, but then again, he hadn't specified. And she hadn't lied to him either; she'd go to the doctor to find out why she was sick.

Within two hours, she'd obtained the results she expected. *Not* pregnant, but she'd been seen going to Dr. Weatherly's office. And John's truck had been seen each night at her home by Paul and, she suspected, by the killer. His tinted windows hid the fact that he sat inside the vehicle, which would work to her advantage now.

During the drive to Valdosta, her queasiness came back with gusto, and she ended up pulling over twice. The timing for the stomach virus or nervous stomach was both horrible and perfect. Horrible, because she felt lousy during the drive to Valdosta and wanted to be home in bed. And perfect, because from all appearances, she *could* be pregnant.

Lexie arrived at Murrell's Assisted Living, exited the car, took a deep breath, and fought the impulse to get sick again due to the smell of full magnolia blossoms. "God, help me." She leaned against the Lexus until she got her bearings.

"Are you okay?"

Lexie turned toward the voice and saw a young man, around Phillip Jr.'s age, walking down the porch steps, then crossing the parking lot toward her. "Stomach bug."

He had sandy hair, long on top and clipped short on the sides. Brown eyes surveyed her with obvious concern, and his mouth formed a definite frown of disapproval. "Granted, I'm not a doctor, but you don't look so good."

She laughed. "No offense, but doctors aren't the only ones

who need good bedside manners, and yours need some work. If I didn't feel bad before, I do now."

His smile claimed his entire face, reminding her even more of her son. How she missed him, and she wouldn't forgive herself if she did something tonight that cost her more time with Phillip, Jr. Or Angel. Or John. But she had to do this to make sure the killer didn't take two more people she loved.

"I'll work on my bedside tactics, should I decide to go pre-med." He grinned. "By the way, I'm Jacob. Jacob Zimmerman."

Lexie's eyes widened. "You're the teen from the local church?"

Another laugh rumbled from his chest. "I am from the church, but I'm in the college program. I'm afraid I look young to the Murrells, and they keep forgetting I'm not one of the teens."

"After you get a certain age, I guess everyone younger looks like a kid. You're here to see my grandfather?"

"I came this morning to see him. Ms. Murrell called me at lunch, though, and told me you were coming this afternoon. Even told me what kind of car you drive, so I could watch for you. This time, I'm here to see you—and to apologize."

"Apologize?" Lexie started walking across the parking lot with Jacob Zimmerman alongside. "What for?"

"Easter morning. Ms. Murrell said she kept meaning to ask me if I knew anything about where your grandfather went, and I hadn't even realized they didn't know he was with me. I should've made certain they knew, but I assumed he told them."

"He talks to you? In sentences?"

"Not all the time, but yeah, sometimes. However, he gets my name confused. Or thinks I'm someone else." He grinned. "That happens a lot with the folks I visit."

"What does he call you?"

"Phillip."

Lexie's chest tightened, and her stomach tensed, but it stayed settled for now. "That's my son. His great-grandson."

"Ms. Murrell told me."

"So where did you take him Easter morning?"

"I didn't know where we were going at first. When I came by to visit him before church, he'd dressed in his suit. I asked where he was going, and he grabbed my hand, then led the way out of the house."

"No one saw you leaving?"

"We went out the side entrance, the one that leads to the garden. At first I thought he wanted to go out by the pond and sit, like the other folks here often do, but he started toward the parking lot and pointed to my keys. I knew it was okay for the residents to leave, so I didn't think it'd hurt to take him where he wanted to go."

"So you took him."

"Yeah. I thought he wanted to go to church, since it was Easter and all, and I thought it'd be nice to take him to the church he wanted to attend. As we started driving, he pointed down the streets where he wanted to go, or told me to turn. So I did."

"And you didn't go to a church?"

"No, but he did have a definite destination. It was kind of far, and that's why we were gone so long, but I think it meant a lot to him."

"Where did you go?" Curiosity made Lexie's skin tingle.

"To a cemetery in Macon. He led me through the plots and we went straight to his wife's grave, your grandmother's grave, I assume. Then he showed me the three tombstones beside hers—the ones for his daughters."

Lexie's throat tightened. She couldn't speak. She'd taken him there a few times, but she didn't even realize he'd remember the way. And he'd wanted to see them on Easter, on the day the killer had murdered again. The same killer that put Aunt Bev in her grave.

"I just wanted to apologize in person for worrying you. Ms. Murrell said she kept meaning to ask me about it, but she never did, not until this morning, or I'd have told you before now. Anyway, I'll try to keep you informed if he wants me to take him anywhere else. I do like visiting with your grandfather, by the way. He's a very tenderhearted man. I could tell by the emotion he had when he visited their graves. He misses them."

Lexie swallowed back the tears.

"Well, I've got a class this afternoon, so I better go. But I wanted to apologize and tell you how much I've enjoyed spending time with him."

"Thank you." She squeezed his hand. "I can't tell you how much that means."

She watched him leave then turned to enter the home.

As she'd told John and Angel, she visited with her grandfather, but instead of staying overnight, she remained for an hour. During that time, she made her grandfather a solemn promise—by tomorrow, the monster that destroyed their lives would be gone.

And then, with Nicholas Truman's nod of agreement beckoning her forward, she returned to her car, returned to Macon and returned to the killer.

John and Angel kept their poker faces in place throughout the morning task force meeting, but by afternoon, after Lexie left to see her grandfather in Valdosta, they were busy preparing a welcome package for the killer. They met with Angel's backup, Federal agents currently positioned strategically down the street and in the lobby of her hotel. They'd planned tonight's arrest perfectly and were beyond ready.

All they needed was the killer.

Angel checked her Glock again, while John scoped out the parking lot from the bedroom window. Because this assignment was potentially long term, the department had splurged, putting her in a two room suite at the hotel. It'd felt expansive and roomy, until tonight. Right now, the two rooms felt as though they were closing in, smothering Angel and her baby.

She thought about the child growing inside of her and of how much her appreciation for life had increased over the past few weeks, since she learned she was now responsible for two lives. Yes, this baby made her the perfect candidate to serve as bait for a killer. But she couldn't deny that there'd been a couple of times over the past few days that she'd felt the desire to do what every other blonde, single and pregnant female in Macon had evidently already done.

Protect her child and get far away from the killer.

But this man killed her mother and nearly took Angel's life before it even began. And if she didn't stop him, he'd kill more mothers—she swallowed, thought of her baby again—and he'd kill more babies.

Angel couldn't let that happen.

But she'd also realized something else since learning about her baby. She wanted desperately to protect the child, but she couldn't do it alone.

While John remained in the darkness of the bedroom scoping out the parking lot, Angel sat on the couch in the main room and closed her eyes.

*It's been years since I've talked to You, years since I felt I needed You.* She swallowed past the urge to cry. There was no time for tears tonight. *I blamed You for what happened to my mother, and I've never given You a chance to have control of my life.* She slid her eyes open, saw that John was still in the other room, then closed them again. *But I'm asking for You to take control now. I may have denied You, may not have wanted to think I need help to accomplish this goal, but there are more people involved now than just me. And I need You, I'm begging You, to help me keep my baby safe tonight. Let us stop this guy, and protect my baby too, God. Please. You know I've never been so scared as I am right now. And I am asking You to help me be strong and help me protect this baby.* She opened her eyes once more, took a deep breath, then slid them closed again. *And God, if we get through this night okay, help me to trust in You the way Lexie does. I've never had You in my life before, but I want You. I want peace. Watch over me tonight, and watch over my child. Amen.*

"Something feels odd." John's voice echoed from the other room, and Angel was glad she had a moment to wipe away the tears that had, in fact, slipped free during her prayer.

"The hotel? I told you, it shouldn't matter to him whether it is a house or a hotel. If he thinks that he is being led to do this by that Supreme One, then he'll think he won't find any obstacles to completing his plan."

John stepped into the main room. They had all of the main lights out, with only the moonlight spilling in through the shades providing any illumination, but she could still see the hard planes of his face etched with undeniable concern. "I'm thinking something isn't right. What if he wasn't as drawn to you as a target as we hoped? What if another blonde, single and pregnant woman is somewhere in the city."

"Do you really think they haven't all left? With all of the warnings, not only from the media, but from their doctor?"

He shook his head. "I don't know. It just seems…"

"Too easy?"

"Maybe."

"It means we're prepared. Besides, we've got our backup outside." She sure hoped that was the reason the setup felt off to John, because she also felt like something wasn't right. Then again, it wasn't midnight yet, so there wasn't any chance of their killer striking here yet.

He looked at her sitting on the couch. "You always this calm?"

"I'm trained to be more calm as tension increases. Let's just say the tension is at a fever pitch." And she was glad she appeared calm. Inside, she was anything but.

He moved to the window, fingered the shades and looked out. "I'm still not certain your guys can watch this place and be discreet enough if our killer ends up being a cop."

"They're good. Haven't lost a profiler yet." She tried to put his concern at ease, but she'd wondered the same thing. This killer was sharp, methodical and strategic. He'd gotten away with this bizarre scenario for twenty-eight years. But Angel hoped his ego came back to haunt him this time. He undoubtedly thought that, with the Supreme One on his side, he was untouchable. And she hoped he showed up here tonight believing that.

And finding himself in the crosshairs.

John's attention zeroed in on Angel's hand, draped over the side of the couch, thrumming against the soft material. "You think something's not right too, don't you?"

Her confident smile slipped a fraction. "It's gone too smoothly. I want to think it's because we've done our job, but this guy is smart. And would a smart guy come after me now? But, if there is no other potential victim in Macon, and assuming he's counted Macon as part of the rule scenario he's developed, then it seems logical he'd have to come after me, right?" She wanted words of wisdom, of assurance.

John had none to offer. "How many serial killers have been known for their logic?"

"He's not coming here, Tucker. I can feel it. But I truly believe I'm the only target left in town. He *has* to come."

"Maybe he doesn't believe you're actually pregnant."

"I have a file at Dr. Weatherly's office that has me three months pregnant. And I've tossed my lunch every day, and anyone who has seen me running to the bathroom at the station knows I wasn't faking that."

"Maybe he hasn't been at the station. Maybe he's one of the guys that fits the profile, but he's further from the case than we thought. There are others who fit the profile, you know."

"Like?"

"Elijah Lewis, for one. That photographer has popped up in odd places several times in this investigation already. And I'm sure there are others close to the case in that type of capacity that we may not have considered closely enough."

She knew he was grasping at straws, but she wasn't going to point out the fact. "Elijah is the one who started the pregnancy rumor in the first place."

"Still feels like something's off."

A sick feeling washed over Angel, and she didn't think it was because she was about to toss her stomach. "What time is it?"

They'd been sitting in the dark since 9:00, and the time seemed to drone on like an eternity. "Five past midnight. It's the day. You should move to the bedroom."

She did, climbing beneath the covers while John disappeared in the darkest corner of the room and waited. They both sat silent in the darkness, neither knowing what to say. The day had come. The killer would strike *if* he found a target. What if all other females fitting the description hadn't left town? What if he knew which one, or ones, stayed? What if he stood outside another person's house right now and prepared to fulfill his goal, accomplish his mission, claim another mother and child?

*God, be with us. Please.* Angel couldn't believe she was turning to Him now, but then again, even through the years she'd denied Him, she'd believed He was there. She merely thought He didn't care about her. But now she wanted Him to care, not only about her, but also about her baby. *Protect us.*

"I'm glad Lexie's safe," John whispered into the night.

The ringing of Angel's cell phone made her pulse triple.

"Answer it." His blunt demand highlighted the intensity of his apprehension. "Hurry."

She snatched the phone from the bedside table and wondered—hoped, prayed—that she was about to learn the killer had been caught. "Jackson."

John watched as Angel grabbed at her phone. He held his breath and wondered if the caller on the other end was about to inform them that the killer had been caught. Was the nightmare already over?

"Etta?" Angel's confusion was evident in her tone. Why would Etta be calling her now?

He took a step toward Angel. "Tell her you can't talk."

"Etta, I'll get the recipe from you another time. No, Lexie had to go out of town. If she's not answering your calls, she's in a dead zone." She paused. "You saw her when? No, I don't think that's possible."

John's back bristled. Where had Etta seen Lexie? And how could she have seen her if Lexie left this afternoon, right after she got off work?

The lighted display on Angel's phone illuminated her face, and he saw her shock. "Etta, are you sure? Are you absolutely sure?"

He stared at Angel. Something *had* gone wrong and it had to do with Lexie.

"Yeah, do that. And we'll get right over there." Angel hung up the phone, grabbed her gun and raced for the door. "Come on!"

John followed her from the room and sprinted after her toward the side exit of the hotel and toward her car, with the Feds from the lobby right behind them. "What did she say?"

"I'm not the intended victim. Lexie is."

# CHAPTER EIGHTEEN

Lexie washed her face. Nothing different tonight, she'd follow her evening ritual: wash face, brush teeth, comb hair, everything the same as the nights when she didn't expect a killer.

Her decision had been easy to make when she realized that her stomach bug—and the fact that John's truck had been outside her home every night—made her perfect in the killer's eyes. Blonde. Single.

And supposedly pregnant.

The fact that she'd asked for a pregnancy test at Dr. Weatherly's and then left her doctor's receipt on her desk at work didn't hurt. The receipt showed a pregnancy test had been administered. It didn't, however, provide the results.

Lexie had placed the receipt out in plain sight and then left the rest to Melody. True to form, Melody wasted no time. Paul called Lexie in Valdosta and told her to stay put. He also said he wouldn't tell Tucker about the baby, but said she'd better tell him, since Melody had already broadcasted it to the entire town.

On Lexie's way back to Macon from Valdosta, she decided to make certain the killer knew he had a new target. She went to the drug store closest to the police station, in case he was on the task force, or a cop, as Angel suspected. Then she bought all three brands of pregnancy tests.

Last but not least, she returned to Dr. Weatherly's office with questions about "her condition." True, she'd only asked the doctor how long she thought the stomach virus would last, but those in the waiting room, as well as anyone watching, would have seen her at the doctor's office.

John and Angel had been secluded in her hotel all afternoon with the additional federal agents standing guard outside. Believing Lexie had left town hours ago, they prepared for the killer's strike. Little did they know, so did she. She'd saved Angel from this killer twenty-eight years ago, and she didn't want to give him another chance to take her away, especially since Angel had a precious baby on the way. And Angel had acted different lately, talked more about life and the baby. She suspected that Angel was finally finding God.

*Let me save her again, Lord. Give her the chance to know You, love You, the way I do.*

She finished scrubbing her face then brushed her teeth. No reason to have the gun yet. He wouldn't come until the chosen day, and that day wouldn't occur for—she looked at the clock—twelve more minutes.

Leaning over the sink, she pulled cool water into her mouth, swished it around and rinsed. Same old, same old. Nothing different than normal. If the killer could see her now, he'd see her getting ready for bed. No big deal.

She sighed, picked up a bottle of leave-in conditioner and sprayed it over her blonde waves, the signal of purity according to the Fellowship and something the killer required in his victims. Good. In his eyes, if her trips to the doctor today worked, Lexie met every requirement.

Stroke by stroke, she pulled the comb through her hair and watched the thick waves loosen with the silky substance. She finished and placed the comb back on the counter. Then she looked in the mirror. A blonde, single and supposedly pregnant female in a silky white nightgown stared back. She produced the picture-perfect image of innocence...with an exceptional aim and a quest for vengeance. "Ready."

The verses John quoted about God's vengeance played through her head and she wondered...was she trying to "play God" by taking matters into her own hands? What if this wasn't His plan for taking care of the killer? Would He approve of what she was doing? Would He help her succeed?

*God, please forgive me. And please, God, stay with me now. Protect me, Lord.*

She looked at the clock. 11:55. She'd purchased several indiglo nightlights and had placed them throughout the house. They cast the interior of her home in an eerie blue haze.

Moving to the bedroom, she flipped the switch on her radio and listened to the DJ on the talk news station. While he continued with the same topic he'd featured all week, the Sunrise Killer, Lexie slipped her hand beneath the pillow and touched the gun.

"As I mentioned earlier, we are mere minutes away from the day the Sunrise Killer is anticipated to attempt another murder. If we've done our job right with the media, and I believe we have, this killer won't be able to complete his goal. Why? Because, thanks to broadcasts like this, as well as local television and newspapers throughout the Macon area, women who fit his criteria have left the city limits."

*Be with me, Lord.*

"We've had several women call in from various parts of Georgia, as well as neighboring states, letting us know they not only left Macon during the time period of this scheduled attack, but they will not return until the killer has been caught. Due to safety issues, we won't release the names of our callers; however, we can allow you to listen to some of their feelings regarding the fear this killer has instilled in all of Macon."

Lexie listened to a blonde, pregnant and single female from Macon describe how she'd driven to Tallahassee to visit friends and family until this "horrible man is taken care of." Then she heard another hiding out in Atlanta. After her description of how scared she'd been in Macon and how she hurt for this year's two previous victims, the announcer broke back in.

"One minute until midnight. Please, all Macon residents, take extreme care during the next twenty-four hours. Although we believe we've done everything in our power to eliminate his chances to find a victim, we have no idea how this killer thinks or what he'll do when provoked. And if you see anyone or anything that seems suspicious at all, please dial 911."

The small wooden clock above Lexie's mantle chimed at the stroke of midnight, and her hand curled around the handle on the gun. She hoped he didn't wait too long.

"We'll continue with our taped conversations from women who've left Macon, but our phone lines are open if you have any thoughts or concerns you'd like included in our broadcast. Again, we're covering Macon's Sunrise Killer..."

Lexie leaned over and twisted the dial on the radio, dropping the sound of the DJ to a light whisper. She wanted the company of his voice so she didn't feel quite so alone, but she also wanted to hear the killer's arrival.

Her ears pricked at a sound that seemed close. In her home? Or in this room?

One of the things she loved about owning an older home, those tiny creaks and groans that occurred with the house's "settling," would be her undoing tonight. How would she tell the difference between the sounds of her house and the sounds of an intruder?

She took a deep, calming breath and lay still in the darkness as her clock struck the last chime of midnight.

Silence.

Lexie waited, keeping her eyes open as long as possible before blinking. Straining her ears to hear every tiny sound, every creak, every breath.

*Breath?*

Had she heard someone breathing? An exhalation, like a soft mist within her room? She scanned the bedroom and despised her decision to purchase the indiglo lights. The blue haze made it appear like something straight out of a horror movie and sent a frisson of pure terror down her spine.

Her hand tightened around the gun. The red digital numbers of the clock beside her bed glared in direct contrast with the blue haze filling the room and identified four minutes past twelve. Lexie's pulse drummed in her ears way too fast, and way too hard, but she couldn't make her heartbeat slow. Breathe in, breathe out. Watch. Wait. Hand on gun.

Angel's words from the firing range filled her head. Time and time again, her cousin had instructed her on what to do. At the time, Lexie joked and laughed about Angel's serious instructions. She didn't laugh now. Oh no, she remembered, and planned to adhere to every word.

*"One of the first things an FBI agent is taught is you only*

*shoot to kill. If you draw your weapon, you have made the decision to shoot. And if you have made the decision that the situation is serious enough to warrant shooting, you have decided it is serious enough to take a life."*

Lexie blinked, then popped her eyes back open. Without a doubt, serious enough. But could she, would she, pull the trigger?

More silence. Then another sound. A little louder than the one before. He's here. Or is he?

She would hear him breaking in, right? Maybe, or maybe not.

Lexie kept her breathing low and steady so she could focus on the sounds. She strained her ears.

A bang echoed from the front of her house, and Lexie's hand squeezed around the handle, her pulse skyrocketed on its own accord, and a hot wash of adrenaline surged through her veins. She steadied her wrist, moved the gun forward beneath the sheets.

Another loud sound, then another. Then rapid banging in succession.

Then she got it. Knocking. Her eyes blinked while she wondered what to do. Did he knock on the victim's door? Was that why there was never any sign of forced entry? What woman in her right mind would open the door after midnight? The questions spun through her head and made her stomach lurch. Oh no, she would not get sick now. She couldn't.

More knocking. Louder. She pulled the sheets aside, slid her feet from the mattress to the floor and stood with the gun clutched in her hand. No, this wasn't the scenario she'd planned, but even so, she could do it.

She had to.

One step away from the bed, with the cold hardwood floor against her bare feet. Another step. Then another, while the banging grew to a fever high pitch.

Didn't he care if a neighbor heard?

But Lexie's home wasn't all that close to her neighbors' houses, and even if it were, most of her neighbors were elderly and couldn't hear banging on their own doors, much less hers. The crazy thought flitted through her mind as she reached the hallway, took a deep, thick breath and progressed toward the large shadow on the other side of her door.

"Lexie, open the door!"

She stopped. Familiarity rang through the voice, but in her frenzied state, she couldn't place it. She *knew* the killer? But who?

Another step. Then another. She had the gun ready in her right hand. Her left hand stretched forward, primed to unlock and open the door. Or could she shoot him from this side? Would the bullet go through? Could she kill him without the confrontation?

Did she want to?

*And*, the back of her mind whispered, *what if this isn't him?*

She couldn't do it, not until she learned the owner of the voice, and determined for sure whether the man who killed her aunt stood on the other side of her door.

*God, please. Help me know what to do.*

"Lexie, open up!"

She stopped walking and recognized the voice.

*No.*

"Listen, John called me because I was closer. They know who the killer is, Lexie. We've identified him. The Feds tracked him through his computer, but they haven't got him yet, and we need to keep you safe. John knows what you're trying to do, and he asked me to watch after you until he gets here. You should've left town when I told you to. And why didn't you tell me that you hadn't told him about the baby?" Paul Kingsley asked from the other side of the door.

"There is no baby." Her whisper wasn't loud enough for Paul to hear.

Paul, John's friend. Paul, member of the Fellowship, who seemed angered when she'd called it a cult. Paul, mid-forties, the right age to fit the profile. Paul, who knew Hannah Sharp, as well as Abby Tucker. Paul, who'd been involved with the case and had known every move the task force made, thanks to Lexie's careful reporting.

Paul.

Lexie reached the door—and the killer on the other side— then she stretched her left hand forward, twisted the lock and backed up, ready.

Paul flung the door open and bounded inside. "Lexie—"

She forced her hand not to shake...and pulled the trigger.

# CHAPTER NINETEEN

"What time is it?" John asked, pressing the accelerator so hard he could feel the vibrations from the motor against his sole.

"Midnight, straight up." The Grand Cherokee hit a railroad track while doing eighty and went airborne. "Hurry!"

"Where are your men?"

"Right behind us." She jerked her head around to make sure. "She'd better be okay."

"Etta called the police, right. You're sure?"

"Yes."

"Try Lexie again—now!"

She withdrew her cell phone and dialed Lexie's number. Like the other two times, the ringing continued. "She's got it turned off. I'm sure of it."

John's hands flipped over each other on the steering wheel through another hard turn. His jaw clenched tight. "Paul better have gotten there in time."

Lexie stared at the body face down on the floor. He wasn't moving, but was he still breathing? With the muscles in her arm and shoulder still burning from the first shot, she lifted the gun to shoot again. Finger moved to the trigger.

*Vengeance is mine, I will repay, says the Lord.*

She couldn't do it.

He wasn't moving, wasn't going anywhere, and wasn't going to hurt any woman—Lexie or anyone else—tonight. As much as she wanted to, she couldn't release another bullet. If he died from the first shot, so be it. But she wouldn't do it again. She'd call John and Angel, let the authorities handle it now. It was over. Finished.

This man, this monster, had taken Aunt Bev's life in front of her, taken John's wife and his father, and taken countless other women's lives, along with the children they carried.

The gun still in her hand, she backed across the room to find her purse and withdraw her cell. Within seconds, and while keeping one eye, and the gun, on Paul's body in the foyer, she fingered the contents of her purse then located the phone. She'd turned it off, not wanting it to ring when the killer came. She'd planned everything, and she'd caught him, after all these years. The phone came to life, and she glanced down to dial John's number.

The blow to her extended arm sent the gun flinging to the floor, then skittering across the hardwood. She opened her mouth to scream, but a gloved hand stopped her cold, while his other arm circled her torso and yanked her against his muscled frame.

*No!*

As he jerked her backward down the hall toward the bedroom, she stared in horror at the man she'd shot.

*Paul.*

Panic, fierce and commanding, filled her senses, made her vision blur. The killer had her, like he'd had her aunt, and Lexie knew what he planned to do, but she didn't know how to stop it. She jerked within his grasp, moved her legs to kick against his shins as they rounded the bedroom door, but her bare feet did little damage against the hard male. Gritting her teeth, she tried to move her neck, to get her mouth free so she could scream, but his tight grip and the leather of his glove pressing against her nose made her short, sharp breaths come out in spine-chilling hisses.

He turned her toward the bed, released her mouth, and before she had a chance to force a scream from her throat, he covered the lower half of her face with a rag, then secured it behind her head, jerking on her hair so hard her eyes watered. Then he twisted her to face him, and Lexie's eyes bulged wider. Her heart hurt in her chest, and her mind raced to the past, to that day so long ago, when her world changed forever by this man. This man, whose face had aged twenty-eight years, but who Lexie could see now, her fear and terror pushing the memory forward.

She saw him then, a teenager with sandy hair, an evil glint in his dark eyes, and a sadistic smirk on his face. And she saw him now, with less hair, but the same intense eyes, and the smirk that had so often appeared on his face when he voiced his objections in the conference room.

Lexie couldn't control the tears that burst forward, dripping down her cheeks to pool against the cloth binding her mouth. She couldn't control the agony at realizing all this time he'd been so close, yet so far away, his image locked tight in the recesses of her mind. She saw Aunt Bev's eyes, wide with horror, and the way she'd shaken her head to instruct her to be silent. She saw her blonde hair, tumbling over the back of the seat as he slammed his fist against her face. Then she heard the sounds. The hideous grunts and growls from the man who killed her aunt, while the eight-year-old in the back floorboard listened in terror. And she heard the whimpered pleas, Aunt Bev begging for him to save her, pleading for him to have mercy for her unborn child.

And then Lexie saw his face. The face of a teen possessed by something too horrible to name, a determination to conquer, to kill, to destroy Angel's mother.

The face of Ryan Sims.

"Well, Lex, you worked this out right nice, didn't you?" He shoved her on the bed, then laughed while he yanked her hands above her head.

Lexie stared as he bound her wrists and gloated about his victory. "Just think, in a little while, I'll get to visit the scene of the latest crime, like always, but this time, what do you know? I'll find the killer. All dead and taken care of by his victim. I couldn't have planned it better myself. Even setting up ol' Tiny Tina to take the fall for the beloved sheriff didn't work out this nicely. And who'd have thought? Paul Kingsley, my old buddy from the Fellowship, the Sunrise Killer. Sounds like lead story material, huh? A shame you won't be around to air the details."

He leaned over her, pressed his wet lips against her ear. "You remember when you first moved to town, Ms. McCain? I tried and tried to get you to pay me a bit of attention, have coffee, dinner, anything. You were so pretty and so smart. I thought you were the perfect one, the one meant for me. Well, you're smart. Smart enough to find someone to take the blame for the murders. Poor Paul. Bet he never saw it coming."

She cried out, the sound muffled within the cloth boundary.

"Funny thing will be when all those girls who left town come back, then one of them has to die in forty days. Real hilarious, don't you think? I'm guessing that pretty profiler will peg it as a copycat killing, and then they'll start the search all over again, looking for a different kind of guy, one totally different from me."

Lexie's eyes darted around the room. What to do? Angel had taught her so well. Gun use. Self-defense. Everything. Why couldn't she make herself remember what to do now?

"You're still trying to think of a way to do me in, aren't you, McCain? Yeah, well, go ahead. There's nothing you can do to stop me. Don't you understand? You hold the power. It's in here." He pressed a palm against her belly and pressed down hard. "And soon, I'll claim it. You have no right to that power, and you don't even understand. It's for the chosen, the ones who've refrained from the sin, who are willing to adhere to the plan. I knew you and Tucker had been together. And then your office buddy saw your doctor receipt and called the police station so you'd be protected. Wasn't that...thoughtful?" He laughed, the sound sinister, cold, evil.

She shook her head, willing him to stop.

*Stop him, Lord. This is the time for Your vengeance. Please, save me.*

He glared at her, the whites of his eyes looking sick in the blue haze of her bedroom. "It can't be undone. You did this, like Hannah. She did this. She started it all, when she chose Finley over me, when she let him do the things to her that I never did. And then she carried the power, power that should have been mine. Now you have to pay the price. It's decided. It's done."

Lexie's tears came harder. She couldn't stop the flow, and she couldn't stop thinking of John.

*John.*

She'd found love again with John. And now, because of her stupidity, she'd die without knowing how far their love would've gone.

Determined to save herself, she kicked out, but his hands tightened against her neck.

"I'd thought the perfect one was the profiler. Imagine my surprise today when I learned it's you."

Lexie closed her eyes. She'd failed. She'd tried to avenge her aunt's death, to make the killer pay for what he'd put her through back then, for what he'd put her grandfather through, and Angel, and all those victims' families in the years that followed—and John—but she'd failed. And she couldn't bear to watch him complete his goal.

The shot rang through the bedroom. Then the second one followed.

Lexie jerked her eyes open, saw Ryan's body tense above her as a trickle of blood spilled from his mouth. Then he dropped to the floor.

She jerked her head to the doorway to view her rescuer.

There were two. Angel and John rushed into the room. John removed the boundary from her mouth and pulled her close. "Don't *ever* scare me like that again." He cradled her head. "Promise me now."

"I promise." She waited for him to untie her hands, then raised up to see Angel hovering over Ryan's body on the floor. "He's dead?"

"Oh yeah. I shoot to kill, remember?"

"*You* shot him?" Lexie looked at John.

"We both took a shot. If she wants to think hers did the trick, that works for me."

"Mine did do the trick."

Lexie remembered her boss and jerked upright. "Paul!"

"He's going to be okay. The medics were right behind us, and they're working on him now. *You* weren't shooting to kill." Angel cocked a brow at her cousin. "Which, in Paul's case, is a good thing. You hit his side. He's going to be in some pain, but I figure he's gonna have you indebted to him for life, as far as working at the TV station. Might as well be ready for it."

John wrapped Lexie in a blanket then scooped her into his

arms. "I could've killed you for what you did."

"You wouldn't have had to. He'd have done it for you."

He didn't laugh, though Angel did manage a chuckle.

Ed Pierce and Lou Marker entered the bedroom with their guns leading the way.

"It's all clear here." John still cradled Lexie.

"The Feds were right," Pierce said. "They traced TRUTHLUVR to Ryan's IP address, but I still didn't believe it."

"Believe it." Angel stepped away from the body. "He fits the profile, remember?"

"I know, but I never saw it."

Zed Naylor entered, jerked his attention to the floor. "Dead?"

John nodded.

"Ryan." Zed shook his head, strands of his gray hair catching the blue light and looking like neon silver.

"The CSI van is here." Lou leaned back to peer down the hall. "And the medics have hauled Kingsley to the hospital. Who shot him? Sims?"

"No, I did."

"Lexie? Why'd you do that?"

"I thought he was the killer."

"Man, talk about the wrong way to go about getting a raise." Lou grinned. "You okay, McCain?"

"Yes, I'm okay."

Two hours later, the CSI team had completed their evaluation of the scene, the coroner had pronounced Ryan Sims dead, and the task force assembled once more, along with Etta Green, who'd hurried across town to verify Lexie was safe. This time, they weren't gathered around a conference table at the police station to share lukewarm, bitter coffee. Instead, they gathered around Lexie's kitchen table and sipped on hot, delicious coffee.

"So, you and Jackson are cousins?" Pierce stared at Lexie and Angel. "Guess I should've seen it. I mean, you favor in the eyes, but it isn't a strong resemblance."

"I favor my mother," Angel said, "Which is nice, since I

never had the opportunity to know her."

"And I favor my father," Lexie completed. "But we both have Granddaddy Truman's eyes."

"Who we'll go visit tomorrow," Angel added, "And let him know the killer is finally gone. Who knows? Maybe that's all he needs to bring him out of his self-inflicted barrier and let him face the world again."

"Wouldn't that be wonderful?" Lexie looked from Angel to John. "If he could come back to us?"

"And get to know his future grandson-in-law." John's comment caused all heads, including Lexie's, to turn toward the handsome detective.

"You trying to tell me something?"

"Trying to ask you something. And if you say yes, I hope your grandfather will be able and willing to give you away."

Lexie's chest flexed tight around her heart, overflowing with emotion for this man who'd given her a life she thought couldn't exist for a girl terrorized many years ago. With lip quivering, chin trembling and tears trickling, Lexie McCain looked into the brilliant blue eyes of the man she loved and gave him the answer he wanted. "Yes."

Etta Green pumped her arm in the air and let out a loud *whoop*, at the same time that Lexie's cell phone beeped from the living room floor, where she'd dropped it when Ryan grabbed her.

"It's after two in the morning. Who'd be calling now?" Angel crossed the room, picked it up and viewed the caller identification screen. "It's the hospital." She handed the phone to Lexie.

"Hello."

"McCain." Paul's voice, thick and gravelly, rasped through the receiver.

"Oh, Paul, I'm so sorry. I am *so* sorry."

"You're fired."

"I'm fired?" She listened to his laughter, which sounded painful from the way he also groaned. "Paul?"

"I'm joking, Lexie. But if you ever shoot me again, you can kiss your career goodbye."

"Deal. Are—are you okay? I really am sorry."

"I'm fine. Way I see it, I'll get my own story on the news, and I figure the reporter will talk up my heroism, how I took the bullet with gusto and kept on ticking."

"You can count on it."

"Who knows? I may even land me a few dates from this gig."

Lexie laughed.

"Hey, McCain."

"What?"

"Reckon you can run the fort until I'm back at work? I figure you're up for the challenge, given how you don't mess around with things. Even guns."

"I'll be glad to."

"Good. Now let me talk to that future Daddy."

"Oh, Paul, I told you the truth. I'm *not* pregnant. John isn't a future Daddy." She held the phone toward John. "I think he's mad at me again, and he wants to talk to you."

Lexie watched John chat and nod to Paul on the other end, while Angel touched her arm.

"Hey, I need you to know something." Angel's words were whispered, but intense.

"Okay, what?"

"Tonight, I prayed again. Really prayed. Asked God to save me and my baby, and then, on our way over here, I asked him to save you. And He did."

"Oh, Angel." Lexie hugged her cousin, tears streaming down her face at the beauty of knowing after all this time, after so many years of pain and struggle, Angel had found God.

Then her attention was pulled back to John when she heard him ask Paul Kingsley to be best man in the wedding that, according to John, would occur as soon as possible. Good. She didn't want to wait, either.

"And Paul, about that future Daddy thing." John glanced at Lexie. "Don't count me out just yet. But let us get married first, and then we'll see." He smiled, looked again at his future wife. "What do you think, Lexie? No more fears?"

She smiled. "No more fears."

He hung up the phone, pulled her into his arms and whispered, "Future Daddy. Sounds good to me."

She nodded, brushed the tears from her eyes. "Sounds good to me too."

*The End*

# Coming August 2013

Angel Jackson is back...

HUNTED, book two of the Profiled Series by Renee Andrews

A decapitated body is found in Tennessee. The head is found in Alabama. What was thought to be a drug deal gone bad ends up being something else entirely, when two more headless bodies are found.

A serial killer with a pension for chainsaws is baiting a pretty blonde profiler. And based on the identity of those gruesome bodies, this killer knows her secrets. Now it's up to FBI Special Agent Angel Jackson...to learn his.

But identifying the killer isn't Angel's only problem with the murder series. The fact that the bodies are found in multiple states equates to a need for multiple profilers. And she fears the man Quantico will send for the joint effort is also the father of the child she carries. Stanley Carlton won her love and then broke her heart. Now he's back, and Angel has to deal with an attraction that is even stronger now because of the bond they'll forever share, a precious child.

Can she keep Stanley Carlton from learning her biggest secret? And will the two of them find a way to work together to stop the killer and, with God's help, resurrect their love?

# ABOUT THE AUTHOR

Renee Andrews spends a lot of time in the gym. No, she isn't working out. Her husband, a former All-American gymnast, co-owns ACE Cheer Company, an all-star cheerleading company. She is thankful the talented kids at the gym don't have a problem when she brings her laptop and writes while they sweat. When she isn't writing, she's typically traveling with her husband, bragging about their two sons and daughter-in-law or spoiling their bulldog.

Renee is a kidney donor and actively supports organ donation. She welcomes prayer requests and loves to hear from readers! Write to her at Renee@ReneeAndrews.com or visit her Web site at www.reneeandrews.com.

Renee Andrews on Facebook:
www.facebook.com/AuthorReneeAndrews
Renee Andrews on Twitter:
www.twitter.com/reneeandrews

Made in the USA
Lexington, KY
01 March 2016